Fundamentals of Organic Chemistry

A Love Story

Also by Andrew S. Levitas

Alumni Notes

The Third Book of Samuel

Fundamentals of Organic Chemistry

A Love Story

By

Andrew S. Levitas

As always: For Phyllis, lifelong friend, colleague and partner

One might well wonder why a whole branch of chemistry is centered on a single element. ...The uniqueness of carbon atoms...from the fact that it customarily forms strong carbon-to-carbon bonds, which are also strong when the carbons are in combinations with other elements...customarily, carbon completes its valence-shell octet by sharing electrons.

– From "Basic Principles of Organic Chemistry", John Roberts and Marjorie Caserio, (New York) W. A. Benjamin, 1964, Chapter 1: Structure, Identification and Nomenclature

How on Earth are you ever going to explain in terms of chemistry and physics so important a phenomenon as first love?

– Albert Einstein

There is no truth but makes increase of loyalty nor true loyalty but it ravish the heart

– Theodore Roszak

In human relations one should penetrate to the core of loneliness in each person and speak to that.

– Bertrand Russell

What he hated most about retirement was the periods of fallow inactivity, when despite new books, new ideas in his medical journals, a challenge in one of the endless handyman tasks it took to maintain a house older than he was, novelty, even the possibility of novel thought, threatened to dry up. He'd hesitated at taking his license and diplomas down from his office wall, said "Teddy screwed us. Won in the end. Or Harvard did. They won in the end." She'd said, "We don't work for Teddy Edwards, or Harvard. We never did. We work for the Clinic and our patients."

What the Department Chair had done was insist on promoting him to Full Professor from Associate, which mandated a salary increase the Free Clinic couldn't afford. A clever way of getting a troublesome subordinate he couldn't fire out of the way, or if not, of undermining the Clinic's finances and thus its services and existence. His retirement as Full Professor had given the Clinic some temporary financial breathing room. He'd boxed up the laminated diplomas and certificates, witnesses to a lifetime of study, thinking *One day when I'm gone the kids and maybe grandkids will sift through this old Rubbermaid tub and find grandpa's credentials and wonder at the antique Latin Or use it for firewood*

He kept up a Retirement License so he could continue ("for convenience") to write his own prescriptions. The license also enabled him to continue on the Volunteer Faculty, teaching; one of the things he loved in retirement was keeping up with the latest, by attending conferences and Grand Rounds (easy to do in a city with three medical schools), and with old friends and colleagues (and thereby getting the necessary Continuing Education credits). But the months he loved most were when he made Teaching Rounds, where he sometimes saw the Clinic's patients; occasionally some who had been his. It was, he thought, the best part of Medicine: Passing on skills. *Being a doctor without the daily agony of watching the profession I loved and respected, and for which we sacrificed our youth, reduced to what I regard as the industrialized conversion of human suffering into investment capital.*

He'd struggled with Electronic Health Records not made for Community Medicine's real issues (made, rather, for the billing convenience of insurance schemes *one thing Morty had been right about Computers are the future little bro Big Bucks*), hated spending time with computers instead of with patients, hated reducing his patients' complex histories to digital codes, knowing that a worsening in their conditions would add a "severity code" that translated into higher billings, knowing it was all mostly going to enrich insurance companies. *At least we do something about the suffering she said* And trying to put out of mind the fact that he really was tiring more easily, and making simple errors in his prescriptions, taking increasing numbers of error calls from pharmacists pointing out his amounts and numbers of refills didn't match (or from younger pharmacists who didn't understand his Prescription Latin; didn't they teach this anymore?), or he'd forgotten to write his DEA or NPI number. He felt guilty at enjoying being out from under that, free to criticize a system he had grown to hate.

Most men his age would have driven into the city; he drove frozen streets to the Alewife T station and boarded a train. He still loved the trains, full of pretty undergraduates, enjoyed mixing with the young students of Boston's many colleges and universities, remembering when he was one of them, and what it had cost him. He was stunned when a girl offered him her seat. *Do I look that old to them? Yes* His mind immediately turned to last night's email. *Half a century It's really that long And yet this girl reminds me of her* In among the spam and emails from the kids was

alumnirelations@columbia.edu
Sent 11/13/17
To: Benjamin Rothstein, M.D.<RothsteinB@harvardmed.edu>
Subject: 50th Reunion History

Dr. Rothstein:

We greatly hope to see you at your 50th Class Reunion May 25—28th 2018. This is a most significant anniversary in the University's history, marking a half century since that tumultuous year, 1968. In addition to the usual chance to reconnect with old friends and celebrate memories, your Alumni Committee, in conjunction with the

History Department and the corresponding bodies at Barnard College, is planning a series of panels and other activities around the events of that year, in hopes that other participating Reunion Classes can discuss and put in context and perspective those events. We hope to start by creating a documentary "oral history", drawing on the memories of those who were there. Attached is a form to which we hope you will respond, as a first step in creating an archive and a 50th Reunion Remembrance Book, to be sent to all members of the Class of 1968. The compilers ask that you please complete and return the attached pdf...

1. Were you on campus for the weeks of the Gym Crow demonstrations and "campus takeover?"
   Yes____   No____

2. Did you participate in the "Gym Crow" demonstration?
   Yes____   No____

3. Did you favor the "campus takeover"? Yes____   No____

4. If **YES**, did you participate? Yes____   No____

5. If Yes, in which of the following ways?
   Building takeover____
   If so, which building?_____
   Support for building takeover____
   Anti-police demonstration_____
   Other (Explain)_____

6. Were you a member of:
   Black Students Alliance (BSA) ____
   Students for a Democratic Society (SDS) ___
   Other_____
   Unaffiliated____

7. If **NO** did you participate in the counter-demonstration?
   Yes____   No____

8. Which to you was/were the most important issue(s)?
   (Check all that apply)
   School/Community Relations____
   Racial attitudes on campus____
   Gender issues on campus____
   University participation in military research/contracts____
   Vietnam War in general____
   Other

For Questions 9 through 11, please use box below.

9. Please describe your participation.

10. Please describe (briefly) your life and career(s) since the events of 1968.

11. What effect(s) did these campus events of 1968 have on your life?

Not Enough Space In Box Below. *There would never be enough space to relive the hurt   Never enough   Is some grad student doing a study of student radicals   Is that what we were she had once said   or were we students who once did a radical thing   Still doing   I said   What's more radical in America than a free medical clinic* He returned to the world when the girl repeated her offer of her seat. *Her face   The apparitions of these faces in a crowd   Petals on a wet black bough* He smiled. "Thank you," he said. "I'm fine." *No I am not fine*

He got off at Massachusetts General Hospital station, crossed the street in blustery cold, (reconsidering his plan to later make the rounds of the bookstores in Harvard Square), warmed quickly in the overheated hospital building, pulled off scarf and gloves in the elevator and prepared for the doors to open on the ward... "Rounds, rounds. Everybody awake?"

They wore scrubs now, not the Whites he had trained in. "Dr. Rothstein, these are the new Third-Years, Drs. Kumar and Majunder," the Resident said.

"Thank you. Shall we? Who's first up. Dr. Kumar? Talk to me."

"One of your Clinic's patients I think, admitted from the ER."

"Ah. So...Dr. Kumar?"

"Sixty-two year-old white male in no acute distress, presents with palpitations and shortness of breath..." He loved the hint of ancestral Hindi musicality. *Second-generation American, like myself* "...Denies chest pain, edema, dizziness, fatigue, perioral numbness. Admits to two beers a day, four glasses of wine a week but I regard him as an unreliable historian."

"You should. Meaning?" *The mantra: Always at least*

double the stated consumption
  "Meaning four beers and eight glasses of wine, minimum. Unconvincingly denies other substance abuse, blackouts, confusion, memory loss, DUIs. Review of systems is noncontributory. Pulse is 90, occasionally irregular, BP 140 over 85, respirations ten per minute, afebrile, face shows spider angiomata..." she went on; he tuned out slightly, tuned back in when she got to the chest. "...clear to percussion and auscultation; Cor: S1, S2, no murmurs or clicks. I thought I felt a liver edge at half a centimeter, no splenomegaly..."
  He tuned out again. When he realized she'd finished speaking he pushed himself off the edge of the table he'd been sitting on. "Well, let's go have a listen, shall we? And see about that liver edge." On the way to the bedside he said, "Usually exam first, then labs, right? But for this we go out of order—for once the labs might inform the exam rather than the other way around. I assume you ran an EKG."
  "We did, with a long rhythm strip. Only thing was low voltage, PACs, and the PVCs and occasional bigeminy that got him admitted."
  They reached the bedside. "Good morning Mr. McHugh. I'm Dr. Rothstein."
  "Not as good-looking as the other Dr. Rothstein."
  "So true. Actually *I'm* the *other* Dr. Rothstein."
  "You look to be older. Say, around seventy? You're a lucky man, doc. She's a beautiful girl."
  "*You're* a lucky man, because she's a very good doctor."
  "She says it's probably the drink."
  "She's usually right. I would take that to heart. Which we're all going to have a listen to, and help her figure out what's causing the problem." He took his stethoscope off his neck and listened. Lungs first; clear as the proverbial bell, as the student said. But didn't advance to the heart. "Peripheral pulses," he said to them. "Where do you look?"
  "Wrists, ankles, groin."
  "And?"
  "Neck. Carotids," the other Third-Year, Majunder, said.

Pretty girl Very

"Exactly. So…come." They took turns palpating Mr. McHugh's peripheral pulses. *"Now* we listen." He listened to the patient's heart, moving swiftly over the sternal border, the atria, the valves, the apex, the carotid arteries, with diaphragm and bell. "Here," he said, "Take my scope. Hear what it really sounds like." Last he had Mr. McHugh take deep breaths while they felt for the liver edge. He thanked him and they walked back to the lounge. "What did you feel, see and hear?"

"The liver edge is about 0.5 to 1.0 centimeters. He's done some damage. Pulses were weak, except the carotid, but no bruit, rhythm was mostly regular but he says that's not always the case. And I picked up a rale or two."

"And?" *Silence.* "Put it together with the EKG."

"Low voltage, PACs, PVCs; you think…cardiomyopathy?"

"Due to…"

"Alcohol. Alcoholic cardiomyopathy."

"Yes. Sometimes the differential is huge, sometimes the patient just tells you. The other Dr. Rothstein is seldom wrong, except perhaps in her taste in husbands."

This got grins. "Dr. Rothstein?" One of the Third-Years said. "I'm unclear about the mechanism of alcoholic cardiomyopathy." *Majunder, the very pretty one.*

"Ah. Well. What do you know about the toxicity of alcohol?"

"It's toxic to liver, heart muscle, some very specific parts of the brain…Temporal lobe. Hippocampus. Memory function, conversion of short to long-term memory."

"Causing?" He pointed to the other Third-Year.

"Korsakoff's Dementia, Wernicke's encephalopathy."

"Yes. What else? What other toxicity?"

"To peripheral nerves."

"Exactly. What's the mechanism?"

"The nervous system pathology is indirectly from alcohol," Majunder said. "Chronic alcoholics have B vitamin deficiencies; the alcohol inhibits folate and B_{12} absorption, causing Pernicious Anemia."

"Could that affect cardiac muscle?"

"Presumably." She hedged. "Possibly."

"How does alcohol cause intoxication?"

That she knew. "It blocks the frontal GABA receptors, causing disinhibition."

"Exactly. Blocks Gamma-aminobutyric acid, inhibitory neurotransmitter, hence disinhibition, the polite medical word for drunk. What else hits the GABA receptors?"

"Barbiturates. Benzodiazepines—Valium etc. Some anticonvulsants."

"Right. Do they cause cardiomyopathy?"

"No. Nor cirrhosis," Majunder said. "So that's not the reason."

"Exactly, Dr. Majunder. So is it the vitamin deficiency?"

"You don't see cardiomyopathy in Pernicious Anemia. So, no."

"Or liver damage. So."

Silence. A Teachable Moment if ever there was one "What does that leave? *I have to ask the right question. This is my job Teaching Organic Chemistry to pretty, intelligent young women Come, Socrates, the Youth of Athens awaits.* He turned to the whiteboard, found a marker. "Alcohol," he said. "What's the formula?"

Silence.

"Come on, you remember. C_2H_5OH." He turned to the board, wrote

```
H    H
 \   /
H-C—C—OH
 /   \
H    H
```

"How does the body rid itself of alcohol?"

"The enzyme. Alcohol dehydrogenase."

"Good. Located in…"

"The liver.

"Right And what does alcohol dehydrogenase do to alcohol? Turns it into what? Take away a hydrogen atom and you get what?" *Silence.* He turned back to the board, wrote:

$$\begin{array}{ccccc}
\text{H} & \text{H} & & \text{H} & \text{H} \\
\backslash & / & & \backslash & / \\
\text{H-C} & \text{—C—OH} & \rightarrow & \text{H-C} & \text{—C=O} \\
/ & \backslash & & & / \\
\text{H} & \text{H} & & \text{H} &
\end{array}$$

"Which is what?" he said. "Come on, you guys took Organic Chemistry." *What these kids need is a short book reviewing clinically useful Organic Chemistry Connecting it with clinical issues Actual patients*

Kumar looked up from searching her phone. "Acetaldehyde?"

Okay, maybe a phone app "Yes. Acetaldehyde, first cousin of formaldehyde."

"So…acetaldehyde does the damage?"

"Pretty likely. More toxic than alcohol, concentrates in the liver, where the reaction takes place, and travels right up what?"

"The Inferior Vena Cava…"

"To?"

"The heart."

"See, you did know this."

"Dr. Rothstein?"

"Yes, Dr. Majunder."

"As a matter of curiosity. Alcohol isn't a nutrient. Why does the body have an enzyme that metabolizes it? To a toxin? *Silence. Long silence.*

"That, Dr. Majunder is a show-stopper of a question. I will hide behind the old shuck that science tells us what and how, but not why." *And I will take that question home to dinner. And maybe there is some lucky man out there who will hear it from you tonight.* "But is that the last step in the metabolism?" No eye contact. They didn't know this, or were too uncertain to risk answering. "No? The next step is conversion of toxic acetaldehyde to harmless acetic acid by acetaldehyde hydroxylase. As an old chem major, I could venture a guess for you. There are a zillion possible ways to get from ethyl alcohol to acetic acid in the lab. In the liver, no. Mother Nature, unlike laboratory glassware, can't get from ethyl alcohol to harmless acetic acid in one metabolic step, with the enzymes available from evolution. It has to go by way of acetaldehyde. Things in the environment that primates—that all animals—are bound to ingest, can ferment, so there has to evolve a way to metabolize this potential toxin, alcohol. Nature didn't anticipate our fondness for intoxicants, and for too much of a good thing. Since it's not a critical pathway, mutations can survive and accumulate, so there are multiple isoenzymes of acetaldehyde hydroxylase, with variable effectiveness at breaking acetaldehyde down to acetic acid. Does that answer satisfy?"

"It does, but—you can't prove it."

"True. It's speculation from the known. Not proof. Most of medicine is like that. We operate one step ahead of certainty. So. There are several isoenzymes, some more active, some less. Acetaldehyde hydroxylase is a critical reactant, and this is a rate-limiting step, like the neck of a funnel, so some unlucky drinkers run higher levels of acetaldehyde for longer than their luckier friends. No one's tried to correlate low isoenzyme activity with the cardiomyopathy, as far as I know. It would be a nice test of the hypothesis. Worth trying. Worth a literature search, anyway." He turned to the interns. "So why is Mr. McHugh here?"

"Monitor. Echo. If negative, cath."

"Exactly. If he had chest pain and no booze history he'd probably have what?"

"Ischemic cardiomyopathy."

"Yes, and we'd do it exactly the other way around. Of course he could have both, but his EKG shows no signs of ischemia."

"Is this just all about chemistry? What about treating his alcoholism?" Majunder asked.

"Yes, Dr. Majunder, what about it? First we had to cut

through the woman-discounting alcoholic bonhomie to remind him that the other Dr. Rothstein seems to have made a start."

"Antabuse?"

"Ah. Problem there. How does disulfiram work?"

"It makes them nauseous if they drink…" She grinned.

"Oh. I see. It inhibits acetaldehyde hydroxylase, so he can't detoxify the acetaldehyde, causing nausea. If he does drink on disulfiram, it might worsen his cardiomyopathy, if your theory is right."

"Yes. If. See how it helps to know the chemistry? Medicine is the art of connecting the science to the patient. *They really could use that book* You need several levels of knowledge. You need to combine the knowledge of chemistry with the knowledge of human behavior. If he does have alcoholic cardiomyopathy, he'd have to be engaged in an active detox program and AA *before* we'd risk Antabuse. Hence his admission…" *You could write that book, Socrates You have the time Something to do in my No, our? old age*

The ward Social Worker waylaid him on his way out. "That Medicaid number he gave us in the ER is bogus," Shelly said.

"Really? Huh. Let me just call the Clinic…" He took out his cell and called. "Mr. McHugh's here. And you know what? His number's bogus."

"As you perfectly well know, that's why he was sent through the ER. Are we playing with Shelly again?"

"Yes. I can hold." And to Shelly, "They're pulling the chart now." Shelly rolled her eyes.

"You want me to sound like Muzak?"

"No. That's okay. There's likely going to be a stern lecture about medical economics at the next faculty meeting."

"Good news. Membership in Physicians for a National Health Plan is all paid up. Pick up some tuna in oil for pasta tonight. And give Shelly a big wet kiss."

"Thanks. Will do." He put away the phone. "You're right. No number. One of our drop-ins. No home address. Guess you'll have to make him eligible while he's here."

"Yes, you've made me expert at that. Come to my office for a minute." They stepped into a staircase landing. "Ben, get these people on Medicaid before they get here."

"Me? I'm retired, remember?"

"Sure you are. They're going to put the name Rothstein on that clinic before you're even dead. It's your baby. But it has to grow up. You guys can't keep this up."

"We can until there's a decent health care system. Come on, Shelly, these are great teaching cases, and we can't afford a Social Worker anymore."

"So you send them to the ER in a condition that under Federal law they can't be discharged or transferred until stabilized, and we have to admit them. It's very clever, and I love you for it, but it's been noticed. I'm trying to warn you."

"When the goal of medicine was to take care of people and the state subsidized the Clinic decently we had a great Social Worker who got these guys on Medicaid when they walked in the door. You. If your department wants to send you down again as liaison, even part time, we could solve this. How about: It costs less to have you at the clinic than to have these uninsured admissions. Department of Medicine can chip in. Joint financing. This shit doesn't happen in civilized countries."

"We live in this one. Which is industrialized, not civilized. Trump is proof."

"Where we've decided health care is like a people garage. Put 'em up on the lift, change the oil, street 'em. If they can afford it."

"I love the liaison idea. I'll see what I can do with the 'it's-cheaper-than-The Clinic-Gaming-the-System' approach."

As Shelly walked him out he said. "They *are* great teaching cases."

"I told you. Teddy is going to give the clinic shit about filling these beds with Medicaid patients. Even legit ones. Something's going on in Admin."

"And you know what I think of Teddy Edwards and where he can shove it. Aside from our duty as human beings and medical professionals: as you know, poor patients are sicker.

They need more expertise, not less."

"And you know I share your sentiments. But I can't keep covering for you. Even if I can get them on Medicaid, I told you, Teddy is trying to minimize Medicaid admissions. Bare legal compliance minimum. Rumor is he's going to put The Freak on notice any time now, Ben. Probably about its survival."

"I know it's to the point that only dicks like Teddy can become Chairs. And satisfy the business desires of the even bigger dicks further up the pecking order. But Medicine isn't a damned business. In the *civilized* world it's a human right. A public service. Part of infrastructure. Police, fire, transportation, water, health care."

"Thank you for that trenchant analysis. You know, don't you, that you're *Doctor* Benjamin Rothstein, not *Saint* Benjamin. You can't save them all…"

He faced her; old comrade in arms. "I do know that, Shelly." *Especially today* "But we can do our damnedest to save the ones who come to us."

"And it isn't Teddy's fault health policy has taken this turn."

"I know that too. What I detest him, and this institution, for is not fighting back. So that I have to sell these patients as Great Teaching Cases, when what they are is suffering human beings, and The Freak as a Great Educational Experience when what it is, is a humanitarian community institution. Teddy goes along to grease his upward career trajectory. To whatever is higher. For as long as I've known him. Which is since we were all trainees. I don't worry. The Free Clinic can handle Teddy Edwards. Believe me."

"Really, Ben? Do you think you're going to occupy the place? We all know your student radical past. What do you think you're going to do?"

"What *they're* going to do. It's a collective. And I'm retired. And I don't know that I can be called a student radical. A student who's done a few radical things, maybe. But yes, occupying a building is well within our skill set. Could always happen, Shel."

On the train home he ran through the questions in the email in his head. *Yes Yes Yes Yes Yes-Mercer Unaffiliated All apply What effect(s) did these campus events have on your life? Petals on a wet black bough Her face Still in my mind After more than fifty years Back then: Lost her With today's technology: Could have found each other on the Internet in a few keystrokes Dear Alumni Committee: It doesn't start with The Occupation The events of 1968 were only a beginning No No A middle If you really want to know let's start where it starts With my first teaching job Teaching organic chemistry to one pretty, intelligent girl*

She was the only girl in the class. At Barnard there was the choice to take Organic Chemistry at Barnard or cross the street to Columbia to study it with the men. She knew; had been advised, by her faculty advisor, quite candidly, if not clandestinely, that to have taken Organic at the men's school would boost her chances for medical school admission. Would increase her competitiveness, as the phrase went. And she had been told, over and over, that anything she could do to increase her chances she should do. Prove she could stand toe to toe with the men. Nothing new, to her. She was the only one of her classmates to take the advice. She felt like a creature in a zoo. Conscious, in a way she had not been since high school, of the boys quickly glancing away when she looked up, of just missing their stares every time she moved. She dared not cross her legs for fear of setting off sighs. She dared not raise her eyes from her notebook in lecture for fear she would have to deal with some awkward or embarrassing situation, make some boy angry, perhaps even insulting, for having excited him. As if it was her fault. She sucked it up, gave no sign of discomfort, kept her eyes down, sat as far back in the room as she could, beat the bell out the lecture hall door and walked as briskly as was consistent with inconspicuousness to the 116th Street crossing and the safety of the Barnard gates. *Make yourself small and the predators can be evaded They weren't called sophomores for nothing*

None of this worked in Lab. There were two three-hour labs a week, and she might as well have been naked. Like high school but worse; no other girls to hide among, to draw some of the attention. She had been assigned the central bench in one nine-stand lab room, the center of the tick-tack-toe board. No place to hide. The fire shield was transparent. The stone bench top was high, the stools high; she knew a skirt would ride up every time she clambered onto one, or climbed to reach a reagent bottle on the top shelf, had anticipated this and thought to wrap herself in a long lab coat. In this and safety goggles, long hair tied in a ballerina's bun, she still drew attention. She couldn't win; if she exposed herself she drew their stares, if she covered up the braver ones ragged her about being afraid to show herself.

As if dipping her pigtails in the inkwell was the way to her heart, or some other part. Or worse. She bore it as best she could, kept her eye on the goal, imagined synthesizing something highly flammable, stepping to the door and striking one of the Bunsen burner igniter flints.

Until one day two weeks into it she couldn't get the distillation apparatus together. This was the first part of the three-step synthesis. The retort fit the riser/connector to the condenser, the ground-glass making a tight seal. The hoses hooked to the condenser; check. The condenser did not, however, fit into either side neck of the receiving three-neck round-bottom flask at the correct angle. It looked decidedly unlike the lab manual diagram, which anyway showed a piece of glassware, a sort of adaptor, taking off from the exit end of the condenser and connecting to the central neck, not a side neck, of the flask. She checked the diagram again, inventoried the equipment at her stand. No connector. That was when she noticed how everyone was looking away, some actively avoiding her glance, some grinning slightly and trying to hide it. Pathetic. She looked one last time in her stand's drawer. Nothing. "Excuse me," she said. "Anyone have an extra connector piece to the three-neck flask? I seem to be missing one."

Two boys seemed disposed to help; they were held back by what she supposed now was the Alpha Male of the group. "Tough luck, Barnyard. Maybe you can go back across Broadway and find one."

Not for the first time she thought *Maybe I could just go take this class there Or maybe I can find my connector and shove it straight up your ass.* She smiled sweetly. "Sorry, no time for that. I'll just have to walk around and see if anyone in the room is bright enough to be able to count to two." And she walked over to the big one's lab bench, expecting to find the missing glassware in his drawer. When she came over he actually pushed her away. *Didn't anybody tell you, you aren't supposed to hit girls?* Then she remembered the student, or whoever he was, the lab assistant, who laid out the equipment and set up the demonstration apparatus before class, and went to find him.

He was a kind of short but gangly guy; a junior; in Advanced Organic she thought she'd heard? She found him in a supply alcove, a sort of walk-in closet, wiping down some unfamiliar apparatus. "Excuse me," she said *I'm getting to say that a lot today* I'm in Lab 4, and I seem to be missing the connector piece, from the condenser to the three-neck."

"Ben," he said, not yet looking up.

"What?"

"Ben. My name is Ben. Rothstein. And you are?"

"Lisa. Lisa Mautner."

"So, Lisa Mautner, you tried the drawer, under the lip of the fire screen? Because I'm pretty sure I can count to nine." He smiled slightly; his tone was ironic, but kind.

"Tell you what, Ben Rothstein, I have good reason to believe I'm being hazed. A fairly large gent with an odd sense of humor I think maybe has it."

Ben sighed. "That would be Boland. Total jock frat-boy schmuck, you'll pardon the expression."

"No, that's my diagnosis too."

He took a length of half-inch-diameter metal pipe from a low shelf. "You up for a little counter-hazing?"

"Oh, I think I could be." Which would be interesting, she thought; Boland looked bigger than both of them put together.

They went back to Lab 4, where Ben announced their entrance by whacking the reagent rack with the pipe. The resulting bang got their attention. "Good afternoon, gentlemen. It has been brought to my attention that an important piece of Miss Mautner's experiment is missing. She will of course have to stay late to complete it, having lost the time it took to determine the absence. I think it's only fair that you all lose the time it takes to find it. So let's all look around for a 3 inch double ended angle connector."

"Why would we do that?" Boland said. "We already looked,"

Ben ambled over to him, the pipe still in his hand. Boland loomed. "Because I'm responsible for all the equipment. I inventory it, I have to account for it. That's my job. I know how to count to nine, so I know there were nine connectors here an hour ago." He turned away, addressed the other seven. "So we're going to turn this place upside down until we find it. Anything missing comes out of my paycheck. One of those things is worth about five bucks, and you aren't worth a nickel to me."

"What happens if we don't?" Boland said.

Ben turned back to him. "First thing that happens is you all get zeros for this lab. Nothing is going to happen in here until we turn it up. After that, I might forget how to count to nine. Next time there may be only eight or seven of something, and it might be hard to find replacements, and who knows how much time you're all going to lose, having to repeat labs on Saturdays. Me, I have work to do. I don't have time to waste on this junior high crap." He tapped the pipe on the stone bench. "Your move, asshole."

Boland looked around. No one was looking back. He reached into his drawer. "Here," he said. "It was just a joke."

"Is anybody laughing? No? Here's another joke. At the ends of semesters I collect the products of the complex synthesis exercise. It's a third of your lab grade. Most of the time my coordination is pretty good. Could slip though. Terrible spillage problems, Boland. For everyone. A room full of pre-meds should be laughing their heads off. No? Tough room. Now. Miss Mautner isn't going to have any more lab problems, is she?"

"I could take that little speech to the Dean, Rothstein."

"And I could take this (he held up the connector) to the Dean. Shall we go now?" Turning to the rest of them he said, "Here's a little tip for the rest of you, from your olders and betters. You don't deserve it, but here it is. A woman in the lab is a huge asset. Organic lab is more like cooking than science. Think, idiots." He handed the little glassware section to her, watched her return to her lab bench. Watched everyone return to work. Went back to the equipment room. *Mission accomplished* he thought. *Cute girl.*

When she went to find him later, to thank him, he was gone. She left a note:

Thanks, I guess. What makes you think I can cook?

At the next lab she found a note under a folded lab towel:

I took a shot. The point is THEY think so. They'll come to you for help instead of hazing you. With chemistry, not cooking.

When she thought about it, it had been annoying to have him step in as a protector. She had only wanted another glass connector, to defuse the situation and avoid giving them the satisfaction of inconveniencing her. But when she was completely honest with herself, when he asked her if she was up for a little counter-hazing, it had been exhilarating to see Boland have the tables turned on him. And it was, she had to admit, exhausting to have to deal with this crap, nice to have one less stress to deal with. And he had put the responsibility on them for keeping a leash on Boland, had done it without undermining her in any way. Put it in terms of *his* demands. And he was right, they did come for help with what was, in fact, just a big fancy kitchen. She got some respect, even deference. He was, she found out when she asked ("Who was that masked man?"—the story had got around, even crossed Broadway) a star student, a chemistry major; not a pre-med, a genuine chem major. That's how he had the grant-in-aid job. Was the Word.

She was doing okay, more than holding her own, in the quizzes, the labs, but midterms loomed, and her faculty advisor's advice haunted her *you have to be twice as good as the guys.* She was mostly confident, but she needed an edge. Would feel that much better having an edge. It seemed to her this shouldn't be public. She stopped at the supply room on the way to lecture, hours before the afternoon lab, and left another note.

I need to talk to you about something. Meet me at Jack's tomorrow at 10? –LM

Under the towel at her lab bench she found his reply: **Sure.**

When he pushed into Jack's next morning it was, as usual, mobbed. Not exactly a campus hangout; it caught a lot of the commuter and neighborhood crowd off Broadway, Amsterdam and Columbus. He almost didn't recognize her with her hair down; with it framing her face *she isn't cute, she's beautiful Rothstein.* The long brown hair framed delicate features; eyes wide, deep brown pools behind those glasses, eyes that lit her face with intelligence, eyes that missed nothing; classic high cheekbones, bowed lips with—in no need of—lipstick…dynamite in a slim, compact package. She saw him looking around and waved. He slid into the booth, ordered coffee and a Danish. "What can I do for you?" he said. *Please let there be something   Oh yeah Rothstein*

"First, I wanted to thank you for that, umm, counter-hazing. I haven't had a moment's trouble since. In lab, anyway."

By now he knew they called her Mount Her or Mouthner. And that the profs hazed her just as much, calling on her relentlessly in lecture sessions "No thanks necessary," he said. "I don't like bullies. I had enough of them growing up."

"Tough neighborhood?" She expected somewhere in the City.

"Jersey. The Oranges. We lived in Brooklyn, then we moved to East Orange when I started junior high. I was the new kid, and they didn't especially like Jews." He shrugged. "I had an older brother. Who helped. What did you want to talk to me about?"

"I guess, sort of…more brotherly intervention. It's like this. I'm pre-med. And I don't know if you know this, but girls' odds of getting into med school are pretty lousy, unless their grades are stellar. And they need an edge. That's why I had the idea of taking Organic at Columbia instead of Barnard. That'll look better on the transcript, and I hope med school admissions committees will get the message that I can hold my own with the boys. I figure, on my own, without any help I can pull a B+. Studying with someone who really knows his stuff, I can ace it. I'm asking you to tutor me, or anyway study with me. Keep me sharp." She watched his face.

He struggled with what to say. She didn't know the profs talked about her; she was acing it already, in spite of their riding her. *Don't blow this Rothstein* He hesitated a moment too long; he had always been awkward with girls.

"I can pay you. As a tutor."

So, no hope here "I usually dislike pre-meds," he said. "Cutthroats, the lot of you. *But she's the best looking cutthroat you've ever seen*

"What choice does a woman have? I want to be a doctor."

"So might I. So what?"

"But you're not pre-med."

"Because I don't really know if I want to be a doctor. I'm really interested in chemistry. Organic, especially. I think it's the key to everything. Life, anyway. Plus I love literature, poetry. As a chem major I get time for electives I wouldn't as a pre-med. There's no rule that a chem major can't apply to med school. If I wanted to."

She thought about this. *A few lit courses wouldn't hurt* "A girl doesn't have the luxury to deviate from the prescribed path. And to not be cutthroat."

What a stupid thing for me to say "Well…okay, yeah, I guess I can see that."

"Do you really have to pay for missing lab equipment? Because, I'll pay you."

"That was bullshit, to scare Boland. You don't have to pay me. We can be study partners. It works for me, too. You'll be a one-woman review course for me."

"And we're a year apart, so we're not competing. With each other."

"True. Sure. I'll do it, if you want. *Sure, of course, Jesus, Rothstein.* But it's only fair to tell you, you don't need it. The profs talk about you, the only girl in the class, you're already on the road to an A, without any help. Not a B+, an A."

"I can't count on that continuing. It isn't going to get easier, I know that."

"I said, okay, if you want. Sure. Two person study group. You can't do this with some Barnard junior or senior?" *What's*

wrong with you Rothstein Idiot
"They don't use Roberts & Caserio. Different textbook, different curriculum."

And, he thought, *they're the competition. Cutthroats, the lot of them. And they probably already resent her for crossing the street.*

"Just one thing," she said. "It has to be…secret. I mean, it can't get around."

"What, like I'm going to write to med school admissions committees?"

"No, just…these guys could be my colleagues someday. And the profs…I don't know. If they doubt a girl could do it on her own, they'd give you the credit."

"You just thought of that? You haven't thought this through."
He watched as those alert eyes narrowed. "I thought of it."

"If you're afraid someone will think I'm slipping you exam answers, I can't. I'm not a teaching assistant, just a glorified dishwasher. Not that that will stop them thinking. And thinking other things." He sipped his coffee. "This still comes under the heading of me hating bullies. Since we can't be seen on campus we'll have to meet somewhere…"

"Yes. We both live in the dorms, so that's out. Here?"

"Jacks's? In favor: the Preppie crowd and the hick town shitpickers are mostly scared to venture this far off campus…"

"You don't like people too much, do you."

"Not many like me too much. Anyway, we couldn't just sit here all day."

"So…I don't know…The Hungarian Bakery?"

"Good, but too close by. Coffee houses in the Village. The Borgia, the Reggio. You can have a table for the whole day, as long as you occasionally order coffee."

"That's brilliant."

"That's why you thought of me." *Atta boy Rothstein*

It troubled him; he wondered if she was perhaps making too much of this. Meaning, if she was just an even bigger cutthroat than the male pre-meds he knew. He dropped by his advisor's office, just casually. "Professor, if you have a moment, just a quick question. My cousin wants to be a doctor, and she asked me if it was true that it's out of reach for a girl. A woman."

His advisor looked over his bifocals for the time it took to see if this was some sort of prank. "Surely, Mr. Rothstein, you're aware the medical schools have quotas for female admissions. It wasn't so long ago they had quotas for…your people."

So his instinct, that they were not dissimilar, was correct.

They traveled separately to the Village that Saturday ("Saturdays," he'd said when they parted. "I can't do Sundays") and met up at the Reggio, both carrying notebooks and Roberts & Caserio, the second half of which was his text for the Advanced Organic course. They ordered espressos, worked quietly, reading. Their silence was broken only when she had a question, which wasn't all that often, and to which the answer was almost always, "Yes, that's right." After an hour his feet were propped up on the bench beside her and hers on the chair next to his. Helpless, he dropped a pencil to get a look at her legs *fabulous*; hoped she didn't notice. After an hour and a half they ordered another espresso apiece. This went on for two more weeks. He watched her eyes move over the text, watched her face change expressions, watched her tap her lips with her pencil, suck on her pen, bite the cover off her yellow highlighter. And watched as much of the rest of her as he could. *So, what? Purposeful. Self-contained* The fourth week she asked him to quiz her for the upcoming midterm, and they had lunch. Then they had to celebrate her 97, top of the curve, so it was lunch again, and he bought. The week after that he came up from the subway and the Waverly had *What's Up, Tiger Lily*, and he asked her if she felt like a movie after lunch.

"What, you mean like a date?"

"Just like."

"You're asking me out."

"I believe I've made that clear. Is this somehow more difficult than the synthesis and reactions of aldehydes?"

"When did you decide to do this? How long have you

been plotting this?" *Since you looked up my skirt a month ago?*
Maybe since we met at Jack's Or before "Since I noticed
this morning the Waverly has the Woody Allen movie."

She put her book down. It wasn't as if she hadn't looked
at him before, but she really looked at him now. He wasn't bad
looking. Okay, he was in fact passably good looking, or would
be if he grew his hair out a little *I can work on that*. His eyes
were the blue she liked, and by now she knew his intelligence.
Adolescent acne seemed to be gone. Mouth that looked always
ready to smile. He was gangly but moved gracefully. And he
was just her size. Perfect fit. And she realized she had noticed
all this before. Had occasionally thought about him. *If I wanted
a boyfriend* That dry wit. Aldehydes, right. And she realized it
had been quite a long time since someone *a boy* had shown any
interest, since there had been *anyone* in her life she liked this
much. "I could stand the break. I could stand Woody Allen."

"Sure. Plus, we already have…"

"Don't say it. Please don't say it…"

"…great chemistry."

She groaned. They stood. He took her hand. She looked
down, looked back up at him, raised an eyebrow. *Smooth,
Rothstein Like I taught you You're in*

"What?" he said. "It's a *date*."

After the movie, which was moderately funny, he said,
"I propose we make this a standing routine. We study, then we
go out."

"Maybe you can afford the time. I can't."

"You have to. R & R. Mautner, you have to. Or you burn
out. I know."

Was he right? The next week he suggested taking in
Fantastic Voyage. "Let's ease you into this R & R concept gently.
It's got a medical theme."

"It's got Raquel Welch."

Somewhere in the middle, where a white corpuscle
attacks the miniature sub, he felt himself, as if pulled by
magnetic force, drape his arm over the back of her seat, then let

it fall on her shoulder. *That's it Rothstein* He wasn't sure how this would work out; he was prepared to retreat to the seatback, then withdraw, but to his delighted surprise, and to her own, she put her hand over his and moved closer to him. *Mission accomplished* It was getting colder, getting ready for winter; he walked her past the broken-down used book and record stores on Bleecker to the subway entrance at Christopher Street with his arm still around her. At the head of the steps he stopped, took her hands. *Should I kiss her Yes, idiot Is he going to try to kiss me* she thought. In the end he only said, "Next week let's meet here and go on to the Reggio together. I'm tired of this…"

"Okay," she said. Which was ridiculous; they would see each other twice in the course of the week at her labs, but they couldn't risk acknowledging each other. All the way back uptown she agonized over it. *Did I want him to kiss me? Was he going to? Did he chicken out? Did I put him off? Did I want to put him off, or did I want him to?*

The next week they went to see *A Man for All Seasons*, and ended up kind of making out during the second part of a very, very good movie, so they stayed for the second show and only made out during the first part. When they walked out into the dusk, mouths still dry from extended kissing, she noticed he was having a little trouble walking, and was shaking his left arm as if to unkink it.

"Are you okay?"

"What? Sure. Why?"

"Because you're limping slightly and shaking your arm like, I don't know…"

"You're going to be a doctor, Mautner. Figure it out."

"Enlighten me," she said. "I haven't taken androcology."

He grinned. "Chemistry. The arm is afflicted with paraesthesias. Pins and needles, caused by nerve hypoxia due to compression of the blood vessels of the arm against theater seat backs. What emergency room docs in college towns call Saturday Night Palsy."

"What about the limp, then?"

He winced. Decided to talk to the future physician;

thinking *she'll appreciate being taken seriously, not patronized.* "The limp is caused by attempted guarding of pain and tenderness caused by prolonged cramping of the cremasteric muscles that attach the testes to the abdominal wall. The condition is technically referred to as Blue Balls." She exploded in laughter. "Oh, sure, you can laugh. I can barely walk, Mautner."

"Well, whose fault is that?"

This time, in front of a used bookstore on Bleecker, he did kiss her. They separated to catch different trains as usual, and all the way uptown, grimacing slightly every time the train bounced over a set of points, he thought *I want her because she has guts and brains and I never knew this before but that's what I want*

The next week she suggested the Museum of Modern Art, and he wondered did she do this to avoid another makeout session. Had he moved too fast? *No you didn't Shut up* By this time they had bookbags to carry the heavy texts through the posh midtown blocks, and despite the extra cost they checked them, tired of hauling them around. It meant he could put his arm around her again. The Matisses excited him, and he unconsciously pulled her closer, felt her pull slightly away. Too fast, he had moved too fast. *You can't heat the reactants too fast, you could blow up the apparatus.* They went for coffee at the museum cafeteria when they'd had their fill of art.

"I loved the Pollock," she said. "You know what I saw? Electron clouds. Orbitals."

"Jesus, Mautner, don't you ever lighten up? You're already a tool; you're in danger of becoming a power tool. I ought to know. Stop. Stop with the chemistry." She was hurt, he could see. He had hurt her, *stupid, stupid.* "I'm sorry," he said, "Of course you're right about the paintings. I see the orbitals too. That was supposed to come out as a gentle joke. It came out all wrong. I'm sorry. Hey. There are only two Organic Chemistry jokes. Want to know them?" It was a desperate try.

"Sure. Why not?" *Let him try to recover It's the mark of*

a gentleman

"First one: Why is Purim the organic chemists'
favorite holiday?"

"No idea."

"Because it's the Feast of Ester." She groaned. "Wait,
here's the other one. You mix ethyl alcohol with acetic acid and
you get what?"

"Ethyl acetate."

"And ethyl alcohol plus benzoic acid?"

"Ethyl Benzoate."

"How about ethyl alcohol plus fornic acid?"

"There's no such thing as fornic acid."

"But if there was, you'd get Ethyl Fornicate." She
laughed. "Look," he said, "I've been walking around all
day thinking I did something wrong last week, because we
didn't, ah…"

"Go to the back of a movie theater this week."

"Well, yeah. So I'm sorry for whatever I did…"

"You didn't do anything wrong. You know about as much
about female physiology as I do—did—about male." When he
looked blank she lowered her voice, beckoned him to lean over
the table, and said, "I'll enlighten you. My aunt Flo is in town."
When he continued to look blank she said, "My period. Menses.
Menstruation. Technically known as Being On The Rag."

He leaned back in relief and renewed affection. "Jesus,
Mautner." He grinned.

"Are we supposed to wear a sign?" she said. She could
see his relief. "So. About those orbitals—that the artists couldn't
have known about…"

"And the Surrealists. Man Ray's photograms…"

Clouds had descended; a frigid wind sliced through gray
crosstown streets, from river to river. They walked to Columbus
Circle, separated to take the two different subway lines that
shared the station. On the way uptown he again thought *guts
and brains*

Then it was Thanksgiving, home to family, and then it

was Christmas Break and papers were due and Finals just over the horizon. He couldn't stop thinking about her, couldn't keep his mind from slipping off the pages onto her body, the feel of it. Which was still, of course, mostly hypothetical. She called him in East Orange, Christmas Eve day, asked him to meet her for a study session, she was stuck on some points about stereoisomerism. He took the train in, met her at the Reggio. The windows were steamed over. They ordered; the espresso machine hissed for cappuccino. They split a Baba-au-Rhum, unable to afford two. "What's your problem with stereoisomerism?" he asked. Wondering *hoping* if maybe she had just wanted to see him.

"Not so much a problem as curiosity. I have a feeling there's a trick to this, a shortcut, especially to double stereoisomerism. That's one part of it."

"Okay. Yes, there's a simple trick. It's especially good on exams, where you're so nervous your spatial reasoning goes to hell. You don't have to picture it in your head; use your hands." He held up his hands. "Your hands aren't identical, right? You can't superimpose one on top of the other. They're mirror images (he held his hands up as if they were object and reflection), right hand and left hand…"

"Right, I get that part, sure. It's the practical part about seeing a stereoisomerism in a diagram. It's just a chain of carbon groups."

"And your hands are just hands *except when they're in mine* but there's a left and a right, because there's an axis of symmetry at the middle finger of each one, and there are two different ways of arranging the four different types of fingers around it. The thumb can go on the left, or on the right, pinky on the left or the right." He held up his hands, wiggled the fingers as he named them.

"Of course I get that, I'm saying I don't see it in the diagrams of molecules. I'm having trouble making the visualization."

"I'm saying, use your hands. Imagine the middle finger is a carbon atom. Imagine each finger is one of the four groups bonded to it. Any time there are four different groups around a carbon atom, you have stereoisomerism, the molecule can exist in right and left handed forms. He drew a simple diagram of a branched alkane. "Here":

$$CH_2-CH_3$$
$$|$$
$$CH_3-CH_2-CH_2-CH_2-\mathbf{C}-CH_2-CH_2-CH_3$$
$$|$$
$$CH_3$$

"The only carbon with four different groups bonded to it is the fourth in the chain. You can imagine the molecule in the mirror, but you don't have to. You just go methodically down the chain, looking for four groups at a single carbon, and to check your work, hold up a hand, the middle finger is a carbon, tick off each group as a finger. After a while it becomes second nature. And it's easy when the different groups are, like, Benzene rings, carboxyl groups, amine groups…"

"Neat trick."

"Quick, Mautner. Name that alkane."

"d,l, 4-methyl, 4-ethyl octane."

"Give the lady a cigar."

"I get it, I get it. I'm curious. Check me out here. I think this works for cis and trans too, only you treat the double-bonded carbons like your central carbon in an alkane." She flipped the notebook page, drew a diagram and passed it over to him:

"You got it, Mautner. What's the curiosity part?"

"I was wondering if this is the basis for enzyme action."

She knows Advanced Organic includes some Biochem.

"Sure. Their action as catalysts is entirely about the shapes of the molecules. You want a lecture?"

She settled back in her chair and folded her arms.

"Shoot, professor."

"Okay. Enzymes are proteins. Made of twenty amino acids in long chains. There are four levels of structure. Primary structure: the sequence of amino acids in the chain. Secondary structure: how the bonds and attractions between the amino acids in the chain bend it onto shapes. Twirls and helices."

"Which make, like, pockets and passages that hold other molecules for reactions to take place?"

"Which is called tertiary structure. But. One more level of complexity. Many proteins are actually made up of more than one amino acid chain."

"Hemoglobin," she said. Two alpha, two beta chains."

"Exactly. Held together by their structures, which is…"

"Quaternary structure."

"You got it, Mautner. All held together by complex chemical bonds. And the coenzymes can change the shapes too, get the enzyme ready for action. Which means the equations for the reactions aren't simple; they're curvilinear, with multiple factors."

"So I'll need my freshman calculus."

"Mostly for Physics, but yes. You will."

"And a sharp study partner."

"I'm in for the duration, Mautner."

"In that case, give me a Christmas present."

"What did you have in mind?"

"Call me Lisa, Ben."

"Lisa."

"Much better."

"Lisa?"

"What?"

"I'd like to see you independent of these study things. School's out. I'd like to go to a movie. I'd like to walk you home. Where is home, anyway?"

"The Stuyvesant Town apartments."

It was bitter cold, but it didn't matter; they held each other close and made it to the Waverly for *Battleship Potemkin*. And he did take her home, but it was too cold to walk; they caught the subway at Fourth Street to the Fourteenth Street Crosstown. "This was my commuter route," she said "In reverse."

"When?"

"Freshman year. I commuted from home. Then I rebelled, I insisted on moving to the dorm. My mother wasn't too crazy about it. My father was willing to pay." He shrugged; he didn't realize she was telling him something. When they got to the front hall of her building, she thanked him for the escort. They arranged a date for the following week, to meet at Penn Station and go to The Cloisters for the day. He'd assumed he'd get to escort her all the way home, maybe meet her parents, but she said, "My mother isn't home, and the neighbors are nosy. Better to say goodbye here."

He looked around, found the door to the fire stairs, pulled her inside, took her face in both hands, and kissed her. "Lisa," he said. She pulled him back; this time she opened her mouth. Time stopped, until they heard some kids clumping down the stairs. They got out just in time. As she got in the elevator she saw he was limping again. This amused her, until she opened the apartment door, knew it was empty, and then she was sad.

She aced the Final and the semester. A few tips on shortcuts had helped in the lab. Second semester began, and with it the clandestine romance. *Is that what this is? We can't even send each other Valentines cards.* He thought. *The Saturdays aren't enough* In the lab she poured toluene into a burette and opened the ground glass stopcock to draw off the first moiety. She leaned against the lab bench, closed her eyes, thought *stopcock*. In the supply room, his train of thought left every two minutes *she's maybe twenty-five feet from here*. She glanced around. No one watching. She pinched off the gas hose to the Bunsen burner; it went *phhht*. "Damn," she said.

At the next bench a guy, (*Firman? Firman.*) said, "Problem, Lisa?"

"Bunsen burner burped." She relit it. About ten minutes later she did it again. "Damn." Firman didn't even look up this time. The third time she did it, close to the end of lab, she said, "Shit." She looked over at Firman. "This burner's had it," she said as she shrugged out of her lab coat. "Gotta see Rothstein." Firman nodded, uninterested. She took as long as she could cleaning up, fiddled with the burner, pretended to scrutinize the intake valve. When all but one of them had left, she unhooked the hose, went to the supply room and banged on the door. Ben opened the top half. "Rothstein," she said as the last of them filed past, "This burner's shot."

"What's the matter with it?"

"It keeps sputtering, going out. I have to keep relighting it."

"Really." He opened the bottom half of the door. "Let's have a look." She walked past him as he looked down the hallway in both directions. Empty. He pulled the door closed, pulled her to him, into a deep kiss.

"Burner's fine," she gasped. They kissed some more, ran their hands over each other. "I couldn't wait till Saturday," she said. "Must be ovulating, or something."

"I can't either. We have to figure out places to meet. This is crazy, Lisa. And it's going to get crazier."

That Saturday he had a list. "Warm places for two people to meet in private," he said. "One, the Library, in the stacks. Two, Cathedral of St John the Divine."

She laughed. "We can't make out in a church."

"Why not? We're Jews, if we're anything. No. We're chemists. SJD professes love of all, invites all, and it has loads of dark places behind pillars and like that."

"You have to have respect for other people's beliefs."

"Do I? Religion doesn't interest me. When I was about ten, my brother gave me *The World of Carbon.*" Made more sense to me than any religion ever did."

"Isaac Asimov. I read that too. There must be an organic chemistry of religion. Of religious belief. Somewhere in the brain."

"Maybe. Huh. I never thought of that. Must be…"

"How does the Library work?"

"There's miles of stacks, floors of them, and there are stairs that connect them. No traffic. Very little traffic, anyway."

"How do we meet up? We can't just walk in together."

"Here's the fun part. I fold a message into your lab towel. Date, time, Dewey Decimal number of the place to meet. You put the reply in the towel and leave it on the bench top. Or just nod on the way out, or shake your head No."

"You mean like this?" she said, shaking her head No, "Because this is nuts, Ben."

"Yes it's nuts, but we aren't. It's the nutty situation, Leece."

On her lab bench, as on all of them, lay a towel. As promised, folded into it was a note. Just a slip of paper, torn from a notebook as if at random: **217 1930 547**. Today was the 16th; she could arrange her homework schedule. Next night at 7:30 she climbed through the stacks to 547: Organic Chemistry. Another of his little jokes, but she could see there was a staircase nearby. It all seemed pretty empty and disused; faculty and grad students would be using the departmental library, which, she realized, Ben knew. He had a real feel for this *Where did that come from?*

"Boo." He had whispered, but in the empty silence it had made her jump.

"Shit," she said. "Don't do that again. Promise me."

"Sorry. Promise."

"Listen, I know it isn't Saturday, but I have a question." He leaned on a shelf. "Is this stuff with hydrogen bonds going anyplace important? I mean, it's fascinating, but…"

"Hydrogen bonds hold the DNA helices together. And give enzymes and other protein molecules their conformation. It's actually pretty interesting stuff. Know what else is interesting? I've gotten to know every nook and cranny in this building."

"Show me."

220 1845 150 (*Psychology*)

224 2000 170 (*Ethics*)

305 1915 440 (*Romance Languages*)

308 1945 610 (*Medicine*)

310 1930 611 (*Human Anatomy*) Right, of course Ben.

313 1930 599 This one she knew from a Bio paper she had researched last year. She giggled to herself at an idea. Well, it was starting to be warm enough. When she showed up he saw she was wearing a ski jacket; the pockets were puffed out with something. She was trying not to grin. *What the hell?* He led her off to a stairwell behind a door, a poorly-lit spiral cage. He started to take her in his arms, but she held him back with a hand. With the other hand she took hold of the jacket's zipper.

"I know 599," she said. "Mammalia." When she unzipped the jacket there was nothing underneath. He gasped in delight, and something like awe. She smiled and laughed. She didn't exactly know what to expect, hadn't known, but she saw the look on his face, and it transformed him. "They're perfect, Leece," he whispered. "I've imagined your body a thousand times, and it's better than anything I imagined."

She had expected him to grab her to him, to have to say something like "Down, boy" and treat him like a child, but instead he gently ran his hands over her breasts. It felt even better than she had imagined. She thought *This is the first time anyone's ever touched them but me* He kissed her gently as he held her breasts, as if they were made of glass, or something even more delicate. Then he very gently kissed her neck, kissed down her chest while he slipped his hands around to her shoulders, *and here was a new sensation, her bare shoulder blades* and bent to ever so gently kiss one nipple, then the other. It was as if a butterfly had flitted from one to the other. As if a rose petal had brushed them. She buried her hands in his hair, moaned slightly, felt herself melt. He stood and she felt him hard against her. "Oh God," he gasped, echoing her exact thought, "We have to find a place to lie down."

"We can sit," she said. "Against the wall." This was no

better than satisfactory, but it had to do. They stopped when they both sensed things had reached the point of really bad decisions. When she had breath she said, "I wanted to surprise you."

"That you did," he said quietly. "You're beautiful, Lisa. More beautiful even than I imagined." She smiled, turned to him. He reached out to touch her again, tentatively. "I don't mean…that wasn't the surprise. My imagination often fails me where you're concerned. I mean, I've imagined you often, but the reality…"

"A pre-med took a lit course. Zelda Fitzgerald used to surprise Scott this way."

"I guess we'll have to meet in American Lit. I'll have to find the Dewey number."

Which was when they heard footsteps on the stairs. She froze. "Zip up," he whispered. "Go out into the stacks. I'll head down, slow him down. Meet me at Jack's." She nodded, and he galumphed down the steps, making as much noise as possible. He whistled. "Evening," she heard him say to whoever it was as the door started to close behind her, "Do you have the time?"

He found her at Jack's. "Are you still…?"

She unzipped the jacket. "I brought a top and bra in the pockets. I put them on in a bathroom at the library."

"Leece…"

"It was worth it, Ben."

"So next time we'll meet in American Lit."

"I don't know if I could do it again. I was so scared when…"

"I know, Leece. But, oh God. You're stunning, Leece. Gorgeous. You're…"

He dropped into a whisper. "They're perfect, Leece, so soft, and I'm crazy for you."

Well she thought *That was pretty much the idea* "You're pretty good at this clandestine stuff," she said mischievously. "Have you done this before?"

Clandestine stuff He made a face. "No. I…We can't go on like this, Leece. I thought I was going to lose it. We have to do this right. I want this to be right."

On the way back to her dorm she thought *Reverently.
That's the word. He touched me reverently*

They were never caught. They were perfect. It was part
of the fun, the excitement, she thought. They never thought *No
one is watching*. Hero and heroine of their own little drama, the
centers of their own universe, it never occurred to them they
weren't the center of anyone else's. The fact was, no one ever
suspected the grimly serious female power tool and the geeky lab
assistant. Ever *imagined*.

He found her note under the lab towel: *Have to see
you*. Well, he had to see her too. But it said *J 2030*. Which he
figured must mean Jack's. He got there at 8:15 and ordered
coffee. She looked unhappy when she slid into the booth.
"Something wrong?"

She passed over her last weekly quiz. "It's a B, Ben."

"So?"

"So? So now I need two A's to maintain the A. Or
three. We've been slipping, Ben. The last two Saturdays we've
been staring into each other's eyes instead of into Roberts
and Caserio. Don't tell me you haven't been having the same
trouble, and don't tell me it doesn't matter. For a girl pre-med it
matters, Ben."

"It's an academic double standard," he said, suddenly
fully realizing this.

"That's a great way to put it. So it's back to business,
Ben. I'm missing something here and I may need your help to
find it, before the midterm."

"Listen, Zelda…"

"Zelda won't be back until Lisa's got an A quiz average.
It's back to work, buddy. You know how much this means
to me."

"Relax Mautner. The lowest quiz grade is dropped. But
we'll work you like a rented mule if you want."

"We're back to Mautner?"

"We're in Mautner mode, Lisa, for as long as you need. *Till I can have you back* Let's see this quiz…"

"Saturday. I have to get back and study for this week's."

They went back to the Reggio, feet propped up, heads back in the books. She aced the next two quizzes. She figured three would restore the average. By now it was just warm enough to be sitting at an outdoor table. "Tell you what," she said. "I have about five pages left, but I'd like to be doing this lying in that park over there."

"Done," he said, signaling for the check. He threw a few coins on the table and pulled her out of her chair before she could change her mind. After that, as spring accomplished, they lay reading and making notes in the greening lawns of Washington Square Park. Around the fountain NYU students chased Frisbees. At the Arch some gathered around a young man with a guitar and a girl with a fierce contralto. Trees came into full leaf. They started to lie next to each other in the sun, until the day she shut Roberts and Caserio, sat up, looked him over, lay her head on his chest and pulled his arm over her. He stroked her belly, laid his book aside and stroked her hair.

"Tell you what," she said, looking around the crowded park. "I have a dream. What I'd really love to do is get out of the city entirely."

"Simple, if you have a car."

"A car? I don't even have a license. I'm only seventeen."

What? "What? How the hell are you in sophomore year and just seventeen?"

"I skipped a grade. The SP classes—did the three years of junior high in two. It's why I never drink. Can't, legally. Relax. I'll be eighteen in a few weeks."

"Then you can get a license." *And this too will be legal*

"No car to drive. We live in Stuyvesant Town. Go everywhere by bus or train. Or walk. Occasionally, cab. When we can afford it. When my father's around I get dropped off and picked up by limos."

"Who is he to rate a limo?"

"He's an orchestra conductor."

"He's a …Mautner. Jesus, your father's Kurt Mautner?"

Oh, Rothstein

"That's him. Kurt Mautner, not Jesus."

"Might as well be. We must have half a dozen of his recordings."

"He'll like that. If you ever get to meet him, give him my regards."

"Not around much?"

"Never was. Then gone completely. They aren't good friends. He pays the tuition. Not much else, but he does do that. That's why I was a commuter. One reason."

"Jesus, Leece."

"This is why I'm a woman of mystery."

"So why did they get married in the first place?"

"Guess."

"I don't…Oh. Oh shit. I'm sorry. I…"

"Nothing to be sorry about. I was an accident. A temporary impediment to someone's career. Two people's careers."

"God bless the accident." He bent his head to kiss her, but a premonition was there. He wondered if he could do this. *She wants to get out of the city.* "…I can get us out of the city."

"You have a car?"

"Not a car."

"How then?"

"A motorcycle."

She sat up. Looked at him. "You're a biker?"

"I'm a biker, Leece, because I can't afford a car. You up for this?"

"Maybe. Where is this motorcycle?" *In Jersey, must be*

He decided. "Come on," he said, standing and offering her a hand up. "I'll show you. It's a bit of a hike." He led her off south and east, to Broadway, across bustling Houston, just missing being hit by a truck making a turn, on south to Delancey. The Lower East Side. Quiet suddenly, the traffic a distant mutter. Unfamiliar territory; one ancient tenement with dark street-level store after another. Textiles, clothing, Judaica. In front of a shuttered dry goods store on Orchard Street he stopped, fished out a ring of keys. The sign said ROTHSTEIN'S. He opened a huge lock on the anti-theft shutter, then a series of locks on the front door, pulled her into the alcove, reached around and pulled the shutter down again and locked it by putting his hand through the grate and relocking the huge padlock, obviously no stranger to this procedure. "Behold," he said. "Rothstein's Dry Goods. Need any sheets? Pillowcases? Quilts? Bedspreads? Towels?" The place was dim, and he didn't turn the lights on, instead walking through to the back of the store. Dust hung in the wan sunlight from a set of dirty back windows that lit the stairs to the basement. More inventory was stacked ceiling high, but there was a space at the rear with a desk and chair. He unlocked another door to steps to a tiny courtyard at the extreme rear. A high fence blocked the view to a street behind it. It smelled... "Like shit," he said. "Once upon a time there were outhouses back here. Classic tenement."

"Why is the store closed on a Saturday?"

"Think, Mautner. Saturday. In this part of town, this is the Sabbath. Shabbos. Sunday is the Big Day at Rothstein's, when we make our nut."

"Which is why you're never around on Sundays?"

"I help my father at the store. That's where the money comes from. Plus the lab job." Against the fence was something covered by a stained tarpaulin. He whipped the tarp off. With obvious pride he said, "Honda CB450. Also known as a Black Bomber. Road bike, 444 cubes, enough horses to get us anywhere you want to go, pretty cheap."

Well, she thought, *It's a motorcycle.* "It's yours?"

"It was my much smarter brother's. He had it at school. Harvard." He bent over to check the wiring and brake lines. "I have to look it over," he said. "I keep the registration current but no one's ridden it in...a while." He checked the tires. *Needed air.* He took out his Swiss Army knife, "Also once my brother's," opened the screwdriver blade, bent, squinted, tested and tightened a loose screw, and returned the knife to his pocket.

"Why hasn't he ridden it in a while?"

"Because he's dead." When he looked up she was staring at him. "He was four years older than me. A math whiz. Morton Rothstein, Harvard class of 1964. Pre-med, supposedly. Only he never made it."

"You want to tell me what happened?" she said gently.

He had picked up a stick and a rag, put it down and faced her. "Stroke."

"I'm sorry," she whispered. "I'm sorry, Ben."

"He called me Rothstein, after... When he came to pick me up the first school day we were in Jersey, the little bastards were whaling on the new kid. He waded in and started throwing them off me. Throwing them. Big guy, Morty. They took one look and ran. They were calling me Rothstein the Jew Boy, hey Rothstein, little sissy New York kike faggot. When it was down to three of them I was able to get up and kick some ass. Not much. After, he said, Never be a coward little brother, cowardice is the ice that never melts. And after that we always called each other Rothstein. We were the Rothstein Brothers. Want to know what we did next?"

"Yes," she said.

He laughed. "We…he…no, we, had a chemistry set. Used to go into the city together, down to Radio Row, where they're building the Trade Center now, and buy chemicals and glassware at the scientific supply places. By the time he left for Harvard we had made everything we could that stunk, burned or exploded." She laughed. "So that night," he laughed again, "We made stink bombs…"

"Organosulfides," she said.

"Very good, Mautner, exactly. And I stink-bombed their lockers. Very few people messed with the Rothstein Brothers after that." He opened the gas cap, put the stick in, withdrew it, sniffed it. "Nada. Vaporized. Probably no spark either. Know what we need now, Leece?"

"A few gallons of a mixture of short and long chain alkanes."

"Again, we award the lady a cigar." He pulled out the key ring. "We can leave the books in the basement. We can push the bike to a gas station on Delancey, get some gas and a charge, fill the tires. It's work, but we ride back in style."

"You can really drive this thing?"

"He taught me. Took me to abandoned parking lots, up back roads in the Watchung. When I was old enough, seventeen, I got a license. We were going to get me a bike when I was old enough and do a Kerouac. Ride together cross country, to Frisco."

She made up her mind. "You can call me Mautner if you like, Ben."

"Thanks, but no. You're Lisa. I'm an idiot." He unlocked the back gate and they pushed the bike out into Allen Street, one on each side at the handlebars. He took the street side *Gallant Ben*. It was five blocks to the gas station; they were honked at the whole way. "Black Bomber," the pump jockey said. "Cool bike." He filled the tank, hooked up the charger. They pumped up the tires. When Ben turned the key and kicked down the starter the bike roared to life on the second try. He straddled the seat, beckoned her over. Putting his lips to her ear against the roar he said, "It always takes two kicks to start. Get on behind me. Put your feet up on the stirrups. Tuck your hair into your jacket. We tilt around curves. Hold the grab strap. Or put your arms around me and hang on."

"Oh, this is why you…"

"Partly, yes…" but it was lost in the roar of the bike as he took off down Delancey. Two blocks later he stopped at a light. Her face was buried in his back, her arms tight around him. He imagined he could feel her breasts against his back, but really the layers of jackets were too thick to feel anything. "You like?" he shouted. The bike vibrated under them.

Kind of "Yes," she shouted into his ear. "Where are we going?"

"Over the river. Brooklyn. Test Ride." They roared onto and over the Williamsburg Bridge. He threaded the way through the streets to the Brooklyn-Queens Expressway to test it on the highway. All around her the city roared. Buildings, overpasses flashed past when she peeked out from behind her streaming hair. When he felt her grip on him tighten he turned off onto the

Manhattan Bridge and ran off on the ramp to Chrystie Street. Minutes later they were back at the gate.

"You like?" he said.

"Yes. But (she was looking at the license plate): current inspection sticker?"

"They can't stop you in New York for an out of date Jersey sticker. I can sneak over Sunday night, on Monday get it inspected. We just gave it a more thorough test."

She was exhilarated and terrified. "Were you testing me or the bike?"

He grinned. "Both. You passed." *Guts and brains* he thought. He threw the tarp back over it, went through the elaborate ritual of locking, unlocking, locking. They shouldered the bookbags. He put his arm around her. "It's like he's alive again, Leece," he said. "Thank you." *I had guts and brains Rothstein   But no conscience Rothstein*

Back at the dorm her roommate asked her about the grease stains on her slacks. She hadn't even noticed, thought how she had ridden all the way uptown not knowing. "Over-friendly dog in the park," she said. The roommate, with whom she was not close, didn't ask what park. Going to sleep she thought about all they had learned about each other that day. She knew he was resourceful, and kind and gentle, and skilled in all sorts of unexpected ways. And that she was not afraid to stretch her experience. And, clinging to him, she felt safe. Protected. Immune. And she knew he was as lonely as she was.

When he opened the store the next day he had part of a Twentieth Century Poetry assignment read and written *In the Four Quartets Eliot proposes that all time, past, present and future is contained and experienced, or perhaps imagined, in every moment* by the time his father and some customers showed up. After a few hours business slackened. He asked for a few minutes off.

"Sure," his father said, wondering, but not looking up. He raised an eyebrow when Ben returned after a half hour with a chrome piece that looked like a tall letter A.

"It's a part for the bike," Ben said. "A backrest. I can rig luggage to it."

"Will it run?"

"I was here yesterday. I got it running."

WQXR, the classical station always on in the background, played Dvorak. His father grunted. "Be careful Benny," he said. "Don't go killing yourself on that thing."

"Don't worry," he said, and went out back, pulled out his old Boy Scout backpack full of tools and bolted the backrest on. Twisting the straps around it, he could carry the pack. Some belts would hold the old sleeping bag, or a quilt. *Ready.*

The note said *J 1745*. He was late; some numbnuts had dropped a big Florence flask full of glacial acetic, a tough cleanup. He still smelled of it. "It's late," he said. "You want to risk having dinner?"

She was hungry, and tired of all the secrecy. "I risk a biker boyfriend, don't I?"

"That's what I wanted to talk to you about. If the weather is right, you want to get out of town Saturday?"

"Where to?"

"Bear Mountain Park. I know a place. And I got you a present."

"What?"

"I put a backrest on the bike."

"How much will this little jaunt cost, Ben?"

"Not much. I have a few bucks. We'll pack a lunch."

"Let me take care of that. There's a little deli near my mother's."

"How about I roar up to Stuyvesant Town in my Hell's Angels colors?"

"How about I meet you at the Reggio and we get the bike out together?"

"Where's your sense of adventure, Mautner?"

She held on with eyes mostly closed until they were

across the George Washington Bridge, but found herself becoming comfortable when he opened it up on the Palisades Parkway, where there were no trucks. The city dropped behind, then the suburbs, and they were in the mountains. Everywhere was starting to be green, mostly just shoots, but among the rock formations and moraine were the evergreens, and many trees were starting to be in leaf. It didn't matter; it was warm and green and blue. He had attached the Boy Scout sleeping bag, backpack, and an old bedspread to the backrest with bungee cord. They roared off the Parkway onto ever smaller roads, finally creeping along an unpaved track between rock upthrusts. They pushed the bike over a little rocky rise. Behind it was a tiny jewel of a lake, a pond really. She heard splashes of, she thought, frogs. It was too soon for insects. She explored the pond edge while he tried to deploy the bedspread. When it just folded under she came back and helped. "Teamwork, Rothstein," she said, and started unpacking sandwiches. As they ate she said. "I'm not the first girl you ever brought here."

"No, Leece, you are. I know the place from Boy Scouts. They used to take us to Bear Mountain Park for hikes. I kinda sorta got myself lost and found this place..."

"I'm having trouble picturing Boy Scout Ben."

"I told you," he said, "After the stink bombs no one messed with the Rothstein boys. But we weren't loved either. I read books, and fooled with the chemistry set, and our microscope. So my parents put me in Scouts, to make friends, make me a regular guy. You know how in war movies there's always a guy in the platoon the regular guys call Professor? I was that kid. On this one hike...I'd read in deKruif's *Microbe Hunters* when Leeuwenhoek invented the microscope he looked in pond water and discovered microbes. Microscopic life. Which I couldn't see in purified tap water. We were on that ridge over there, and here was this pond. So I drifted to the back of the line and hid. Calculated where they'd be; used my compass to find them. They were in a panic. Scoutmaster was really pissed. But. I had a canteen full of pond water. Full of amoebas and paramecia. "

"I read *Microbe Hunters* too. I was the girl that went to Bronx Science."

"Holy shit, Leece. You never told me. I'm impressed."

"Well, I should have gone to Stuyvesant, five minutes away from Stuyvesant Town, but it's all boys. You know, not one of those Science geniuses ever had the nerve to even ask if he could carry my books, much less for a date."

"Probably scared you were smarter than they were."

"What happened with Boy Scouts? Did it make you a regular guy?"

"Nothing did. But. When I was fourteen Morty got the bike. That made us some friends real quick. He rode my new friends all over town. I showed him this place, once. He might have brought girls here. I think…I'm…I'm pretty sure…" he said vaguely. She brought out Roberts and Caserio. "Jesus, Mautner, you never quit."

"I have some questions about amide reactions. We're here to study Organic Chemistry."

"We are studying Organic Chemistry. All around you is Organic Chemistry. What it *does*."

"So, God was an Advanced Organic Chemistry student?"

He knew she was teasing him, but to him this was serious business. "What god? Been doing David Hume in Philo…"

"His refutation of The Argument From Design. The Watch–in–the–Desert–Argument. If you find a watch in the desert, there must be a designer."

"Yes. Which I can see, because a watch is made of metal and glass, inorganic chemicals. But you and I know that carbon molecules are capable of self-assembly. All they need is solvent and heat. Mautner. It's a World of Carbon. You were asking about Hydrogen Bonds. Did you know that DNA isn't really a molecule at all? It's two molecules. The Double Helix. The two helices are held together by hydrogen bonds. They can zip together or unzip to be the bases for two new helices. Self-assembly… "

She put the book down, picked her head up above the gently waving grass stalks. "That's how you think of this? Just Organic Chemistry? Where's the *wonder* of it, Ben?"

"For me that *is* the wonder of it. That Chemistry can *do* all of this. Every tree, every blade of grass a chemical factory, making wood and energy out of air and water. Us, all of us, chemical factories…"

"So that's what I am to you, a chemical factory?"

"It's all, the whole world is, one big organic chemistry reaction…" He had wanted to share this idea with her. "A series of chemical states, every moment a chemical state, unfolding from the previous state. Every tree, every flower, every grass stalk once a seed. Us once fetuses, sperms and eggs made by our parents who were chemistry labs, and them once babies. Back and back and back. Our brains: Huge organic chemistry labs with how many thousand reactions running at once. In series. Every thought, every feeling, a chemical state proceeding from the last one…" He was suddenly overwhelmed by the breadth of his own vision. "Life is an epiphenomenon. An emergent property of a fifth level of protein structure: Organisms. Quintenary structure? Quinary structure?"

"So, the brain is a biochemical engine? That explains consciousness, to you?"

"Very complex systems of molecules, neurotransmitters; you did the Bio 1 lab throwing acetylcholine at frog gastrocnemius muscle, right?—move across the synapses, activate the next cell in the system…"

"How can a thought move a molecule?"

"The moving molecule *is* the thought. Thought is an emergent property of the system."

"That isn't an explanation, it's just a way of talking about it. How?"

He knew he was on shaky ground. "I guess…in a way we can't imagine yet."

"Or maybe ever? Pretty smug view. Chemical determinism. Except, *you* don't know what the next state of the chemical factory's systems is going to be, do you? No surprises possible?"

The sun had warmed them; they had been able to shed their jackets, and shoes. He started unbuttoning his shirt. "Well, it's had four billion years. It's all surprises, I guess, even to itself.

What might it do in the next few billion years?"

"What might it do in the next few minutes? What might your quintenary structure do if it collides with some other quintenary structure?" She looked at his chest, pulled her sweater over her head, reached around and unhooked her bra.

"Lisa…" he kissed her, pulled her to him, felt her breasts against his chest; she kissed back, felt herself flush, felt his fingers and lips gently on her. They took their time, rising, lying back, rolling over each other. How long? They didn't know, didn't count. Once again they reached a decision point. He was panting. She pointed. "Did I do that?"

"Yes, Lisa, you did. Through the wonder of Organic Chemistry." Silence, except for tiny splashes at the pond, a breeze in the branches at the woods on the ridge.

"Can I…" she said, and stopped.

"Can you what?"

"See. Can I see it."

He was hesitant, then thought *guts and brains* and slowly unzipped his jeans. Slid them and his shorts down. Thought *What the hell* and took them off.

She reached over and touched him. "So smooth," she said. He gasped. "Sensitive too," she murmured. "It's been like that for quite a while."

He was breathing strangely. "Tumescent," he said, "Is the word you're looking for."

"Yes," she said. Suddenly she arched her back, unbuttoned her jeans, and slid them and her panties off. "It's only fair," she said.

"Only fair? No," he said. "It's beautiful Leece. You're beautiful. Beyond belief." He groaned, almost cried with frustration. "Leece, I'm not, uh, prepared. I never thought…" *Yes you are Rothstein*

"A Boy Scout not prepared?" she teased him.

"Protection, Leece. We need another organic chemical. Latex. We're not going to risk this. We can't. Shit. Oh, god."

She closed her eyes. "We can touch and kiss each other," she said.

"Yes, we can do that…" He reached over tentatively, then more surely.

She had a small orgasm almost immediately; lay back lazily. "Thank you, Ben," she said, eyes closed. "That was nice." When she opened her eyes, she saw he was still aroused. "Oh," she said. "Oh, Ben. I remember. Blue Balls. How are you going to stand driving a motorcycle…"

With effort he said, "I've been asking myself the same question." He lay down, turned away from her, ashamed, suddenly. *Interruptus isn't safe little bro* He didn't know what to do. Or rather, he did, but didn't know how to…ask. Or what to do if she didn't…

But she knew; whispered to him, "Turn this way. To me." And she kissed him and took him in her hand, tried to be as gentle as he had been with her. She felt him gasp, buck slightly as he came. He regained his breath slowly. "I'm sorry," he said.

"Don't be sorry," she said. "They weren't *actually blue,* you know."

They both laughed. "Thank you, then. For this relief, much thanks." He sat up, looked around. *This has to be right* he thought. "We have to do this right," he said.

"Yes. Ben, listen. I'm going to be eighteen in a few weeks. I know what I want for my eighteenth birthday."

"What?"

"I want *you.*"

He laid back down and held her. "Are you sure?"

"A girl hydrogen atom says to a boy hydrogen atom, Hey, I lost my electron. Boy atom says, Are you sure? And she says, I'm positive." He laughed. "I want to not be a virgin anymore, Ben, and I want *you.*"

"Then we have to find a place, Leece. It has to be right."

"Yes. Right. We'll give it some thought..." *Silence.*

"Yes. We certainly will. So…Uh…You had a question about amides?"

He thought about it in bed that night. How her touch turned a familiar simple bodily function into music. *Got a hot*

one there Rothstein Shut up Shut the hell up
* * *

She thought about it in bed that night. It had been like touching herself; she'd done that. The older girls, the ones who had "done it", said it was much better than that. She felt almost sure it would be; she knew what she felt when she saw him. She wanted him inside her. She wanted him to be her first.

The note said *J1845*. "Have you been thinking about it?" she asked him when he slid into the booth. "Because I have."

I've been thinking about almost nothing else "What's your conclusion?"

"Hotel."

"Right. Same conclusion I reached. Here's the bad news. New York hotels are about the most expensive in the world. Must have gold toilet seats. They're a little cheaper on weekends. There are Lyons Houses and SROs for winos and crazies, some right down Broadway, but we're going to do this right." When he told her how much a decent hotel cost her face fell; all their serious money *almost* was going into accounts to cover possible med school application fees, travel to interviews (the advice was: apply to ten schools minimum, to assure acceptance to one), microscope purchase and lab fees. "That's only the beginning," he said. "We'll need rings, to get past the front desk. And for me to legally buy condoms."

"You're kidding."

"I'm not. But I think I can get rings at a pawnshop. We can keep them or bring them back and hock them again."

She looked away. "I didn't think this was going to be so complicated."

"We could go back to the pond," he said. "Wait for warmer weather, score a pack of Trojans somehow, bring an air mattress, get bit up by mosquitoes…"

"Let's keep thinking."

They were both going home for Passover. She would travel to cousins on Long Island, he to Newark to change for the

Public Service bus. *Same station, going in different directions*
He put away the thought. It was a nice enough spring day to
walk down Broadway. He waited at Jack's until he saw her pass,
swung his backpack onto his shoulder and caught up with her.
When they were well clear of the campus he risked taking her
hand. There was no rush; as usual they looked in shop windows,
made a note of what was coming to the Thalia (but it was too
close to the campus to risk that), steered clear of the panhandlers
and junkies in Needle Park, admired Lincoln Center, strolled
through Times Square. They could have taken Eighth Avenue
south from Columbus Circle, but the Long Island Railroad
end of Penn Station was on the Seventh Avenue side, and the
working girls worked Eighth around the bus terminal; it was, he
realized, part of his ingrained, automatic deference to her needs,
his father's treatment of his mother, and look where that had
led. Then again, why make an issue of walking down Seventh
Avenue, through Times Square, vs. Eighth? *Why not*, he thought,
*ask her which way she wanted to go? Why did this never occur to
me, at least not before this?*

   He was in the midst of this reverie when she brought him
back to full consciousness by pulling him across 34th Street, and
he looked up and saw the solution to their problem staring him
in the face. It had been staring him in the face since he was a kid.
She started down 34th to the station entrance, but he pulled her up
short. "Leece, wait. Stop. Look. It's our answer."

   She didn't have to ask him what to. "The Empire
State Building?"

   "No..." He pulled her across Seventh and down to 33rd
Street. "There."

   "Macy's?"

   "No, The Hotel Pennsylvania, just south of Macy's. Right
there. It's a railroad hotel, Leece." She looked blank. "You know
the song? Pennsylvania 6-5000?"

   "Glenn Miller."

   "Right. You know the lyrics?"

   "It's an instrumental. There aren't any lyrics. Just,
wait, yes, 'Pennsylvania Six-Five Thousand', a few times, like

a chorus."

"And one time, 'Pennsylvania Six Five Oh Oh Oh'."

"Okay. So?"

"A railroad hotel, Leece, my father told me about these; he used them during the war, on leaves. You can get a room overnight or for a few hours, to wait between trains when you're transferring. You can check in without luggage, which presumably is in the station checkroom or on the station platform waiting for your next train. So anyone could check in for a few hours. To have Oh Oh Oh."

She looked over the shabby, graying building. It looked no worse than their dorms. "How much do you think it would be?"

"How about I find out? Wait here." Why he was reluctant to reveal in any way that he was there to find out how much a room would cost for the purpose of having sex with a girl he was crazy about, and wanted him, in a world that wouldn't allow it he couldn't say. *More of that phony gallantry, that patronizing I'm starting to see through her eyes.* The lobby was shabby, the carpets threadbare; obviously the place was a shade of its former self, like the ruin of the once grand terminal across the street. "Excuse me," he said to the desk clerk. "My mother's coming through on her way to DC to see my sister, she wants to see if she can stay here for a few hours to visit me, or for the night."

He thought the clerk's eyes said, *Yeah, sure kid, is that your best story?*, but he said, "It's fifteen a night." *You can afford that, Rothstein*

"Can you still get rooms by the hour?"

"Not anymore. It's fifteen a night. Nobody says you have to stay all night."

"We should be able to come up with that," she said when he told her. "Did you see a room?" He went back in, asked to see a room.

"Look kid," the clerk said. "I got nobody to cover the desk. The rooms are clean, there's nothing living in them but you and whoever you're with. The walls are thick, so it's quiet. They're gonna renovate all this," he pointed to the lobby, "And we're very understanding about being between trains."

"Wouldn't they have one of these around Grand Central too?" she said when he reported back. They agreed to meet and walk over on their way back. He insisted on staying with her until her train was called. "I know how to catch a train," she said.

"That's not why I…how about we go down to the platform and see if there's a dark end, behind a pillar?"

"That's different." There was.

The house was dark and dreary. Once his mother would have been buzzing around the kitchen, making dinner for aunts, uncles, cousins. Since his brother's death she had no interest. She had taken to bed most days, rarely leaving the house, which was in a perpetual state of mourning. His father greeted him at the door. He smelled chicken, knew she was at least up and cooking. He dragged his father's old Army B-4 bag full of laundry up the stairs. Pictures of Morty as a baby, a toddler, in his Little League and football uniforms, carefully arranged and dusted. A few trophies and ribbons and his books, he knew, were all in place behind the closed door of his room. A single 11 by 14 frame next to his own room held two baby pictures, himself in a Boy Scout uniform, in High School cap and gown. Mahler drifted up the stairs from his father's office.

She had set a fourth place at the table. Not just the traditional glass of wine for the prophet Elijah. They started to read the Haggadah, but it was clear her mind was on the Winter Break three years ago when Morty died. On his last seder, his last High Holy Days, his Bar Mitzvah. Back and back. *Morton Rothstein*, Ben thought, *Harvard 1964*.

"So what's new, Benny? Tell your mother what's new."

"Not much. Still pulling A's."

"You and your brother," she said. She sighed. "He was going to be a doctor."

No "I've been thinking, Ma. Chemistry majors can apply to med schools."

"Yes?" She sighed. "You never cared about practicality. I thought you wanted just to keep playing with chemistry, like you played with Morty, with the chemistry set."

He looked at her. Realized this had never occurred to him. "I'm…thinking of applying to med school, Ma. Harvard Med." He was stunned when she stood from the table and ran from the room. "I thought that would make her happy," he said to his father.

"It will. She'll come around." his father said. "It will me, too."

"Because of Morty?"

"Going to Harvard is special. Was special to Morty. To us."

"Columbia is Ivy League too. What's more *special* about Harvard?"

His father stared off. "In the war. My unit CO was a rock-ribbed Republican. From Bahst'n." He took a sip of Passover Manischewitz. "The Army put Jews into anything to do with numbers. They think Jews are so good with numbers. So, especially the Air Corps. Bombardiers, navigators, weathermen. Also, Quartermaster Corps. What I did in the war, same as I do now; I moved dry goods. Also truck and jeep and tank parts. Colonel Worthington. Hahvahd man, he never tired of telling us. Hated Jews, especially Jewish officers. Made it difficult, almost impossible, for me to get leave, to be with your mother. Hated *schvartzes* too, even though after we broke through in Normandy and ran across France, it was an incredible Negro Quartermaster unit, truckers, the Red Ball Express, who pardon my French were also treated like shit, kept Third Army in socks, boots, ammo and gas. Asshole." He took another, non-ceremonial, sip of Manischewitz. "That's what makes going to Harvard special. What's the point of fighting Nazis in Europe if we leave them the power here? Fuck the lot of them, again pardon my French, is my attitude. Morty's too." He took another sip of wine. "He wouldn't let me go home, Worthington. Quartermaster officers are in charge of cleaning up. Have to account for every one of those socks, boots, every other damned thing an army carries. The combat troops started to go home right after the Krauts surrendered. Worthington put me in command to keep me there counting everything, clearing the inventory and signing it out, telling me you're the best I have, Rothstein, such bullshit, he was just riding me, keeping me there and sending his friends home. I didn't get home until late '46, and your mother was at home with Morty, alone with him and Grandma the whole time." Another sip of Manischewitz. "There are assholes everywhere. Even at Harvard, still. But. It's also a place to meet rich people, make connections. Move up. Meet a rich girl, hey? Infiltrate *Bahst'n*." His father's tone was bitter; his face betrayed nothing but what Ben thought was avarice mixed with revenge. Or contempt with envy.

"It's a pretty damned good medical school. Best in the world, maybe."

"How did you decide to be a doctor, all of a sudden? You know we'd love that."

"It's not all of a…"

His mother returned, dry-eyed. "If you go to Harvard you can't help out in the store. Morty had to quit that too."

"In med school you don't get weekends and summers off. I'd have to quit the store no matter where I go after the first year, anyway."

"I'll hire an assistant," his father said. "You think it wouldn't be worth it?"

Ask him Rothstein "Maybe the first year I could come down weekends," he said, "On the train. I'd get in real late, stay like you did on leave, at the Hotel Pennsylvania." His mother looked up sharply. "Does the New York Central have one too?"

"The Commodore," his father said shortly. "Like in Commodore Vanderbilt."

His mother started to cry again. "Sophie, stop," his father said.

"I'm sorry," she said, sobbing. "I miss Morty. And now Ben will go away."

"I might not get in…"

"You might not. If you do, there will be no hotels. When you visit, you come home. This is your home." She looked at his father. "And there will be no assistants. We can't afford it. If he goes to Harvard I'll come back to the store." *That might be a start for her A good thing* he thought. But she didn't stop crying. Not altogether.

When she kissed him goodbye the next day her face was wet again.

***

    At Penn Station he went to a phone booth, found a phone book, looked up the Commodore. He met her train and they walked through the springtime city, holding hands, trying not to think *We're looking for a hotel to have sex in.* The Commodore was definitely a cut above the Pennsylvania, with, unfortunately, prices to match. "It doesn't matter, Ben. What matters is who, not where." He had long ago come to that conclusion, was relieved she had as well. A passing rain shower chased them into the subway, cheating them out of a walk back uptown. On the train something that had been bothering him, something seeing her again had driven to a far corner of his mind, popped out. The penny dropped. Railroad hotels. Army leave. Why did he need *Back and back and back*

    The pawn shop was on Eighth Avenue, the part of Times Square populated mostly by pimps and prostitutes of all persuasions. He got offers of things he'd never heard of. The shop had numerous rings, ruins of failed marriages or desperate situations. He only considered those that had been left for a hopelessly long time. "Kid," the guy said wearily from behind the wicket, "You'd be well advised to throw in a suitcase too, something that doesn't look brand new." Clearly the Voice of Experience *He's right Rothstein.* He took the advice. At a pharmacy somewhere on Broadway he asked for a three-pack of Trojans, careful to be wearing the ring. "Lubricated or unlubricated?" He felt mildly humiliated. *Rothstein you never told me.* Lubricated sounded better.

    Under the towel he left: Mission Accomplished.

    She was having second thoughts. Was she? If she thought she was having second thoughts…It wasn't him. *Ben wouldn't hurt me* He could have forced himself on her at the pond—no, it wouldn't have taken any force, she'd have been, pretty much, willing, she knew—but he didn't. Wouldn't. She *thought* knew she could trust him. Both to not hurt her, and to keep the secret.

She thought. *What am I afraid of?* It wouldn't hurt all that much. But after…How would she feel after? *And how would he*

When they met on a Friday night, at Jack's, he was already wearing one of the rings. She had the suitcase, had asked for it. He smiled at her, took her left hand, looked deep into her eyes, and slipped the second ring onto the fourth finger. "Happy Birthday," he said. She smiled, spread her fingers, looked down at the ring on her hand. Suddenly it wasn't funny. "Okay?" he said. She said she was, but her heart fluttered a little. She didn't know that his did too. He took up the suitcase. "You don't have Roberts and Caserio in here do you?" he asked.

She punched his arm. "I do not," she said. "I have a birthday surprise."

"What would that be? Aside from no Roberts and Caserio."

"Is there something about the concept of "Surprise" that escapes you?"

The suitcase was heavier than was comfortable for a walk from 112th to 33rd Street; they went into the subway at 110th. In the train she put her head on his shoulder. They had tried to dress like a young married couple traveling by train. However that looked. In the event, the bored desk clerk hardly looked up. Ben thought he quickly looked for rings and luggage, but couldn't be sure. *Better safe than sorry*. He signed the register Mr. & Mrs. John Roberts. On the way up in the elevator he said, "How you doing, Mrs. Roberts?"

"Still okay, John." But her heart still fluttered.

The room was small, the door thick and heavy, with an alarming security chain and large directions to fire exits. The curtains were wide open; he pulled the shade and closed them. When they put the dim lights on, the walls were cream colored, all the way to a shadowy ceiling higher than in a more modern building. The furniture was scarred, the carpet worn. There was a faint musty odor. But the bed was large and high off the floor, the mattress soft. The towels were a little coarse. "If I'm any judge of dry goods," he said. She took the suitcase into the bathroom, and emerged with a box of incense and a lab Bunsen igniter. "Is that stolen lab equipment, Mautner?"

She winked. "Borrowed. But it's okay, I know the lab guy." She lit two incense cones. He came over and took her in his arms, kissed her. "You might want to make yourself comfortable, Rothstein," she said, and disappeared into the bathroom. He took his clothes off. He popped a peppermint Lifesaver into his mouth, feeling like an idiot, but this was a birthday present. *He* was a birthday present. No. He was *delivering* a birthday present. He was a conveyance. Like a United Parcel truck. He wondered suddenly *Morty wouldn't* if he was up to this. If he could do this; do it right. Do it at all. His heart was beating wildly. He knew they were about to cross a line *but we've already crossed so many* He took the condoms out of his wallet and put them in the bedside table drawer. *These things can break, and then* He recognized his anxiety just as she came out of the bathroom, wearing a long white nightgown with eyelets and lacy straps.

"Oh," he said. "Oh, Leecy."

She pirouetted. "You like, Mr. Roberts?"

"Very much, Mrs. Roberts." He rose and embraced her. "I like *you*, Mrs. Roberts."

She had taken some time adjusting the gown, brushing her hair, facing her anxiety in the last moments, realizing that desire had surprised and overwhelmed her at the pond, had driven her past any anxiety. When he kissed her, tasting like peppermint, kissed her neck and her eyes it began to happen again. He ran his hands down her, kissed her down the straps of the gown, across its neckline, the tops of her breasts and shoulders. Then he knelt down and lifted the hem of the ankle-length gown, as slowly as he could, running his hands up the backs of her legs and thighs. She was naked under the gown. He kissed her at the tops of her thighs where they met her belly. He touched her so carefully, so tenderly, almost hesitantly, as if she were made of glass *as if I might break*. Then it was like at the pond, like when she touched herself. The roller coaster rose in a steep curve toward a peak. "Bed," she gasped, and pulled him to it. Desire warred with anxiety and inexperience *do I want this now, or just to get it over with?* He was aroused, she saw.

Driving himself past anxiety, he dropped down next to her and grabbed a condom, couldn't get it open, finally tore the wrapper with his teeth. She had to laugh, and this partly broke her mood, but not, entirely, his. "I want you," he half whispered, half said.

"I want you too," she said, and opened her legs slightly. He pushed gently into her, just hard enough to enter, then push… "Ow." She jumped slightly.

He stopped "Okay?" he gasped, anxiety returning.

"Yes, yes, it's fine. It's okay, Ben."

He thrust once, twice, felt himself starting to come and held her tight. He tried not to thrust too hard, worried she might be dry; he wasn't sure, couldn't tell with the condom on…didn't really know what that might mean. He held her, whispering her name.

She liked that, liked that she had given him obvious pleasure. But it hadn't been that different from when she pleasured herself…"Thank you, Ben," she said. When he withdrew she drew her knees up, covered herself with the nightgown and looked at him.

"Was that okay for you?" he said.

"Well, I'm not a virgin anymore, and the nicest boy in the entire world did the job, tenderly and gently, which felt good, so I guess that was more than okay."

He lay back, then after a while jumped up to the bathroom to take the condom off. When he returned she had pulled the covers up. In repose her face looked angelic to him. At length she went to the bathroom to clean herself. There was a little blood spot on the sheet. She couldn't resist looking at herself in the bathroom mirror. Did every woman do this at this moment? Every one with access to a mirror? *Nothing different.*

He wondered what she was really thinking. He felt he had made a botch of it. He had wanted to do it as she deserved, to mirror how he felt about her, with full orchestration; at best, he felt, it had been a decent string duet. *At best* She came back to bed, pulled the covers up again, rose up on an elbow and kissed him. He would have liked to talk or watch a little of the "Tonight Show", just to cool down, but from the looks of things the nicest thing the nicest boy in the world could do was go to sleep with her. He turned off the light and put his arm around her.

He woke from a dream of her. He was hard as rock. In the dream they were...he had...in the half-light of the City That Never Sleeps, there she was. There was the face he had just...he bent to kiss her.

She stirred. She dreamt she was experiencing the best kiss ever, a kiss that included soft fingertips circling her breasts through a diaphanous fabric. And then she was awake, and it was not a dream. She put her hand in his hair, opened her mouth under his, rose to meet his hands and his tongue. The roller coaster began to rise. He started to pull the nightgown up; she sat up and pulled it over her head; naked, she pulled him down and he gently sucked one breast, then the other. She moaned; felt the roller coaster rising higher and steeper on its track, rolled over on him, kissed him deeply, pressed her breasts over his mouth. He rose and licked one while caressing the other, then switched. She felt him hard against her. He rolled her on her back, ran his tongue down her belly and between her thighs. She moaned; he paused to catch his breath, grab a condom pack out of the drawer and tear it open, and returned his tongue to her. He could taste the center of her, heard her cry out. The roller coaster had seemed to reach the top but it suddenly rose higher and steeper, higher than it had ever risen, higher than she thought it could rise. For him it was a revelation. He licked her gently, then insistently; she held his head, cried his name. He grunted, was past speech. He only knew he could happily drown in her. His hands ran over her breasts, under her thighs, her buttocks, raising them, raising her to his lips and tongue. Her hands in his hair, she felt the roller coaster rise higher than she thought possible. "Ben, now." She all but screamed it. He rolled the condom on with the last rational thought he had and plunged into her; even through the latex he could feel her heat. She pulled her knees up, pulling him into her, wrapped her arms and legs around him. He covered her mouth with his, buried his face in her neck, *Lisa, Lisa, Lisa,* feeling her body rise to meet his, the roller coaster reaching a new height together, and suddenly plunging over the edge, down into a tunnel, up another rise, down, around, up a little and down and around, slowing, running quietly and coming to rest along a flat to a little pond surrounded by waving grass, in a quiet wood.

They held each other, breathless, stunned, awestruck at the audacity of what they had done, what they had discovered. A simple biochemical act, one their parents knew, that common act that had started the long chain of chemistry that was themselves. In the half-light they looked at each other, wide-eyed, still joined at their centers. He couldn't hold himself up; he collapsed into her embrace, whispering her name in her ear, feeling her breathe, that miraculous process. Their breathing synchronized, slowed. He felt her contract a few times around him, *what an unexpected pleasure*, felt himself shrink, but not unpleasurably. He came out of her to assume a new and pleasing embrace. The nightgown was on the floor. Bedclothes were everywhere. They could not let go of each other. When he could speak he said, "Happy Birthday, Lisa. *Now* you're not a virgin anymore, and neither am I. *We* aren't a virgin anymore."

"What *was* that?" she whispered.

"Some more organic chemistry? An emergent property?"

"I didn't know," she said.

"Neither did I," he said.

"I didn't know it was possible to feel this good. I want to stay here forever. I want to feel like this forever. I want to do that again."

He ran a finger over her cheek. "Yes," he said. "Oh, yes."

When they woke it was full light. He grabbed his watch; nine thirty. Damn. Checkout time was eleven. "No," she said. "Ben, I don't want to go. I don't ever want to get out of this bed. I don't ever want to be anyplace but in this bed with you."

"I couldn't want anything more, Leece. There'll be other beds, other times."

"When's your birthday?" *Today, he thought; today's my*

birthday. "Past. I was twenty last month."

"You never said."

"I didn't want you to get me anything. I thought I'd get my present now. And I did. Leece, we have to go. We have to shower and go…Hey, we can save time, shower together." She liked that idea, giggled and laughed when they soaped each other up, when the inevitable happened, when they couldn't figure out how to do it standing up. "I can't see getting a condom into this situation anyway," he said. That brought her back to earth. "Agent XX" he said. "We have to figure out how to get you back through the German lines with the radio." When she gave him an Are You Crazy look he said, "Clandestine stuff. The suitcase. You left the dorm with it; you have to go back with it. And we can't be seen together on the train, especially with that."

"Or the rings, Agent XY." She was, unexpectedly, sad when she took the ring off.

In the mirror she still looked the same to herself, but thought, *I'm Having An Affair Now I know what my mother knows* and *What would the other girls think if they knew* She knew she wasn't well-liked. Not disliked, just not well-liked. Would she be better-liked if she were the Voice of Experience? Or just a braggart? Would they like her even less, being, as she was, younger than them all? *Would they even believe me* And there were, of course, The Rules. She felt pretty sure she could suffer some penalty. Expulsion, even. They all knew that. *So maybe I'm not all that unique Maybe I won't be the only one pretending to be a virgin Being secretly proud not to be*

Back in his dorm, he lay thinking. *What did I tell you Rothstein? Was that great or what. You nailed one. Shut up You can shut up now Morty I don't need you anymore*

"How often do you think we can afford to go to the hotel?" she asked. She was sitting, naked, on the soft fleece of the Boy Scout sleeping bag, which in turn lay flat on the air mattress he had picked up at Hudson's Army & Navy. She was brushing away flies and gnats, which had begun to swarm at the pond. He reached out to touch her breast. "Back to business, Rothstein," she said, pushing his hand away. Two copies of Roberts and Caserio lay beside the mattress.

He lay on his back, naked; closed his eyes. Insects whined. "Well, the initial expense of the rings and suitcase are behind us, and we'll eventually re-hock those. Incense we have. Condoms could be considered an expense, but we should move that to the investment side of the ledger. That leaves the room rate of fifteen bucks, which at my current rate of pay and your allowance leaves us flat broke. *No it doesn't* No. Seriously? If the bike holds out, and we come up here most Saturdays…once a month? Two months?"

She flung herself on him. "I don't know that I can wait that long."

"Finals are coming up Leece. We won't have the time anyway."

"I meant to ask about the Complex Synthesis Exercise."

He heard the capital letters. "It's no big deal, really. You get a compound to synthesize. You have a few days to plan it, you work out what you need, hand in a list of necessary supplies and equipment—to me, by the way—and then you carry it out."

"It's scary, Ben." She pulled on an army surplus OD T-shirt to keep the bugs off. "I dream organic chemistry."

"Waste of time, Leece. The only useful organic chem dream was when Kekule couldn't figure out the structure of Benzene. C_6H_6, it kept going around in his head…"

"Do you really believe that story?"

"Truth or legend," he said, "It gets passed on. I never dreamed anything that coherent." *Not exactly about chemistry, anyway*

"It wasn't that coherent. C_6H_6. How can that even *be*? He dreamt the six snakes with their tails in each other's mouths, and he made the leap to six carbon atoms in a hexagon, the benzene ring, but that wasn't the important part."

"I see what you're saying," he said. "The important part was when he woke up and saw the connection between the dream and the structure problem."

"No," she said, "The even more important part is that he had to imagine and prove chemical resonance to explain the bonds…"

"And discovered the resonant bond, which wasn't in the dream. Damned good point, Mautner. Resonant bonds. It started in a dream but it needed work."

"I just dream I'm in this big empty kitchen."

Resonant bonds… "Leece, I'd do anything for you. Anything. I could look over your list of supplies if you thought you needed me to."

"Really? You would do that? Why would you be willing to do that, Ben? You think I can't do this on my own?" He realized she'd mistaken his meaning.

"Because it has nothing to do with being a doctor. You aren't going to be synthesizing organic goop; that's for the chemical engineers and flask jockeys. But you don't need me or anybody to do anything for you, Leece. You've memorized a zillion rules about how to make an aldehyde into an acid into a ketone into an alcohol into an amide into an amine…who knows that better than me? It's cooking. If you had to make, something complicated, like, say, what, a risotto, what would you do?"

"Look up the recipe, gather the ingredients, study the recipe and make notes on the best sequence of steps, and light the stove."

"Same exact thing. No sweat, Leece. You've got this knocked."

Resonant bonds He was washing glassware. Rinse, load machine, empty machine, acetone rinse, let dry, replace in closet. Repeat. As if he were part of the machine. He always smelled like nail polish remover. She didn't mind; she often smelled like the last thing she'd made in Friday lab. Rinse, load, unload, acetone rinse. Think about the next time they'd be together. He realized *This is the way maybe 90% of the world lives. Numbing physical labor while imagining a good fuck.* It was the same when he was trying to study some dull course. Statistics, say.

The sum of the…divided by the square of…He would close his eyes, feel her skin. Taste her. *I told you Rothstein Quit with the studying bro Whoever she is she beats the hell out of chem lab It's just a big chemistry set We outgrew that didn't we And stats and calc Jesus bro It's just another version of The Store* Even when he was reading something from a favorite *fun* course. Chaucer. Eliot. American Lit. *Guts and brains* he thought. And heart. And humor. In that body. *Tell you what, Mautner* he thought, *I love the way you…*he stopped. *I love the way you do anything. I love…you.*

Did he? What was love? Another emergent property? *A desire to always be with someone?* Check. *For the rest of your life?* Yes. Probably. *Till death do us…*he shied away from that one. *I've never said it to her And she's never said it Doesn't seem to care.* What would she expect if he said, "I love you?" A pin? A ring? A wedding? He didn't know. For all he knew it would scare her off. She had places to go. *Both of us do.* She was every bit as good as he was, he knew that. Better, at some things. And maybe that's not what she felt at all. *Anyway, people you love make demands and you never know what they might be* Did she have moments like this? Did she think about this? He had no way of knowing that, about a thousand feet away across Broadway, she did.

He was lying in his rack reading when his roommate, less a friend than a fellow lab rat, crashed in the door, slightly drunk. "You dog," he said. "You lucky dog." Ben looked at him quizzically. "Word is you're banging some chick from the Barnyard."

Exactly what they'd been afraid of. He realized in an instant how his stock would rise in the dorm, on the campus, if that got around *Tell him What's to lose, Rothstein Be the Big Man on the floor, maybe the whole dorm Change the way the jocks and preppies see you* was ashamed of the thought, knowing he thought more highly of her than that, valued what he had with her more than that, knowing how much this could cost her, how much actual trouble she could be in *I'm not you, Morty.*

He smiled wanly. "I wish," he said. "They run that place like a nunnery. Who's this lucky chick supposed to be?"

"Girl in one of your lab sections," the roommate said, trying to lean against the wall and almost falling. "Starts with an M. N? M."

"Mautner?"

"That's it."

Tempting, ain't it "Nah. Nothing to it. Who says?"

"Jock named Boland."

"Boland's a prick. And she ain't that great. Cold fish. Total power tool. Nope. Sorry." He went back to his book. Realizing *Resonant bonds* how much she had to trust him. Realizing he truly was falling in love with her. Had fallen.

When she came in from her lab her roommate and two of her friends were sitting on her bed. "You have to tell us all about it," her roommate said. "That's the rule."

Trying not to betray too much anxiety, trying to sound bewildered, she said, "About what?"

"You know about what. About the guy. About IT."

"What guy?"

"The guy across the street you're Doing It with."

She kept up the bewildered look, *insides turning to water*, shook her head. "Still not getting it," she said.

One of the roommate's friends said, "I have it from my roommate who's dating a Phi Delt whose frat brother is in your lab, that you're Doing It with this Junior."

"A Junior? There's no Junior in the...Wait, the lab guy? The tech?"

"That's the one."

Tell them. Be one of the girls Why not "He's a total tool. Not my type."

"The Phi Delt says."

"Then the Phi Delt is full of crap, and so is your roommate. And I need to study, which is all I do for that damned course."

"You're sure?" the roommate's friend trilled.

"Sorry to disappoint you," she said.

* * *

She couldn't risk a phone call to his dorm, so it had to wait until she could get a note to him. They met at the Reggio. "I know," he said. "It's Boland. I denied it."

"And they believed you?"

"No guy would deny it. My br…most would say it was true even if it wasn't." She realized this was true. *In fact he could have been bragging all along, and obviously hadn't.* "It's just Boland," he said. "And I thought about doing a number on him again, but I thought that would just blow it up. So, just a simple denial." She nodded. *Best idea.* "Close one," he said. He took her hand. "I know how much it means to you to keep this secret," he said. "I would never, ever hurt you, Leece. Never." He looked away. "I went so far as to call you a cold fish, to really clinch it."

She looked down. "I did the same thing," she said. She looked at their still-joined hands. She realized she was truly falling for him. Had fallen. "Maybe we didn't have to go that far."

"Given how I feel about you, Leece, it about tore my heart out."

"Mine too," she said. They sipped coffee quietly. "How is that?" she said finally.

"How's what?"

"How you feel about me."

He thought quickly. "Do I really need to put it into words?"

She thought quickly *Mistake Mistake Don't push Not now Don't risk* "No," she said. "We don't have to put it into words. What we have to do is cool it for a while."

"Yes," he said miserably. "Well. Finals are coming up. Maybe we would have had to do that anyway."

"Yes. Probably."

"And we should go back separately. I'll kill an hour at Bleecker Books." She got up to go. "Leece. Wait. I'm going to put it into words. You're the most wonderful and beautiful thing that's ever happened to me."

Unexpectedly, her eyes filled, and she touched his cheek. "After exams," she said, "We'll celebrate, Mr. Roberts."

They aced their courses. They celebrated with a night at the hotel. "I have a surprise for you, Mr. Roberts," she said. "I have a summer job." He did too, but at the store, earning the allowance he got the rest of the year; no addition to the income side of the ledger. So this was big news. "At Macy's," she said. "Perfumes and maybe lingerie counters." His eyes widened. "Right next door. And pretty good pay, Ben. We can do this without bugs. And in air conditioning." And they did. Nearly every week, telling her mother and his parents that they were visiting school friends in the country. "Hello Mr. and Mrs. Roberts." By August the hotel staff greeted them by name. He met her at work; she could get things at employee discount, looked like a fashion model. They took their time now. He enjoyed undressing her slowly. "You're like this incredible gift I got," he said one night. "I so love to unwrap it." She grinned; for the first time in her life she felt as attractive as her mother and cousins told her she was.

One Friday night he was late. "Couldn't take the bus through Newark. Orange Avenue is in the riot zone. Had to take the Lackawana to Hoboken, then the Tubes. Takes twice as long. Newark's burning, Leece. They have army in the streets. I think…" The room, on a top floor, faced west. He raised the shade. "I thought so." They watched smoke rise from the fires far across the river. "Can't blame them," he said. "You remember the fire hoses turned on the kids in Birmingham? The bomb in the church?"

She nodded. "What can we do, Ben?"

"I don't know," he said. "I don't know what any two people can do."

One Friday night she arrived slightly irritated. When he embraced her, started to work on a button, she stopped him. "Problem?" he said.

"My aunt Flo was late and has overstayed her welcome by a little."

"Did we miscalculate…? *Did a condom break*

"No, it just isn't a clock. Most likely no problem. Should be no problem by morning. It does leave us with an open night."

"Movie?"

"Nothing worth seeing. I checked."

He looked out the window. "Ever been to the Empire State Building at night?"

"Never." It was two blocks away. A brief thunderstorm had cleared a humid haze. The steaming streets had cooled just enough. The line late on a summer Friday night was long, but had some interesting people on it. One couple carried a picnic basket and chatted in rapid-fire Quebec French, which they were able to understand just enough of for the couple to catch them eavesdropping.

"Parlez Francais?"

"Oui," Ben said, "Un petit peu, si vous parlez tres lentement et avec un accent *Brooklynoise*."

The man grinned. Slowly, as if speaking to a child he said, "Nous sommes marrié aujourd'hui."

"Ah, oui. *Felicitations*," Lisa said. This elicited a barrage of more complex French than either of them could completely understand, involving some romantic expectation of the Empire State Building. The view on a storm-cleared night was, in fact, spectacular, canyons of light becoming strings of jewels leading in all directions through the outer boroughs and suburbs; distant lightning. They took several turns around the 86th floor terrace, Ben pointing out landmarks in Brooklyn and Jersey, Lisa paying a quarter to look through a telescope into her own window (she thought) in Stuyvesant Town. They found the Columbia campus by following Broadway north to a patch of relative darkness, joked about it. When they got to the 101st floor there was the sound of a cork popping. The honeymooners had opened their picnic basket and were sharing champagne. The small crowd applauded as they deployed a tiny portable record player, carefully placed a 45 on the platen, and danced a slow foxtrot.

Two other couples laughed and joined in. Lisa took Ben's hand. "Dance with me."

Ben froze. Then he awkwardly, reluctantly, took her hand, clumsily put his arm around her waist and revealed a total lack of terpsichorean skill. On the walk back to the hotel she needled him. "Finally found something you're not good at, Rothstein."

"Sorry. It's my brother you want. He could dance any girl around a room."

"You did that like you've never danced with a girl before."

"I never have. Once with my mother at Morty's Bar Mitzvah, once with her at mine. Never really learned. About my Bar Mitzvah, the less said the better."

Which was of course her cue to say, "You must tell me all about it."

"For a start, my Torah portion was Va'yeshev." She looked blank. "Genesis 38. The Story of Onan." She shook with laughter; she laughed so hard she doubled over and he had to help her up the steps to the hotel. "Oh, yeah. I had to make a speech about the meaning of the story to me. Morty never got over it. He had stopped believing in God years before. I don't think I ever did." He put on an imitation of the cracking voice of his thirteen-year-old self. "The Story of Onan teaches us of our duties to our family before HaShem. Only HaShem defines what is sin and what is righteous." She had to hold her sides. "But when seed is spilled, does not something grow?" She exploded again. "Morty about shat himself. I could swear even the old men, even my father, even the Rabbi, everyone who stuffed a check or Series E Bond in my jacket pocket, were biting their cheeks to keep from laughing. Who could learn to dance?"

When she could, she said, "That won't get you out of it. I learned at summer camp. We had dances with the boys. Our counselors taught us."

"Not a lot of dance instruction at Boy Scout Camp."

"I'll teach you," she said. He was doubtful. But realized she wanted to teach him something, that this was important to her. Back in the room she searched the radio dial, found the Jonathan Schwartz show, a mix of Sinatra, Bennett, Peggy Lee, and Big Band. "Start with a foxtrot," she said. "All you have to do is hold me and step around."

"I know how to do that naked."

"It's a social skill, Rothstein. You have to learn to do it with clothes on."

"I've heard it said it's a vertical expression of a horizontal desire."

"That too. That's it. Be inspired. It's impossible to be bad at this."

"We're alone," he said.

"So? Oh, I see. It's…you can't dance in front of an audience. You aren't uncoordinated, you're self-conscious."

"Exactly. Yes. I really don't know what I'm doing."

"You must know something. You're leading."

"I am? What's leading?"

"You're setting the pace and the route and moves. You don't know you are?"

"No." To "String of Pearls", she began to turn him, set the pace. "I see." He said. She stopped suddenly. "Now you know how it feels."

"How what feels?"

"To be female. You had no idea you were leading. You just did it. A natural male thing. No idea what you're doing, but you lead. Instinctively. And I was taught to follow. Instinctively." He heard her bitterness.

"I'm sorry." he said. "This was supposed to be fun."

"And all of a sudden it wasn't," she said. She sat down on the bed. "It took me by surprise. The idea of it."

He sat next to her, put his arm around her. "Anything I can do?"

She thought. "You could learn a dance that doesn't involve leading, or where I could call the shots. The Lindy." She showed him, and, slowly, he seemed to get it; two steps on the lead foot, two on the back foot, backstep, repeat. When he got it, and "In the Mood" came on, she said, "Twirl me." When he looked blank, she threw his hand up and twirled herself on the end of his arm. She showed him a few other steps, told him when to do them, and was happy again. So was he. "Think you could do this on a dance floor?"

"I might," he said, and wondered when and where that could be. A part of his brain said, *Awkwardly. At our wedding. Our children's Bar Mitzvahs and weddings. Morty would cut in and dance her around the room*

She went into the bathroom. "Good news, Rothstein. I think Aunt Flo will be gone on the morning train."

And then it was Labor Day, school around the corner; she would be quitting the job, and he was saving money again. He would be starting the application process to med schools in the fall; fees, travel expenses... "Why travel expenses?" she finally asked, one night when they were wrapped around each other at the Pennsylvania, listening to the off-hum of a faulty air conditioner.

"I've decided to apply to med schools."

"When was this?"

"I started to feel...I got sick of being a lab rat. Test tubes and equations just aren't doing it for me anymore."

Why travel expenses "In the City?"

"Sure, of course, and that's where I'll probably end up, but I have to apply to some others, to be safe. And, Harvard."

She pulled back. "Big step, Rothstein."

"I know it. You inspired me. I've been toying with it for...I decided. "

"Pretty far from here." *From me, I mean*

From her, she means. But also "About five hours by Black Bomber."

"In the winter?"

"Train. I can sleep on a train, be right here by Saturday morning, do it in reverse and be back by Monday class. After a year you'll be there too, and we can stop living like the French Resistance."

"You have it all planned out, do you? You know the chances of a woman getting into Harvard Med are about zip."

"There's BU and Tufts..."

"There too, my advisor told me." *And they're not Harvard* "Not even Columbia. My advisor told me my best shot would be at Woman's Med in Philadelphia."

"You're a 4.0 student, Leece."

"And from a Seven Sisters school. Means nothing if you don't have a penis."

Can't tell her why "Leece. Harvard is The Best. My advisor told me the definition of an Expert is someone from Harvard with slides. I have to try."

"I want to be The Best too. Where do I go? Sure as hell not Harvard."

"I might not get in. But I did once. I did it once already, Mautner." She had never seen him angry. No, not true. She had met him in a rage. She had never been on the receiving end. His anger was an ugly thing. "I got into Harvard, just like my brother. That's one reason he was home that weekend, to celebrate with me. *You have to get out of The Store, Rothstein It's the only way out of The Store* The Rothstein Brothers were going to take Harvard. When he died, my mother folded up. Took to bed for weeks at a time. Cried, wouldn't eat. Couldn't or wouldn't go to the store. Still won't. That's one reason I help out my father on Sundays. I couldn't leave them." He looked away. "That wasn't the only reason. My Harvard money went to pay for Morty's funeral. I was accepted at Columbia too, and they offered a partial scholarship and the Grant-in-Aid lab job. I took that. I walked away from Harvard once, Mautner." He caught himself. He softened his voice, took her hand. "I'd only be a phone call away. You could call me whenever you…"

"Need help? You think I can't do this without you? Is that what you think…?"

"Shit, I saw this coming from the get-go. Remember, I told you, the first night at Jack's, you didn't need me. You were acing the course on your own. I'm the one who told you, you could do it on your own."

"So you think I need you for that?"

"For what?"

"To tell me I can do it on my own?"

They made it up, apologized, but knew it lay between them, an unwelcome third in the bed.

She would eventually be taking Biochem at Barnard; he gave her his Baldwin text. They traded in their Roberts & Caserios at Barnes and Noble on 18th and Broadway; a few blocks south his turned into an army surplus field jacket at Hudson's Army-Navy. It looked great on the bike, flying up the Palisades to the secluded little pond at Bear Mountain. He'd grown his hair longer now, the way she'd said she liked it, and he talked about growing a beard. But not before his med school interviews. He ran around the city on trains; he dared not treat a suit to a ride on the Black Bomber. He vanished for two days; she knew he'd been to Boston.

"How'd the Harvard interview go?"

He looked away. "They were interested in me being a chem major. Asked if I might be interested in research, eventually, an M.D/PhD. Leece, it's pie in the sky."

At the pond it was silent. Brown leaves crunched underfoot, and late in the day a cold breeze stirred them into rustling dances. She looked around silently as he rolled up the sleeping bag and blanket to stow on the bike. He watched her stare around, put his arms around her. Gently he said, "It germinates and blooms and then it dies, Mautner. That's how the chemistry works." *He says it like I don't know it*, she thought, *but I do.*

It started to turn colder. Too cold for *al fresco* sex. They approached the problem scientifically, dismissing dormitories, homes of first and second degree relatives, friends' homes, as ridiculous. Gas or train costs, not to mention winter trips on a motorcycle, eliminated cheap motels out of town. They calculated how often the Roberts could check in to the Pennsylvania: once every six weeks, if they skipped meals. That left only two possibilities: empty classroom buildings, to which he had access only to labs and the equipment room (and the eternal odor of glacial acetic acid or worse), and were anyway patrolled, and the basement of Rothstein's Dry Goods. The first time they tried this was almost the last. They had the air mattress, and all the bedding they could ever want, but it turned out there was a rodent problem. They set out traps on two successive Friday nights and hauled away the massacre on the Saturdays. The third Saturday the traps were empty and there was no detectable rodent presence. He smuggled in a hot plate and incense, hid them behind some detritus in the back room. Such was their hunger for each other that, at least at first, they found the stamped tin ceilings and exposed pipes romantic. He hummed tunes from *La Boheme*. "Someday," he said, "We might regale each other with this memory." He didn't see her wince.

Finally, though, the day came, with a wind howling outside, and snow beating against the single window and covering the Honda's tarp, that she said, "Don't you begin to find all this a bit…sordid? Because, I do."

"You know I imagine it as an artist's garret," he said.

From under two quilts (pulled from open stock) she said, "No. It's a tenement dry goods store's cold, dank basement. I have two pairs of socks on."

"Spring will come," he said, "Warmth will return to the parks and bosky dells."

"When real warmth comes you'll be gone. You've been going to interviews for weeks now, Ben. And you won't talk about it."

"We're talking about it now. I probably won't get into Harvard. All the others have been in New York. From which Philadelphia can be reached overland via the negligible crossing of New Jersey. I could apply to Penn…"

"But if you get into Harvard you'll go. You should go. It's the best. I know you want to. You know you want to. That's something no one should pass up. *Say no*

"With us ther was a Doctour of Physik. He was a verray parfit practisour."

"No need to bring Chaucer into it. I wouldn't pass it up either." *Say no*

"I don't want to pass *this* up either."

"Yes, sex under two quilts in a damp tenement basement, who wouldn't give up Harvard Med for that?"

"It's sex with *you*. Come with me, Leece."

"And do what? *Be* what?"

She's right. "Yeah. Bad idea. Look, my first year, I can catch late trains weekends, we can meet at the hotel for whole weekends…"

"Oh? Every weekend? That's possible? You really think you can do that?

"Okay, every other weekend, and you apply to the Boston med schools… "

"And you think I'll be accepted just because you wish it? I'll apply, but I won't get in. My advisor says no chance. I'll try Tufts and BU *they aren't Harvard*, but I'd bet against them taking me. Taking *women*. They think they'll train us and we'll just get married and quit. That we're taking the place of a man who will give his life to Medicine. They say that to girls at their interviews, see how they answer. As if there's an answer that matters."

He turned, held her shoulders, looked deeply into her eyes. "Leece," he said, "If I could, I would get into Harvard and give you my place."

She pushed him away. "I don't want your place. I want *my* place."

He looked away, abashed. "Yeah," he said. "I'm sorry. I get it."

"Do you?" After a minute of rage she said quietly, "I'm sure I can get into Woman's. And Albert Einstein has started taking more women per class. This new City U med school at Mount Sinai is bound to. But nothing in Boston. If you get in, and you go, there's no guarantee I can follow next year."

He couldn't admit why he needed Harvard. Even to himself. Couldn't know if it would make any sense, or any difference, to her. Or even make it worse. *Right over there, at that desk. Going over the numbers with his father* But he needed to be with her. He needed her. It was terrifying. He couldn't choose. He knew she was right. There was, could be, no

guarantee. They couldn't know where she'd end up. Maybe even in Europe, if she didn't get one of the rare women's slots at an American school. Or Guadalajara. *Maybe I won't get in. Maybe I won't have to choose. What do I want What can I want*
She needed to be able to see him. She needed him; hated *needing* him. She knew she was right; there was no guarantee. The roller coaster still ran most of the way to the top. They were young. They needed each other. Each of them loved exciting and then satisfying the other. Each took pride in it. In Being The Best.

The note said *J1515*. "A rare daylight meeting, Agent XX. What gives?"

"A solution to our little problem. My mother will be out on a regular basis weekends, or anyway weekend days, for the foreseeable future."

Jackpot. It required finding out, by trial and error, which was more acceptable: making love in her childhood bed or her mother's queen. "I can't do this with teddy bears watching," he said. Which was a lie; he wanted the queen bed; hell, it wasn't *his* mother. There were a few pictures of a much younger Lisa, and a picture of a still-attractive middle-aged woman, like an older version, on the dresser. There was a music stand and sheet music, Vaughn-Williams' *The Lark Ascending*.

"She's a freelance violinist," Lisa explained. "Used to be with the symphony, now she plays in pickup quartets and orchestras, and gives lessons. The violin is wherever she is. She tunes it, carries it, cleans it, buffs it with a cloth diaper. I used to think, that violin is my little sister. It goes where she goes. Um, there's the laundry problem." That was easily solved via the good offices of Rothstein's Dry Goods, which supplied a set of sheets that could temporarily replace her mother's, repeatedly, and hidden in her own closet other times. The warm room, having a whole apartment to play house in (she could, in fact, cook, and he was, of course, rather good at washing up), restored their spirits.

"What about the nosy neighbors?"

"Good question. I'm a big girl now."

He left it at that, *knowing they shouldn't.* The time for
med school acceptances was approaching, they both knew. And
avoided. Skill had been added to ardor, could make up for the
increasing tension. Views of the river and its bridges out one set
of windows, of the midtown skyscrapers out another, made a
bubble for them, around them. Or there had long been a bubble,
and its walls became stronger, thicker. Mostly.

"The chemistry is back," she said, gazing at a ceiling she
saw in a new way.

"It was never gone."

She ignored this. "It's all chemistry. The arousal, the...*the*
worry...We're hostages to the chemistry. Says you."

"We *are* the chemistry," he said.

"No more to it than that, for you?"

"Of course there is, but the chemistry is what's under it.
Behind it."

"Then nothing is anybody's fault? It's all out of our
control?"

"No, not..." He wondered, suddenly. "I think...the
control is part of the chemistry. I mean, the controller, the brain,
the thing that controls, is also chemistry..."

"I don't know," she said. "Then the *control* is *just*
chemistry too." *And love is*

"I really don't know either, but I know I love talking
about it with you. I know I can't live without this. Leece.
Here's an idea. Tell me if it's crazy. I take a year off, work in
the store. Then we both apply to Louvain, or Milan, or Rome.
Or Guadalajara."

"That is crazy. You'd be drafted. There's this war thing
going on."

She was right, of course. He could be draft-exempt only
if he went straight to med school from college, and he'd need a
year to put together money for them to live abroad.

"Yeah," he said. "It's like we're stuck on flypaper, or in
quicksand. Can't get loose of it, break out of it, it's all around
us." *In us, even   Now you're getting it, Rothstein*

I think I know where you're stuck she thought. It was the

crack in the bubble. But the roller coaster again ran all the way to the top, and beyond. In afterglow he ran his hand down her hip. Thinking of the Man Ray photograph, he said, "If you were a violin you'd be a Guarneri." His eyes were closed; he didn't see the pained look cross her face, or he'd have known to apologize, or ask what was the matter. He just lay beside her in the big bed, eyes closed, gently caressing her thigh. "I love this," he said.

"What? The bed? The apartment?"

"No. This. This feeling. Being at peace. Content."

"Yes," she said. "Happiness. Is that what you're saying?"

"Yes. Complete and utter happiness."

"And you're content to give that up, to go to Harvard?"

His eyes snapped open. "If I get in? That's hardly certain."

"But if you do, you'd be ready to go."

"Honestly? I don't…Maybe. Almost…"

Almost she thought.

Quicksand. He thought: *NYU or Harvard?* No. No. *The original dream, or the new one?* No. Not that either. Hurt himself *hurt his family who he'd already hurt, hurt grievously* or hurt her? Stay, let the letting go of Harvard fester, break them up later, end up with neither. Or hurt her now.

She thought, *let him go. Tell him to go, I'll follow.* But I might not. Might not be *good enough* for Harvard, or any med school in Boston where women aren't welcomed, *have to be twice as good as a man to get in.* Or, any med school. Be good enough but be kept out by being a woman. Do something else? Teach? Biology, chemistry? Have babies, be nothing but a doctor's *wife? His* wife, yes, but nothing else. Lose *myself.* Let that bitterness grow until I leave him, or he leaves me. Hurt him now or hurt him later. *Hurt him or hurt myself Bastard*

In the black-and-white of adolescence, no alternative occurred to either of them. Except to keep making love, with an intensity and desperation that left them, still, breathless. Hold each other tight enough to get through this. He still touched her as if worshipping; she still touched him as if she would never let go. And it still built to the pleasured frenzy, the calm afterward when nothing else mattered. One Saturday they had to end early; her mother would, unusually, be back that night. Hurriedly changed the sheets back, folded theirs and stowed them behind the old dollhouse in her closet. Showered, hurriedly kissed goodbye. They'd usually left more time, in case her mother came home early. More than a year of clandestine life had made them expert at deceiving the world. And themselves.

When she came out to breakfast next morning she was greeted by her mother's unhappy look, the one that was a prelude to anger. *Allegro moderato.* Or maybe was just the cover for the anger that was already there. It didn't matter. Her mother's reply to her "Good morning" was to hold up a torn condom wrapper. "Can you explain this?"

Shit. Had they forgotten to empty the bathroom trash? There would have been plenty of damp Kleenex too. She couldn't think of anything plausible to say, suddenly didn't want to. "I'm having an affair. We came here yesterday."

"How long has this been going on?"

"Here? A few weeks. Elsewhere? Months."

"And you thought, well, I'll just do this at home."

"We can't really afford hotels, and it's pretty cold out."

"Can't afford…Who is it?"

She shrugged. "A boy from Columbia. He's a senior. Going to med school. I asked him to tutor me in Organic Chemistry."

"And he did, didn't he. You've doubtless heard the one about why buy the cow when you can get the milk for free."

"I'm not a cow. And who says I want to be bought? I wanted an affair. He didn't seduce me or anything, mother. Nothing happened that I didn't want to happen. He's a very nice guy. Probably going to Harvard Med."

"He'll be leaving, then. Quel surprise. Or perhaps you'll want to go traipsing off to Boston after him. Leave everything and everyone here and just go..."

"No. I don't see myself doing that. They don't want

women. It's just an affair."

"Well. Do I get to meet him?"

"That would be rather awkward after this, wouldn't it? Besides…I don't know if this is a meet-the-parents kind of…"

"You don't see this as lasting."

She realized, suddenly, painfully that she truly didn't. "I don't know that anything's lasting."

"So, you're eighteen, nineteen, you just say, 'Oh, I'll have an affair'."

"Why not? You do. Where are you on weekends?"

Her mother reared back as if slapped. "I'm an adult. My life didn't stop when your father finally left, Lisa."

"Actually, mother, I sort of thought it didn't stop even before he left."

Her mother went past anger to rage. "You dare say a thing like that to me? Before? Before what? Your father was all over America and Europe conducting orchestras. All of which had string sections. You think there was ever a before? I think maybe you ought to go back to your dorm after breakfast."

"Why wait that long?"

She risked calling Ben at his dorm an hour later; they met for coffee and eggs and rolls at Jack's. "She found a Trojan wrapper?"

"We were apparently a little careless with organic waste removal."

"So. Look. We can make this up. Invite me to dinner. To meet her. It's fine."

"I didn't tell you the rest…"

When she finished he put his coffee down. "So you told her you're just having an affair?"

"Right, and what's her beef? She is too. That's where she's been, Ben, why the apartment's empty Saturdays. Weekends."

"So, this, us, is just you having an affair?"

"Well, isn't it? What else is it? You're leaving for Boston, probably, in a few months, so isn't that what you wanted? Want?"

"No. I want… Then you'll apply to med school, and after

a lousy year with me burning up the roads on the bike, you'll be in Boston too."

"Are you not listening? What does it take to get through to Planet Ben? What if I don't get in anywhere in Boston? Or New York for that matter. I can only count on Woman's in Philly, if anything. I'm not giving up being a doctor."

"I've applied to NYU and Columbia and Downstate and Einstein too, Leece. I still could apply to Penn. I don't have to go to Harvard. *Yes I do* I might not get into Harvard myself."

"But if you do, you'll go. How long have you known this is how it would end? From the beginning I bet. At the latest, since you applied. You wouldn't miss out on that just to stay with me."

"And what did—do—you want? Why should I stay if this is just an affair?" It was out on the table, along with the sugar, salt, pepper, ketchup, opened containers of butter and marmalade and jam, egg-smeared knives and forks. "We have to think about this,"

"What I don't want to do is think about this, Ben. Not right now."

Reluctantly, he dropped it. Knowing it was the wrong thing to do, that he could *would* lose her either way, and later was better than now. "I have to get to the Store."

Could he not see how important he had become to her? Not that she couldn't survive without him *I lived quite successfully without him* She thought she understood. *Morty my smarter brother Morty who could dance me around the room*, implying: *steal me Any girl Away*. She could understand this; it was a version of what *Am I good enough* she herself felt. Being important to him was important to her. Being more important to him than Harvard *Not something I'm proud of* and it seemed he could just walk away. With him she had felt *immune*, somehow *protected*. Her rage at this surprised her. *They're all like this. What the hell was I thinking The lonely girl The easy mark I fell for that* Hormones. Simple organic chemistry. Not the first girl, the first woman, who thought a boy, a man, really, *truly*, cared.

About anything beyond sex. Beyond *getting laid*. Her mother knew. Knew how easily attachments are broken. Take your pleasure; the chemistry of *that* is simple *Once you get the hang of it* and move on. *But, Ben was…*

And then she called him. "My father's coming to town for a conducting gig. He wants to meet you."

"How does he even know about me?"

"Best guess: my mother deigned to contact him to check you out. That being a father's duty. To protect his daughter's, the family's, honor."

"I'd actually like to meet him. I admire his work."

"He'll like that; I told you. You'll get to see him treat me like an eight-year-old, which is how old I was when he split for good."

"He doesn't scare me," he said.

"It isn't a matter of scary," she said. "It's just…he's very old-school European paterfamilias, which makes a weird mix with having abandoned us, or anyway my mother. He has some pretty old-fashioned attitudes."

"Towards women going to med school?"

"Towards women, period. Let me think about it." In the end she agreed. Hesitantly. Not really sure why. What difference could it make? *Do I think my father will talk sense into him? Or bring a shotgun? Would I want that Is that really me*

Her father took them to the Russian Tea Room, for which they had to dress formally. One more tour for his interview suit. She was, as usual, he thought, breathtaking. Kurt Mautner was on a first-name basis with most of the staff; he was probably there every day after rehearsals at next-door Carnegie Hall. Lines vanished; a table appeared before them, seemingly by enchantment. They shook hands, sat down, got orders out of the way. They made small talk about school. Ben tentatively expressed a growing interest in Mahler, whose symphonies were being explored in a series of recordings by one Kurt Mautner, whose vaguely Central European accent Ben couldn't identify. "My parents are also big fans," he said.

"Ah. They keep a shop, I believe, yes?" Salads. "I'm pleased to meet the young man who has been such a help to my little girl."

Little girl? "She never needed any help, sir."

"No?"

"It was just how we met." She shot him a look that he missed.

"Well, I always watched over my little Liesl very carefully, just between you and me, Benjamin, made sure she had the best, every success." Main course. "I worry about her, I'm sure you understand, so I must be sure she isn't—do I have the expression correct?—punching above her weight."

As if she weren't sitting right here "She aced Organic Chemistry, Mr. Mautner. Which is a very difficult course." *Why wasn't she speaking up?*

"No doubt thanks to your expert tutelage, Benjamin." He pulled out a checkbook. "For which I would like to take the opportunity to thank you, recompense you, for your time and efforts."

Ben turned, looked into her eyes briefly, saw there *Please* and didn't know for what she was pleading. *Has she not told him Did her mother not* As evenly as he could, he said, "Mr. Mautner, I think you are very much mistaking the nature of Lisa's success. I repeat, she aced Organic Chemistry. She got an A in the course crucial to entering medical school. She did that with nothing from me but some encouragement early on that she was getting it just fine. We studied together but…I think you are very much mistaking the nature of our relationship."

Her father turned to her. "Is this true, Liesl?"

"I think Ben is underestimating his contribution, the encouragement, but yes, it's true, with very little but that encouragement, and a little Socratic method when I had a question, when something wasn't perfectly clear, I did it on my own."

At which point Ben let anger take over. "Just as she can do in any course she takes, and at any med school, Mr. Mautner. You can put away your checkbook."

Her father returned the checkbook to his pocket. The silence lasted just a beat too long. "Well. Thank you, Benjamin, for straightening me out on this point. You are obviously a young man of integrity…"*Why, because the shopkeepers' son wouldn't let you buy him off?* "…and obviously a great friend to my little Liesl."

It seemed obvious to Ben that he was holding rage in check by a hair. The rest of dinner was a chilly affair. When he left them momentarily to deal with some perceived anomaly in the check she said, "We have to talk."

"Oh yeah."

"Tomorrow. He'll be gone. Dinner. Jack's, at six."

She was clearly unhappy, anxious, even agitated, when he met her at Jack's. "So you feel a need to take on my father?"

He was surprised. "Well, somebody ought to."

"Do I figure anywhere in this, or is it just between the two of you? And what do I do when you're gone? What does he do? Did you even think of that?"

"You know what your father is? He's…"

"I know exactly what my father is. He's *my* father. And I know what I need from him. I need to be able to talk to him, be on speaking terms with him, after I graduate, because he's my father, and I need to go to med school and I need his support— his money, okay?—to do it. And whatever else he is, he's *my father.*"

"His money, yeah, what was that with the checkbook, trying to buy the shopkeepers' son off? How does he know about the store anyway? From you?"

"Of course."

"What you need…"

"Oh, now *you're* going to tell me what I need? You're starting to sound just like him." That stopped him, sat him back against the booth's cold vinyl. "You think you can just do that, piss off my father, screw up my relationship with him, and then vanish out of my life?"

"I'm not going to vanish out of your life. I'm going to Boston, not the Moon. If I even go."

"You think I don't know why? It's Harvard med, not undergrad. You'll be that much better than your brother. You'll win that one, Ben."

He was confused, angry. Didn't know how she'd come to that. *Didn't know you're that transparent, Rothstein, did you* "Win what? What the hell are you talking about?" *Can't tell her What would she think of Or her father think of* "The competition with your brother. You think it isn't obvious? So go. Go win. Meanwhile, I'll need my father." *Knowing she was wrong. Knowing she was right.*

Anger took over. "You have no fucking idea what was between me and my brother. None. But hey, you get to have an *affair*, just like your mother." It was the first time he had ever said something deliberately to hurt her, and was stunned he had. He got anger under control, or thought he did. "Look, let's drop the Psych 101 crap. We were talking about your father. What has this got to do with..."

"Right now it has to do with your attitude being just like his. There's a difference between being *cared about* and being *taken care of*, Rothstein."

He thought he saw what she meant. "Okay," he said. "So?" When she made no response he said, "I'm sorry. I took the wrong tack with him. I get it. I'll ask you—what do you need from me? To apologize to him? What?"

But she was, he hadn't seen, way past that. "What do I need from you? Right now? Nothing. Not a goddamned thing."

He rose, threw his napkin on the chair. "Then that's what I'll do." And he walked out. *Asking himself What am I doing? How am I doing this? Why am I doing this? I'll call her later. I'll call her in the morning. Or she'll call me. Chemical reactions are reversible, can run in both directions, if the conditions change.*

But she didn't. And he didn't.

In the wake of the Tet Offensive that made it obvious the war was lost, Johnson opting out of re-election, the King assassination, an anti-War march of half a million people to Central Park, and a lemon meringue pie to the face of

New York's director of Selective Service, anti-war activism came to Columbia. The arguments that had formed a distant background hum to his life with Lisa, arguments against the school's involvement in the War, in defense research, the taking of adjacent Black neighborhood land for the new gymnasium, suddenly turned militant. He woke to the full realization of a bullying society, bullying Southeast Asians who only wanted their own country, and Harlem residents who only wanted to keep their homes and park. City police turned back an assault by a large group of students on the gym construction site; there were clubbings and arrests, maybe some tear gas. The bubble was definitely broken.

There were murmurs of bringing the institution *down*. He recognized, or *felt*, the inherent racism and militarism, manifested in the med school admission quotas, the park land takeover, and the War and the Draft, as components of a thing that had also driven him and Lisa apart. He found himself increasingly angry at what they all increasingly thought of as The System. His acquaintances among the activists were surprised by his sudden interest and involvement. One or two suspected him of being a police informant, but people who knew him pointed to his lab job and his work in the family store to explain his absences from campus life. There was promised, *predicted*, militant action, but no provision for casualties when, their demands having been rebuffed, the Black Students' Alliance and SDS began occupying campus buildings. He had a premonition about this; thought *medical supplies*. Their grim determination sent him to the lab. Clean sheets would make good temporary bandages; he raced down to the store and helped himself to a few white sheet sets *Not the first I've taken No this is different* stored them *with a pang* in the lab supply room. He started making up methylcellulose and tincture of iodine. He "liberated" bottles of ethyl and isopropyl alcohol. He made small, easily-concealed draw-offs of glacial acetic acid from the carboys and diluted it down (it washed off tear gas, he'd read). He stole ten feet of glass tubing, as much as he thought he could conceal the absence of, sawed off three inch lengths, drew up the methylcellulose *You can make more interesting stuff than this little bro*, lit a Bunsen burner, fired up one end to seal them off, heated the open ends and drew them out with pliers to make sealed ampoules. He worked as fast as he could to make forty of these. And thought *Not enough*

When the first building, Hamilton Hall, was taken over by the Black Students Alliance and their allies, Black Power considerations outweighed student solidarity, so white students took over the Low Library administration building (famously supposedly smoking the president's cigars). The red-armbanded factions split, each to a building. Ultimately, they took over Fayerwether, Mathematics, Architecture and, almost as an afterthought (because it was the anarchists), Mercer. Classes stopped. Students, faculty, press and spectators milled in the Quad. *You stay out of this little bro Turn On Tune In* He went to the empty lab and assembled a kit for each building, went around to each to survey the numbers, back to the lab to assemble final kits for each group. The Black students thanked him but a Medical Committee for Human Rights doc had already joined them. Lawyers, too. The others had got to know him and took the boxes. "It's food we need, man," they said, but that was beyond his powers of organization—and scrounging connections. He passed the word to green-armbanded sympathizers. He was on his way back to the lab to make a few more methylcellulose ampoules and more iodine when a roar went up as several dozen Barnard girls marched in. He thought she'd be in it somewhere *guts and brains*, thought he saw her, made one more set of rounds to show them how to use the methylcellulose and acetic acid, urging them to cut up the sheets for bandages. But really hoping he'd find her. *If I could just get her alone for a minute Chemical reactions are reversible, can run in both directions, if the conditions change*

He thought she'd most likely be among the anarchists and unaffiliated at Mercer Hall. Mercer looked north to Hamilton; farther away, the view was of College Walk. The statue of Alma Mater at the foot of Low's wide stone stairs was easily visible. To the south were Butler Library and an exit to 114th Street. He didn't find her on his first visit, but still thought the best bet was Mercer. *Just long enough to*

On Day Three blue-armbanded jocks and frat boys formed a siege line around the buildings to prevent food and supplies getting in. In his field jacket, length of pipe in one pocket, he pushed past them. He'd brought his own kit of first aid supplies; he searched the buildings for her group as sympathizers formed another, protective line blocking the jocks and frat guys. He was in it now. He took out his Swiss Army knife, cut a length of sheet, found a red pen in an office and made a Red Cross armband. This was the first Campus Occupation. There was not yet an established script; they were all improvising.

On Day Seven he found her group, finally, a feminist-anarchist outfit, part of the motley crew occupying Mercer. *I should be angry at her* he thought. *Mad as hell*. Except he'd been the one who'd walked out. So he was angry at himself. Or himself and her. Both. Neither. Both. He took her aside and told her what he was doing; she listened, face turned away from the noise from the Quad. He persuaded her of the importance of cutting up the sheets for bandages, preparing gauze for makeshift gas masks…a roar went up from the Quad and he looked out the window. *Jesus* he thought *The idiots have used my sheets for banners*. "So, Ben, are you here for political reasons, or what?" she asked him.

"I told you, I don't like bullies. And I don't like The System. The quicksand we're caught in. There's MCHR in some of the other buildings. You got me. I'm your medic."

The de facto leader of her group, a hawk-faced girl, asked, "And your qualifications are what, exactly?"

"I know first aid. You could use some help if things turn violent."

"They won't. This is a peaceful demonstration. What are they gonna do, beat up their own students? Shoot us?"

"They arrested and clubbed a bunch of us at the Gym Crow just days ago. I was there. That's what sparked this. That's why I'm here. There are cops gathering on Broadway and on Amsterdam."

"We know that. That's why *we're* here."

Someone at a window called. There was a scuffle between the jocks and the sympathizers. As they watched, a group of faculty broke it up, talking to both sides; more showed up and they formed a third ring, separating the jocks from the friendlies.

"I told you," Ben said.

"Yes, Ben," Lisa said, "And a bunch of faculty talked them down."

He squinted. "That's our old friend Boland out there." People gathered at the windows to watch. The parlay broke up after an hour; the jocks were signaling to each other to disband. Cheers went up from the occupied buildings. He turned away.

"You see?" she said.

"I see that the cops are pulling those clowns out so they don't get in the way when they charge." *This isn't the best There's no time*

"You're paranoid."

"Wasn't that you sitting next to me at *Battleship Potemkin?*"

A few kept watch; they split up what little food they had left. Conversation slowed, died. A cry from a window; a girl and her boyfriend had cut themselves trying to open a stuck sash. He opened a sheet set, took out his Swiss Army knife and cut two strips, opened a flask of tincture of iodine, bathed the cuts and tied a bandage. When he looked up they were looking at him differently. And he saw them differently. Suddenly they were his patients.

A girl at a window said, "What's going on at Hamilton?" In the gathering darkness the Black students were coming out, fists raised in the Power Salute, escorted by community leaders. They walked peacefully into the quad, to applause. Elation spread through them. Suddenly everything, anything, seemed possible. A new world.

"They're negotiating," the hawk-faced girl said. "We just won on the gym, now they'll talk to us about the Defense Department contracts."

But they didn't. They watched as a phalanx of cops, clubs

swinging, rushed Low Library, the heart of the protest, watched
them drag out unresisting demonstrators by the feet, their heads
banging on the stone steps, leaving them bloodstained. Cries of
"Pigs Off Campus" echoed across the quad.

"Meeting," the hawk-faced girl shouted, "Meeting."
They gathered in the front hall, some hanging over banisters
and railings. It took minutes for quiet. "We have three choices,"
the hawk-faced girl said. "Resist, resist nonviolently, or
surrender and walk out. The Low crowd may have resisted.
They're hard-core."

"I say surrender," Ben said. "The BSA did, and walked
out of Hamilton heads high. The other ways you just get
beat up."

"Are you a narc?" the hawk-faced girl said.

"I'm your medic. This is my job. Telling you the risks.
Lacerations, fractures, head injuries, tear gas."

"Can anybody vouch for this guy?"

"I can," Lisa spoke up. "He's no narc, and he knows what
he's talking about."

"Ever been beaten up?" Ben asked the hawk-faced girl. "I
have. It's no pleasure, unless you get to hit back. And you won't.
We're outnumbered, outgunned and outclassed."

"Sure, we'll get hurt. Our wounds are our weapons.
Shock the conscience of the nation."

"If it had a conscience we wouldn't have to be here,"
someone said.

"Our friends and our classmates won't tolerate this. Pigs
Off Campus. They're already chanting it."

"You don't seem to understand what you're risking,"
Ben said.

"You're chicken."

"He isn't," Lisa said.

"Well, neither am I," the hawk-faced girl said. She raised
her voice. "People, we have right and history on our side, and
we can put our bodies on the line with our brothers and sisters at
Low and Fayerwether, or not. This is an anarchist body. Anybody
wants to leave, walk out with their hands up, can. But I don't

know that you stand any better chance with the Pigs that way."
She looked at Ben. "Any arguments?"

Ben considered. "No, actually. You make a good point.
But if we go through with this we'd better be prepared. I'll
prepare bedding strips. Wrap them around your heads. Scalp
lacerations bleed like crazy; it'll keep the blood out of your
eyes and keep the wounds clean. Women with pierced ears, take
your earrings out; they use them as handles. If there's tear gas,
get away and get some eyewash, and wash any exposed skin
with acetic acid. Dilute vinegar. I brought some of both, but not
enough if we're all out in the open. I can make a few makeshift
masks, wet gauze in a sheet strip, but it isn't much protection. If
you're getting beat, protect your head, eyes and neck. Everything
else will heal." He went to his pack, pulled out the sheets and the
knife and started cutting.

Lisa came over to help; he started the cut, she tore. "You
sure sound like you know what you're talking about," she said.
"Where did you learn all that stuff?"

"Except the part about the earrings, and tear gas, the Boy
Scout handbook."

"There's a merit badge in political protest?"

"First aid. Are you down with this?"

"I don't know, Ben."

"Stick close, Leece. Stay right with me. These people
want to get hurt. Or they don't really believe they will, they don't
know it's become okay to hit girls. At Brooklyn College six
months ago a protest against army recruiters went that way."

She felt he was right, but didn't feel like agreeing with
him. "It makes a statement. It reveals the brutality of The
System. It mobilizes support."

"At what price? First choice, in these situations, nobody
gets hurt. Second choice, the other guy gets hurt." He saw the
look on her face. "In my opinion," he said. "Stay close, Leece.
Please." She kept tearing sheets, feeling an edge of real fear,
thinking *He might be right.* The group had meanwhile decided to
make a show of nonviolent resistance, sitting down and linking
arms on the little terrace at the foot of the building's portico, just

east of the Library. He took two sheet strips, used a red marker to make two thick red crosses and handed her one. The cops had apparently finished clearing the buildings north of Campus Walk, and were advancing in line toward them.

The first gas arced in over the heads of the kids concentrated on the grass terrace. It was meant to herd them away from the building, toward the advancing line of cops waiting to club or arrest them. Instead it scattered them. Ben grabbed a handful of his homemade gas masks and soaked them down with a flask of distilled water. He shoved one into Lisa's hands and tied one around his nose and mouth. "Put it on," he shouted over the din of screaming, crying students and the hiss of the gas canisters. "Keep it wet." He waded in, trying to distribute the few pitiful masks, planning to make more. It was hopeless. Distribute a handful, live to fight another day.

She was doing the same, and quickly came to the same conclusion. She somehow heard him shouting, "Leece. Lisa. MAUTNER. OVER HERE," above the din, just as two gas canisters landed and one popped right in front of her. She gasped. He saw her through the dispersing cloud, ran in and grabbed her. And picked up the dud canister. "Leece, come on." She resisted his pull, but her eyes were starting to burn. "Leece, we can't do anything more here." He pulled her south, toward a building they both knew backwards, forwards and in the dark. They ducked behind the columns of the Mercer portico, then the shrubbery, climbed the little hill beside Butler Library. The clouds of gas helped to hide them. She realized what he was up to. Her vision cleared for a minute; when he turned to make sure they weren't pursued she found a basement window, just big enough to slip through. Pulling the length of pipe out of the pocket of his field jacket, he smashed the window, quickly but methodically knocking stray shards of glass out of the frame, and opened it. "In" he said to her.

She rolled through, then let herself down carefully from the sill. "Watch the glass," she said, and he did. They both knew where they were. Under Life Sciences. Under Mammalia.

"Upstairs," he said. "If they search the building we have

to be one step ahead." She needed little urging. But he stopped to toss the dud gas canister under the window. "Let New York's Finest take the heat for the window," he said.

"It's pitch dark," she said.

He reached into another pocket of the field jacket. "I have a flashlight," he said. "Be Prepared." He partly covered the lamp end with his hand and turned it on. They reached the landing alcove at Mammalia. He tore off their gas masks, saturated with gas and useless now. "Nobody ever thanks the masked man," he said.

"True. Thank you, Ben." She pointed to the flashlight. "Boy Scout issue?"

"I hereby abjure the uniformed services."

"How do you make jokes in a situation like this?"

"I'm scared shitless, Leece, if that makes you feel better."

"Just making sure. What now, do you think?"

He snapped off the light. "We wait."

"My eyes are still streaming. I think I caught some gas."

"You did. The gas is likely allyl chloride. Are you okay?"

"I don't know, Ben. It hurts. A lot." He heard fear in her voice.

"Stay here. No matter what happens, stay here. I'll get some water."

"In what?"

"Stay here, okay?" He snapped on the light, covered it with his hand, tried to remember where a bathroom was. He found it on the second try. There was a towel roll on the wall. He tucked the light under one arm and used both hands to pull at the roll until he was finding only clean new towel. He propped the light on the sink, opened his knife, used it to slash the used towel away, pulled out a good length of clean towel, slashed that off the roll. He put away the knife, soaked the towel in cool water, and made his way back to the alcove. "Lay your head on my lap," he said, sitting. "Squint your eyes." She did it, and he gently wrung the towel, irrigating her eyes. He made two more trips for water. On the second trip he dumped the cut-off length of dirty towel in a trash can. *Leave no trace. This never happened.* On the third trip he chanced looking out a window. The cops were herding or dragging the remnants of the occupying students out to waiting paddy wagons. The red and blue lights of the police cruisers made flashing patterns on the drifting clouds of tear gas, weirdly beautiful. A few rocks and bottles flew from the sidelines. No one was coming into the library.

He threw himself down beside her in the dark alcove. "Eyes okay?"

"Much better. Okay, I think. Thank you, Ben."

"How are you doing, Leece?"

"Okay. I'm okay." *Bullshit.* "You?"

"I'm okay. More or less." *Bullshit.*

They sat in uncomfortable silence, *Maybe now is a time to What to say* until she said, "Did you hear about the girl in my class who got expelled for living with her boyfriend? It was in the New York Times."

"Yeah. Good thing we kept quiet. Leece, I want to…"

"Why did you? You know what happened to her boyfriend? Nothing. Which is what would have happened to you."

Anger warred with knowing she was right. "I know. In fact I'd have been famous for nailing a beautiful Barnard girl. Been a Big Man On Campus. It's a sick system."

"You mean the System where you get to go to Harvard Med and no matter what I do, how well I do, I don't? That's why we came over. One reason, anyway. You are going, aren't you? Got in, didn't you."

"Yes. System's sick, and sickening."

"But you are going." *And will forget all about me*

"After we…yes. I am." *And I can't tell you why It would make no sense*

"So. Congratulations." *Silence   Still too angry Not the time*

"I should have been expelled," he finally said. "Or arrested. You were jailbait, and we got to Bear Mountain through Jersey, so I transported you across state lines for immoral purposes. That's a Federal rap." When she didn't laugh, or even smile, he said, "At Bear Mountain I sometimes felt like Winston and Julia in *1984*. Now, even more."

"You think anybody's been killed?"

"I don't know. Maybe at Low. Got fucked up pretty badly, that's certain."

"This whole thing is fucked up," she said.

"At Low…maybe they're trying to scare the rest of us, if they're thinking at all."

"It's working. My eyes hurt." They sat in a long silence until she said, "Ben? At the end of my block, there was this nice policeman that stopped traffic for us on First Avenue so we could cross to go to school. He said hello to me, to all of us kids."

"They hate us, Leece. Over-privileged, draft-dodging spongers, drinking and fucking and smoking dope while they and their kids do the work and the fighting and the dying. I can understand that; half the guys in my high school class, maybe more, are cannon fodder over there."

"They don't get that it isn't our idea for it to be this way. We don't want that for them. Or anybody."

"But they're okay with it, they do it and expect respect and gratitude for defending the so-called Free World. Each of us thinks we're doing it for the other, and we end up at each other's throats."

"The difference between being cared *for* and being cared *about*, Ben."

His turn to be silent, until he said, "Easy for our Administration, for whom we are a problem, to call them in. Probably be mailing us happy-talk alumni magazines, and asking us for donations, for life." She was silent. "April is the cruelest month," he quoted.

"Breeding lilacs out of the dead land, mixing memory and desire," she said, finishing the quote.

A mixed message, he thought. *But try* "Remember the last time we sat here?"

No answer. There was nothing left to say. They sat in the dark, silent, waiting for time to pass, two strangers in a lifeboat, staring at each other. At one point they fell asleep briefly, but he dreamt they were being assaulted, and jolted awake, knew they had to be out of there before someone came to inspect the place.

In the morning, probably. Would there be cops outside? She stirred. "We'll have to go out a side door, Leece."

"Won't they have those covered?"

"It's still chaos out there, or it was when I looked. I don't think they're thinking that far ahead. Anyway, what choice do we have?"

"Wait here until…no, I can't imagine they'll just open up like nothing happened."

"Who the fuck knows? I vote we move. You?"

"Ayes have it."

He smiled. "Can you see?"

"Yes. You done good, Ben." *Good enough?* Dawn was still some time off, but there was a lightening in the sky to the east, over Harlem. On the way down the steps to 114th they caught another whiff of drifting gas. "Allyl chloride, right," she said. "Organic goddam chemistry." It was only a whiff, and it didn't affect him much, but her eyes, already irritated by the previous exposure, started to tear. "Ben, my eyes are burning again."

"How bad is it?"

"Bad. I can't see, Ben. It hurts too much when I open my eyes."

He put his arm around her, felt her shaking. "Keep your eyes closed. I'll guide." Across Amsterdam was St. Luke's Hospital. The Emergency Room entrance was screened by police cars. Even if they got past that she could spend hours filling out forms, waiting for the urgent cases, maybe be arrested; he didn't know…

A rhythmic clop, clop, clop came from 113th Street. "I hear horses," she said.

"Mounties," he said. The squad of horse-mounted cops turned north on Amsterdam, toward them. They'd be on them in seconds.

"Kiss me," she said.

"What?"

"Kiss me, Ben. Now."

He did, realizing what she was doing. He pulled her to

him in a doorway, kissed her, his heart thundering. He tasted her tears. The lights from the police cruisers across the street lit them intermittently, dimly. When the mounted squad came abreast one shone a light on them. "Get on home," he shouted. "Get on out of here."

"Get a room," another one said, and they all laughed. Ben held up a hand, waved, lingered a second, and walked her on. Down 113th he could still see cops on Broadway, *can't get her back to her campus that way*. She moaned in pain. Having hurt her so much himself, he wanted to kill the brutes who had done this to her. "Keep your eyes closed," he said. He suddenly realized he still had the towel in a pocket of the field jacket. Ahead, at 112th, loomed the bulk of the Cathedral of St John the Divine. He remembered: as part of its mission, it was open at all times. "We're going up some steps," he told her.

"Where are you taking me, Ben?"

"St John the Unfinished. There'll be water there." The great cathedral was deserted; the menacing police presence had cleared the streets. He laid her, moaning, on a pew near the doors, but access to the floors below, where the restrooms presumably were, was locked. They wanted the prayerful, not vagrants. *This is not*, he thought, *over. This is not fucking over*. It wasn't; the students would be blamed for the damage actually done by the police, there would be a second round of protest, the administration would be shaken up, President Kirk would resign, classes would be, effectively, suspended. The University would not press charges against any of the students, would withdraw from war work, and end ROTC (for a time). He and a large part of the class of '68 would walk *en masse* out of their Commencement in this very cathedral for an impromptu gathering on the Quad. But that was weeks away.

Where was water? And he knew. "Up, Leece. One more short hike and we're there." It was dim in the soaring nave; he took out the flashlight, covered it with his hand and snapped it on, helped her down the aisle to the transept and laid her on a front pew. He took out the towel and crossed the transept to the altar, knowing the font must be adjacent to it. He found the Baptistry in a side chapel, soaked the towel in the ornate font, returned, knelt, and irrigated her eyes. Five times he did this, thinking *He so loved the world* After the fifth irrigation he dug into the pack and found the homemade methylcellulose ampoules. "I'm going to use some organic chemistry, Mautner," he said, "Open, and I'm going to put a drop of this in the corners." He broke open one amp for each eye, dropped the contents at the tear ducts. She blinked, sat up, looked around in the dimness. *Missa est*

"What was that?"

"Methylcellulose. Active ingredient in eyewashes. Allyl chloride irritates mucous membranes. Eyes are the most sensitive. Chemistry, Mautner…"

"It *hurts*, Ben."

If we'd been at Low they could have dragged her down the steps Banged her head on the stone Hit her with a club They could have broken her. What to do then "I have a bunch of it. You'll take it with you when I…"

"Ben, did you just irrigate my eyes with water from the font? Holy water?"

"I guess." Now he knew he would do anything for her. And she knew it too.

"Jesus, Ben."

"He appears unmoved. And the font is this huge fountain. It refills."

"They're probably going to have to resanctify it or something."

"I don't think I profaned it much."

"It doesn't matter what *you* think, it matters what *they* think."

"I'll come back tomorrow. I mean, later today. I'll tell them. I'll leave a note."

"Promise, Ben."

"I promise." *Anything*

He walked her down 112th and up Riverside, checked for cops and edged up 116th toward the Claremont Avenue entrance, avoiding the police on Broadway. He thought *If there are cops on*

Claremont I'll take her home We'll slip through the Park down to the subway at 96th Or I'll get us to the store Hide out for a day But we still stink of gas This was a tough neighborhood; he kept his hand on the little length of pipe in his pocket. "Which dorm are you in now?"

"Just drop me at the gate, Ben. Thank you. I'll be fine now."

At the gates he said, "Leece, I need…We need to talk."

"No, Ben, we don't."

"Leecy…"

"Ben. Stop. Please."

"Leecy…"

"Ben, I'm begging you." At first he thought it was the gas irritation, then he realized she was, had been, crying. "Ben, I can't do this again. I'm evened out, I'm back on course, please, please go now. Leave me now." She turned, and he grabbed her arm.

"Leecy, I can't just…"

"Ben," she shouted, "Let me go." It was the cry of someone being torn in half. Then, more quietly, "Let me go, Ben. Please. I need you to let me go."

And he did. *Anything* he thought. And as he let her go he knew how much he had hurt her, and that the feeling he had when his brother died was nothing to this, because he really, really had done this. He was really, truly responsible.

He **thought** maybe she might come to his Honors Chemistry presentation. Well, people were always a disappointment. Especially the ones you loved. There was that word again. He felt like punching a wall. He wondered how many towels he'd have to wrap around his hand to avoid fractured carpals and metacarpals (widely known in emergency rooms, he would later learn, as Friday Night Fractures). *This is what men and women do* he thought *We love for a while then we lose each other and move on Covalent Bonds, resonant Bonds easily broken with enough heat Now you're getting it Little Bro* He thought about riding out on the Black Bomber, anywhere. *Like we planned Rothstein* He angrily joined the graduation walk-out, to his parents' anxiety and chagrin. He'd missed her terribly, through all the turmoil of the post-occupation upheaval. He missed her body, of course, but knew the sex would have been nothing without her sharp wit, the look on her face when, looking up suddenly from a textbook, she found him looking at her, the greeting in her face when he walked into Jack's. Teaching him to dance. To love.

The summer at the store before he left was interminable. "Another Rothstein at Harvard. You'll show 'em, Benny." His mother sad, resigned, caught, he thought, between Morty being somehow alive again, and (he hoped) some fear of losing him, too. But she did begin leaving the house, coming to the store to take inventory and keep the books, gradually returning to life, to take over sales from him. That was something.

There was plenty of time for thinking. Through the whole summer, he knew she was out there, knew he could walk into Macy's, ring a doorbell in Stuyvesant Town…but why risk, why set himself up for, that kind of hurt again? The conclusion Ben came to, after considerable thought, was that the kind of girl he wanted wouldn't, by her very nature, want him. Or anyway wouldn't want him as much as he wanted her. Or wouldn't for long. His grief began to turn to anger. Her driven self-containment, so attractive at first, he began to think of as self-centeredness. Competition with Morty? How could she misunderstand so completely? She should have understood

Harvard *meant something* to him, and how much *she* meant to him, but evidently she hadn't. Didn't. *But how could she know the thing that, as her self-containment made her* her, *made him* him? Which led him to absolve her, by becoming angry at love, the idea of love, itself. *Ma Nature doesn't need Love to propagate the species Impulsive sex is enough We are all self-contained. We are all selves. We can have pleasure with each other but in the end we're just ourselves, with our own needs There is only the chemistry, the hormones and the pleasure. Not real, molecular bonds, ionic, covalent, resonant Hydrogen bonds That can unzip The Double Helix falling apart* It freed him to just remember the pleasure she had given him. The pleasure she, Lisa Mautner, had been to him. *Guts and brains.*

Then, finally, Harvard. There was almost no time for thinking. For recreational reading. Recreational anything. There were five women in his class. Two were so remote they were too much loners even for him. Nothing beyond acknowledgment of his presence, if that. One was engaged, or anyway wore a ring. One was, and there was no getting around this, ugly as the proverbial mud fence. That left the woman they all called, in the locker-room atmosphere that was no different from the colleges they had just left, Nola Mae. She was friendly, interested, interesting, with all of them, but slid away from anything deeper. Everybody's sister. *Or a lesbian, was whispered by some.* These were all, he realized, survival strategies. And it wasn't lost on him that, if he was being this analytical about it, none of them attracted him enough to want to try to penetrate that. None of them was Lisa.

The first time he had The Dream, it was of seeing Lisa dragged down the stairs of Low Library, head bloodied. Other times, she was emerging from a cloud of tear gas being clubbed by a helmeted cop. The dreams always woke him.

He was buried in work. College had been mere preparation for this. The unfamiliar material of Gross Anatomy and Histology was killing him. This was time to be endured, like his first two years at Columbia *before the best friend I'll ever have showed up out of nowhere.* He didn't really want a relationship now, he thought, working on the bike in the student parking lot. It had shaken bones, teeth and kidneys the 200 miles to Boston, but it looked to be one of his few friends, so he kept its points and plugs clean and everything lubed. He knew he could gun the bike and be at Barnard in maybe five, maybe six, hours *But why set myself up for that kind of hurt again?*

The bike gave him a certain notoriety, but was not the draw, at a medical school, that it had apparently been for Morty. *Or maybe it's that I'm not Morty.* As his first winter in Boston approached he knew he'd need to get a tarp, take the battery indoors; the bike would be useless to him until spring. That was one reason Morty had gotten the bike instead of a car; it meant he couldn't be tapped for work at the store. "Rothstein," he'd said, "You have to get free of The Store." Ben could hear the capital letters. "The Store will eat your brain and leave you poor, leave you a zombie like Dad. Come here, I'll hypnotize you. You…Must…Leave…The …Store." That had been why Morty had taught him how to drive and service the bike. "This," said Morty when he'd brought it home, all black and shiny and shaking and roaring, "Is the antidote to The Store." By which, Ben knew, he meant dutifulness, the Boy Scouts, Hebrew School, *menschlichkeit*, Jewishness. *Only*, Ben thought, *Morty, you took way too much of the antidote.*

When Nola Mae began disappearing on weekends Ben naturally assumed someone had landed that fish. He never noticed how this tiny event, seemingly unremarked by anyone else in the class, coincided with the first of a crescendo of sexual fantasies that reached a pitch endangering his concentration, especially on neuroanatomy. At first they fastened on one of the younger librarians, later on a series of grad students and the odd girl spotted on the T. Boston had more colleges per square inch than any place outside of Oxford, most coeducational, and in his imagination he fucked his way through the lot of them. He didn't know a soul in the city, or at any of the colleges, was all day every day either in a lab or a class or reading for one, so imagination was the only outlet he had. Columbia was all men, his hometown wasn't worth considering, and the young women coming into Rothstein's Dry Goods had always been there with their mothers, buying the prenuptial bedding and towels for the first apartment.

The thing he began to notice about the sexual fantasies was that he had to work to keep the face of the girl in the fantasies from being Lisa's. Also the fantasies almost always involved doing things he'd done with Lisa. His favorite was the one when he'd brought creamy pastries from the Hungarian Bakery to the hotel and they'd eaten them naked in bed and she'd had a smear of cream on her face and he'd licked it off and she'd fallen over laughing and said So…you'll lick it off any place I smear it? And she'd

Harvard, having legendary access to centers of power, did not require (or tolerate) full campus occupation. Demonstrations, teach-ins, student strikes (sometimes with faculty), walkouts on Commencement (and other invited) speakers were sufficient to make news. The War, to him, had become a distant idiocy; by the time he'd joined the occupation of Mercer it was obvious to the whole country that the thing was not only unwinnable, but was turning the nation into some kind of police state. He wasn't, he knew, a complete pacifist; he'd pieced together the horror of the Bocage campaign and The Bulge from casual remarks and, later, close questioning, during all the hours at The Store *being a Quartermaster officer was just like the store except for German artillery. Except when they busted through at the Bulge and they gave out rifles and ammo.* But in this war, he was certain, *we're the bullies.*

He stumbled on and began listening to WBCN, the underground station that broadcast news of the many community events and gatherings, mostly political, along with an eclectic mix of folk, rock, jazz, some classical, and comedy. When hippies began assembling on the Common, dancing, smoking weed, flying Frisbees, the outraged citizenry sent in the police. He had no greater faith in the Boston police force than in New

York's, or Chicago's after the other police riot at the Democratic Convention. Every time, it stirred the dreams, and memories of Lisa, in pain, blinded, eyes streaming, *hurt*. And how he had hurt her, how being here, in this place, hurt her *but if it was just an affair* He worked to keep those memories limited, marginalized. He began to have more time; he'd already taken Biochem as an undergrad, and physiology, pharmacology, were essentially applied biochemistry. He volunteered at the Free Clinic, founded by students and young faculty a few years ago, that everyone called The Freak. The kind of place he might find *But it would be a needle in a haystack, kid* It was exposure to suffering people and their needs, before official introduction to The Wards, and he found himself caring about some of the poor, some of the hippies, the winos, the down-on-their–luck, in ways he had cared about no one but his family. And the people at Mercer. And Lisa.

On April 4, 1969, practically the anniversary of the Columbia Occupation, Harvard undergraduates, outraged as Columbia students had been at encroachment on the local community and the University's involvement with ROTC and war work, occupied the administrative offices; in a replay of Columbia the University police, then State Police were called in, with exactly the same result. Ben cut classes to join the Student Health Organization, the student wing of the Medical Committee For Human Rights, as an official medical aid, and was there in his field jacket with the clinical year students, interns and residents, on hand for whatever first aid was needed. Good sense prevailed in the ensuing police riot (this was *Harvard*); rather than taking any action that would bring charges of vandalism, while police battled students in the building and yard and surrounding streets, the occupiers stole stacks of files documenting the university's deep involvement with the likes of the military, CIA and Dow Chemical. Smuggled out of the building in the chaos, the files were read over WBCN, printed in The Mole underground newspaper, and eventually by the standard print media. When the police riot in Harvard Yard led to a city-wide student strike, and mass actions on Boston Common, Ben was in it, with his MCHR armband, at first mostly directing people to clinical year students and young faculty members from Boston's medical schools with actual medical skills. It all culminated in a Fall Moratorium called by the Boston Peace Action Coalition that shut down every Boston area college. *Look what we helped start, Leece Pebbles that started an avalanche* He wondered whether Lisa might be in the National Moratorium March On Washington. He never told anyone about Mercer Hall, or what followed. *She still has to negotiate the medical school admission process.* Now they all had war stories, and he didn't have her consent to tell theirs.

At first every trip across the street senior year, for classes, or, especially, to use Butler Library, stirred increased pulse and cold sweat. And the dreams. She dreamt she was blind, being chased by screaming police. Her roommate had to wake her once. She avoided passing close to Low Library, now being renovated, and passed up taking a literature class she very much wanted because it met at Mercer Hall, but was able to take Embryology, and take an Anthropology course second semester, when the dreams had abated. And learned things she wished she could share and discuss with B*astard*.

She concentrated on work, found herself sought-after in study groups. But she took Biochem at Barnard. *Bastard's textbook Bastard's name on the flyleaf* Introductory lecture: "The only way to promote chemical reactions is with heat and catalysts, which with organic chemicals means risk of explosion, and toxic heavy metals. The challenge before living organisms is to carry out complex chemical reactions without excess heat or toxic catalysts. They manage to accomplish this with enzymes. Organic catalysts, complex proteins that can bring reactants together not far above room temperature..." Borderline sarcastic. *Bastard could have given that lecture So could I*

At all her New York City med school admissions interviews she was, as she had been warned she would be, asked, Why should we give you a spot that could go to a man who will dedicate his life to Medicine, when you're probably just going to get married? She could answer (honestly): "There is no prospect of that on the horizon." The sole exception was Woman's Medical College of Pennsylvania. When her mother moved in with Richard she told herself *I'm free to accept admission anywhere*, and she did feel free. *But, also, abandoned*

At a pre-Christmas (1968) party to which she had asked her roommate to get her invited, she got drunk for the first and only time. She didn't do anything unseemly, just retreated to a soft chair from which she told a considerable number of young men, including one who, many years later (in another America entirely), would become wealthy enough to buy a Senate seat, to leave her the hell alone. Her head and her gut spun on different cycles. The roommate, greatly annoyed, helped her back to the dorm. At the 116th Street crossing she gently vomited into the gutter, not the first time, and absolutely not the last, that such a thing had happened at that spot. More commonly to freshmen, but she had started college at sixteen. So. She woke feeling even worse, and, quite involuntarily, made the second entry in an involuntary mental ledger headed Things Benjamin Rothstein, B. Sc. (Columbia 1968) Didn't, Wouldn't or Couldn't Do. *Boy Scout Ben didn't drink. Or hadn't. Maybe he'd started Or smoking dope Bully for him. Well, he probably wouldn't have even gone to the party. Oh, enough with men.*

Summer 1969 seemed endless. The tedium of the Macy's job grated on her. She turned down her father's offer of a summer at Tanglewood, knowing she would have to share quarters with his latest companion, and endure her mother's response. And then she was called to an office and told she was being transferred to the Lingerie Department. "Because," the new department manager said, "A pretty girl in Lingerie is a real asset to sales." When she bristled he said, "Unless you want to pass up the raise." She considered the state of her finances and swallowed what she had intended to say. She learned to deal with the creepy men who browsed the silky racks and when asked if they needed help said, "No, thank you; she's just my size." When the manager began hanging around, finally asking if she had plans for the weekend she decided she'd *really* had enough.

"**Rothstein**." He looked around at the man who had hailed him and drew a complete blank. "Michael Firman," the man said, pointing to himself. Seeing Ben's face devoid of recognition he said, "Organic lab. I had the spot next to that Barnard girl."

His stomach turned over. "Sorry," he said. "It was just a job. You were all a blur."

"But you remember her. And Boland. You shut that motherfucker *down*, man."

"Oh, right. That." He got himself under control as best he could, and when he trusted himself to sound casual he said, "Whatever happened to her, anyway?"

"Who, the Barnard girl? Mautner? She took a few more courses across the street. I was in Embryo with her. We studied together and…" *I know how that goes* "…you'd never have guessed it from how she was in Organic, but by senior year she was a stone fox, man. Total knockout. We all wanted her. I tried; she shot me down through the floor. No more hazing, believe me. She got into Woman's, in Philly. She should have been here, man. She should be. Her grades beat the crap out of mine."

And his heart thawed, melted. *Yes she should*, he thought, *damn it*. And he realized what he'd been to her, what they'd been to each other: First Love. *I guess*, he thought, *we did teach each other more than chemistry. And when I'm with a woman, later, I'll think of her, for just a moment, fondly.* And maybe he'd given her something equivalent to what she'd given him, he thought. *We taught each other what love is.* Just another branch of Organic Chemistry? But there never seemed to be a Second Love.

With one of the Long Island cousins she took off for Woodstock. They never made it; the Thruway had been closed, other roads were blocked or gridlocked. When they turned back, she thought *Bastard wouldn't turn back…Tell you what Mautner, what I'd really like is to get to hear the music And he'd stand by the bike and cock his head the way he did, look away, think, look back, the way he did, and say We should be able to get there* *on back roads.* But he liked her parents' music, would more likely be at Tanglewood. She had her ears pierced, grew her hair even longer.

He had started seeing patients in the Clinical Examination course. Once a week, out of the lecture hall and off to a clinic or hospital to examine and present cases. They had all been given black bags and stethoscopes by pharmaceutical companies that would be ever more grateful to them in the coming years and decades as the medical profession became the Health Care Industry; he bought the otoscope/ophthalmoscope, reflex hammer and other impedimenta out of the earnings from Rothstein's Dry Goods. Sheets and towels transformed and transmuted, by the alchemy of monetary exchange, into the next step for the Rothsteins out of Eastern Europe and into America. So he thought on bad days; on good days he took pride in knowing how to use these tools.

Before seeing patients they learned how to examine a chest, examine an abdomen, how to draw blood, in the time-honored way: on each other. Through the luck of alphabetization his lab partner was Nola Mae, whose real name was Margaret Roth. They had been thrown together over the corpse in Gross Anatomy and were again brigaded together for Clinical Examination. The night before learning the art of percussing and auscultating a chest she knocked on his dorm room door and pushed her way in.

"Rothstein. You're rumored to be involved in some radical stuff. True?"

"I suppose," he said, shutting the pharmacology text he'd been falling asleep to.

"So, I wonder if I could enlist you in the cause of feminism."

Her manner was straightforward but he could feel her distress. "Depends how."

"Tomorrow afternoon we're supposed to strip to the waist and examine each other. There's an obvious issue."

He sat up, gestured to his desk chair. "For all of you?"

She sat. "The other women are going to ask their lab partners too, if that's what you mean." She pointed to the button-down shirt she was wearing. "I'll be wearing this. If I go bra-less, I don't have to take it off, or unbutton completely. If I unbutton the bottom buttons, you can just slip your stethoscope up under it and listen to both upper and lower lobes, and under in front for the right middle lobe..."

"Yeah," he said. "The heart will be harder."

"Yes, but not impossible. I can put your scope over the apex, sternal and side landmarks."

"And," he said, if we stand in the corner of the room, with you facing the wall..."

"There you go. You in?"

"Absolutely, Mags. You're being bullied. It's fucking outrageous the women don't have their own room for this."

"Isn't it. We tried suggesting that, but we didn't get faculty support. Tradition. Told us on surgery we'll have to share changing rooms with the men, or gown up with the nurses. Be tough, girls. Thanks, Ben. I'll tell you, the one thing I'm scared of—terrified really—is, if we get the wrong prof, he'll ask me to be the demo."

"Not a problem," he said. "I'll volunteer to be the demo." Next day he struggled to keep her real name firmly in mind as he maneuvered them into a corner. He gallantly looked away as she maneuvered his stethoscope over her heart. She was stoic, but her racing heart gave her away. "Thanks, she whispered as she buttoned up.

At dinner he got ragged. "Thanks for blocking our view, Rothstein. You trying to get in her pants, or what?"

Am I? "Fuck you all," he said genially. On the other side of the dining hall the women were discussing—what? *How would Lisa feel, doing this*

Assigned psychiatric patients at Mass Mental Health, he offered her a ride; she was unprepared for it being on a motorcycle. "I don't think so," she said. "I've never ridden one of those things."

"You just have to hang on. Arms around me, or use the

grab strap and back rest.

"Nice try, Rothstein. Grab strap it is." She held on, but accepted a ride back from a Fourth-year on a psych subresidency. *Well, the backrest didn't go to waste*

At Woman's she was no longer a *girl*, no longer in a nunnery. The campus strikes, marches, rallies, anti-War and early feminist demonstrations had blown parietal hours and *in loco parentis* off the planet. Even in the dorm, no one stopped male visitors. The campus was relatively isolated, but the women here were more like her, all determined med students; she made friends more easily than she ever had. Many were either local or had attended nearby colleges; through them she met guys. These were mostly set-ups, blind double dates, guys met at parties (male med students and grad students from Penn and Jefferson and Hahnemann). A few dates were modestly successful, but the failures, and one aborted fling attempt, were more memorable…

"This is weird," he said. "Brainy chicks usually don't dig bikes." She rode, knew how to lean on curves. But when he took her to see "Easy Rider" she started sobbing, and ran out. *Crazy*, he thought. *Probably no action there anyway.*

Some turned into second dates. One turned into mild making out. "You want to go somewhere after?' he said when he caught his breath. "Your place, my place?"

"Maybe," she said, closed her eyes, went back toward him, and found—empty air.

"I want to see this movie," he said. "This is a very good movie, and I'm seeing it for a course…I'm a Film Studies student, remember?"

"So we can stay for the second show."

"I need to see it in sequence. I can't keep up with the titles if we're…"

"Okay. Watch your movie. Enjoy."

One, at a turnout along the Schuylkill, invited to her room, said, "So I finally get to see the Holy of Holies." She looked, he didn't know, quizzical? Insulted? She'd taken that all wrong. "I mean your room," he said. "You said, come back to my place."

"I did, didn't I. Yes." By this time she was sharing a house on Queen Lane with three classmates; the lease was in one's name, the phone in another's, the water bill in a third's; she had the utility bill, and they evened up the expenses monthly. He turned off Kelly Drive on to Midvale, started looking for a place to park, not having to find a space hidden by trees; she had invited him up at last (and none too soon; she hadn't been touched in what felt like too long). She smiled at him as she closed the door. "Make yourself at home," she said. "I'll be right back." He could hear conversation, perhaps argument, beyond the door. What exactly did *at home* mean, he wondered as "be right back" turned into a lengthening while. Get into bed? Take off his clothes, and get into her bed? Too risky. Nothing to read except medical books. Maybe there was a bottle, a little Peppermint Schnapps, Southern Comfort. He got up, opened the top dresser drawer. Jewelry, socks. *Wait. What's this?* The door opened. "What the hell do you think you're doing?"

"I was just…"

"Going through my things."

"I was looking for…"

"Nothing in there is your size. I think you'd better leave."

"Hey. Yeah? What's this, then? Looks a whole lot like a wedding ring."

"I said, you'd better leave." She reached behind a night table and came up with a miniature souvenir baseball bat, banged it against the metal of the bedstead. "NOW," she said. He ran, thinking. *Crazy bitch.* She wondered if *Bastard* had kept his length of pipe.

In Gross Anatomy lab, they had dissected their corpses' abdomens and chests, and, at the end of second semester, were down to head, brain, and limbs. Her tablemates had covered the emptied abdomen and chest cavity; the man's dry, dead eyes stared at the ceiling lights as they had all year as she laid back the muscles and tendons to expose the wrist bones. "Nice job," said the professor, who had materialized behind her. He had her stop, and turned to her three partners. "Can you name the carpal bones?"

"Scaphoid, Lunate, Triquetral, Pisiform, Trapezium..." Norma said, and faltered. He turned to Laura. "Trapezoid, Capitate..." They all went blank.

"Hamate, he said. "Class?" Everyone looked up from the cadavers they were working on. "There are three simple mnemonics for remembering the carpal bones. The most popular is Some Lovers Try Positions They Can't Handle." When no one laughed, he said, "All right, if you don't like that one, how about Scottish Lads Like Taking Prostitutes To The Caledonian Hotel. Or a variant, Students Like Taking Prostitutes To The Carleton Hotel. When no one laughed, he said, "It's a joke, ladies." They were silent. "Tough room," he said.

Is that how *Bastard* had thought of her? No, wait; *she* had been the one to call it *just an affair* and *he* had been the one to walk out angry.

He let his hair grow even longer, grew a beard and mustache. He attended a few of BCN's live concerts, was there the night Bruce Springsteen blew the roof off the Harvard Square Theater, but never went to the club concerts. He told himself this was because he couldn't dance, but knew it was because he couldn't dance without Lisa. He favored classical music when he studied, always had; it centered him; there were no distracting lyrics. But Kurt Mautner had been appointed assistant conductor of the Boston Symphony Orchestra; his name was all over the radio. He couldn't forget her if he tried. *I could have taken a year off. Worked the store, taken a few courses, applied together this year. No. Draft bait.* He wondered what she was doing right now. Probably the same thing he was, or damn near. *But inferior, of course, because: at* Woman's. *What bullshit.* Well. If some of the reactants are left in the vessel, a little heat, a little catalyst, should be sufficient to restart the reaction. He could hop on the bike, be in Philadelphia in, what? Six hours? Eight hours? But he didn't know Woman's schedule. Or where he might find her.

A dorm would be easy to find, but what if she had an apartment? With another girl? Two or three other girls? *Women.* Or a guy? Okay, say, dorm. What would he do, stand out front like Brando shouting "Liiisaaaa?" None of this completely discouraged him. What stopped him was, she'd said "Let me go. Let me go, Ben". And he had. When people said that, when you did that, it seemed to him, you couldn't go after them. They had to come back themselves. If they were ever going to.

Her skill at drawing blood surprised her. *Bastard's* competence, in the lab, with the motorcycle; maybe it was the Boy Scouts, maybe Morty and the chemistry set. *I should have been a Girl Scout,* she thought, but she doubted the Girl Scouts taught those skills. She was good at starting IVs, other scut work, then at more complex procedures. On Surgery, to her surprise, her sewing talent (from a grandmother?) was the basis for some moderately skilled suturing. But she had no desire to be a surgeon; her dissections in undergrad Comparative Anatomy and in Gross Lab in her first year were no great thing; she didn't enjoy cutting. Besides, Surgery was the ultimate boys' club. It was humiliating just to hear their banter with the nurses. But she was allowed, even encouraged, to do some pretty fancy suturing on minor trauma in the ER.

His Pediatric clerkship was split between children (sticking sharp objects into very tiny, very vulnerable organisms) and adolescents (sticking sharp objects into larger, vulnerable organisms capable of resistance and immune to cajolery from medical personnel barely older than themselves). She was reputed to be movie-star gorgeous, seventeen years old, from a wealthy suburb, and this was her fourth admission for Crohn's Disease flareups. He went in with the Peds intern and the surgery resident, found her sitting on the bed beside one of the nurses and living up to the reputation. She was also bleeding into her bowel; a section had necrosed and had to come out. They told her to get undressed and into a gown, "We're coming back to examine you;" she knew the drill. The surgery resident lingered; to Ben's shock said to her, "I'm going to enjoy this." Ben and the intern exchanged a look; the resident, watching her undress, told them he had little time, they could come back and do their admission histories and physicals later.

"Did you see that?" Ben asked the Peds intern, who grimaced. When he went back in he found her crying. "He's a jerk," Ben said. "A real schmuck. I'm really sorry."

"It isn't for you to be sorry," she said through tears.

"No, I…but I, we, have to examine you too."

"That's okay," she said. She had stopped crying. "I'm used to it."

He got her history, did a quick physical (adolescents, even with life-threatening illnesses, were usually completely healthy otherwise) and started an IV. When he came to the lounge to write his student admit note the intern was arguing with the resident.

"…was completely uncool, man."

"Oh, grow a pair Christiansen. She took it as a compliment. And she could use it. She's going to come out of this thing with a belly scar, and if she isn't lucky you people will start her on steroids and her looks are going to go in the toilet."

"For what it's worth," Ben said, "I found her crying. And if you don't go in and apologize to her and make this right I'm going to take it to the head of Peds."

"And who are you, a fucking little pissant Third-Year I can ruin for life?"

"He's the guy who's going to the head of Peds," Christiansen said, "And I'm the guy who, if he does, and you try to give him any shit, is going to back his story."

The surgeon looked from one of them to the other. He broke into a laugh. "Yeah, I had you going there for a minute. Sure, I'll apologize to her. Shit. Come on."

They went back in, and waited for her to get off the phone. "These guys think I owe you an apology," he said to her. "I was, I don't know, too crude, in my appreciation of your… You're a beautiful girl. We're going to try to keep it that way. Okay?" She nodded and looked away.

The next time Ben came in she said, "You didn't have to make a big deal of it."

"Sorry. I thought he'd upset you. Insulted you. Was creepy." She sighed. "Creepy, yes. Nothing I can't handle. I said, I'm used to it."

He walked out thinking *You'd think she'd be grateful Why get involved? She's just a bundle of chemistry Yeah But Why should she have to be used to it   She's the same age Lisa was when we met*

She had questions about a visiting professor's lecture on burns and burn healing, but instead of taking questions he said. "I have to run, ladies. If any of you have a question, come see me." His office was in a labyrinthine building at Penn. A grad student at a lab bench *familiar lab odors the familiar glassware* in a long white coat, directed her to a nearby hall. Nister beckoned her into his office. "Miss Mautner. Welcome. Sit." He pointed to a couch. And closed the door. "What would it be my pleasure to do for you?" Her radar buzzed slightly, but she ignored it.

"I have questions about electrical burns," she said, taking out her notebook.

"Ah. A prominent part of my research work. Which I could make you an offer to join, if you're interested. You appear enthusiastic." He joined her on the couch. "Could be a real career boost for you." He smiled. You're a very pretty girl."

She retreated from him. "Join. Perhaps," she said, glancing toward the door.

"The topic will be prominent on your next exams, on which I'm sure you're eager to do well. I'd be as happy to offer you a leg up on that as you would be to accept it." She watched, paralyzed by disbelief, his hand advancing toward her along the couch back, and twisted away when she felt his other hand on her knee. She sprang for the door, slammed out of the room and ran, blinded, numb; thinking *Did that just happen? What just happened?* Blundered down the hall. *Do I report this? Who to? Does he do this every year, run out and offer to take questions at his office Doors like huge refrigerators Cold Rooms?   Hot rooms? Tissue Cultures? Familiar odors of acetone, glacial acetic acid, toluene* One of the big doors opened. The grad student was suddenly there. "Are you okay?" he said. "You look upset. You're shaking."

She suppressed a sob. "Yes. I'm fine. Just a bit lost, again. I forgot my notebook in Professor Nister's office, and I have to find it again…"

"Come down to the lab," he said. "Catch your breath. Have some tea. I'll go for your notebook." *Does he know Does everyone* He retrieved it for her, and began calling (her address and phone number were on the cover: If found please contact…). She made excuses for a month, but when she felt she should try to overcome her feelings from that day, she finally, tentatively, agreed to a date.

That was how she met Robert.

He couldn't believe the War dragged on. He remembered a phrase of Morty's *Losers always double down, Rothstein* He still went to the teach-ins when he could but the Spring and Fall Mobilizations, the Mass Marches On Washington were too distant to make it there and back in time for his ward duties. His, and Boston's, rage boiled over when the students were killed at Kent State. After four days of mass demonstrations downtown, he took an "emergency leave" to join the spontaneous protest in Washington. He blasted down I-95 on the bike, found a SHO formation to join, took off the field jacket and set out in the brutal heat distributing water and salt tablets to the crowd. At one point he could have sworn he saw her on the Mall, but by the time he could push his way through the mob, she, or the girl he thought was her, was gone. He grieved, knew he wasn't over her, *maybe never would be.*

A volunteer assistant at The Freak one night had auburn hair down to her waist, long legs and long dangling faux Native American feathered earrings. "Come to my place after?" she said casually. He was going to say "Sure" when she said, "There's hash, and. we have three girls and only two guys, so…"

Jackpot Go for it bro Cowardice is the ice that "Sorry, not my scene," he'd said.

Well, but. In the midst of death we are in life. There was the sheer physical need. *Why that one girl little bro?* If the kind of girl he wanted wouldn't, by her very nature, want him, or anyway wouldn't want him as much as he wanted her, logically it was a matter of a search for an un-Lisa. Or a non-Lisa. Or an anti-Lisa. There were plenty of (well, a few; enough) nurses, social workers, OT's, PT's, lab techs, ward clerks, and departmental secretaries who were mildly charmed by Biker Ben. The Boy Scout backpack was now an ironic statement, given the hair and beard. The Adolescent Ward nurse who had witnessed it all thought he had made just the right size deal of it. She was the first real *date* he'd had since he'd left Lisa. Not the last. In the casual way of that time, they had sex. That was the difference, he thought. *I had sex. With Lisa I made love.* He was writing a progress note, back against the lounge wall, when he realized the conversation he was overhearing between two nurses was about him. "Word is," one said, "He's good in bed." *Good in bed. Is that what I am* What exactly did that mean? Good at the gymnastics? *I'm no athlete* "I mean," the nurse said, "Sheila says he takes time, cares that *you* come too."

If so, *I learned from Lisa.* No, they had learned together; she had taught him to care that a partner had pleasure too. That a partner's pleasure heightened one's own. To be considerate. To be kind. Had he always been? He didn't think so. Not until her. Before her he'd been a fighter. Morty had been a fighter. He'd fought his way to Harvard and almost fought his way out. She'd been a fighter too. But a different kind. Walking past Stuyvesant High, the science high school she could have walked to but was all male, to travel over an hour to Bronx Science. Morty would have wanted to set fire to the place, or anyway stink-bomb the teachers' lounge (or maybe the Board of Education; it wasn't the teachers' fault the place had been built without facilities for girls). She fought a different way, but she was just as tough. Would make a hell of a Rothstein, he thought. He could hear Morty's voice again. *Plenty of action. I told you the, bike brings in the action. Loosen up. What did I tell you. The Rothstein boys can take this town Fuck our way through Boston   You need to get experience, little bro. Radcliffe is a cliff we can climb Cliffies, Rothstein Money coming out their ass There's more than one fish in the sea Plenty of tuna out there."*

None of these things lasted long. There came a point in each relationship when he felt either disappointed, or, worse, felt exhausted and disappointed in himself. On a beach at Cape Ann waves pounded the driftwood to splinters, the splinters to dust. "Rub some sun block on me?" she said.

"Sure," he said. He felt the warmth of her skin, accented by the sheen of oily cream. "Oxybenzone," he said dreamily. "Methyl parabenzoate."

"What?"

"The active ingredients in sun block."

"You would know that."

"Ful redy hadde he his apothecaries, To senden him drogges and his letuaries."

"What? What the hell was that?"

"Chaucer. The Canterbury Tales. It's a poem."

"Well. I know that much. Hey. I know this, too." She gestured vaguely in the direction of the sea. "There's these rocks off there. They're supposed to be in a poem."

"*The Dry Salvages*. T.S. Eliot. Third of the *Four Quartets*. 'I think the river is a strong brown god'. 'You are the music while the music lasts'."

"Jesus. Do you, like, know everything?"

"I know a lot of things. I don't know everything."

"No, I mean, do you *have* to know everything?"

"I know stuff. I'm supposed to know stuff. Does that bother you?"

"Yes. Yes it does. I guess."

"Why?"

"I don't know why. Because I don't know everything."

"Would you like me to play dumb?"

"I guess I would. For a while, anyway. Can you?"

"Tell you what. You cut off the left half of your hair and

I'll turn off the left half of my brain. That's how it would feel."

She just looked at him. "This isn't going to go any further, is it."

"I guess not."

And He was late again. A patient had started coughing up blood and he stayed to learn how to drop a tube for a bronchial sample. He called to apologize, reschedule.

"How much later, Benjamin?"

"I think maybe an hour."

"Meaning two hours, Doctor Standard Time."

"This isn't a nine-to-five job. You know that."

"Here's the deal, Benjamin. I'm going to the restaurant. If you're not there in an hour don't be there at all. I'll be gone."

"Save yourself the trouble," he said. "Be gone now."

And what he came to think of as his all-time favorite: "I've never been with a Jew...a Jewish guy...before." For what she really wanted to ask she substituted, "Do you, like, not eat ham? And wear one of those beanie things?"

"A yarmulke. They're called yarmulkes."

"So, do you?"

"I'm not observant. I don't practice a religion."

"You don't believe in God?"

"I would put it that I believe there's no such thing as gods."

"You think there is no God?"

"I said, *believe* there are no gods. I can't prove it. It isn't susceptible to proof."

"How can you say that? I mean, twelve years of Catholic school, I came out without much religion, but I believe in God. A God."

"I took a lot of chemistry and biology and physics, and I know how it works, and I think the universe can do its thing without anything supernatural behind it."

"You don't feel a God out there?"

"Out there, in here, nope, nothing. Just all this. What you see. Chemistry. It's a marvel. An incredibly intricate, interlocking dance. It made itself. It runs by itself, and produces marvels. Isn't that a greater miracle than something made by an all-powerful being? That all this, that life, can arise out of chemistry?"

"You're serious."

"Perfectly serious. Why would I not be serious?" He moved his hand over her.

"Because you can't be."

"Imagine there's no heaven," he sang. "It's easy if you try. No hell below us. Above us only sky…"

"You're scaring me. I don't know if I can…I don't know that I can…"

And the ultimate "Hey," she said. "Med stud. That your bike?"

"Nah, I'm stealing it from a Hell's Angel. I just beat the keys out of him."

She laughed. Looked like what she probably was, biker chick in a nurse's uniform. "Give me a ride to Southie?" *Told you little bro*

"Sure. Why not?" Turned out she was a P.T. Shared an apartment with two others in South Boston, filled with Red Sox and Bruins paraphernalia. He wasn't sure he would survive the sex. Wasn't sure he was really there at all.

He lay staring at the ceiling in the dawn light, feeling ashamed, wondering how best to leave. *Was that great or what No. I'm not you, Morty* What was the Woody Allen line? *Sex without love is an empty experience, but as empty experiences go it's one of the best there is.* But it wasn't. Not anymore. It was starting to be like gym class. Yeah, at first it had been fun, the sex felt good, but he had to admit, part of this was that before Lisa he had been awkward with girls, and after Lisa he was confident to the point of cockiness. Trying, he realized, to replace quality with quantity. The perfect one with three, or however many it took, imperfect ones. And it wasn't fun anymore. The bike had helped. The Harvard med student, no movie star but not bad looking, a little dangerous perhaps. *Of course you'll get in I'm here so you're a Legacy It's a pussy bonanza That's not what I'm here for Morty Of course not It's a perk Radcliffe Wellesley BU BC…BC, that's Catholic girls Morty… And Simmons What's Simmons? Kind of a finishing school, and we get to apply the finish Rothstein I'm going with a Cliffie right now, I can get you a date You're in little brother In Harvard and In*

But none of them had ever helped him push the derelict machine up Delancey Street to help revive it. Or up a secluded mountain road to a tiny, peaceful pond. The woman beside him stirred, opened her eyes. "Who's Leece?" she said.

"Huh?"

"You said Leece while we did it. I'm Lucy. Luce. Is there a Lisa in your past?"

"Not in my past," he said.

She came home to a dinner with her mother and Richard to celebrate passing her Part One Boards and transition from her classroom to her clinical ward years. "We have an announcement too," her mother said. "I'm giving up the apartment. We're engaged." At first she felt the loss of her childhood home. "You won't be home anymore," her mother said reasonably, "You'll be at the hospitals nights and weekends, won't you?" Then she felt freed, in a way she didn't completely admit or understand.

On OB-GYN she was surprised by her response to the babies. New life, coming from, seemingly, nowhere. Only not nowhere. In the miserable inner-city hospital in North Philly from exhausted, sweating, screaming women, and girls sometimes half her age, with no insurance, often abandoned by the fathers and by other family. She held their hands, tried to substitute for the missing support. *Something not new for me, mothering the mothers* Cold cloths for foreheads, ice chips for thirst, runs to the harried labor deck nurses to try to squeeze out an ounce of pity. Holding on, herself, until the moment when she could step in, in the delivery room, and the little head appeared, the little face, the tiny body, that might or might not heal it all, make it all worth it. Or make it worse.

This labor had been a nightmare; a tired, woeful woman in her mid-thirties for whom this pregnancy had meant the end of the relationship that had produced it. Before her contractions had become too serious to carry on a conversation she'd been hopeful that the child would fill the void left by the man who'd left her. Lisa got the medical and pregnancy history and felt an alarm go off. "She says the baby was never very active, and fetal movements seemed to slow even more in the last trimester, or anyway the last month," she told the resident.

"Which is it, the last trimester or the last month?"

"She isn't sure."

"And now labor isn't progressing?"

"Not well."

"Could be a breech. Or worse, nuchal cord. How long has she been in labor?"

"Almost thirteen hours now."

"We may have to do a Section, if we can't turn it. Monitor hooked up?"

"Yes. No distress yet, but I'm worried."

"We should be," the resident said. "What about?"

"Well, if breech, fetal distress; if a Section, all the complications of surgery, infant respiratory distress…"

"True. Why should we think it would be breech?"

"Why would we…?"

"She told you it's been underactive. That sometimes means a baby with a congenital defect. Used to be we thought breech babies were damaged by not enough oxygen on the way out. Now we know the reason they're breech in the first place is they're hypotonic in utero, and don't turn. Maybe symptom of some congenital defect."

Oh no. "What can we do?"

"Nothing. Watch, wait, do what's indicated." Which in the end was a C-section, when the breech-positioned baby showed signs of fetal distress. She held the tiny, floppy, blue, barely crying little one for the briefest of minutes until the pediatricians came roaring in to spirit him to Neonatal Intensive Care. Long enough to note the epicanthic folds, the downturned mouth, the tiny hands and feet of Down syndrome.

"Probably cardiac cushion defect," the Peds intern said. "We need some O's here, people." The baby pinked up slightly with the oxygen.

The mother was stony-faced next day on postnatal rounds. Lisa sat with her for the long minutes until she was ready to talk. "He's a mongoloid," the woman said.

"I know. I held him when he was born."

"They say he's got a hole in his heart. He's going to need heart surgery. Then he'll be able to breathe easier. But they say it's hard to get for kids with...."

"Yes. *Silence.* "What's his name?"

"I don't know. I had names picked out, but now...I don't know."

"She's right," Robert said. "The cardiac cushion surgery is pretty new. There aren't a lot of people doing it, and on a mongoloid...I don't know, babe. Not good."

"It's called Down syndrome. And that's all you can say?" *Don't call me babe*

"What do you want me to say?"

She knew the time had come that she was too deep in her books, burned out on the daily grind of scut work and on-command recitals on the wards, and had to get out of town. She asked Robert if he wouldn't like to get out of the city for the weekend. "Can't do it, babe. Cell culture medium doesn't change itself."

"Please, Robert. Get someone to cover. I'm going crazy. Or will do."

"So take a road trip, babe. It's a good idea."

"You know I don't drive. And anyway, I was thinking, together. Please, Robert."

In the end he grumpily asked a colleague *Now I'll owe the guy a favor* to change the cell cultures' medium for a day (sheets of epithelial cells for possible burn grafts; it really was delicate work, *but if a bunch of Nister's cells die what do I care*); he'd do it just as they left and just when they returned. She thought, *a run up to Bear Mountain with Bastard, on the bike, hair flying, arms wrapped around him.*

* * *

She tried to persuade him to join her at the Fall Mobilization. "It's only a day trip," she said. "DC is only a two-and-a-half, three hour drive, tops."

"Enormous traffic jam. Why go?" he said.

"To protest the war, Robert. Stop the killing. Save a bunch of kids' lives."

"Of course the war is stupid. But...Enlistees? Draftees? They're fools."

"They're poor, ignorant kids just off the farm and out of the ghettoes. Led by men who don't give a shit about them. To say nothing of the poor Vietnamese."

"Yup. Wouldn't catch me falling for that."

"Is that all you can think to say?"

"What do you want me to say? They're all fools. Right up to Nixon."

"That we're supposed to heal."

"That you're supposed to heal. I'm a scientist."

"You're an M.D."

"Working on getting a Ph.D. I had enough of healing, thanks. I mean, the work I'm doing is going to heal people, but I don't have to be in contact with their foolishness all day." This rocked her. "I can heal by deciphering the chemistry and fixing it. Maybe I'll stumble on something in the chemistry that will make them less fools, but I doubt it."

"People disgust you?"

"I didn't say that. I just don't want to engage with it. To spend my life catering to their damn foolishness. They can cut and run at any time. Could have gone to Canada, or I don't know, found a deferment. Or deserted. I would have."

"They were too scared and angry to think." She recalled her Anthropology. "They have kinship ties. Of friendship and loyalty."

"In a bad cause."

"Absolutely. But they don't see it that way. That's part of the tragedy."

"I refuse to engage with it."

"Wait. You think anyone who fights is a fool? I

mean, with weapons, in armies, maybe, sure, but anyone who protests...?"

"Yes, babe, I do."

"You're no pacifist."

"No, I'm...I don't know. Uninterested. I'm interested in the biochemistry, not the organisms. If you see what I mean."

"I see what you mean. More interested in the chemistry than in its epiphenomenon. It's emergent properties: Life. Robert, I cut class to go to DC to the Kent State protest last year. I took part in the campus occupation at Columbia."

"Did you really?"

"Yes I did. And I've been to four Marches On Washington. I've yelled stuff and at Columbia I helped take over a building and I was teargassed..."

"Well, I hope you've outgrown that. I refuse to have any part in the madness."

"By withdrawing from it completely," she said.

"By refusing to engage with it," he said, "Or refusing to let it engage me." She couldn't see a difference, but let it pass. "Did you smoke any of the President's cigars?"

"No. That was in another building. And it's propaganda, anyway."

He shrugged. "Babe, are we having an argument?"

"Yes, Robert. I believe we are. And please don't call me *babe*."

"I've always called my girlfriends that. It's an endearment."

"Not to me. To me it feels demeaning."

"It does? I'll try to remember."

The dream confused him. He was on psychiatry; dreams were supposed to be the Royal Road to the Unconscious, but this one led nowhere. He heard a choir in a Mormon Temple, which meant Salt Lake City, singing, "You are not salt salt is inorganic." It was two days later, at a grocery, by chance walking past the condiments, he became aware of the blue Morton's Salt canisters. So the dream, he realized like a thunderbolt, meant

"You are not Morton. Morton is inorganic". Well, he was, by now. Inorganic is the most common thing in the universe to be. *But I'm organic. Still*

It was a standing joke that on your Psychiatry rotation you psychoanalyzed yourself, but she was surprised to find it actually happening as she read the textbook's capsulized Freud. *So I'm drawn to older men of course I am my classmates have always been older Robert isn't my classmate Neither was Ben Of course Always trying to replace my abandoning father So obvious Is that what I really What do I really want To escape that dynamic completely would be nice To want something more*

She woke to the sound of him rattling keys She sat up to the odor of fresh coffee, was shaking out her hair when he came in, fully dressed. "Morning. Lab calls."

"What's going on in the lab?"

"Something maybe significant, maybe not."

"Tell me about it."

"It would just bore you."

"I took biochem, Rob. I wouldn't find it boring, I assure you." When he didn't reply she said, "When will you be back?"

"I don't know. Late afternoon? Have to harvest some cells, while they spin I might as well feed the cultures, and by the time I'm done with that..."

"I could help. I'm pretty good in a lab…"

"Nah. No, stay here."

She swung herself out of bed. "I have work too. I'll go back up."

"Figured you'd say that. Here." He handed her an envelope. "Lock up, put the key in here, drop it in the mailbox. I'll just take my mail key. Have some breakfast, I left some coffee." He kissed her quickly. *Perfunctorily* she thought.

She showered and ended up having the coffee. *He didn't have to harvest the cells; he could have left them for later To be The Best, Lab Comes First.*

She'd thought that a man so focused on his work would

understand her focus, and support it. Leave her to it. He was in fact content to see her take off back uptown, but what had felt like support now felt like indifference. She felt *detachable*, and that was supposed to be part of the attraction, except *she* had in fact made the coffee, set it up in the percolator last night, so what was she? She didn't want to be dependent on a man, but was loving a man a form of dependence? Did it have to be? He had his career, she had hers; it should feel like independence, but increasingly it didn't. Even with the demands of her own medical career: cook, dishwasher, eventual hostess for his colleagues when Rob inevitably became Department Chairman? Which was exactly what she'd feared if she'd abandoned her medical aspirations to follow Ben to Boston.

She was going to take the trolley to Center City but turned away at the last moment; it was a fine day and she had the time she had made for Robert. She could easily walk to 30th Street Station and take a Chestnut Hill train, but that would leave her with a walk through a dicey neighborhood at the other end. Some kinds of independence were dangerous and she had no Ben with a length of pipe in his pocket. When she thought of Ben now, she thought *We should have stayed at the Hotel Pennsylvania. Better, we should have built a cabin at the pond. He would never have left me like this; he would at least have offered me a ride home Wanted to be The Best, but was at least considerate.* She added one more thing to the List Of Things Ben Rothstein Would Never Do (it was, had she been counting, #173). *Bastard?*

Since she had the time, she walked east on Walnut (to avoid the equally dicey porn theaters on Market West and Chestnut). She stopped at the middle of the bridge for the view up the Schuylkill. Just below her a train struggled through the maze of tracks into the Station, on its journey, she knew, to New York. And beyond, to Boston. The Station, the Post Office, the stone bridges with their warrior eagles; Ben would have said, "Beautiful examples of WPA architecture." The way she and Ben had strolled the city, seeing everything, looking in store windows, pointing out little architectural details, an ornate cornice, a daring bay window, old people, druggies, books in used bookstores, funny ads on buses (YOU DON'T HAVE TO BE JEWISH TO LOVE LEVY'S REAL JEWISH RYE), smelling the cheeses in Little Italy, the pickles on the Lower East Side. *In fact, Ben, the eagles, according to this plaque, were salvaged from the demolition of New York's Penn Station.* And the bike. God, she'd been terrified the first time, and not all of that. Then she was exhilarated. *Because, with Ben He took care of me. Took care, period, so naturally of me too Why do I miss that now? Ambivalence. Want it and don't want it. Balance of reactants driving the reaction back and forth around a precarious equilibrium. When Ben touched me, it was with reverence.* Sex with Robert was the first real sex she'd had since Ben. It was okay. Sometimes better than okay. Sometimes the roller coaster even went past the top. Well, that was realistic. In bed he was good, technically. As *considerate* as Ben? Often. Well, mostly. (#s160 through 165). *Or just wanted to be The Best?* She walked on.

She sat for a few minutes on a bench in Rittenhouse Square. Panhandlers approached. She read their diagnoses in their faces, their movements. The exploded facial veins *spider angiomata* of the alcoholics, the stooped, shuffling gait *drug induced-Parkinsonism* of schizophrenics on antipsychotics…She thought, *Ben ruined me for adult life. For real life.* Robert was real. Robert was the reality. He was intelligent (very), dedicated (driven, rather), attentive (sometimes), a decent lover (mostly). He was, at almost thirty, *settled* in the sense her mother meant it: on the way to a probably brilliant research career *so, competition no issue,* probably a department chairmanship; anyway some eminence, in a very promising field. The Chairman's Wife. Dinners, children, planning faculty events—Rob would always be *IN THE LAB.* His tissue cultures would come before his children, as they came before her, now. His needs would always come first, and she'd be left to clean up and administer the rest.

Her mother thought he was a nice guy, when they met ("Well. Finally one I get to meet"). Her father, in town on a road trip with the BSO, thought so too (despite the fact that Robert was tone deaf). Not as—what was the right word? *Passionate*, about some things as Ben. Luckily he'd been there after the thing with Nister; she'd heard a door open in the hall behind her, and when Robert said, (sufficiently conspicuously, or did she just think this later?), "Are you okay?" she'd heard it close. Ben might have kicked the door in and made a scene (#135). Would have four years ago. Would he now? She realized she was comparing 1972 Robert with 1968 Ben. A fantasy. A Ben preserved in memory's amber. Robert was real. *Or was it the difference between* First *and* Real *Love?*

When she got tired of brushing off panhandlers she continued east on Walnut, north on Broad, past the Academy of Music and City Hall, and east on Market to Reading Terminal. *Take a ride on the Reading.* The train from here would mean a longer walk, but through safer territory. She bought her ticket and went to the waiting area for her train to be called. The seats were like pews. Probably from the same supply company. Who had said railroad terminals were the cathedrals of the nineteenth century? *Had he really bathed my eyes with holy water and anointed them with oil?* He hadn't said "I'm taking you to St John's" or "Just come along, babe", or anything like that. He'd said We're going up some steps, into St John the Divine. There'll be water there. She'd been as helpless as a baby, crying and in pain, and he'd still talked to her as if she were a fully functioning member of the team. Well, she had found the window. And thought of the kiss trick. And he hadn't mistaken that, had realized what she was doing. Clever and resourceful, was Ben. *Wait; I was every bit as clever and resourceful.* Her train was called. *Theophile Gautier. That's who'd said it. I think. God, I spend half my life waiting for trains. Ben would have driven me home. Not controlling; considerate.* Which was when the thunderbolt hit. She could hear his voice. She knew perfectly well the idea was her own, that she had just associated it with Ben, but she still wondered if anyone else in the train had heard him say, "*Are you waiting for Daddy to show up with the limo? Take driving lessons, Mautner. Get a damned license and buy a car.*"

Well, why the hell not? She had or could get the money. She could drive herself anywhere she wanted. Robert could come and go to his damned lab without it mattering a damn. Robert could stop seeing her entirely, and she needn't care. Ben could go to Harvard; so what? Ben could die like his brother; so what? Whoa, where had *that* come from? *Because, when I occasionally masturbate, it's Ben in my head, is where.* The train bumped over onto the Norristown branch amid a tangle of sidings and old factory buildings. *Bastard. (#1: Never called to apologize)* She left the train at East Falls and started up Queen Lane, ducking overhanging crape myrtles, not yet in bloom. Soon there would be azalea. What made this self-determination thing so damned important, such a conflict? Easy—so she would never again have to feel what she felt when her all-loving father left, never again have to be a terrified eight-year-old. If she had a car, she could easily take electives at Penn and Jefferson and Hahnemann. Really polish the resume. Get an internship anywhere she wanted. *Maybe even Boston* Which was when lightning struck a second time. Principles of Organic Chemistry, by John Roberts and Marjorie Caserio. *Marjorie.*

She could drive to Boston any time. *Not as Little Liesl. As Dr. Mautner.*

The chemistry was always wrong; some final step always missing from the equation, some final reactant missing from the synthesis, so no *resonant bond* formed…One brilliant Saturday in spring, a rare conjunction of off-time and weather, he tied the backpack full of sandwiches and a canteen to the backrest and blasted west on the MassPike to the Berkshires. He had acquaintances, people he ate with, worked with, teamed with, but no one he was close with to share the trip. There were many side trails on Mt. Greylock but even these were crowded, and he struck out between trees, over a grassy ridge and sat to admire a view of green mountains stretching in every direction *that she would love* He crossed his arms over his bent knees, rested his forehead against them and closed his eyes. A breeze sighed and brought odors of fresh grass *aromatic benzyl ketones* he thought. There was a rustling off to his left. In his closed eyes, he could see her clearly: Lisa, wearing shorts, tennis shoes and a T-shirt tight across her breasts, carrying a textbook. *Every one of them, a little piece of her   Added all together nothing close to what I felt for her   Felt?* He'd promised himself not to, but gave a single sob.

She was on the permanently-jammed Schuylkill Expressway, slowly inching forward in traffic, hypnotized by the swipe of windshield wipers, fallen into a fugue. She knew she was liked. Even well-liked. When she knew something, which was most often, she shared it. She was even, maybe, loved (Robert). What she missed was being adored. Ben, she'd realized, had adored her. *The French make this distinction: Je t'aime; Je t'adore.* She thought she liked Robert, even maybe loved him. Could come to love him, anyway. Ben, she had adored. The sad, important thing was: past tense. *Face it I have a wish to be adored   No   Unacceptable   I need to be independent No   Incomplete   I like* sharing *a relationship What I need is to love and be loved and* valued *Equally In equal measure   To be close enough with another human being for that   Acceptable, surely*

When she got to Robert's she used the mailbox key, found the apartment key in the envelope. Shouldn't she have a key by now? He could have a key to her place, if he ever came as far from *THE LAB* as her place. She checked the time; he was late, probably something gone pear-shaped at *THE LAB*. She put the bag of groceries down, unwound her scarf and set water on low heat for eventual pasta. She unpacked the bag and put away the food, started a salad. *What's wrong with being adored, if you're valued?* An hour later he showed up, kissed her perfunctorily. "Sorry I'm late." As usual he smelled like toluene and acetic acid. *And* respected? *Intellectually respected?*

"Something going on in the lab?" But he was gone for a shower; her words, she knew, hung uselessly in the air. When he came back he didn't smell like the lab anymore. Was drying his hair with one towel, another wrapped around his waist. She liked his chest, and he knew that. She set out plates, glasses, cutlery, napkins while he watched. "Car's wobbly again."

"I should have a look at that for you," he said. "What's for dinner?"

"Pasta al tonno."

"Which just means pasta with tuna."

"And garlic and oil, capers, and Romano cheese," *and work.* "Try."

"Good," he said, rolling it around in his mouth. They ate. "Thanks for getting dinner, Lisa."

"De nada. What else is on the menu tonight? There's a good movie at…"

"I thought, maybe, early to bed." He grinned. "Celebrate something gone well in the lab."

"Could do," she said. "Tell me about the lab. What went well?"

"Like, now? It's complicated. How about later."

"How about, as a turn-on for me, you show some respect for my knowledge of biochemistry and tell me about the lab."

"You're my break from the lab." He buried his face in her hair, her neck, as she scrubbed the pasta pot, which he was supposed to dry. Which she found vaguely irritating rather than romantic. She shrugged him off. "Come on, Lisa, enough with the dishes." He took her hand—really took it, as in she couldn't get out of his grip—and pulled her to the bedroom. She still had the dishcloth; he took it from her and threw it in the general direction of the sink. Began pulling her top out of her jeans, pulling her toward the bed. It was take it off or risk tearing a perfectly good top, and once that was gone, might as well shed the jeans.

He was neither clumsy nor careless, he knew what she liked, she knew what he liked, but it had been a tough week, and tonight she wanted something, oh, extra. Something novel. He'd said, *celebrate.* She climbed on top of him, planning to…he rolled her back over, rolled back over her, reached for a condom he'd placed on the bedside table already partly unwrapped *probably when he'd showered,* she figured. As he reached for it she laughed and rolled him over, climbed on top again and reached for the condom herself. Their hands collided and the condom slid off the table and under the bed. "Shit," he said. He rolled her back on her back and leaned over the edge of the bed, searching among, she knew, the abundant dust bunnies and other wildlife for the errant contraceptive.

"Get out another one," she said.

"Last one," he said.

"It's filthy under there. That thing isn't going in my..."

He rolled toward her. "So let's just do it bareback."

"Are you nuts?"

"Come on, Lisa, what are the odds of getting pregnant the one time you..."

"Not a risk I'm willing to take, Robert. No way. There are alternatives."

"None I can't do better myself." And he started to roll on to her.

She pushed him away, sat up, stood, started gathering clothing, dressing.

"Come on, Lisa, don't be like that."

"How dare you. Don't be like what? Don't be unwilling to risk getting pregnant so you can get your rocks off?"

"Come on, babe."

That tore it. "Jesus, Robert. Talk about not getting it. Well, you're not getting it."

"Oh. I'm sorry I called you babe, I really am. Look, the risk really isn't that..."

"The risk for you is zero, isn't it."

"Lisa. I hate condoms. Why the hell are you not on the Pill?"

She paused, a shoe halfway on, halfway to being thrown at him. "Because at Woman's Medical College we happen to know about the side effects, and we're waiting for the next generation of lower-dose pills, which will be coming out in a few months. There's some biochemistry I know that you evidently don't, or don't care enough about. Which is now irrelevant to our current, and future, situations." She got her purse, threw the mailbox key at him as, suddenly realizing she was seriously, for real, leaving, he started to get up from bed. "No need to see me out," she said. *Son of a bitch*, she thought. *God, I hope the goddamned car starts.* It did.

At his cousin Ellen's wedding he was seated with the other ushers and the bridesmaids when his mother came over to ask him to dance with her "just once."

"Excuse me," he said to the bridesmaid with whom he had been making desultory conversation. Gallant Ben. When they got back, Ellen, making the rounds of the tables, had just reached the bridal party.

"I just got my son to dance with me," his mother said, smiling to the bride and bridesmaids. She patted his head. He took a swig of wine. "He's become a decent dancer—who taught you to dance?" she said. "Was it Morty? That was my other son," she said to the bridesmaids. "He was Ben's older brother. So good with him. Taught him everything. He was good at everything."

"Except one thing," Ben said. "Keeping on breathing. It seems I'm better than him at that." He walked away from the shocked silence, out of the synagogue's party room, out onto the terrace. He sat on the steps, traffic on the nearby Long Island Expressway keeping up a steady hum in his ears. He still had the wine glass, was halfway down it when he heard the rustle of crinolines under stress as Ellen sat down beside him and kicked off her shoes. "A visit from the Rebbitzin?" he said.

"I thought I'd see why my favorite male cousin walked out of my wedding."

"I'm your only male cousin. Only living male cousin. There's no contest. Any reaction from the Rabbi when his bride's favorite male cousin pulled up on a motorcycle?"

"He's a Reform rabbi. I doubt he'll ever have a congregation. Teach, probably."

"So they're not going to lift you both up on chairs and dance around?"

"Nope. We can even drive on Shabbos. So. What's

with you?"

He nodded. "I'll never be anything to her but a dim shadow of her lost favorite. You know what, Ellie? Morty would have thought that was the exact right thing to say. He would have laughed. He would have said it himself."

"I know, Ben. That's the irony. He always stuck up for you. She was alone with him and Grandma for almost three years before your father came back from overseas."

"I barely remember Grandma."

"She loved you. We all did. You were such an engaging little one. Beneleh, she called you. Little Ben. She always said, Sophie you saved the best for last." They looked out into nothing. "You wouldn't dance with me at my Sweet Sixteen or your Bar Mitzvah, so who finally taught you to dance?"

"Girl I knew in college."

"Must have been some girl."

"She was. She didn't just teach me *how*, she taught me *why*."

"So where is she now?"

"I don't know. We broke up when…because…I went to Harvard. To fucking Harvard. And I did it for my mother. For both my parents. *That's* the irony of it."

"To actually *be* a doctor. Morty just wanted to *play* doctor."

He heard the suppressed anger. "He tried that with you?"

"When I was eleven, twelve. Starting to show. Surprised? Come *on*." He shook his head. She took the wine from him, took a long sip. "So. About the girl."

"She was a year behind me. I could have stayed in the City, but I had to go to fucking Harvard. She was pre-med. I helped her—no, we studied together. I don't know for sure where she ended up. Went to Woman's in Philly, I was told, but a lot of the women there transfer out for their clinical years so the diploma doesn't say 'Woman's.' Not to anywhere in Boston. It's tough for women, getting into med school."

"Tell me about it. You helped her?"

"She didn't need help, but yeah, I think I did. I think she

helped me at least as much. More, maybe." He took another swig of wine. "I think I decided to go to med school because of her." Another swig. "Good decision. Except for *where*."

"She taught you to dance."

"She gave me a reason."

"You going to get plastered?"

He looked at the wine glass in his hand. "No. I have to ride the boneshaker back to Boston. There are old bikers and bold bikers, Ellie, but no old bold bikers. I've seen too much in Emergency Rooms. This was probably my last road trip. I'm going to be an intern, a resident, I'll have to cover all over Boston, in all kinds of weather. I'll need a car. My first paycheck as an intern, plus I sell the bike, I can probably get a used VW."

"Morty's bike."

"Yeah."

She started putting her shoes back on, winced slightly. "Want to come back inside, be properly introduced to some bridesmaids?"

He looked back at the synagogue. "I don't fit in, Ellie. I never fit. With her, I felt like I fit. It was like a great pair of shoes."

"The girl who taught you to dance."

"Yeah. With her I fit. I don't fit up there. I haven't ever fit. I've tried on a lot of other shoes. Well, a lot. Enough. And they never fit, and I know there's shoes out there that are a perfect fit…I should never have left. Should have stayed in New York."

"Shoes is the best simile you can come up with?"

He lifted the wine glass, pointed to it. "Okay. How about this. She was the perfect counterpoint, like in a Bach fugue. A complimentary strand of DNA, how about that?"She put an arm around his shoulders. "I have to think of something apologetic to say to my mother. She just crumpled when he died. Got this… ideal picture of him…"

"No, Ben. She always had that. She always doted on him. Come back inside."

"I will. As soon as I think of something apologetic to say

to her."

"Morty wouldn't."

"I'm not him."

Ellen hugged him. "No," she said. "You aren't."

She watched her mother get married, surrounded by a new family of stepsiblings and their young children. (Plenty of money there; her mother had taken her to lunch to tell her, said she didn't care to get married again, but Richard had gone over the tax advantages, the need for her to be provided for after he's gone, that his kids can't easily challenge, and be able to sign stuff for each other if we...If he's hospitalized Lisa had said). Richard seemed a good man, a nice guy, something her mother maybe deserved, someone for whom her mother seemed like a human being deserving of some devotion. To the extent of putting up with a sometimes prickly stepdaughter, occasional visitor— apartment crasher, rather—from Philadelphia. Or from Medical Land. He tolerated her warnings about his penchant for cigars and Porterhouse steak; he was enough older than her mother that she worried about his long-term health.

"Do I have a new Grandma?" a little girl asked her mother.

The new stepsister smiled at the awkwardness. "Not exactly, sweetheart. Grandpa Richard has a new wife, you know, it's his friend Lilian. And this is her daughter Lisa."

"Is she...my new aunt?"

Lisa took the little girl's hand, felt her fidgeting in her dress and Mary Janes, jumping clumsily in frustrated confinement. She knelt down, herself suddenly clumsy in the unaccustomed Maid-of-Honor gown and heels. "Do you want to call me Aunt Lisa?" she said in her best Pediatrics voice.

"Yes. Aunt Lisa. Aunt Lisa."

"Then I guess I'm Aunt Lisa. What's your name?"

"Courtney." The new stepsister smiled. Awkwardly. *Perhaps icily.*

As she watched the brief ceremony Lisa thought how long her mother's search had been. *Do I really have to settle for Robert? Evidently I do not.* When the music began, and especially when she danced with her new niece balanced, giggling, on the toes of her shoes, she inevitably thought of Ben. In the hotel that night, taking off the evening dress, she inevitably thought of Ben. *Mom has Richard Now I can go anywhere I want Maybe now I can go traipsing off to Boston* The longing, she realized, was part of the attraction. The anger gone, she had perhaps, she thought, now replaced the real 1968 Ben with an idealized version. *He hadn't taken the money He could have As annoying and dangerous as it had been he'd stood up to the old man Saying stuff I should, arguably, have said* Was he still the same guy he had been? Leaving aside for the moment the question of whether she was the same person she had been. It was a risk, who people were. How they changed. Would 1972 Ben be attracted to 1972 Lisa? Only one way to find out. And only one way to find out where to find out.

She had to cruise around for close to a half hour before she found a parking space; it *was* crazy here on a Sunday. A small lump came to her throat when she saw the sign. ROTHSTEIN'S. The man helping customers was obviously Ben's father; he looked like an older version. "Can I help you, young lady?"

"You can, Mr. Rothstein. My name is Lisa Mautner. I'm looking for your son. We…" and she burst into tears. She was shocked, hadn't expected this, hadn't felt it coming, or had ignored it. Now, looking around the familiar shelves…

He stiffened, but, "Come," he said kindly, "Come in the back." Down the familiar stairs, she was suddenly in the back room, there was the little hot plate…she burst into another round of sobs. A formidable-looking woman came from behind a busy desk she remembered as dusty and unused. Could only be his mother. "She's here about Morty."

"Oh. No, Mr. and Mrs. Rothstein. About Ben."

"Go tend the store, Solly, there's customers. I'll take care of this." He vanished back upstairs. The woman turned back to Lisa. "Sit," she said. "Take a load off."

"Mrs. Rothstein," she got out between sobs, "I came here

looking for Ben. We…"

"You're late."

Oh no. He's married? "Late for what?"

"No, I'm asking you: Are you late?"

Pregnant. She thinks I'm pregnant? "No, no, Mrs. Rothstein, we haven't seen each other since college, and…"

"You were going around with Ben in college?" She saw the long hair, the hoop earrings, remembered the chaos and craziness in which his college years had ended.

"Yes. For over a year. We were…"

"So how come he never mentioned you?"

She knew she couldn't explain. "Mrs. Rothstein, I want to get back in contact with him and I hoped you could tell me where he is. I mean, I know he's at Harvard…" and she broke down again.

His mother passed her a tissue. "And he's going to stay at Harvard. And he doesn't need any crazy girl that if he wanted to be with her he would be."

That angered her. She forced herself to stop crying, took a pad and pen from her pocketbook and wrote her name and number. "Here," she said. "Just give him this and he can decide for himself. If he calls me, fine, if not, not. I'm at Woman's Medical College of Pennsylvania. In Philadelphia. Tell him Lisa Mautner would like to speak with him." When the woman didn't take it she placed the slip of paper on the desk. The woman just glanced at it, as if perhaps a fly had landed. His father was busy with customers when she came back upstairs; there was nothing to do but leave. She was almost sure his mother would tear up the note, but she had revealed something important. *He was going to stay at Harvard*, meaning *intern there, go on to the Residency there unless the damned War went on and he was drafted after his internship Damn*

His mother did in fact tear up the note. *Another crazy girl.*

He'd arranged a brief vacation for Yom Kippur and slept on the train to arrive before noon, in time for the Yizkor service. His parents bustled around, delighted to see him for the first time since his med school Commencement, which had been a great deal more normal than his Columbia graduation. Then he had vanished into the internship. He was exhausted. "You'll come with us to say Kaddish for Morty," his mother had said.

The synagogue in Livingston had absorbed the oldest Newark Jews, all the old prayer books and prayer shawls, refugees from the riot-torn city. He remembered the odor, of old books and old men, from Brooklyn. *One more place I don't fit in* As they stood for the mourners' prayer he had a sudden memory of his grandmother, hugging him, smiling, kissing his cheek, whispering *Beneleh, shayne punim*. Little Benny, beautiful face. *Yis gadal v'yiskaddash sh'may rabo*. *Morty was dead before he died* What he mourned for had no formal prayerful acknowledgment.

At dinner, breaking the fast, his father asked, "How do you like being a doctor?"

"By this time, Dad, I've been doing it for a year, really, at half speed. This is just more of the same, but twice as much work. No time for anything but work and sleep."

"No women in your life?" he teased.

Ben sighed. "Nurses with orders to be signed. X-ray techs who lose my patients for hours at a time. Little old ladies in congestive heart failure. I said, no time."

"Because, a girl came to the store, asking for my son," his father said. Ben froze. "I thought she meant Morty, but she was looking for you."

That could only be one girl. He chewed, swallowed, put his fork down slowly. "When was this?"

"A few months ago. She came in the store, asking for you. She started crying, so I took her down to your mother. I saw her go back out, she was okay. I remember. Lisa Meitner. Like the famous chemist."

"Mautner," he said. "Lisa Mautner."

"Like the orchestra conductor?"

"His daughter."

"You know Kurt Mautner's daughter?"

"That's a story. Did she leave a note, or say where I could

contact her? Ma?"

Her best defense had always been a good offense. "How come we never met or heard of this girl?" his mother said. "You were going around with the daughter of a famous orchestra conductor and you never told us?"

"Yes, and right there is why I never told you."

"How is it she knew to come to the store?"

"She knew, Rothstein's on Orchard Street. How hard is that to find? How is it you never told me she came in?"

"How are we supposed to know you wanted to know? She says she hasn't seen you since your crazy college, she's sitting there crying like a baby, with the hippie hair and the earrings like an immigrant, how do I know she isn't just some crazy girl?"

"She left a note. She always left notes. Where is it?"

"I don't know. I left it on the desk in the store. It probably went out in the trash. She said she was at some girl's school in Philadelphia."

"Woman's Medical College of Pennsylvania, Ma. I *cannot* believe you did that."

"How was I to know she's Kurt Mautner's daughter?"

"By God damn it calling and telling me, is how. And what does it matter whose daughter she is?" He rose and threw his napkin on the table, as angry as he'd let himself be. *Maybe she's home too.* They were dead silent as he called 212-555-1212.

"What name and address, please?"

"Mautner. M as in Mack, a, u, t, n as in Nancy, e, r." He gave the address in Stuyvesant Town.

"I'm sorry, sir. There is no one by that name at that address."

Shit. Her mother had probably reverted to her maiden name. What was the area code for Philadelphia? He pulled out the phone book; 215-555-1212. "Name?"

"Lisa Mautner. M as in…"

"I'm sorry sir, we have no listing in that name."

"Woman's Medical College." He wrote it down. Returned to the table. His mother was crying. "You don't need some crazy girl…"

"She's not a crazy girl. She's a very sane medical student. And she is *exactly* what I need." He took her hand. "If she ever comes back. If she ever comes to the house. If she ever calls. If you ever see her on the street. You take her in, you give her a cup of coffee, and you call me. Right then. Have me paged. And. You give her my number. On the spot. You promise me this. God damn it, I've been wanting to contact her for…"

"What's between you and this girl, Ben?"

"Remember the summer I was visiting college friends on Saturdays? She was the friends. We broke up because I *had to* go to God damned Harvard. What's between us is what's between us. This girl made me feel *alive*. You promise me. Now. Both of you."

No luck at Woman's next day; they wouldn't tell some guy on the phone. She wouldn't be in the dorm anyway, she'd have her own place by now. In some nearby town? Doing clinical rotations elsewhere to sharpen up the resume? Or what? On his way back to Boston he had an idea, caught a local train to Penn Station, took the subway downtown, then crosstown, maybe she *was* home for the Holidays, but there was no answer to doorbell or knock. He ran down to the mailboxes, found the name of the next-door neighbors, ran back up and rang their bell. An elderly woman answered the door, looked him up and down. "Mrs. Bronstein, I'm so sorry to disturb you, I'm a cousin of the Mautners, but there's no answer, do you know where they might be?"

"You're a cousin and you don't know she moved out?"

"Well, it was the daughter that I…"

"You think I don't know who you are, that I don't remember your face? I'm old, I'm not deaf, blind or stupid. If she wanted you to know where she is you would know."

He smiled at her. "Thank you for your help, Mrs. Bronstein. And from the bottom of my heart, let me say: Go to hell." He was regretful by the time he got to the street, and in the subway, yet when the train to Boston was speeding him over Hell Gate, he was glad he had told *somebody* to go to hell. But he knew why his mother had acted as she had, and it saddened and terrified him.

The internship year ground on. Graduation had meant he was no longer entitled to live in the dormitory. Every night he wasn't on call, or volunteering at The Freak, he came home alone to an empty apartment, full only of used furniture *You need sheets and towels* his father said *I'll send you What size Twin* The lack of sleep, the approach, he knew, of the endless winter, the endless responsibility and decisions, the wounded lives, the deaths, days and nights listening to the stories, listening to the failing hearts and lungs, palpating the bellies and the groins, saying *this is going to hurt a little*, trying to cure the dying, and the merely suffering, ruined bodies. The loneliness of all of that and the empty return to the empty apartment, eat just to keep going, sleep just to be able to wake up, alone, alone even with people all around him, like college but worse because he knew what it could be like, with someone. *Just an affair* Her face, her voice, in his dreams now, the feel of her body, waking to the fleeting feel of his arm around her, or her leg thrown over his, her hair spread over his chest as it had been mornings at the hotel. But it just went on, Time, the eternal laboratory, the chemistry going on and on, an endless chain of reactions, each moment an instantaneous equilibrium, every product a new reactant. Equilibria? He fell into sleep, another equilibrium state.

It came to him: one more chance. He had a salary now; he could afford a ticket. In the cheap seats. He took the T; a suit and motorcycle still did not go well together, and he still hadn't had the heart to trade it for a car. From near the roof of Symphony Hall he watched her father take the podium, nod to the concertmaster and give the downbeat. Sat back and tried to enjoy the concert. *Might as well.* The Mahler Fourth, ending with the soul-piercing soprano solo. He pushed through to the crowd backstage, using his MGH ID, was about to be spotted by Security when he saw Mautner, called his name. He turned, and Ben saw recognition in his eyes.

"Mr. Rothstein, isn't it?"

"It's Dr. Rothstein now, sir."

"Dr. Rothstein, then. I trust you enjoyed the performance."

"I did, sir, very much. I've come to love Mahler."

"Wonderful. Is it an autograph you wish?"

"Sort of, sir. I was hoping you could give me Lisa's phone number."

"Were you really? If she wanted you to have it you would have it, wouldn't you."

"She does, sir. She contacted my parents to ask for mine. They didn't know who she was, so they..."

"They didn't know who she was. You never told them about her, then. I see when I called you a young man of integrity I overestimated you."

He gritted his teeth, bit back anger. Saw that her father was, perhaps, right, and softened. "That may have been true, sir. I'm older now." It sounded lame, even to him.

"You're more experienced. Shrewd. Character doesn't change." He turned away.

Past time to be a responsible adult in the vehicular transport department. He calculated the assets. It broke his heart. Garaging the bike, versus letting go of the last vestige of Morty, saying a final goodbye to him. And to Lisa. *Maybe she'd only wanted to ask about Boston internships No She wouldn't have cried*

And then it was Thanksgiving. She sat with her mother at the end of the table nearest the kitchen. Richard, her you-can-call-me-Dad-if-you-want-to, sat at the far end after carving the turkey. Between them were his assorted children and grandchildren. *Well*, she thought, *I'm the stepchild.* The hubbub eventually quieted as they all settled down to eat. Conversation lagged after Richard finished carving.

"We're disappointed not to see Robert," her mother said. "Is he with his family?"

"There is no more Robert. Not for several months, mother. Many months. Not at the wedding, remember?"

"Oh. I thought he just couldn't get away from work."

"I'm sorry to hear it," Richard said. "Nice young man."

"Nice enough to come and be introduced," her mother said. "Ben. His name was Ben Rothstein," Lisa said. "Probably still is."

Richard said. "He goes by Dr. Rothstein now." Her mother shot him a look.

She put her fork down. In fact, carefully lined up her silverware. Looked from one of them to the other. "He would be Dr. Rothstein, as of last June," she said. "I would very much like to know how you know that." The table quietened again.

"Richard," her mother said.

"She has a right to know." He turned to Lisa. "He approached your father in Boston, after a concert. Wanted to know how to get in touch with you. Your father called to ask if he had tried here. He was concerned."

"And you were going to tell me this when?"

"I wasn't going to tell you at all," her mother said.

"When was this?"

"Maybe a month ago? After the High Holy Days…"

"Mother. If someone approached me to ask to contact you I would get the address and number and tell you. It would be up to you after that. I'm not a child anymore. Or didn't you notice? In six months I'll be a doctor. Does that make any difference to you? Any at all?"

"Lisa, we can discuss this privately, later."

She rose. "Privately, yes. Later, no. Now. Kitchen." Unexpectedly, Richard followed them. As they left the dining room for the kitchen she heard her favorite step-niece say, "Mommy, is Aunt Lisa mad at Lilian and Grandpa?"

"He was…" her mother started.

"He was a boy I loved, and who loved me, and now he's a man who wants to contact me, and after Robert, who was nowhere near as *nice* as Ben, I would very much like to speak with him. Am I getting through to you, Mother? Richard?"

"I'm sorry, Lisa. Your father seemed to think poorly of him."

"And he's a terrific judge, is he? I get to make this call, not you, not him. Me. If Ben Rothstein calls, if he sends a letter, if he knocks on the door, you are to give him my number. You are to call me immediately. I'll be calling Father to make this crystal clear."

"Lisa. He left you. Went off to Boston…"

"Which was my doing, mother. But he came for me at the campus Occupation."

"You were in that?"

"I was. So was he. He pulled me out of teargas, got me back to my dorm, and he wanted to talk, and I was a fool, I told him to leave me alone…Is there something you don't understand? I started this. I tried to contact him through his parents right after your wedding. I ran into this same crap from them, but it must have gotten back to him somehow, I bet at the High Holy Days. Huh."

"I'm sorry if I…" Richard said.

Her mother glared at him. "Lisa, I just don't want you to make the same mistake I did about a man."

"I'm that mistake."

"*Lisa.*"

"And I was just as afraid of that as you were. I see now I was so afraid of it that I made exactly the opposite mistake. And now I have a chance to repair it. Mother. I know you want the best for me. But it's your idea of best. I have my own. Thank you, Richard."

"I want Grandpa," the little girl had been shrieking. She ran in, wrapped herself around Richard's leg. He picked her up. From his arms she pointed at Lisa. "Are you mad, Aunt Lisa?"

Lisa reached out and touched the tip of the little girl's finger with her own. "No, honey," she said. "I was mad, but now I'm happy. Happier than I've been in a long time."

When she got home she thought about how to try to contact him. She knew he couldn't have found her; the phone was in the housemate's name. She knew neither of their schools would help. Call Mass General and have him paged? Might work, but he could be anywhere in Boston, not on call, beeper off; she might have to bombard them with calls. Try his parents again, tell them he was trying to reach her? Then she'd have to explain her family's actions; they could refuse, humiliate her again. And maybe he'd approached her father to get her number so he could tell her not to bother him. But the only reason for that would be that he was in a relationship and his parents would know that; would have said. Or maybe they wouldn't know, as they hadn't known about her...*Oh, no.* But that seemed very unlikely *He'd just have told my father...*

From the next room Judy Collins' voice sang, "Blow you old Blue Norther, blow my love to me..." *He didn't just love me, he adored me He would do anything for me,* she knew. Anything except maybe the one thing she'd dared not ask. She'd had the chance the night of the campus assault, the police riot, *and instead of asking him to stay I asked him to let me go. Begged him to.* Knowing if I asked him to stay he would. Or had been too scared he wouldn't. She shook her head. *Fool. Idiot.*

His internship year ground relentlessly on. A new low point, at the middle of winter, was the summons to his draft physical. After taking the group's pulses and blood pressures a crew-cut sergeant singled out the three doctors, then pointed to a row of small plastic bottles on a table and shouted, "The rest of you numbnuts strip, drop your socks and grab your cocks, go in that latrine and fill those. Write your name on the label if you know how. *Move,* asswipes." He turned to the three doctors and said, "If you gentlemen would please go to the officers' head and bring me back a labelled sample?" When they complied and returned he directed them to a cubicle where a bored man just older than they were, with a caduceus on his uniform lapel and captain's bars on his shoulders, said, from a long-memorized script, "I'm going to get your individual histories and do a quick physical. First, do any of you have any medical reason you think will keep you out of the army?" He pointed to the man nearest. "You?"

"Gilbert's disease."

The doctor/captain laughed and turned to a set of forms on his desk, "Cute. He gestured toward a tiny exam room. "Go strip and contemplate your harmless and clinically meaningless liver enzyme elevations. You?"

"Migraines."

"Yeah? Me too." He gestured again, and pointed to Ben. "Care to try your luck?"

"I have a GI problem. Visceral disgust for the military, this nation, and this War."

"Hilarious. Think I don't?"

"Okay, then, can you do something about it?" Ben said. "Can you stop these sergeants bullying these poor kids…"

"No. It's part of the Machine. Step One in indoctrinating teenagers into subservience. But not you; you could be one of their next commanding officers. The joke's on them. They're closing down the War. We're all getting early discharges, and you'll probably never even be called. Cheer up. Hey, Nixon may be in big trouble, too."

The rumors were true; troops *were* coming home, the doctors were returning to the positions they'd been drafted out of. "I have good news and bad news," Billy Mortenson said. "The good news is, Teddy Edwards is back six months early. The bad news is, Teddy Edwards is back six months early."

"Who's Teddy Edwards?" Ben said.

"Resident I had on my third year clerkship. Earl of Groton, Duke of Harvard. Blue blood in both veins *and* arteries. Twenty-third generation Harvard. Attitude to match. Might show up as our rezzie on the next rotation. How lucky do you feel?"

"Good morning, children, are we ready for school? I'm Doctor Edwards. Teddy. And you are?" The interns, fourth years, and third years rubbed sleep out of their eyes and gave their names, the last of them a woman named Sally Eliot. "Well," he said, "This *is* the Wasteland. In the room the women come and go, talking of Michelangelo. No pending emergencies, we can distribute the sign-out cards and read our colleagues' off-service notes. Now. On my team, we pitch in and help wherever we can. Only good thing I learned in the Army."

They made rounds and were reading the off-service notes,

writing their on-service notes, when a nurse popped into the ward lounge. "Whose is Mr. Kaplan? He's very uncomfortable, needs to be disimpacted stat."

"Mine," Ben said. "My lucky day."

"Good man, Rothstein. Puts me in mind of a joke. Miami Beach, an elderly man falls over on the sidewalk, an ambulance comes, they hustle him onto a gurney, tech says, "Are you comfortable? Old man says, 'Vell, I make ah livink'."

They looked at each other. Uneasy smiles. "Right," Ben said. "On it. But first, let me pitch in, Teddy. One, the women come and go in *The Love Song of J. Alfred Prufrock*, not *The Wasteland*. Two, you'll need to work on your Jewish accent if you insist on telling that joke. I'll be here to help you with that, too. Every time."

Winter deepened, and froze the streets, rimed the windows, iced the downspouts. On a dark, shivering trudge from the hospital to his apartment he paused to look up at the sky. Iron gray clouds thinned slightly to form a pearl gray mist that blurred a crescent moon. He thought his blood barely flowed. He had made it this far partly numb, telling himself *she's gone* but now it hurt worse, the anesthesia wearing off, knowing she wanted to talk to him, knowing how badly he wanted to talk to her, *but just out of reach* he knew despair.

Her senior year ground on. Winter deepened, and work only got harder, because now, she admitted to herself, lonelier. There was a halo around the moon: ice crystals. The first snow fell; application time for internships. She knew it must have long since snowed in Boston. The old challenge, the old anxiety. *So I'll have to take the risk I was too afraid to take the first time*...Hell, why can't I get an internship at Mass General? Or somewhere else in Boston? I'm at the top of my class and I'm a damned good doc. And just by the way, I'm attractive, personable, my father conducts their damned orchestra. *Any relation to Kurt Mautner? He's my father.* I'd rather they picked me for my grades, but when did I stop trying to have an edge?

When did I get so pure? *I need an edge, Rothstein Now you're thinking, Mautner*, his voice said. *The way things are going, they might just be looking for women* You're *the edge.* Who would he be? *Same old mix of apprehension and determination If he's turned into a jerk or the chemistry's just not there anymore I'll still have Harvard postgraduate credentials What can I lose*

```
Gentlemen,

       Please send application materials for
the Massachusetts General Hospital Internal
Medicine Internship, July 1973 through June
1974, to me at the above address. Thank you
for your attention.
```

Lisa Mautner
```
Lisa Mautner, Woman's Medical College of
Pennsylvania, Class of 1973
```

Where he was, *resourceful Ben* was on the phone to Woman's Medical College, asking about their Graduation Day. And calling the House Staff Office to arrange vacation for that weekend. *Guts and brains.   I know where she'll be on that day*

Beeeeeeeeeeeeeep His beeper's tiny screen showed an unfamiliar callback number. What the hell? "Dr. Rothstein here."

"Dr. Rothstein. This is almost-Doctor Mautner. It's been a while, Ben."

He was shocked; shocked to hear her voice, on the grayest of gray days, suddenly her voice, out of nowhere, out of nothing, shocked at the rush of conflicted emotion he felt. "It has been a while." He swallowed. "My fault, I'm…"

"No fault. No fault, Ben. Please."

He breathed again. "Where are you calling from?"

"The Information Desk. They want their phone back. Could you come down?"

Could I come down? I could fly down. "Billy. Cover for me for a half hour."

"What for?"

"Just do it. Go restart Mrs. Jackson's IV and I'll do two for you later. Three."

"Sure. But it's busy. Half hour. No more."

He met her in the lobby, the run down the stairs just long enough to realize how delicate this could be. *How would this go Be cool No way to know what to No rule book for this.* She almost didn't recognize him when he pushed through the stairwell door, then smiled at his obvious eagerness. The smile he'd so missed for years awoke his own. Those eyes, come alive with seeing him, the eyes he could lose himself in; the eyes, the mind, that missed nothing. But her moment of hesitation when she hadn't recognized him unnerved him; approaching her, he blurted, "What are you doing here?"

She felt joy awaken, and its lifelong companion, distrust of joy. *Who is this man* "Is that how people say hello in Boston?"

"Cut me some slack, I've been up all night. On call." *Is this a dream Oh God She looks* "You…you look terrific." She did. Her hair, even longer now, cascaded over her shoulders, some clipped at the center. Suit, heels. *Interview* "Are you applying for…?"

She saw him take her in; relief flooded her "Internship,

yes. And I asked if I could shadow an intern, and they gave me the rotation list, and said I could page you, and ask if it's okay… God, I was kind of afraid you might just hang up on me."

"Never. Never. Come. Coffee. First coffee. First I buy us coffee." He steered her to the cafeteria. Sat her down, brought coffee. Sat. Stared.

"What?" she said.

"Nothing. I mean…uh, you. Here. You…uh…got your ears pierced."

"Yes I did. And you grew your hair! And the beard and 'stache…"

"Leece. I was an idiot. A complete jerk. And I stayed a jerk until five minutes ago. Leece, what did I do? What did we do?"

Not now Not yet "Went to med school. What's dumber than that? So is it okay? To shadow you?" She touched his hand. That simple touch electrified, then relaxed him; seeing his face relax, she felt hers do the same. Shy, still a little wary, they sat back and examined each other properly, she now an elegant young woman, he a tired, unshaven young man in stained whites, stethoscope hanging off his neck, tunic pockets bulging with test tubes, the Washington Manual bedside reference book, tourniquets, reflex hammer…both knowing that back at work she would look exactly as he did now. They drank each other in. "You're at Woman's, I heard?" he said.

"Yes. Looking at medical internships up here. The Boston Women's Health Collective is here, Ben. Thought I'd shoot for the stars. I'm pretty far up in my class."

Is that all she wanted to call me about, at the store No She'd cried "No surprise there. So, you want to follow us around for a few hours? See what this joint is like?"

"Yes. And. I want to see you, Ben. After. If you want to see me. after."

Relief "If? Don't be ridiculous," he said. They sipped coffee, pretending not to look at the fourth fingers of left hands. Knowing it should wait, but each knew the other had tried to make contact; unable to postpone asking, knowing… Said at the same time, or a microsecond apart: "Is there anyone…" And laughed. "Ladies first," he said.

"No one. Were. But now, no. You?"

"Same here." He thought a minute. "I counted on seeing you again, finding you, somehow. When I found out my mother had thrown you out I…"

"So you *do* know about that."

"My father brought it up when I was home Yom Kippur. Then…I tried to track you down too. In Philly, then at Stuy Town. Got thrown out by your nosy neighbor." He told her the story. "Then by your father, too."

"I finally heard about *that*, no thanks to my mother. Or to him. Your mother said, you were staying in Boston, so I knew you'd be interning here. It's…what finally decided me to come up here. Apply here."

"Good news. They maybe don't know this at Woman's, but the rumor is, the Doctor Draft is ending; they've started discharging some of them early, right back to their residencies. So, yes, I'm here to stay. You really applied here because…? Lisa. I'm so very, very glad to see you. See you here. Anywhere. More than I can ever say." He glanced at his watch. "Shit, got to be getting back. Let's get to it." He turned his beeper back on, led her to the elevators to the wards, introduced her to Billy Mortenson and the two Third-Year medical students. She followed them around, followed him mostly. He could see how she itched to join in, stepping forward before remembering she wasn't on home ground. After lunch there was an admission, an elderly woman in congestive failure. He picked up the chart, found Lisa a white coat; she sat in on the history.

"Mrs. Cullen. Welcome to The General."

"I've been here before."

"So I see. Well, we'll try to make it a short stay. This is Dr. Mautner, she's visiting us from Woman's Medical College in Philadelphia, and this is Dr…"

"There's a medical school for women?"

"Yes there is, Mrs. Cullen. I'm visiting today, thinking about interning here."

"So," he said, "What seems to be the problem, my dear?"

The patient frowned. "They could use some women doctors here," she said. "I can't breathe. Going up stairs. Have to sleep on two, three pillows."

"Let's let Dr. Phillips take it from there."

The Third-Year ran through the standard cardiac history: "Any chest pain? Numbness around the mouth? Arm pain? Palpitations, skipped beats? History of rheumatic fever…?"

"Dr. Mautner, how do they do this in Philadelphia?" Ben said.

"Same way, but they also ask: Any heartburn?" That got a yes. "Nausea, vomiting?"

"Nausea, yeah. Yes."

"Dizziness?"

"Also."

"I see. What medications are you taking for your heart?"

"Digitalis. They say it makes my heart stronger. And a water pill." The Third-Year took the rest of the history, the Review of Systems; they did the physical, heard the rales (the bubbly sounds of fluid in the lungs), pushed fingertips into the swollen ankles. Smiled, made sure the IV was running, said goodbyes, and went to the lounge behind the nurses' station to write admit notes and quiz the Third-Year, but were interrupted by afternoon teaching rounds.

"You came on the right day," Ben whispered to her. "Sachs is one of the top attendings in the place, plus he's on the..."

"Who's this?" Dr. Sachs asked.

"Fourth-Year from Woman's in Philly, sir. Dr. Mautner. Looking at internships. She's shadowing me."

Sachs looked her up and down. "Lucky you," he said. "Welcome, Dr. Mautner."

The Third-Year presented the case. "Sixty-two-year-old white female of Irish extraction with two days of shortness of breath, no chest pain, but heartburn…"

"Stop. What's the significance of the heartburn?"

"Uh, I don't know sir, the…Dr. Mautner asked her."

"Dr. Mautner? Enlighten us in Boston from the wisdom of Philadelphia."

"Cardiac pain often presents in women as heartburn."

"Sometimes in men too. Point goes to Philadelphia. Go on," he said to the Third-Year.

"She also reported dizziness and nausea..."

"Ah. Go on."

The Third-Year ran through the list of meds, the review of systems, physical exam...a routine case of CHF. *Except for what Lisa had found* Ben thought.

"Sum up for us, Dr. Rothstein. Show the young lady how it's done in Boston."

"Subjective: We have a 62-year-old Irish woman on Didge and Lasix, with two days of shortness of breath, chest pain, dizziness and nausea. Noncontributory Review of Systems. Objective: florid facies, rales bilaterally, both lower lobes, chest films not yet back, bilateral 3+ ankle edema, labs not yet back. Assessment: Congestive Heart Failure, possible ischemic cardiomyopathy, possible..."

"Wait. Let the students cut their teeth on this one. What else could account for increasing CHF, in a woman on Digitalis, reporting, thanks to our lovely visitor, heartburn, nausea and dizziness? Third-Years, restore the honor of Boston medicine."

They were stumped. Sachs turned to the blackboard and wrote: "I, Atrogenic". They laughed. "Always, always in your differential diagnosis, people, stop, point to yourself and think, whisper it if you want to, I, Atrogenic. Iatrogenic—caused by us, caused by the doctor, by our very own cures. So..."

One of the Third-Years said, tentatively, "Digitalis toxicity?"

"Absolutely. Too much of a good thing. It's made from foxglove, you know. A potent poison. A little strengthens the pump, a lot weakens it, and causes heartburn, nausea and dizziness into the bargain. All of which can be misattributed to the cardiac disease itself. Also diarrhea. A patient on Didge, always, always get a Didge level. So. Plan..." And so it went, a few more cases from the other team, a few more IVs to restart, time to wind down, make a few last notes, sign out to the night's on call team.

"Was that Alvin Thomas Sachs, the one who wrote the Cardio text?"

"It was. No big deal. Everybody here writes a textbook. I have to pick up some stuff I left in on-call," Ben said. "Wait here? Come with?"

"Let's see how an MGH on-call room compares with Henry Avenue. Lead on."

Across many corridors and skyways, into an older building; suddenly the lighting was dim, surfaces worn, approaching but never quite reaching dingy. "Yesterday's underwear and socks," he said. They both stared at the bed. Looked away. Realized, both of them, how delicate this could all be. Still was. He stuffed the laundry into a pocket, took his coat off a hook. "Where's your coat? Where are you staying?"

"The Training Director's Office, I guess. I'm staying at a place on Kenmore."

"The Combat Zone?" He hesitated, *but she doesn't know the city* "At the risk of sounding like a father: Are you nuts?"

"Any idea where I live in Philadelphia? It's close to the T, and cheap. I thought it would be not much worse than the Hotel Pennsylvania" *He doesn't sound like a father He sounds like a friend But also* "Being a big brother again, Ben?"

"No. Travel advisor. I know a much safer place, and even cheaper. My place." She looked thoughtful. Then quizzical. Lifted an eyebrow. "Relax. I have a couch. I'll take the couch, you take the bed. I'm exhausted, I could sleep on a bed of nails. Come on, Leecy. Give me a chance to make it all up to you. And what time is your interview?"

"Nine."

"I wish...maybe I could drive you. If you want."

"On the bike? Really?"

"I'm a big boy now. I have a car. Almost a car. Used VW. Come on, Leece."

She considered. The hotel and neighborhood had looked, in daylight, even less appetizing than it had at last night's arrival, if such a thing was possible. *They don't call it the Combat Zone for nothing* "It makes sense." *It makes more than sense* "Okay." "And can I take you to dinner? We never got to finish our last dinner." In his elation, he missed her grimace. The hotel was, as he'd suspected, a "hot bed" above a disco. "You'd never get any sleep here." *Or might not wake up* "I pretty much didn't last night. *Couldn't.* I may be as beat as you are." She checked out, handed over the key, argued about the late checkout, settled for an extra half-day they figured the clerk pocketed. They chased some small-time dealers away from the car and left for Ben's apartment near the hospital. Both of them were by now accustomed to 'round the clock ambulance sirens; this was no problem. The size of the apartment, a studio hacked out of an old Back Bay townhouse, was. There was no actual door separating the living room/kitchen/dining space from the bedroom, just one of the bead curtains much in fashion at the time. He showered, shaved and made himself presentable; she hung out the interview suit and changed into jeans. They left from the MGH T stop for a little café off Harvard Square. The Band *Pulled into Nazareth, was feelin' 'bout half past dead* blasted from the New & Used Records; he stopped to listen.

"Your musical tastes have changed," she said.

"Widened," he said. "Funny thing. I knew from my brother's time this independent classical station, WBCN, when I got here I tuned in and it had changed to the damnedest freeform station, anything and everything, and all the Movement news..."

"Turn on, tune in," she said.

"But I still study to classical, that's WBUR, which, they mention your father's name about once an hour. Kept you in my head..." She laughed. The unmistakable odor of weed drifted out into the street as they approached the café. "I promise I won't leave you," he said. "I won't even go to the restroom."

She winced. "Don't joke about that Ben," she said. "It still hurts."

"I'm sorry," he said. "That's why I'm trying to joke."

"Is taking me to a place across the street from Harvard another joke?"

"No, Leece. Of course not. I want to show you…The Square's been the most exciting place in Greater Boston, the center of everything we could... I'm so sorry, Leece.I thought, couldn't hurt. I guess I was wrong." *If this hurts it means what?*

"It's okay, Ben, I was just needling you. I think. I forgot, you're all about people not getting hurt. I should tell you, there were an awful lot of grateful people from Mercer Hall, girls who didn't lose their earlobes, asking about you, wanting to thank you."

"Told you: No one ever thanks the masked man. But you got your ears pierced."

"Don't worry, I always remembered to take them out at demos," she said, and over dinner they recounted some of their Movement activities to each other. And told each other about the dreams they sometimes still had, that woke them, hearts pounding. "I don't know, Ben, it all seems to be dribbling into nothing, since they stopped the Draft. Nixon's still there, our guys are coming home, but the War, everything, just…goes on."

"But I think, Leece, Mercer…we were pebbles that started an avalanche. We don't know where it will end." She shook her head as if to clear it.

"I should thank you, Ben. I never thanked you for what you did that night."

"We did that together, Leece. You found the window. And the kiss thing. That was brilliant."

"I saw it in an old spy movie. You desanctified a cathedral for me, Ben."

"You were in pain. I'd have taken it down stone by stone."

She felt, almost, a tear. "Did you ever leave them a note?"

"I did. I promised you, didn't I? Next day. 'To whom it may concern: I'm very sorry but my companion was teargassed at the Columbia campus and I took water out of the font to bathe her eyes. I'm sorry if this causes any inconvenience'. Signed it John Roberts."

She laughed. "You didn't."

"I did. It was a promise."

"A Boy Scout is…"

"Boy Scouts don't desanctify cathedrals, Leece." They backed away from it again; over espressos they talked about how it was on campus after the takeover, the graduation walkout, where she'd done this clerkship, where he'd done that rotation. Neutral topics. Dancing around it. Re-establishing enough of a friendship to talk about it. She admired his stethoscope, not the standard student "gift" from Parke-Davis; a real cardiologist's scope. "I'm thinking, Cardio," he said.

"I'd have thought, Neuro."

"Too raw. Too close. Couldn't do it, Leece. It just made me angry. Besides, Berry aneurysms are a vascular problem, not neuro. I'll get to treat hypertension, use anticoagulants correctly, and it turns out I have a feel for EKGs. When I read an EKG it's like I'm reading a good mystery. Or a complicated poem."

She knew the feeling. "What happened to research?"

"After Mercer, I lost any interest. Tired of wrangling test tubes…I found, what turned me on was taking care of patients. Like we did that night, but without the tear gas. At the demos here, too, I volunteered. And at this free clinic, everyone calls it The Freak. You mentioned the Women's Health Collective. The Freak is a collective. The disadvantage is, the finances are always hairy, but Leece, I have this crazy idea. What if The Freak was university-affiliated? A teaching center for a med school? Half or more of the med school staff volunteers there now. The University could underwrite it. I'll have to show it to you. Remember when we were looking out at the fires in Newark, the riots, asking what a person, what any two people could do? A free clinic is something. "

"If I get in up here." They stared off, knowing it was premature, even dangerous, to be having any hopes. "Pretty cool idea, but I don't know, Ben. Med schools are pretty paternalistic. Hierarchical. Collective leadership? I doubt they'd go for that."

"It might need a titular Medical Director, or some such bullshit post, to go, like, to faculty meetings, but decisions could still be collective inside the building…" Conversation lagged. Finally he said, "My mother threw you out?"

She looked away. "Your father was very kind. He took me in, took me downstairs. To where we…then your mother took over. I said I was there to ask about their son; they thought I meant Morty." She saw him startle. "She asked me if I was late."

Oh shit They knew They do know "Jesus. Not really."

"Yes really."

"Well. Leece, she was a great mother, when we were young, Morty and I. Then, I don't know, Morty died, and…she just collapsed. Then I guess she got…hard."

"I know, Ben, it must have been terrible for her. My mother was terrific when I was little too. They both got kicked around by life."

"Still," he said.

"Yes. She said, Her Ben didn't need any crazy girl from his past."

"Her Ben, right. Yom Kippur, I straightened her out about that. I told her who you were. And I told her you were exactly what I need, and that if you ever contacted them again, they were to call me immediately."

She looked away. "And then you tried my father. Brave man."

It was time to go. Crossing the Square they remembered how they once had to travel separately to keep their relationship secret. Now they had secrets from each other, and were silent, thinking how to discuss what they most needed to. They lingered at the Square's huge newsstand to peruse the latest Mother Jones and scan The Mole and a few other underground newspapers for any hint about Watergate, postponing having to return to whatever would happen at the apartment. Finally he took her hand to run for a train; she let him hold it as they rode back into Boston.

Back in the apartment, they contemplated the sleeping arrangements. The bed was adequate, but the couch was a sorry thing, one step short of protruding springs. "I can't let you sleep on that," she said.

"It's no worse than an on-call bed at Boston City," he said. And suddenly thought *I don't have any fresh condoms even if No That isn't going to happen* He took out his second pillow, an old quilt for crashers, laid them out on the couch. "I'm too tired to care," he said. "Really, Leece, I don't mind. I invited you. I...want you here."

"If you're sure. I bet I could still get that room back at the hotel."

"Not a chance. I'll set an alarm for 6:45." He fiddled with the bedside clock/radio.

"Well then. Good night." It was all very awkward, suddenly.

"Good night, Leece." They made ready for bed as best they could.

"Are you okay?" she called a few minutes after he turned out the light.

"Yes. Sure. I'm fine. It's fine." But it wasn't fine. He couldn't sleep, even exhausted as he was. The pain, and the anger, came back to haunt. Anger at himself, he realized. Some at her, but mostly at himself. The couch began to seem like a bed of penance. He tossed and turned. What was she thinking? Nothing; she was asleep, grateful for a friend and a quiet, comfortable, safe bed in a strange city. Maybe that was all she had wanted, contacted his parents for...And then he heard her crying softly, and realized she was no more asleep than he was. He rose in the dark, the only light a dim reflection of moon and city glow through thin drapes. He went to the bead curtain. Parted it. Knew he was backlit. Heard her draw breath. "Leece? Are you okay?"

"No. I'm not. I want very much to get in here, and I worry I'm not going to make it. Ben, they asked me The Question." He could hear the capital letters.

"What question?" But he knew.

"My advisor at Barnard warned me, and they asked me at every med school interview except Woman's 'How do you justify taking a spot from a qualified man'."

"What did you answer?"

"What I wanted to answer was, why don't you shove it up your ass, but I pointed out my grades at Woman's and my Seven Sisters 3.6 GPA and said as sweetly as I could, Qualifications are qualifications. But then they went one better. Asked me why they should train me when I was just going to go out and have babies."

"Jesus. What did you say?"

"Told them not to worry, there are pills for that now."

He laughed. "I'm so sorry, Leece. I never knew it was *that* blatant."

"I knew. And you knew. I told you."

He leaned against the wall, ran his hand through his hair. "Leece.? I, Atrogenic."

"What?"

"I, Atrogenic. I thought I was helping. I thought I was doing what you needed, laying it all out for the old man. I see now. I think I even saw then. Too big a dose. We should have talked first, about how to approach him. I see that."

"We were too angry at each other. And I see that he insulted you, and that you could have taken the money, and you wouldn't, and you said things I wish I had said. I thought about it a lot, what I said at Jack's…what I should have said was, there's a balance between being cared *about* and being cared *for*, and I felt like you had the balance wrong. That maybe no man can get it right, but…"

"Did I have it right at Mercer?"

"Yes. I think now…the balance changes with circumstances. And you seem to have it right today. You left it to me to do the arguing with the clerk at the hotel."

"Oh. Well, sure…I mean…I think I get it, Leece. I hope so." He paused. "I kept thinking you'd call, and we'd work it out."

"I wasn't angry about that. What I was really angry about was you leaving me for Harvard." She sat up. "But you walked out on me, Ben. Left me sitting there. It was the most hurtful, worst possible thing, you could have done. I thought, why should I call?"

"I know. I realized later. It must have been like when your father…"

"Yes, it meant to me that you'd go to Boston and forget all about me. I guess it was a test. Plus I thought *you* owed the apology."

"I thought you did. You calling it just an affair. I was so wrong, Leece."

"No, Ben, I realized later what that sounded like to you. That I'd really hurt you."

"The most hurtful thing. Like, you were only amusing yourself with me on the way to your goal, like it meant more to you than I ever could."

"Which is what you going to Harvard meant to me."

"Yes." He looked away. "With your father, I was a bull in a china shop."

"And I was like the owner of a china shop that instead of collecting for the breakage, burns down the shop. Really stupid."

"So why didn't you call me?"

"Because, as you said, when your father walks out on you and your mother and never comes back, you kind of expect when someone walks out of a restaurant on you they aren't coming back. And then, you showed up at Mercer..."

"And when someone says Please leave me alone you expect they have to do any coming back." He sat down on the bed. "I worry now, Leece. After we hurt each other so badly, can we get back together. You were the only person I ever felt like I fit with. I missed you so much. I didn't know how much I'd miss you. I didn't *really* know. I thought it would be just a year, then you'd be here...You were the perfect fit, and I'm scared that... Can you forgive me?"

"I missed you too, Ben. Terribly. For the same reason. I tried not to, worked not to, and I couldn't. I couldn't forget you. Can you forgive me?"

"When I figured out how I'd hurt you, I realized there was nothing to forgive. It's myself I can't forgive."

"I forgave you long ago. Do it. Forgive yourself, Ben. The joy we know we can bring each other is greater than the pain we caused. The joy is more important."

He felt around in the dark for her hand and took it. "Well. You did call."

"We both did." They sat in the dark like that for a while. "Ben," she said finally, "This is ridiculous. Go get the pillow and come to bed."

"It is ridiculous, but I don't have any energy…and I
don't have…"

"Just to sleep."

"Right. Oh. I can drive you to the train tomorrow night."

"I'm not leaving tomorrow night. I have more interviews.
I have two more days. Three more interviews. Tufts, BU,
Beth Israel-Deaconess…"

"I can drive you, if you want. I'll get someone to cover,
and I'll drive you."

"Oh. I got a license. I have a car in Philly. When it runs."

He hesitated only a moment. "Then take my car, if you
want. Boston's a bitch to get around in. Registration's in the
glove box. And here's a map." He felt *responsible*.

"Couldn't be worse than Philadelphia. Are you sure?"

He found and handed her the keys. "You must really want
to come to Boston."

"Where are there more teaching hospitals? My parents
say it's a great place to meet and marry a doctor. After four years
at Woman's, a great place to meet guys."

"Leece…"

"I'm teasing you. I came here first to track down one guy.
Anything after would depend on him." She moved over toward
the wall. Patted the empty space beside her. "Come to bed,
Ben." In the dark she said, "Did I mention I love the beard and
mustache?" *And that I'm wondering if it tickles*

At 6:45 they wakened *New on WBCN From Steely Dan
singing how they're never going back to their old school* wound
partly around each other in the small bed; awkwardly, they
separated. She pointed down. "Did I do that?"

He laughed. "Happens every morning, remember?"
Meaning she'd never been overnight with another guy? "You
might have something to do with it."

They shyly took turns in the shower; he shaved in the
steam, handed a towel around the curtain to her, then a robe. "I
never watched you shave before," she said.

"Not much to shave," he said. He made instant coffee and toast while she dressed and did her hair up. Her entrance stunned him, again.

"What? Do I not look okay?"

"You look spectacular, Leece." *And you're here*

She did a brief pirouette. "I hate to say it, but the key to getting a Boston internship might be to talk like a biochemist and look like a fashion model. Only keep wearing the glasses, to look serious."

"If that's the key, you're in. On both counts. You're whip-smart. And you're a beauty, Leece. You always were. You were a beautiful girl, now you're a beautiful woman."

"In your eyes," she said, and turned away. And suddenly turned back. And kissed his cheek. "For luck," she said. "Let's eat."

He rushed to get his whites on, came back to grab toast and coffee, found her studying the city map. "You sure you know the way?"

"I've left time to get lost."

"You can use the house staff parking at BI-Deaconess. Car has the sticker."

"That will save time. I should go."

"You should."

"…I don't completely want to."

"You'll come back. You have to. Your stuff is here."

"Ben I…Thank you, Ben."

"Leece, I was wrong about something. It germinates, it blooms, but it doesn't die, it hibernates. And it blooms again." He got up. Came around the table, and kissed her. Really kissed her. "For luck," he said. "Now go. Knock 'em dead."

At morning rounds Ben was caught daydreaming when his name was called. "Dr. Rothstein. Where is your head today?" At lunch with the team he was in for a ragging. Bad luck: Edwards sat down next to him. He quickly picked up on the conversation: Where is Rothstein's head today? "Rothstein, is your mind on medicine or is it on that magnificent little piece of ass you were squiring around yesterday?"

"I don't recall anyone of that description. I recall a Dr. Mautner."

"And she is one magnificent little piece of ass."

It was like high school again, or the all-male world of the dorm. It sucked you in, even more if you tried to ignore it. There was no high road to take. "Dr. Edwards, I'll tell you what. She's an old friend, and if I ever hear you refer to her as a piece of ass again, I'm going to hand you yours."

"OOOOOOOOOOO," said the rest of the table.

"What? You think she wouldn't take it as a compliment to be called a magnificent piece of ass?"

"Ask her yourself. She's standing next to you." When he turned, startled, Ben pushed his face into his plate. The table erupted in laughter. "Something my father told me," he said as Edwards wiped gravied mashed potato off his face. "There are schmucks everywhere, even at Harvard."

"I'm not going to forget this, Rothstein."

"Don't. You may need to remember it for a good long time." He imagined the scene perfectly. But Edwards was the kind of prick who would take it out on her if he had the chance. Maybe it would get back to the internship admissions committee, and they'd think twice about taking her, or women interns in any numbers, thinking *Look at what we face* and *What if we admit Blacks* Instead he said, "So if you wouldn't want to say that in front of her, why would you want it to get back to her that you had? What if she were a member of the team, sitting right here? She will be, you know. Or some other woman will." Edwards stared at him. He rose, put his hand on Edwards' shoulder, squeezed lightly. *Wishing it was his neck.* "Come on, Teddy. Let's go save some lives."

He found her just coming in after the day of tours and interviews, asked her how it went, knowing what she really wanted was Mass General, *well who didn't.* Hard to remember how much he'd wanted it, after a grueling day, and nearly five years without her. The sadness of that was only just beginning to lift.

"I'll change into something more casual," she said.

"Only a little more. I have a real paycheck now; we can go to good places."

She had brought only one other thing. Well, two. She was determined to wow him, half knowing she didn't have to, half thinking she was competing with her younger self, so...She came through the beads in a taut black turtleneck, grey miniskirt, black tights, ballet flats. And a beret.

He rose, drinking her in again. He lagged a little, to watch her walk, before taking her hand. He would remember her as she looked that night for decades to come. "You were beautiful, Leece," he said. "You've become exquisite."

"In your eyes."

He imagined touching her, *mixing memory and desire*, didn't know she was having almost the exact same thoughts.

They went to the North End, an Italian place of undoubted quality and reputation, candlelit tables, long local ownership and college-student wait-staff. He glanced at the girls; *well, he's a man, men are pigs; but he isn't*, he kept coming back to her, obviously dazzled. *He's obviously delighted I'm here, he knows I came after him, I know he came after me, what am I worried about* Her eyebrows rose slightly as she took in the prices on the menu. On a Wednesday night the place was half empty. It was like having a private room. He was staring at her again. *Mesmerized* she thought *Well Wow I* He was, in fact, dazzled. She'd gotten where she'd wanted to go. Still driven, but he'd admired, he knew, the drive. As much as he'd often found it a pain in the ass, he remembered, he'd admired it. Still did. They ordered. Continued to fill each other in on some of the missing years. What the campus was like, the lull in the wake of the great spasm of 1968, the years in med school, comparing their experiences over salads. Dancing around it. Finally she said, "This is certainly a step up from Jack's." *Obviously serious business tonight*

"I'd give anything to be back at Jack's, Leece. To do it over." The main course came; pasta with fascinating sauces. The wine was opened. They oohed and ahhed and mmm'd, reassuring the waitress that "everything is okay, great," and were left alone.

"Anything wrong?" he said.

"No. God, no. It's…"

"You're so beautiful, Leece. Gorgeous. Always were. Not just in my eyes."

"I'm glad you think so. Who else's eyes, pray?"

"Well, Michael Firman, for one."

"Who's Michael Firman?"

"Classmate of yours. I mean, you took classes together. He was next to you in Organic lab, and he's a Fourth-Year here. Will probably intern here. Remembered us and Boland. Told me you took Embryology together. Told me you studied together."

"Oh. Right. Firman. Ben. Is this some way of finding out who I've been with?"

"No," he said… "All right, yes. It isn't jealousy, it's…and I'll tell you my…"

"I haven't… No. Not…Ben, let's cut to the chase. You pretty much ruined sex for me." The fork stopped halfway to his mouth; some fascinating sauce dripped back into the plate. He waited for her, having no idea what could follow. "Have I been sexually active? Yes. Did I enjoy sex? Sure. Some of it was good. I was in one long, longish, relationship. But I always knew what better was. Ben, nobody ever talked to or touched me the way you did. You *cared*, Ben. I knew that. I know that." *And I cared, and care, about you* she thought. She put her fork down, sat back, folded her arms. "Your turn."

They had always been frank with each other about sex; it had simultaneously been, he remembered, part of their daring, part of his respect for her as fellow aspiring physician and student of biology, part of what they could be with each other, what they could do and be with no one else. As he searched his feelings, that was the key. "I've been active. I've wandered in the wilderness for five years. I mean, enough casual sex. For a lifetime. It was the same for me, Leece, and thanks for the right words. It felt good, but there was never the glow of just being with you. I knew what better was. Knowing there was already someone out there, and I would never find better. You ruined it for me and ruined something else too. Being alone. I could never forget you. Forget *us*."

"The one that lasted a while for me, Ben, was a guy named Robert. MD-PhD at Penn. Every time I was with him I'd think of you. He was enough like you, it was impossible to forget you. Except he was always in the lab. Lab came first, and I wasn't even second. And over the hospital building: 'Pennsylvania'." He laughed. She smiled. "It wasn't funny at the time. My shop too, every place I looked, Woman's Medical College of…Pennsylvania. When I got the car, the license plate: Pennsylvania."

"There weren't *that* many. Leece. And I wanted them all to be you."

"You don't have to say that."

But it was, he saw, in some way true. "What I mean is," he said, "I wanted to find what I had with you. I never did. I don't think I ever will. Ever could. It was just sex. I don't mean I didn't feel affection, but it never grew into anything more, there was always some disappointing way they…weren't you. When breaking up, I'd be angry they weren't you, didn't have your… intelligence, your…I was maybe angry at *myself*. I mean: we just had sex. With you I made love."

She dropped her eyes, touched his hand. "That's it," she said.

The waitress came over. "Is everything okay?"

"Absolutely, he said.

"Certainly, she said.

The waitress poured water. "We stopped eating long enough to worry her," he said, and took a sip of wine. "I went back and forth about the Harvard thing, Leece. It was tearing me apart. But if it was just an affair…"

"I just said that because I was mad. Because I was scared of losing you. It was better to end it myself. For myself. Pick a fight about nothing."

"I did the same thing, Leece, but I came back for you, at Mercer I…"

"I know, Ben. I would have gone anywhere with you that

night, but then I thought, I was afraid, it was, just, you know, wartime. Adrenalin. Chemistry. You were still going away. And if I went with you, what would I be, if not a doctor?"

"I should have gone to NYU. Or Einstein, or…"

"Ben, I desperately wanted you to stay in New York. But I couldn't ask you to do that. I couldn't say I love you and make you do that. You told me, you'd already given Harvard up once. And believe me, I know what happens to relationships where somebody has to make a sacrifice like that. My father gave up conducting for years. He taught at Julliard until he couldn't stand it anymore. And I knew how it felt when he left. I was terrified of ever feeling that again, Ben. Terrified. So I blew it up."

"Fired me before I could quit?"

"Right…"

"And I let you. I let you do it, Leece. Because I couldn't bear to tell you I had to go to Harvard. *And why*. I did it for a bunch of wrong reasons. So I have this big laminated Harvard Med diploma, Leece, and I'd gladly burn the damned thing…"

"Don't. Those things can come in mighty handy. I'm here to try to get one."

"I should ship it to my parents. Let them hang it in the fucking Store."

"Why?"

"Why? Because when I found out my mother threw you out, I very suddenly got really tired of trying to be both of the Rothstein brothers." He picked up the wine glass, thought about a long pull, but just sipped it. "I think I decided to be a doc because of you. I mean, to not be a chemist. After Morty died… There were few people who liked me, and damned few I liked. I was just, I don't know, numb I guess. Playing with lab gear…"

"So you really lost interest in research?"

"That was Harvard's interest. Not mine. I cared about *you*. Deeply. I started caring about people again. At Mercer…I like taking care of people, Leece. Patients, I mean. Relieving suffering. It comes from being with you."

"I feel the same, Ben." She hadn't expected this, for it all to happen so fast. *He's the same A better version maybe?*

Maybe I am too "I worried some, coming here…I didn't know if you'd be the same person you were five years ago. Then I thought, you couldn't know that about me either."

"Am I?"

"Are you what?"

"The same."

"Better. An improved version."

"Thank you. And…you've grown into yourself." He paused. "But I hurt you."

"We hurt each other. It doesn't matter anymore." They were out of words.

"Would you like me to warm those plates up for you?" the waitress said.

"That would be nice," Lisa said, and they resumed eating the very interesting pasta when it came back. The candle on the table was almost a stub.

"Ben," she said. "I have one more interview tomorrow and then I have to go see my father. For lunch. Come with me, if you can get away."

"I don't think that's wise," he said, and told her the details of his last encounter with her father. "I don't want to blow it again."

"Don't worry. Whatever his Little Liesl wants, she gets." He winced. "Relax. It was a joke, Ben."

"He thinks I was just toying with you, Leece. It was something else. My parents would have…I don't know. My mother was still distraught at losing Morty, was afraid of losing me. And when they heard who your father is…I was afraid they'd see dollar signs. They're not bad people, but they live on the financial edge."

"My father's an expert on toying. Look, this is easy. I'll tell him we didn't ever talk to your parents because we were going to talk to him first."

He laughed. "You can really play him. Probably play me too."

"I never have, Ben. Never. Not that way."

"I know that. Leece. You never would."

"Maybe just a little."

"Mmm. I'm thinking…4-methyl, 4-ethyl octane. Did you really not get stereoisomerism?"

"Of course I did. But I told myself you'd know a trick, like the physics students vaselining their slide rules. And you did. But I needed an excuse to myself for wanting to see you. I was playing myself. The scared part."

It hit him suddenly. "You could have stayed with your father last night."

"No. I couldn't. There's someone there I'd rather not meet." *Among other reasons*

"Can I show you a dessert menu?" the waitress said.

"I'm full," she said. "Just a cappuccino."

"Cappuccino for me too," he said, and when the waitress left, "How come you didn't drive up here?"

"The car's a shitbox. I can't depend on it for anything but local transportation."

"Maybe I could have a look at it."

"That's what the Mud Phud always said, and never did. You always kept your promises. And. You're good at so many things. That was always part of the attraction."

"You should see me sell dry goods. Yeah, I'm good at stuff. Except one thing. I'm no good at giving up loving you. I couldn't manage that."

"You know, you never used that word. Neither did I."

"I was afraid it would scare you off. I'm using it now. I love you, Lisa. I loved you then, I love you now. I've never loved anyone or anything more. I never will."

"Two cappuccinos," the waitress said.

Her heart was beating so hard she thought he could hear it. "I love you too, Ben."

There was, for him, starting the car, still the question of what "I love you" meant to her. What he meant to convey was "Come be with me and be my love." Which would mean what to her? *Frank and straightforward. Guts and brains.* "Leece. we love each other. We've said it. What do you want to do about it?"

"I'm still digesting it. I thought, we'd meet, and talk, and get to know each other again, then maybe…I didn't think this could happen so fast." *Didn't dare*

He maneuvered through the notorious Boston traffic, trying to decide which was the more treacherous navigation: Boston's twisted streets or her experience of her parents' relationship. Relationships. "Assuming you want to be together, we have to decide how."

"I do," she said, thinking *he drives the VW the way he drove the motorcycle, squeezing through lanes and paths he makes through traffic himself.* "It all depends on me getting an internship here, which I'm starting to feel like might really happen. If I do…I'd like to…"

"I'd like you to…"

"You first this time."

"Live with me. Live together, Leece. I'd say more, but I'm afraid of scaring you."

"Take it one step at a time, Rothstein. Easy does it."

"That was my instinct. It's the vibe you give off. I don't care what we call it, I just want to be together." They were in the lot behind his building now, he was backing into a parking space anyone else would nose into; she knew he'd say "It'll be quicker to get out of tomorrow," typical Ben logic. They were at the apartment, through the door. "All I know is," he said, "I know what it's like to wake up in the morning with you, and I know what it's like not to, and I want to. Every day. For the rest of my life."

"We'll be on call some nights," she teased him.

He swept her to him. "Leece, you're the greatest gift life ever gave me, and in an incredible package."

Oh God yes "Sooo," she said, "Would you…like to… unwrap the package?"

It was a new discovery, this; a combination of the ardor of first love and the remembered knowledge of each other. They undressed each other slowly, he remembering all the exact places she loved to be kissed, she moving to let him, remembering where he loved to be touched while he kissed her. When she was down to the tights they moved to the bed, paused while she wriggled out of them into complete nakedness. He paused to take in the sight of her body, so well-remembered, so surprising after so much time. She heard his sharp intake of breath, heard him say "Leece", knew he was going to say "You're so beautiful" but she pulled him down to her and instead he ran his mouth all over her, down to her core, found the exact spot with his tongue, so well-remembered, so many times imagined; she moaned, and he remembered that moan, and he sighed, and she remembered that sigh. She surprised him, rolled over and did the same for him; he groaned, heaved; rolled back over and reached for the restocked bedside table drawer. "No need," she gasped. "There's pills for that." She reached down to rub him against her. They had never done this before without a wall of latex between them, and it was glorious. She saw him close his eyes, he felt her moist and warm, and as slowly and tenderly as he could he came inside her; he felt her like wet velvet; she felt him warm and hard. "Lisa," he whispered, and felt her rise to meet him. "Ben," she whispered, and so they experienced the last inches of each other without any intervening organic chemistry, had another first sexual experience with each other, losing their virginities with each other for the third time, and came saying each other's names, breathing I love you, oh I love you. *So many virginities to lose.* How long they lay locked together, neither knew. There were small caresses, and at last they lay next to each other, at peace.

"You started on The Pill."

"Two months ago. I was hoping this might happen, so I thought, never be unprepared again." Suddenly she got up, ran to the bathroom, came back with an MGH towel. "Need this," she said.

"One thing a Rothstein will always have is plenty of sheets and towels."

"I need things to be dry," she said. To his quizzical look she said, "I brought something else to sleep in." Reaching into her bag she pulled out the white nightgown. "Don't they say in Boston, 'It's wicked cold'? Sorry; I have to re-wrap the package."

He took her still-naked body in his arms. "This is the package," he said. He tapped her forehead with one finger. "The gift is in here."

And there she thought, *is why I called back.*

They woke to *WBCN The Voice of the American Revolution*, "Which is what we seem to have had a tiny part in igniting," he said. In the shower (together, this time) he told her about his draft physical. She laughed. He told her he thought he'd seen her at the Kent State action in DC, tried to reach who he thought was her.

"Could be. I was there," she said. "But *we* weren't ready to happen yet."

"So what's on the agenda today?" he asked over breakfast coffee.

"Interview at BU/ Boston City, and the lunch with my father." When he started to respond she held up a hand. "Just me, Ben. I'm going to say what I told you last night. Can I have the car again? I'd love to drive up in your car."

"Sure. Nice touch."

"He's conducted Wagner. He appreciates theatrics."

"One parent down, three to go."

"My mother won't have much to say. She moved in with a guy…"

"Over a year ago, the nosy neighbor told me. Scornfully."

"Longer. With him was where she was when we used the apartment. So, two down. That just leaves your parents' response to The Crazy Girl."

"They'll cope. They'd fucking better. I don't think they'll have much to say either. I told you I knew about railroad hotels from my father. Don't expect an apology from my mother. Not her style. But they'll love that I'm marrying a doctor."

Marrying?

Kurt had dressed formally, and carried a stick, *As usual looking as Mitteleuropean as possible An aging Viennese* Lisa thought as he hung his topcoat.

"So you're staying with your young man. Dr. Rothstein."

"I was staying at a cheap hotel I'd found, and when I called Ben he explained about the Combat Zone and invited me to stay with him."

"You of course could have called me. Stayed with me. Why did you not?"

"It's simple, and I doubt you really need me to say it. I feel extremely uncomfortable staying with my father when his girlfriend of the moment is quite possibly younger than I am. What Mother would feel, I can't say."

"I hardly expected you to be a prude, Liesl. Since…tell me something, as long as we're being candid. When I met your Benjamin Rothstein for the first time, how long had the two of you been intimate? And are you again?"

In for a penny, in for a pound she thought. "A bit over a year. And, yes."

"Then none of them is as young as you were when you began. Or your mother. Since we're being candid."

She barely knew where the intensity of the anger came from, knew it could be a big mistake. "Are you going to play the indignant father? Really?"

The gentleness of his response surprised her. "Hardly. I was never a father. I know that, Liesl. I never set out to be."

"I was an accident. I know that."

"I tried being a husband and a father, and I wasn't good at either. I did try, Liesl. I wasn't any good at it. You were both better off without me. I'm good at music. I'm good at conducting an orchestra. I set out to do that, and I am very good at it. The music comes to the listener through *me*. I make dead composers and musicians live again. It's intoxicating. The power of that. You want to be the best doctor you can be, correct? Perhaps it is the only thing I am good at. Music is what I had in common with your mother. I used to attend Lilian's performances when you were little; do you remember?"

"No."

"You were there, at some of them. You came to some of mine. After…I sent the cars for you and Lilian. You never liked the music. Fidgeted the entire time…"

"I would have preferred a simple visit." She was surprised at the feeling with which she said this.

"Sometimes Lilian was too angry for that. I never could deal with her anger. I never knew how. I was also never good with children, and I dislike intensely not knowing how to do a thing. But now you are an adult, and I would guess, a very interesting person. One I would like to get to know. I always respected your intelligence and determination. I can only hope Dr. Benjamin Rothstein also does."

"You know he does, out of his own mouth. He not only respects it, he enjoys it. It's what I love most about him. We enjoy each other's intelligences."

"Good, Liesl." he said gently. "That is important. I always respected Lilian's musical talent and judgment." He sighed.

"Are you also interested in getting to know *him*?"

"I feared he was perhaps taking advantage of you. I believed he was not a gentleman…"

"He is a gentleman. Literally, a gentle man. We fit together. We love and care about each other. We quarreled after that dinner with you, but during the Columbia protest he came to find me, and he got us both out of it safely. He has mentioned marriage, if that means anything to you."

"You mean, more than it meant to me once? You're still angry."

"He hadn't told his parents about me because we wanted to tell you first."

He picked at his salad. "I suppose for the sake of a more harmonious future I can choose to believe that."

"If you don't choose to believe it, you'll be depriving yourself of the company of a very intelligent young man who admires your Mahler." The anger she was trying so hard to suppress edged up a notch. "I'm angry because you didn't see fit to tell me he tried to contact me, which I would dearly have wanted to know. You misjudged him badly. You and Mother both. Misjudged him completely. And caused me to."

He just sipped his *kaffé mit schlag*. "I sincerely hope so,

Liesl. For your sake. Why is he not here now?"

"Two reasons. One, he's a medical intern, and can't get away for long enough. Second, he didn't want to interfere with me meeting with you. And why should he want to, when you tried to humiliate him the first time you met, and dismissed him the second time? And, given you and mother did your best to prevent us reconnecting now?"

"Rhetorical questions. What exactly are your intentions now?"

"I've applied for several internships in Boston. My grades are very good, so I'll probably get one of them. And he and I will live together."

"And if he leaves you?"

The anger took her. "As you left Mother? I will have my salary, and my work, and Harvard credentials, and I'll be fine. Nothing like Mother. You ruined her life…"

"I saved her life, you seem to forget."

"No matter. She's quite well set now. Richard is a very nice man. And I will be living with Ben Rothstein. With your blessing or without."

"I see. Well. You are an adult. You are my daughter and I wish you all possible happiness. And if you can overcome your anger at me you will be welcome at my home whenever your adulthood encompasses *my* relationships." He called for the check.

"Only if Ben is welcome too."

"He is truly knowledgeable about orchestral music? Yes?" *And anything on WBCN* "That's your first correct judgment of him."

"Time will tell."

She showed up on the ward again, just before afternoon teaching rounds, found him restarting an IV. "I told him, Ben, that he misjudges you. And I made clear, the next time he sees me it will be with you. If that's in two days or two weeks or two decades is up to him."

"How'd he take it?"

"Very dignified. *Echt Deutsch.*" She was going to go on,

but Teaching Rounds caught up with them just outside in the hall. Dr. Sachs said, "Perhaps the charming Dr. Mautner will join us again." The Third-Year presented the case, a 45-year-old man with a complex history of congestive heart failure, blah blah, blah...Physical findings..."

"Stop," Dr. Sachs said. "Let's see what everybody hears." He listened to the patient's heart first, then each of them listened in turn, from resident to intern to Fourth-Year to Third-Year. Sachs said, "Perhaps a prospective house officer could have a listen." Later Ben wondered why Sachs hadn't merely offered her his stethoscope. Well, she needed an edge, but she didn't need a clue. She took a moment to gain time, dug a hair clip from a pocket, and in a balletic move that brought a smile to Ben's heart, swirled and clipped her hair into a French twist, turned to face him, away from the outstretched student offerings, pointed to his stethoscope and said, "Dr. Rothstein?"

"Certainly," he said, handing her the superior instrument.

She listened anteriorly, posteriorly, across the chest, and at the apex, the classic auscultation landmarks, went back once to listen with the bell, and handed the stethoscope back to Ben as they went out into the hall.

"What do you hear?" Sachs asked her.

"I hear a Grade II to III systolic murmur and click over the mitral valve and a Grade II at the apex."

"Meaning?"

"Mitral and aortic disease."

"Your differential diagnosis?"

"Without a history, just based on physical findings? In an adult, Rheumatic disease of course, but with the number of tattoos and the earring I'd put forward the possibility of luetic valvular disease."

"Anybody have anything to add?"

Silence. The silence which on teaching rounds is the equivalent of thunderous applause. "What workup would you suggest?"

"Chest films, rheumatoid factor. VDRL with titers; could be secondary, active."

"You have a good ear, Dr. Mautner. Must be from your father."

"Oh, no," she said sweetly, "From my mother. She's a violinist. My father's been a little deafened by the brass section and tympany. Too much Mahler."

She left her hair in the twist in case she got a chance to do any more work.

When they got back to Ben's place their hunger for each other overwhelmed any other appetite, and they ended up two hours later ordering in Chinese takeout, eating out of the cartons in bed. Delight prevailed.

"You realize," Ben said, "You have this thing knocked. Alto Sachs is on the admissions committee. You awed him. Not to mention a roomful of house staff and students. Actually he can be a real shit with women. He gave Nola Mae a tough time when she was a Third-Year."

"Nola Mae?"

"Classmate. Maggie Roth. We called her Nola Mae…"

"For Nola Mae Tangere? Cute. Real cute."

"Leece, You impressed the living shit out of him. 'She knew the cause of every maladye, were it of hoot or cold or drye'…"

"… 'and where engendered and of what humour'," she finished the quote, "She was a veray parfait praktisour." He laughed. "What's funny?"

"Remembering something. How much I love you, and why."

"I had an edge, Ben. I don't know that I could have done that without your stethoscope."

"It wasn't only that. It was putting it together with the tattoos and earring. Sachs stresses observation, being observant. Plus it looks like he's a symphony fan."

"Can't tell my father. He'd send him tickets. That kind of edge I don't ever…"

"I know that Leece. Another part of what I love about you."

"It would have been more impressive if I'd done it with my own scope."

"Don't be silly. I think maybe part of what impressed him is you knew which scope to borrow."

"Maybe." She let it go. "Do you really think I'll get in here?"

"Yes. And even if you don't, you get me. It's too important to take risks. I'm going to hedge the bet, Leece. I'm going to call around Philly too. See if anybody wants a Harvard-trained resident."

"Better idea," she said. "I'll list the Boston hospitals on my match list, and next after those, Metropolitan in New York. Call them. They always need people."

"That's brilliant. Metropolitan. Everybody's safe school. Plus: on-call every fourth night instead of every third. We could live on the Upper West Side, Leece. We could walk out on Broadway actually holding hands. We could walk out into the middle of the crossing at 116th and kiss passionately in front of all Columbia University."

"We should do that no matter what happens. You would really leave Harvard?"

"Whither thou goest I shall go, Leece."

"For an atheist you know an awful lot of Bible."

"Five years of Hebrew school in Bensonhurst is perfect preparation for atheism."

"Like the Boy Scouts is perfect preparation for political dissent?"

"Exactly like."

"Yeah. If you're Ben Rothstein."

He rolled a Moo Shu Pork crepe. "I never asked how it ended with your father."

"He wished me well, hopes I'm happy. But you're still on probation, I think. He asked me my intentions."

"What are your intentions?"

She wound her fingers into his. "I'm a difficult person, Ben. I want to do my own thing, but be a part of something bigger than myself. I want to be loved, but I want to be loved the way I want to be loved."

"Lucky you. I want to love you the way you want to be loved."

She shook her head. "I'm kind of afraid that may not be possible. So. My intentions are to take one step at a time, if that's okay with you."

"Then the next step is, I intend to take you to the train tomorrow. Morty will cover for me," he said. And, "Relax. I'm not crazy. Billy Mortenson. Classmate. He'll cover until ten. I'm on call tomorrow night; I'll cover for him until ten next day. He's got a date, hopes to sleep in. After that... Leece..."

"What?"

"I...I'm no day at the beach either and...Um..."

He wants to say more She put a warning finger to his lips. "Okay, look. I *fancied* you..." She bit into an egg roll, dripping soy sauce on the sheets. "Then..."

He tried, and failed, to wipe it up. "And I *wanted* you."

"Before or after you dropped a pencil so you could look up my skirt?"

"Both." He reached for an egg roll, spilling more soy sauce and not caring.

"Just checking. Good. Because then I *desired* you..."

"So did I."

"You desired you?"

"Good one. No. Then I *adored* you."

"Yes. I know that. That's why I was so...I adored you. Then, couldn't forget you."

"And I longed for *you*."

"Yes. And here we are. Step by step." She scooped some Szechuan beef and rice.

"See, there has to be a chemistry of that, that we can depend on despite anything."

"It doesn't mean we know what the next step is. I've been waiting for this, Rothstein. I have a challenge to your chemical determinism. I took Anthropology. Senior year. It met in Mercer, of all places, and I took it my last semester, I couldn't even walk past that building until then. Even then, every time I walked in I could swear I smelled tear gas." She looked away. "Anyway. So yes, there's a chemistry of attraction, I'll give you that. But beyond that? All the chemistry needs to meet its goal of reproducing itself is enough attraction for unprotected sex." In her enthusiasm she missed his fleeting grimace. "It doesn't need (she pointed vaguely out the window) all this."

He forked up some Szechuan beef, spilling some. "All this what?"

"Culture. Cities. Museums. Art. Literature. Religion. Music. Anything beyond the ability to survive in the forest. Everything else, we made for ourselves."

He thought about this, chewing slowly (and dripping more soy sauce). "There's chemistry in our brains that allows us to do all that."

"Yes, but it doesn't *determine* it all. It doesn't *have to* take any *particular* form, or keep it. Cultures. We've made a zillion of them, and we can rearrange their pieces however we want to make more. Others. The chemistry is a limiting factor, but not much of one. The formula for short chain hydrocarbons doesn't determine the rules in the state driver's manual, or where you go on a motorcycle. I kept the course books, Levi-Strauss, Saussure, if you're interested."

"I think I get it. Our brain chemistry determines a *capacity* for belief, for creativity, for social engagement, but not the content?"

She was in the middle of a bite. "Mmmmph. You got it." Swallowed. "Systems theory. I call it a sextenary structure of proteins." He smiled. "Could have gone with hextenary, but... Oh. Reminds me. I still have your Baldwin *Biochemistry*. With your quintenary structure's name on the flyleaf. I hope that didn't inconvenience you."

"Nope. I skipped those classes to concentrate on Anatomy." He took a swig of tea. "Thinking about yours, mostly. Umm. So, since culture is malleable, contingent, not absolute, we can decide on *our own* rules for living, independent of chemistry or culture."

"Structuralism implies we can, since no culture is

superior to any other."

"Thus, we can have dinner in bed, rather than our culture's traditional breakfast, or the avant garde Naked Lunch or *Dejeuner sur l'herbe*."

"Indeed. *Exactement*. And do anything we want for the rest of the evening. And our lives."

"Wait," he said. If chemistry is just the mechanism, if DNA is just the code for the mechanism, another way to look at it…"

"Is like music," she said. "The written score is the code, the orchestra is the mechanism for the music…."

"Which the musicians, the singers, the conductor, can interpret in different ways, from the same score, to evoke the hearer's response…"

"Different responses in different hearers," she said. "So, even the code isn't absolute. The chemistry doesn't *make* life, like a factory. It isn't a factory. It's an orchestra. It…"

"*Evokes* it," they said together. They stopped. Looked at each other for a time.

"Well," he said finally, reaching out for her, spilling more soy sauce. "Solved that one. What *shall* we do for the rest of the evening, Mrs. Roberts?"

They swayed together in the rush hour T. "You think I couldn't have gotten to the station on my own, Rothstein?"

"I know you can, Mautner. But I've missed you for going on five years, and you have to go, and I want every minute together I can get."

"I was just teasing Ben. So do I."

At South Station she bought fruit and a sandwich for the trip, grabbed a cup of coffee. They talked noncommittally about nothing, trying to avoid the thought that they were separating again, until it was time to go out to the morning cold of the platform. Steam rose from ancient pipes. Switch engines clattered over points in the adjacent yards; commuters streamed off suburban trains, around them. Finally he said, "Leece, you'll be here in less than six months, we'll live together and…"

"A lot of ground to cover before that, Rothstein. Maybe we'll be in New York."

"Okay, so in New York. I don't care where we…"

The conductors were calling All Aboard. Sadly she said, "You know, when I was little I used to tell people my father was a conductor and they thought I meant on a train."

He climbed aboard with her, to help throw the suitcase up on the overhead rack; she thought; *Considerate Ben.* They got no further than the entry vestibule when he dropped the case and pulled her to him. She hugged him as if to incorporate him; he hugged her as if he could melt into her. They were kissing as the train lurched forward. "Ben," she gasped. "Train's moving."

He pulled her back. "It's okay, I'll get off at Back Bay. Leece. Listen. I wanted to say this last night. I want you to know how serious this is. How seriously I take this."

"I take it seriously too, Ben."

"But I want you to *know* I do. How much I do. So. Listen. I want to be with you. I don't care where or how. So here it is: an open invitation to marry me. I don't care when. If we live together fifty years without marrying, I don't care. But I want you to know it's a no-limit, open invitation. You say yes when and if you want." The train rounded the curve out of the station, picked up speed toward Back Bay. "Think about it, Leece."

"Ben, there are so many ifs we have to…"

"But that's not an if. It's a when. Whenever you want, if you ever want. I just want you to know, absolutely, that I will never leave you, Leece. One time is enough."

"I don't know what to say, Ben. I just know I want to be with you. I can't imagine wanting to leave you either."

He grinned. "Then you don't have to say anything else. Although I might from time to time remind you of the offer to make it legal in our culture."

"Tickets." She showed her ticket, got a seat check. The conductor looked over his MGH whites. "Sir?"

"We were saying goodbye when the train started up. I'll get off at Back Bay."

"You do or you'll be buying a first class round trip ticket

to Providence."

  The train slowed for Back Bay Station. He threw her suitcase onto the rack, kissed her again, and, painfully, got off the train. *Doing it, as usual*, she thought, *the Ben way.*

  She couldn't have counted on me getting her out of that hotel...She isn't perfect. She's sometimes a perfect pain in the ass. A difficult person Yes That I love. Exactly as she is. Can I ever stop this feeling responsible *for her?* He boarded an Orange Line T. *This might not work out. She might not get any of her Boston choices. Would I leave Harvard for her? I hope I don't have to but I would.* The lights flickered suddenly; there was a popping noise and a flash as the train hit a rough spot in the third rail; he was catapulted back, momentarily, to the tear gas canister popping at her feet. *She's so right. The real injustice is, a guy as bright as she is would have a Mass General internship in a second.* Turning anxiety into political anger, he could go back to work. But it didn't suffice, he could see through himself. *If it's all the System's fault it was never any of her fault, she's perfect, unflawed, just a victim of society's paternalism, so she needed my help. Which I was glad to give. Which she asked for, and takes, up to a point, then gets furious when I cross some invisible line. Was she ever really my student? Hell no* He changed for the Red Line at Downtown Crossing. *She picked up on that patient's Didge toxicity, and auscultated that patient and came up with that possible syphilitic multivalve disease diagnosis without a thing from me. Impressed the hell out of Alto Sachs.... The girl I adored, become a woman, a doctor, I respect Do I really want to spend the rest of my life with her? Hell yes. I can't believe it Here she is and I don't Don't what Little Bro Deserve her You don't, Little Bro*

  Towns flashed past. She thought of Robert. *I didn't lose Robert I never had enough of Robert to lose.* For him the lab would always come first, and not just the lab. *Ben found coverage to take me to the train. Totally unnecessary. Just for the extra few minutes with me. Ben does anything I ask, and sometimes even before I ask. He needs to ask.* But, to be honest, she thought, even when he did things like take the couch, offer to tutor me for free, I felt anxiety and a sense of guilt, even though I knew he delighted in doing those things. Guilt at enjoying it? Guilt at needing, or wanting, anything from anybody? Anxiety? *Well, my father gave grudgingly, and only if there was something he wanted.* Gifts came at a cost. She'd taken the cheap hotel to save for taxi fares; she couldn't sleep at her father's partly because that would have been a gift. Not with Ben. Ben said *she* was the gift. And, she suddenly realized, nothing he had done in the past three days had felt for a moment like an encroachment on her independence. Had he *outgrown* this? *Have I?* He'd offered her a ride, but then lent her his car. She tried to imagine Robert lending her his car. Or her father, for that matter. Or her mother, come to that, if she drove. *If she didn't make a career of being driven around*

You're the greatest gift I ever got Was that him saying that, or just his chemistry She knew what he'd say to that. *Leece I am my chemistry You're your chemistry Quintenary structure* What did that all even mean? Marry him, she thought as the train approached New Haven. Well, it would settle Mother. *Lose my self. Wait, with Ben I never lost my self What did he say? You've grown into yourself No The oldest fear Of the aching, bottomless disappointment of loss That happened twice Once with him*

The train crew by now were talking about the pretty girl with the medical journal on her lap who just stared out the window, passing the story to the new crew. *He adores me. Of course he adores me, I screw his brains out. No, you jumped his bones the first No, the second chance you had That is mutual, shared pleasure. It always was. And not before I asked him to. Because I adored him. He enjoys more than that about me He's never called me Baby. He's never embarrassed or demeaned me in any way, come to think of it. Even as a joke. And, not at Mercer. He took care of us at Mercer. He took care of everybody, then of me. He did anything I ever asked. Help me fight off a bully. Help me get an A in Organic. Help me have an edge. Take me out of the city. Be my first.* And, finally, *Go away.* Leave me alone, I said, and he did. Come back to me, I said, and he has. Is willing to give up Harvard, go wherever I go. Without, she realized suddenly, any hint of subservience, ever. *Desanctified a cathedral He really would do anything for me I must never take advantage* I promise myself, Ben

But…an academic career…you have to move out to move up. *What I'd have had with Robert Always looking for a job wherever he goes No wait, he wants this Freak*

And then the conductors were shouting New York Penn Station New York, and the Hotel Pennsylvania was maybe fifty feet above her, *and I said, I want to stay in this bed with you forever. And he says okay, marry me. I really am a difficult person*

She suddenly realized she'd woken up with him three mornings in a row. The warmth of that. How would it be to wake up with him for a week? A year? Many years? She could feel his hands on her. His mouth. Feel her hands on him. Slowly exploring each other's bodies. Feel him inside her. And, unlike Robert, he didn't fall asleep after. He held her, kept caressing her; the glow of that, and they joked and laughed. She shivered pleasantly. *If he was sitting next to me If he was here right now I'd want to go upstairs to the hotel Catch the next train You're in love, Dr. Mautner* God, I love him. *Structuralism says there is no fixed way no right way of defining art or composing music or composing families Of ways two people might*

Marriage. *Yes, well. I am*, she thought, *aware of the phenomenon.* Mutual subservience. Prelude to divorce, is what it is. Breaking up, yes, you just walk out, or he walks out. Divorce, that's a whole other story, Rothstein. I felt completely helpless. I have to know I'm not risking that. Not risking my life. Or any child's life. Because that's what it feels like. *I knew at the Reggio I wanted to go out with you. Then at the movies I knew I wanted you. And I knew I wanted you to want me. Then I knew I wanted to have sex with you. And then I realized I wanted to be with you, and that's when it got scary. Would maybe have been scary even without all the melodrama of the Harvard thing and Mercer. Okay, Rothstein, we got past that. Desire and friendship pushed me past every scary point. Marriage, though. I don't know what would push me past that fright.*

———————————— ● ————————————

On Match Day she paged him to tell him she'd got the MGH internship. She was breathless with happiness; he was ecstatic and relieved in about equal measure. The Universe had smiled. "Congratulations," he said. "Oh my god, Leece, congratulations." He could feel her excitement through the phone, knew she could feel his.

"There's a lot to plan," she said.

"Yes…I'll call you back around 6:30, okay?" When he did, he said, "We didn't think this through."

"What, again?"

He chuckled. "Yes, again. I'll be a resident, so if we're on rotations together…"

"…You'd be responsible for grading me. Neither of us wants that."

"Right, so…"

"We go public."

"Exactly, Leece. We go to the Training Director and we say we're living together, or we're married, as the case may be…"

"One step at a time, Ben, one step at a time. When you say 'we go', you mean it literally. We go in together."

"Absolutely. Of course that's what I meant."

"So not until I get there. We'll have two weeks between my graduation and July 1. Can you come, by the way? To my graduation?"

"All set. If you hadn't shown up when you did, I was going to find you by going to your graduation. I had already called Woman's for the date and scheduled the time off. I can help you move. Maybe right after graduation we can move you up here and set up house? I'll have to start hunting up a larger apartment. And a bigger bed."

"I can come up some weekends now, haul stuff, if the shitbox holds up."

"I can take a look at it. But you have Part Two Boards."

"And you have Part Threes."

"So…we'll have to do the apartment hunt and bed shopping after…"

"Ben…don't expect any gratitude, but the crazy damned thing is…Rothstein, you bastard, you got us both to Harvard." He grimaced. "Chemistry and Culture, Mautner. They work in mysterious ways." He wanted to tell the world, but between putting down the phone and returning to the ward lounge he realized he could tell no one. Not yet.

A dinner at her father's went surprisingly well, or would have had not the presence of a pretty flutist little, if at all, older than themselves required a level of emotional sophistication they had, despite medical training, not yet acquired.

Kurt made his overture to Ben. "I understand you are an aficionado of my work."

Ben recognized the olive branch, but decided to accept it on his own terms. "Particularly your approach to Mahler, who was, I know, also a conductor. I notice you use the human soloists and chorus as just other musical instruments."

"Indeed. Yes. Precisely, Benjamin. That's what they are."

Ben smiled. "Perhaps when performing music. Not other human activity."

Lisa hid a smile.

And then her mother and just Richard for dinner; no step-family. "Well," her mother said, "At long last I get to meet Dr. Benjamin Rothstein."

"Ben is fine," he said. "And I'm sure you know Dr. Mautner." He saw Richard barely suppress a grin.

Lisa choked back a laugh. "Lisa will do," she said.

"Thank you," her mother said. "I would hate to think you were being formal with me when you aren't with each other."

"Meaning what? His intentions are entirely honorable, mother. He's asked me to marry him."

"And what was your answer?"

"To ask some other time. I have more trust in him than in marriage."

"You must realize I'm concerned about that issue from the way you both behaved five years ago. You know, Lisa, that I think the two of you have violated every rule I know for making a prudent marriage. What I want for you…"

"All *your rules*, mother. Your rules aren't *The Rules*. Anyway, I've become quite certain that there aren't any *The Rules*. First thing I learned in Anthropology is that *all* cultural rules are arbitrary."

"Anthropology," Her mother looked from one of them to the other. "So you just make your own rules," she said.

Ben said, "Your daughter has an open invitation to marry me, at any time…"

"An exercisable option," Richard said.

"Exactly," Ben said, "She'll always have it. Always."

"Well," Lisa said. "We did study Roberts and Caserio's Rules of Order together."

"That's obviously some private joke, and don't explain, I want to finish my thought. You didn't let me finish. Ben. What I always wanted for my daughter is to be certain she has the respect and caring everyone should have in a relationship. I want, no, I need, your promise."

He turned to Lisa. "You have it," he said. "With pleasure. With all my heart."

After, Ben said to Lisa "Your parents. Now…my mother."

Lisa picked an exhausted Ben up at Newark Penn Station in the Shitbox. They drove through the demolished blocks of the still-scarred city to East Orange. This had become An Occasion, he told her; she was invited to sleep over, and they had invited Ellen and her husband for dinner.

"The Rabbi? He can drive on the Sabbath?" she said. "What's this about?"

"A Reform Rabbi. Only family we have left? I promise he won't marry us today."

His father welcomed her warmly. His mother explained that she'd misunderstood, thought Lisa was from some girls' school. "You looked so young, my Ben didn't need that kind of trouble, you'll have children, you'll understand." Lisa had hoped for an apology, not an *explanation*. Or rationalization. She chose to smile and understand. The men went outside to light the barbecue grill. "I didn't know my Ben was going around with somebody distinguished. You should have said who you are."

"I'm not distinguished, my father is. And we weren't going together when I came to the store. It was in college."

She nodded. "When he stopped being home, weekends, we should have suspected something. So, tell me, why when you came to the store did you cry?"

Lisa rose. "If you'll excuse me for a moment. It was a long ride…"

Ellen followed her out. "My Aunt Sophie wasn't always this way. She wasn't always so overbearing. Losing Morty hit her pretty hard."

"I'm sorry," Lisa said. "I needed a minute. I just…"

"Worry that you'll have mother-in-law problems. Don't. Ben can handle her." She told Lisa what had happened at the wedding. "When he walked out I went after him. I found him half way down a large glass of wine. He told me about the girl who taught him to dance, who he missed so terribly, and was afraid he could never find again."

"When was this?"

"When he was in his last year at med school. April of '72."

So, before he knew I'd tried to contact him She felt a little better.

Over dinner ("Kosher chicken, straight from the *schochet,*" his father reassured the Rabbi) his mother said, "So, in Boston you'll probably be seeing a lot of each other."

Lisa didn't understand at first. "We certainly will," Ben said. "We'll be living together. We're in the process of finding a larger apartment."

"Living together?" She laughed. "Oh, when you're married, you mean? Maybe Eli here can officiate, can't you Eli?"

"From the minute she gets to Boston." Ben said.

Her laugh vanished. "Oh? And what does *her* mother think of that?"

"It isn't up to her," Lisa said

"What do *you* think of that, Rabbi?" his mother said.

He paused to interpret his wife's gentle kick under the table. "I think that's between them and God," he finally said. "I'd be happy to officiate, if they ever ask."

"Well," his mother murmured, loud enough for the table to hear. "She's the one who can get pregnant."

"There are pills for that now," Ben said. "And I think it's for the best we sleep elsewhere tonight." She left for the kitchen.

His father looked around the table. "You'll need towels. And sheets. What size?"

Lisa took Ben's hand. "Queen," she said "I'll send a box when it's time." He paused. "Be kind," he said. "Things don't always turn out the way you expect. Life isn't a fairy tale. Always, no matter what, be kind to each other." He followed his wife into the kitchen.

Lisa felt even better. "No wonder you were so eager to leave New York," she said later, teasingly.

"Maybe, unconsciously," he said, seriously. *You have to tell her. You owe it to her*

They had planned another weekend to go apartment hunting, but Lisa called him to ask about another quick trip to New York. It was a real pain in the ass, but it seemed important to her. "Turns out Richard's whole family wants to meet you," she said. "My mother more or less begged. The excuse is celebrating my 25th birthday. We can trade on-calls for Friday-Monday, catch sleep on trains Saturday morning, meet at Penn Station, sleep at the Pennsylvania and head back Sunday. Tell you the truth, they've been giving me the fish eye ever since I showed up in their lives. I think they want to meet anyone who could ever be even remotely involved in Richard's will."

"Okay, I guess. For the sake of future peace. The Pennsylvania might be fun."

Both had run for trains straight from work, with their black bags. This turned out to be fortunate; there was a medical emergency. The patient was her favorite step-niece's teddy bear, which had sustained a severe abdominal wound, caught on a protrusion on the elegant old building's elevator gate. The little girl was crying inconsolably. Her father's offer to repair the wound with duct tape only increased her distress. "Aunt Lisa and Uncle Ben are doctors," he said wearily. "Maybe they can help Pooh Bear."

"We might at that," Ben said. They laid Pooh Bear on a coffee table and examined the wound. "I believe, Dr. Mautner, that we have here a deep abdominal L-shaped laceration. Do you concur?"

"With stuffing herniation," Lisa said. "We'll have to operate, Courtney." The little girl looked suitably solemn. "Will you hold Pooh's paw? We're going to give him something to keep it from hurting." She rubbed the bear's abdomen with an alcohol pad.

"First we'll have to listen to his heart," Ben said. He took his stethoscope from his black bag and applied it to Pooh Bear's chest. "Want to listen, Courtney?" He put the earpieces in the little girl's ears and whispered, "Lub dup, lub dup."

"He doesn't really have a heart," Courtney whispered to Lisa.

"I know," Lisa whispered back as she took two suture kits from their bags. "Don't tell Uncle Ben. Okay. Now we operate. Silk sutures for this, Dr. Rothstein."

"Yes," Ben said. "Anchor stitch at the point of the L." He took a forceps and pinched the bear's torn fabric together. Lisa took a hemostat from the suture kit and closed it on the curved needle. Carefully she pierced the pinched fabric, pulled through, released the hemostat, looped the silk thread around it and knotted it. Ben took a scissor and cut just beyond the knot. Courtney watched, wide-eyed, fascinated. They pushed the stuffing back into what was now two slits. They repeated the procedure ten times.

"I'm out of silk, Dr. Rothstein. Would you take over?"

"With pleasure, Dr. Mautner." He passed her the scissors. 'Will you assist?" He completed close-stitching the other arm of the L. "There," he said to the bear and to a delighted Courtney. "All better." They looked up to find all the step-siblings and older children looking on intently. They applauded. Courtney looked awe-struck. She hugged the bear, and said, "Could I ever learn to do that?"

Ben patted the bear. Lisa squatted down to four-year-old height. "You're a good patient, Pooh Bear," she said. "Courtney, you could learn to do it when you grow up."

"On *people*, Aunt Lisa?"

"Yes," Lisa said. She looked up. "But first we learn by practicing on fruit. Orange and grapefruit skin. When you sew them up feels just like people skin. Uncle Ben and I have refrigerators full of what looks like Dr. Frankenstein's fruit basket."

Everyone but Courtney's mother laughed. "Say thank you to the doctors," her mother said, rather severely. Courtney mumbled her thanks. "Louder," her mother said, pushing her forward.

"Best part," Ben said to Courtney, "After, you can eat the fruit."

On the walk back to the hotel, Ben said, "I thought you were paranoid about them, but I do get a real chilly vibe off Courtney's mother. I don't think she likes the current arrangements. Or us. Now I see why you worry about your mother."

"I do." Lisa looked away. "Thank you for coming, Ben." She paused. "Isn't Courtney's a sweetie? It did my heart good to heal her bear. If it eased my mother's relations with them, so much the better." She wondered, as they registered, if anyone remembered Mr. and Mrs. Roberts, but once in the room (shabby as ever but not as moldy) her mood brightened. "Let's celebrate like we celebrated my 18th, Mr. Roberts," but in the morning said, "This was fun, but I'm more than ready to have our own place."

There was just time for a quick breakfast with his parents at Ratner's before The Store opened Sunday. Quick hugs and his mother's, "You couldn't come and stay by us?"

"The hotel is right over the train station where we both came in around midnight, and they're more comfortable with us sharing a room than you are." Ben said. "So."

His father smiled. "I just remembered something. You asking about railroad hotels. Now I know why. Listen, what color sheets do you want?"

"Light blue," Lisa said. "If you have. And thank you."

"I'll send you two sets. And some velour towels. So soft," he said. "I'll send you a set, with the Queen sheets, light blue." His mother shrugged.

They just made their trains, going in opposite directions.

At her graduation, she introduced Ben to, and said goodbye to, all her friends, everyone promising to keep in touch. She'd sold The Shitbox to a Penn student; they made their long way up I-95 in a rented van full of furniture and books, with a stop at Columbia to jump out and kiss at the 116th Street crossing, knowing how childish it was, this defiance of a culture and its system that they had done a tiny bit to banish to the dustbin of history.

The next big thing was the meeting with the Training Director. When she'd gotten off the phone after calling him about her acceptance to MGH her jubilation was muted. They couldn't ever serve on the same team, anywhere he'd have any supervisory authority over her (which meant grade-giving authority); that was only right and proper. But, she saw clearly, she was back in Organic Chem at Columbia; she'd be *his woman*, any success, any advancement, might be at least partially credited to him, since he was a year ahead. So, again, she'd have to be twice as good as the guys. The System would screw her again, she could see; screw both of them. She had tried to explain her fears to him in bed, when she'd come for an apartment search. "In a weird way we'll be competing with each other." She knew he would laugh at this; he was never in competition with anyone that she could see *except maybe Morty*. "The issue isn't direct competition. You'll be on specialty rotations, consulting on my patients, and you'll do your best, and I'll have to do twice your best to prove beyond doubt that I'm as good as you, so we can be professional equals. You don't know…"

"I'll help…"

"No. That's the damned problem. Don't. You can't.

You shouldn't."

"I don't mean slipping you the answers, Mautner. Okay, we're two very driven people. We wouldn't have gotten this far in a competitive system if we weren't. But hey, maybe you'll help me. We each know things the other doesn't."

"I don't think you understand, Ben. Because…you say you're competitive, but you don't care enough about what other people think to be in a competition. You even purposely evaded competition by being a chem major instead of pre-med..."

"Also, because I'm not a woman?"

"Okay, yes, you don't know what it's like."

"I understood well enough to have conducted a torrid relationship with one that could have gotten her expelled but instead she's going to intern at Mass General."

"But you don't know what it feels like. Not deep down. You can't."

"Maybe I have some idea what it feels like. My brother…until he died, even after, every damned thing I could do, everyone in the family thought it was because he taught me." He took her in his arms. "You be the best ever, Leece. You do what you need to do. Do what feels right to you. Always. Don't ever worry about me. I'm not competing with you, and I won't influence your evaluations in any way. Ever. "

"I know that, Ben. It's…again, it's not you, it's just…the *culture*."

"Dr. Rothstein. Dr. Mautner. You wanted to see me."

"Thank you for seeing us, Dr. Baker. We think this is a delicate matter but probably easily settled." He waited for them to proceed, with a slight sinking feeling. *Well, kudos to them for being out front about it.* "We're in a committed relationship," Rothstein said.

"What does that mean, exactly?"

"It means we're living as a couple, and expect to continue to," Mautner said.

"Without…ah…benefit of clergy?"

"With respect, Dr. Baker, that's between us," she said.

"We, uh, knew each other in college," Rothstein said, "And when Dr. Mautner was accepted for the internship, we knew we wanted to be together, and we knew we should have this conversation."

"I see. Not something you saw fit to mention at your interviews, Dr. Mautner."

"It wasn't relevant," she said. "I expected, and expect, to be judged on my skills and nothing else. Then, now, and in the future."

Well put, Baker thought. *That's exactly what you should be accorded, in a decent world.* "It means you cannot be on the same rotations. That poses some problems in making schedules, but nothing we can't get around. One or the other of you may have to rearrange your elective preferences to avoid Dr. Rothstein ever being in a supervisory position. He may of course not participate in any way in your evaluations."

"Exactly, sir. We wouldn't have it any other way."

"You will, ah, notify me if there is any, ah, any change in the status of the relationship." *Though that would still be a problem*, he thought.

"Immediately," Mautner said.

"Of course," Rothstein said.

"Very well. Thank you for coming to me with this. It does you both credit."

"Thank you, sir," they both said. Separately. *Lovely young woman*, he thought as they left. *I hope they make it. I hope they know what they've taken on.* He sighed. *More women in every class. This could be an issue every year.*

"Are we going to have to take a lot of shit?" she said.

"Constant and unending."

"We're going to give it back, aren't we."

"Rafts of it. Truckloads, Dr. Mautner. As much as is safe."

"The Rothstein Brothers? Only this time you're the older brother, Ben."

He began to sense how very important this still was to her. She was in. She needed to do this on her own, and to be seen

to do it on her own. To be *equal*. His impulse to encourage and
protect and rescue. And her fear of his competitiveness. He shook
his head. "You got me out of that. We're a team, Leece. Like the
night at Mercer."

"We weren't a team. I was the walking wounded."

Not enough "You walked. You found the window. You
saved us with an ingenious kiss."

"I told you, I saw that in a movie. This is different."

He continued on call, dragging himself through the last
days of his internship, while she set up house, *our own place*
waiting to start hers. Dishes and pots and pans from her old
place, a few from his, an espresso maker from her father, small
appliances from her mother, his spavined couch, her desk and
chair, the new bed. She broke open boxes, dusted closets, hung
clothes. He joined her in the evenings to cut open the boxes of
new towels and sheets from Rothstein's Dry Goods. "The velour
towels. Soft, as promised. Queen Size replacements for the
Chinese-Dinner-stained sheets," she said. She sniffed them, "To
see if they still smell of the basement. I wonder if the rodents
are back. Remember how awful it was? The mice, the rats, and
the cold. The arguments about you going to Harvard. The anger.
The disappointment. And the time with your mother... "Well,
remember, *you* can't get pregnant." She didn't see him grimace,
and turn toward her. *If it be not now...*" He put down the Swiss
Army knife.

"There's something I've been meaning to tell you for...
The worst, for me, was when you said me going to Harvard was
about winning a competition with Morty."

"I only said that in anger. You weren't the first man to
leave me for his career. "

"Career? That isn't why either. I said to you once, you
have no idea what's between me and my brother. It's time I tell
you. I owe you that. It will explain a lot, including the reception
you got from my mother. My parents. I couldn't make sense of
why I felt so driven to go to Harvard without telling you things
I'm ashamed of. Something I've never told anybody. It's a

wound I have to drain."

"You said it was about being the best. And I was angry, thinking you thought being the best, besting Morty, would make you happier than being with me could."

"And I let you think that. The best? I don't even know what that means anymore. I want to be a good doctor, take good care of my patients. I don't, and didn't, need Harvard for that." She just looked at him. He paused, looked away "Harvard was my father's, the family's, dream, the ultimate way to become American. Make connections, meet *distinguished* girls." She winced. "And Morty's dream was to get away from The Store." She could hear the capital letters. "He always told me to get away from The Store too. That's what Harvard was all about, for them, and for him." She watched him think. "You're right about me wanting, then, to replace Morty for my parents…"

All right, let's do this "And for yourself. You loved him, Ben. It was a terrible loss. When I had the time, the perspective, I realized how that must have been for you…"

"Yes. But it isn't that simple. I wonder how you'll feel about me after I tell you this. Oh, God, Leece, it's past time to tell this. We have to do this before we start the year. I once thought I'd never tell anybody, but I can't let you go on thinking I left you for…You should know the worst things I ever did. You should know what I'm responsible for. You think of me as some kind of left-wing Boy Scout, but…"

Now she was frightened; had never heard this tone from him. "Okay. Tell me," she said carefully. "What you think I should know." *You promised my mother And me*

She saw the distress in his face, where she had seen it so seldom, and tried to swallow fear. "You're who you are now, Ben. This, whatever it is, is from before we ever met, so it's part of who you were when we met, and since. So don't worry that it figures into what I think of you. How I think of you, now." *I hope* "Tell me. Maybe I can help."

"Help? It's long over. I can only ask you to understand." *Will that help*

"Ben. Okay. Tell me. How bad can it be?" *Obviously*

pretty bad

 Where to start "Morty and I were raised on my father's
stories of being drafted in 1940, never got to finish college;
he was sent to OCS, became a Quartermaster officer, and the
whole War he was bullied and harassed by his anti-Semitic
commanding officer, a Harvard guy. By the time he was
discharged home Morty was two years old, almost three. He had
to make a living. The Store, which he'd worked in as a kid, was
an inheritance from a childless uncle. Rothstein's. He always
said he was still a quartermaster. But with softer towels, I guess.
Going to Harvard was becoming a real American. No. Sticking
it in America's eye. Morty was brilliant. On his way to Harvard
by the time he was ten. Maybe before. From when we were old
enough we helped out—worked—in The Store. And Morty's
goal in life was to get out of The Store. For both of us to get out
of The Store. No. More. His whole life became about trying
to get away from being the Nice Jewish Boy. Away from The
Store to Sex, Drugs, And Rock'n Roll. That's what the bike was
about. The minute he was old enough for Working Papers he got
a summer job as a waiter at a Catskills hotel. The Flagler. Second
tier; not Grossinger's or The Concord but, he said, still decent
tips. And rich girls, from Long Island. Westchester. The first
summer, he made enough to buy the bike. With a little help from
me, because the money wasn't all salary and tips. I told you, I
think, he was a math whiz. Which he applied to poker. He was
just a high school kid, but a big guy, easily passed for college
age, so he got hired. And when he included himself in their poker
games, the actual college boys thought he'd be an easy mark.
Sometimes he did lose, but when he did he'd come home on
his day off and ask me to loan him money to stake him again. I
did, and he paid me back, with interest. Which gave me enough
to stake him when he set up games at Rutgers and NYU when
he was a senior in high school. First Bank of Ben. The parents
never knew."

 "Jesus, Ben, so what? That's not so bad. So he was a card
sharp. So what? He could have made a lot more at Columbia.
Or Princeton."

"That's not the end of the story. Don't risk alerting
the Ivy League. Going to Harvard was part of his plan. My
senior year in high school was his at Harvard. I went up for my
undergrad admission interview. December 1963. It was when
everything was settling down after Kennedy was shot. He had
long since dropped the pre-med courses. The parents didn't know
the math whiz was applying to MIT, to study computers, said
computers not medicine, were the future, the road to riches. I
was going to stay the weekend, after the interview. He was... he
should have been in despair, but he wasn't, he was full of manic
energy. Should have been my first clue. Going on about... Leece,
I'm going to use his words, so you get the flavor of this. He'd
always talked about getting me laid. About the acres of pussy we
were going to plow together."

She rotated the desk chair and sat, her chin on the chair
back. "Acres of pussy."

"Yes. Two of the Seven Sisters are here, he said,
Wellesley and Radcliffe, not to mention BU and BC and
Simmons, and rich bitches all dying to lose it, and I'd be a
Harvard man, he'd be MIT, with a motorcycle, we'd be rolling in
it, he said.

"So, you nailed a Barnard girl instead."

"Stop it, Leece. It was never like that. Never. See, that's
one reason I never told you." She decided to try to let him go on
without interrupting. "He had this whole line, that these were
finishing schools, and we'd be the finish. About how the girls
kept boxes of wedding rings in their dorms so they could check
into hotels..."

So much for that decision "That's how you knew to get
the rings."

"That's how. Leece, please. This is hard enough." He
paced. "Only he couldn't afford it. His first roommate was some
kind of trust fund baby, so he was running with that crowd, or
trying to. At Harvard he found a kind of bullying he'd never
encountered before. One he couldn't fight or cope with. Scorn
for the kids without money. When he started meeting Radcliffe
girls, it was You can't afford Cliffies, Rothstein. Out of your

league. Maybe code for *Jewish*, but if it was about money… He figured the only way to make it at Harvard was to have money. And there weren't many ways. He thought about a job at the Coop, but that was another *Store*. Plus, he told me once, it didn't matter if you *had* money, just that you *behaved like* you had money. By, say, telling everybody your father owns a dry goods factory, not a crappy store on the Lower East Side, and playing high stakes poker at the frats, which *would* bring in money. He won, mostly. Mostly. But by senior year…at dinner he told me he'd set up a double date for Saturday night. Fancy restaurant. I asked him with who, he said who knows, a girl, one of his Cliffie girlfriend's dormmates, probably as up for it as he figured I was. I said, with a high school kid? He laughed, said, You're not, little brother, and I said, So who am I then, you know, being jolly, and he laughed, said *I* is the imaginary number."

"The imginary… *i,* the square root of minus one?" Lisa said. He nodded. "So, identity, for him, was imaginary? Sounds like, by that time, for him, it mostly was."

"Pretty much. Tonight you're a Columbia sophomore, he said. You can pull that off, you know enough chemistry. Then… he handed me a condom, said You never know what they're using, and retracting the landing gear doesn't always work…"

"Retracting the…oh. So, I wasn't really your first."

"You were. That condom was still in my wallet at the pond, but it was years old, I didn't trust it." He stopped, ran his hand through his hair. "My interview was a success. They offered to take me, but no scholarship, because when he graduated, and wasn't a family expense anymore, we wouldn't meet the need criteria. Morty was thrilled; The Rothstein Brothers were going to be in Boston together, I'd be accepted at Harvard and lose my virginity the same weekend. He'd be out late, winning the money to pay for the restaurant, so I could sleep in his room. Which was a mess. It was almost end of semester. Books stacked up that'd never been opened, a half-done paper by the typewriter, on Wittgenstein and the Problem of Identity, his usual brilliant stuff, about how language was inadequate to truth and belief, so the only hope was in numbers, math, but even in math *i* is an imaginary number; "I" is just imagined…"

"Wait. Not so brilliant. Because only in English are the symbols for first person pronoun and for the imaginary number the same. In French it's *je*, in Spanish it's *yo*, and most importantly in Wittgenstein's native German it's *ich*. He missed that, Ben. He'd never have gotten more than a D on that paper in my senior Philo seminar."

"Hell. You're right. That went right by me. Shit. Anyway, the despair he should have felt, that I felt for him…there was a to-do list a mile long by the typewriter; the paper was already weeks late. He was way far behind in his courses. I realize now, he was under incredible stress trying to keep up with the poker and his courses. There were beer cans, a Canadian Club bottle and an aspirin bottle in the wastebasket, but he had more energy than two people, and there was a film can by the typewriter. Full of pills."

"Shit, Ben. You think, Speed?"

"That's what I think now. Benzedrine? Ritalin? I don't know. Meth, maybe? He could have made Meth in the chem lab easily enough."

"Oh my God. They raise blood pressure. And the aspirin… he couldn't clot. The headaches were the aneurysm leaking."

"Right. I didn't put it together then. I was a high school kid. What did I know?"

"You couldn't know *that*. So, you met these Cliffies…"

"No. He came in around three, four in the morning. He was frantic. Couldn't sit still. He'd lost; he apologized, said we'd have to call it off. I said couldn't we take them someplace we could afford, and he said I didn't understand about these girls. I thought, he must have lost pretty big. He was pretty distraught. And irritable. Jumpy."

"The Speed maybe?"

"I think so now, yeah. Anyway he told me to just go home; we'd celebrate some other time. Which I thought would be Christmas break, but he was so far behind he stayed and worked on the overdue papers and studied for Finals. Then he called me during his Finals Week, asked if I could lend him some money.

I was worried he was losing, told him You said I was going to
need it if I was going to go to Harvard. He said True, so okay, no
problem. But a week later he came home unexpectedly during
Winter Break. He usually hung out at ski lodges with friends.
Playing poker of course. And losing. Told us he was looking into
a summer job at the Institute for Advanced Studies."

"Let me guess. The summer job was a poker game he'd
set up at Princeton?"

"Yes. And. He wanted to finance it with the float from
the Store."

"The what?"

"The float. The Store's big day is Sunday, remember?
Banks aren't open weekends. Sundays I took the store's cash
receipts over to the Night Depository chute at the Bowery
Savings Bank while my dad closed up. They wouldn't be
collected and booked until Monday morning. Which would give
him use of the money, the float, until Monday. Deposit the exact
amount of the receipts by Monday morning, keep the winnings,
no one ever knows."

"But if he lost…He was embezzling. From his own
family. *You* would be."

"Technically, yes. He described it as investing The Store's
money in poker futures. A sure thing. He always said he had an
edge: the frat boys were drunk, and he wasn't, he'd always made
good any losses out of past winnings. But, this was more…"

"The speed was disinhibiting…"

"Clouding his judgment, right, so he missed what you
saw in the Philo paper, and maybe a lot more."

"So… you gave him this float money?"

"I told him I couldn't do that. I was a coward, Leece. I
didn't save him."

"Coward? You couldn't save him. You couldn't risk that.
How could you? You'd just seen him lose big, weeks before.
How did he take it?"

"Actually he was apologetic, at first. Said he knew he
shouldn't have asked me, wouldn't have if it was just to cover
poker losses, but it wasn't to cover his losses this time. It was to

jack up the stakes at the Princeton game to pay for an abortion."

"He'd got the Cliffie pregnant?"

"That's what I thought. The girl's family, he said, would never accept this, accept *him*. They'd make her go to a home, adopt the child out. Even if they did marry he would have to drop out of school, work, maybe at The Store, risk being drafted. Or have to go to Canada. And, he really didn't want to marry her. Computers are my future, he said. Our future. I told him, tell Dad, he'll find the money."

"I bet he would have. Your father was always kind to me. He's a kind man."

"He is. But he isn't immune to disappointment. Morty didn't want, couldn't stand, the parents to know, to destroy their picture of him, the Harvard pre-med they knew. Thought they knew. The image..." He went silent.

"The imaginary number."

"Yes. So I kept my mouth shut. I loved him Leece. And I owed him. He ended up winning at Princeton but he was afraid, not enough. Never mind, he said, he'd figure something out. If only I *had* done it. Or just loaned him money when he first asked me. He'd have won enough..." He seemed to her on the verge of tears. "He was my big brother. He took care of me. And I didn't take care of him. I couldn't save him. If I'd gone to my father, he'd have given him the money. But I failed him. I was a coward."

"You're no coward, Ben. Who knows *that* better than me?"

"I thought, for years, if he could have got past this...he said, and I believed him, he could get back on the straight and narrow. But the girl, what would happen to her? I thought, maybe I *will* go to my father for the money, but I couldn't. And then he died."

"You were still a kid, Ben. In thrall to your big brother, I think."

"I'd have denied it then. Been angry at anyone who said that. But now...I think that's true. He begged me not to, don't worry, he'd figure something, was already worried enough, to the point of constant headaches. He was chugging aspirin..."

"Ben, he couldn't know he had the aneurysm, and neither could you. You were just a high school kid. You did everything a kid could do."

"He had to get back to school. He zipped up his leathers, kicked the bike down and roared off. That was the last time we saw him alive. Next thing that happened, we got the call from Harvard that he had died. Autopsy showed the burst Berry."

"I'm so sorry Ben. It must have been horrible for you."

He nodded. "My mother just collapsed. Friends stayed with her while my father and I went to arrange transfer of his body and pick up his things. My father did the body part; I went to his room. His roommate had cleared out the liquor and beer and the pills and the Playboys in case his parents came to box up his stuff, and he told me there were repeated calls to Morty from some girl. Wouldn't leave a name."

"She was a Cliffie. They must have known her. Who she was."

"No. That's just it. They knew the Cliffie. It was *another* girl. He had been *romancing* the Cliffie. This was some girl he was just…having an affair with."

"Just an *affair*. I'm so sorry, Ben. Now I understand how you heard that. I accused you of being no better than him." He nodded. "So who was she?"

"Definitely not Radcliffe. They didn't know. Someone he was bragging about, a local waitress, some townie, maybe a girl from BU or BC or Simmons. Nobody had a clue." He paused again. "It was only later, when I thought about it…he didn't care about this girl. Just the sex, and the bragging about it. Jesus. To *use* someone like that…hell, use me, use all of us…."

"Yes." She sighed. "What did you do?"

"What I was there to do. Put on his leathers—over two sweaters, they were much too big for me, and it was cold as hell—and drove the bike home. First time I ever touched it after that was with you." He paused again.

"What…happened to the money?" *Did you take it*

"There wasn't any in his room. Maybe they stole it. I hope he gave it to the girl. He thought it wasn't enough for an abortion. I got this idea. I'd go to Harvard and I'd be in Boston and I'd find her. I'd find the baby. That's what I told myself. But my mother was too sunk in grief to work at the store, and they couldn't afford an assistant. Then, I found out, my college money had gone for Morty's funeral."

"Oh, no."

"I'd been accepted at Harvard, and Columbia, but with Morty gone and the funeral expenses...Columbia offered me a partial scholarship and the Grant-in-Aid lab job. The family finances were always pretty precarious. Big mortgage, ups and downs at the Store. That's where my father went over it with me. Can't do it Benny, can't swing Harvard now. I should stay here, I said, help in the store. Rothstein and Son. That's how guilty I felt. Don't be a fool, he said, you have the brains to not have to slave in a hole-in-the-wall dry goods store. Your brain is your ticket out. When I mustered out Morty was a baby, three years old. I had to make a living. By the time I got home there were damn few job opportunities for returning vets, even officers, much less finish college, GI Bill or not. You boys were the hope of this family, he said. Become doctors, make a good living and take care of your mother and me in our old age. As much as I wanted to see you and Morty both at Harvard the scholarship will give us the time to put together the money for med school. You could go to Harvard Med. That's what you'll do. It was the new plan. I didn't know that I wanted to be a doctor then, but I wasn't going to argue with him." He stopped. Resumed. "Hell, if all this shit hadn't happened I'd have gone to Harvard and maybe become a jerk like my beloved brother. Part of what was so awful was finding out who he was. Or who he'd become."

"Did you ever try to find her? The girl?"

"When I got here in '68 I went to a private detective. That was a good laugh. He clapped his hands together like Bogart in *The Maltese Falcon*. You want me to find a girl, no name, maybe a college student from who knows where. She may have dropped out. Or died. And you think I can go ask every abortionist, hell, every doctor, in Massachusetts and vicinity about a nameless girl five years ago? Keep your money, son, it's a needle in a haystack, it's a needle in a thousand haystacks, and don't believe anyone who agrees to try, they'll just take your money and keep telling you for a few bucks more they can try harder."

"You've never found her. And you blame yourself for all this?"

"I kept—no, keep—waiting for her to show up in our ER, or a clinic, or The Freak, or someday an office, a woman with a young child, asking if I'm related to a Morton Rothstein..." He went quiet. Paced some more. "The Cliffie called. Once. Frantic. To ask where Morty was, she needed to speak to him. Got my mother, who was crazy with grief; she called my father at the store, is how I know."

"Where a few years later she didn't need some crazy girl from your past..."

"Yes. And our sleeping or living together. Shit, I wanted to scream at them, *I'm not Morty*, but I can't, because...I always hoped they had no idea. If my father knew, he never let on. But, they first thought you were looking for Morty. Then maybe that I had, I don't know, also, got a girl in trouble." He still looked despondent. "There was no stolen money, finally. Just, a girl whose life maybe was ruined. Or maybe had an abortion, or a miscarriage, who knows. And my parents, who all they had was a store that barely paid for a house they couldn't afford and a college fund, and a picture of one ideal son." He went to the window, stared out. "My parents thought they were somehow responsible for his death, pushing him to go to Harvard. I thought I was, for not getting him the money. Telling them after might have relieved their guilt, but it would have left them knowing what he'd become, destroyed their picture of him. Which would have been even worse, it seemed to me. He died, there wasn't going to be any second chance. Except me. *I* was the second chance. My fault, I figured. That I hadn't done what he asked, or told them what trouble he was in, that we, I, could have prevented it all. I owed them. So..." He was staring out the window. "And I never told you. I am so sorry, Leece. For not telling you. Hurting you, and not explaining why I had to go to Harvard. I didn't have it completely worked out, in my head.

And, telling you right now, wishing it all never happened, I'm realizing, if it never happened, if I hadn't done what I did, I'd have gone to Harvard, and never met you, never got the greatest gift the Universe ever gave me."

Her instinct was to leave, walk until she'd sorted out her feelings and suddenly confused thoughts *But I will not leave I will not* Instead she swiveled the chair back to the desk and sat staring blindly *Harrison's Textbook of Medicine latest New England Journal Friedman and Kaplan's Psychiatry* He crossed the room and put his hands on her shoulders, but she shrugged him off and he stepped back, dreading what could come. *The greatest gift* "I have a question. Did you feel so guilty you went to Harvard to punish yourself? Sacrifice the gift? Because the sacrifice was *me*. Was *us*." She stood. "Is it ever likely to happen again?"

"It's what I can't forgive myself for. What I'm afraid you can't forgive me for. If you want to leave…"

The joy outweighs the hurt She turned. "I'd prefer an answer to my question."

"Well, an answer's in the desk drawer." She opened it and found a stamped envelope, addressed to Metropolitan Hospital. Inside it, a completed residency application. "To be mailed immediately if you didn't get a Boston internship," he said.

"You were really prepared to do that?"

"Completely." He stood back. "Morty was far from a perfect person, Leece. And so am I. Now you know what I'm capable of. Lying. Duplicitousness. Cowardice. But not of ever leaving you again."

"No. A Boy Scout is loyal, trustworthy, honest and true."

"You'll have to settle for one out of four, if you still want me."

This is why he needs the chemical determinism idea To ward off this pain Maybe any pain "Kid stuff," she said. "You are all four. You did the best you could. The best a sixteen-year-old could. I don't think anyone at that age could have done better. You took care, or tried to, of Morty, but he didn't let you. Of your parents. You take care of me, when I let you. Of your patients,

I'm certain."

"And you take care of me. You never *really* need taking care of."

"You got me out of Mercer, and the Combat Zone. And I was ready to quit that damned lab. How am I taking care of you?"

"You're doing it right now. Shit, I should have told you all this. I was afraid. I thought I'd acted badly, that I should have risked taking the float money for him. And for the girl. I was afraid you wouldn't understand."

"I don't know if I could have, then. How I understand it now is, you couldn't join him in his dishonesty, his schemes, his *values*, but you didn't shrink from respecting your brother's secrets, and when he died, your parents' grief. And you didn't become a jerk. Even in thrall to him, you never became him. Jesus, Ben. You must have been terrified. Alone with this, all this time." That was when he cried, and she held him, kissed him. After a time she said, "Even if you ever found the girl, what would, what could, you do?"

"I don't know. Tell her what happened to him. Tell her he'd loved her; didn't just use and abandon her. I thought that white lie would at least make it better for her. Do something for the child, if there is one. Ever was one. Introduce my parents to their grandchild, maybe? A piece of Morty…"

"Instead, you took pity on the lonely girl in the chem lab."

"It wasn't like that, Leece." *Or was it?* He thought how to answer. "I don't think I could know for sure that's not how it might have started."

"That's why Freud called it the Unconscious. Ben. His death…it was his doing. And, just the chemistry of a Berry Aneurysm. He put you in an impossible position. There was nothing you could do that wouldn't have hurt yourself or someone you loved. And I see now I did the same thing to you when we broke up in '68. Hurt me, hurt yourself, or hurt your parents. I understand now why you needed to go to Harvard. I do."

"So, you're okay with this? We're okay? Really?"

"Yes Ben. We are. Really. I understand why you acted as

you did…"

Yet at dinner, and after, she seemed to him distant, abstracted. Preoccupied. He thought he knew why. "I promised myself, after all this, to never lie again, never keep secrets. Never. But I did. About you. And by not telling you this."

"You mean lying when you denied being with me? About our weekends? It's not the kind of world where you can make a vow like that. I think it depends on what you lie about, and when. If it hurts anybody, or prevents hurt."

They hung the soft towels, opened a few more boxes, and went to bed. But not to sleep. "You're still upset. I should have told you in '68," he said into the dark.

"I don't think it would have changed anything. I'm not upset; I've been thinking. I think I've been lying too, to and about myself. It's why I understand you, I think. You've never asked about my mother. About my family. Or lack of one."

He realized with a start that this was true. "I assumed you sprang from the forehead of Zeus. Some miraculous process. I knew there were cousins on Long Island. You never talked about it, so I never…I mean, you more or less told me, in the park that day, that you were a Woman of Mystery, so I figured, you'd tell me when you wanted to. I figured, something to do with the pregnancy. Or the War. A lot of people I know have no family. Some of our people were never heard from after 1941."

"It was to do with the War. She almost never talked about it. I had to pull it out of her. So I got in the habit of not talking about it. My mother was born in Prague. In 1938 they started the Kindertransports, out of Austria. She played the violin from very young. She got into a Jewish youth orchestra. It was competitive, you had to compete to get a chair. Then came Munich. The orchestra wangled an invitation to France, set up an invitation to do a concert here…most of the kids never went home. Which was the plan. Some went to Palestine. The cousins in New York sponsored her, took her in. She never saw her parents again, or any of them. She was sixteen." She sat up in the bed.

He sat next to her, put his arm around her. "That explains a lot."

"Not all of it. The conductor. The man who set it all up. Was my father."

"Kurt did that?"

"He created it. Traveled all over Central Europe, auditioning kids. To get out as many as he could he became an expert on Mahler, The Third Symphony, and the Symphony of A Thousand, so not just players; choruses and vocal soloists. They had to be good, to make it credible. So they could go on tour, get to France, and out of Europe."

"That's ingenious. I think I owe him an apology."

"No. My mother stayed with his orchestra here. And started sleeping with him. She wasn't sixteen anymore, she wasn't the first, and she wasn't the last, and then I happened. And he tried to make it work, and he couldn't, and he left her. Left us. Ben. She wouldn't take a penny from him, except for child support."

"Now I see where she was coming from, about...about me."

"She had it all wrong. You're the inverse of my father. He's a bad man who did a good thing. You're a good man who thinks he did a bad thing. And here's the thing I've been thinking. She was all alone. I couldn't leave her. I understand myself, finally. I think now, that's why it just fell out of my mouth, that it was just an affair—I wasn't going to leave her. Guilty, is how I would have felt if I'd ever come with you to Boston. When she moved in with Richard I could go only as far as Philadelphia. And then...I went to the store to find you the day after their wedding."

"Same as me," Ben said. "You weren't free to go. I wasn't free to stay."

She lay back. "First qualification for being a doc—ability to put others' needs before your own. God, I'm glad we unloaded all this baggage before I start the internship." She rolled toward him. "You did find an unwanted child."

"Just because you were an accident doesn't mean you were unwanted."

"I was unwanted. She might have become a soloist. Famous. Glamorous." She stopped. "Would you like to stop me at hopelessly neurotic, before I get full-on crazy?"

"Since October 1966," he said quietly. "Since October 1966 you have been very much wanted. More than words can say." He reached over.

"Just what are you doing there, Rothstein?"

"Proving you're wanted. Or would you rather have a picture in the Post Office?"

Her eyes closed as he moved his hand over her. "Once upon a time there… was a handsome prince who had (he kissed her neck, then her lips) been turned into a dishwasher. And he met a beautiful princess…"

She kissed him. "Who was actually a wicked witch, who cast a spell on him to make…him…believe…that…she was…a beautiful princess…"

"And he …Ahhh…he began to believe he was…a…handsome prince…"

"Mmm. You know what? The spell…MMMMMM… worked on both of them."

Their own place. Little Liesl was happy, ecstatically so. Dr. Mautner was another matter. The question gnawed at her, was she here because of him, would she be here if Benjamin Rothstein had never existed? Or if he'd gone to Harvard undergrad? Only met now, here? Or never? In bed, at peace after making love, she said, "You know the joke, 'Ginger Rogers did everything Fred Astaire did, but backwards and in high heels'."

"So you'll have to figure out how to do a pleural tap backwards and in high heels? Can't help you there, Dr. Mautner. I know a few tricks, but not that one. You know I'm a lousy dancer. Is this a way of saying you're nervous?"

"No, Ben. Terrified."

"Come on, Leece, you're building this up. It's the Harvard thing."

"At Woman's we sort of helped each other through. That's not going to happen here. Every cutthroat pre-med in the country, the worst of them, is here, am I right?"

"The med school was like that. They settle down, Leece. They aimed to get here and they got here. Believe me, learning to do this job swamps them. They don't start competing again until for jobs, in senior residency. We work in teams."

"Do I have to say: not necessarily, if you're a woman."

"Okay. Look. What gets you through. Got you this far, is thinking you have an edge, right? Even if you don't need one. Even if you *are* an edge. So. We're about the same size. Tomorrow I'll ask at the laundry for an extra set of whites. There are two procedures here that med studs learn, most other places they're intern procedures. Bone marrow samples and central lines. I have a bone marrow to tap, and a guy I absolutely know will need a central line. Know how to do those, and you're in. Come up to the ward with me and I'll walk you through both."

"Is that kosher?"

"Is possibly refusing you an internship here because we're a couple, or not working with you as an equal because you're a woman, kosher? Or right?"

"Rothstein Logic. Could be trouble for you. It really isn't exactly legal."

"Neither was occupying a college campus and desanctifying a cathedral, or deflowering an almost-underage Barnard girl, Dr. Mautner."

"That isn't the only thing I worry about, Ben. I've seen internship harden people. I mean, make them hard, uncaring. Numb to patients' suffering. I don't want that to happen to me."

He hugged her. "I know what you mean. I think it was happening to me, to some extent, until you showed up. Maybe we can keep it from happening to each other. Hold on to ourselves and each other. You've seen those procedures, marrow taps and CVPs?"

"Sure. Assisted at several, put in the anesthesia."

"See one, do one, teach one. And. One more thing I can show you. The Freak. Take a tour, introduce you around. After that, you can feel ready."

At Zero Hour they both suited up, Ben now in lab jacket, shirt and tie; Lisa in intern's tunic and floppy pants, pockets full of instruments. They looked at each other. She straightened his tie. Ben was going to sneak a kiss, but she said, "Ben, these last few days…I'm ready. You?" Instead he took her hand and they walked out of the apartment.

$\mathbf{At}$ Orientation, Teddy Edwards, now Chief Resident, welcomed the newbies to Boston. "You all know this is a center of the highest educational standards, with an accent," he said, "Best exemplified by the old joke: Guy gets into a cab at Logan Airport, asks the cabbie, Where can I get scrod? Cabbie thinks a minute, says, That's the first time I've ever heard that question in the pluperfect subjunctive." Nervous laughter, from the men. Lisa turned to a woman next to her (the only other female intern) and rolled her eyes.

And then it started, the 120-hour weeks, the sleepless nights, the exhaustion, the endless responsibility, the enslavement to the needs of others, very sick others, dying others. She'd had a preview in med school, as a fourth-year student, as a sub-intern; half the workload of an intern, but only for eight weeks. This was the full load, and it went on…forever. For Ben as first-year resident it wasn't much better; the responsibility was greater, and he had to supervise and teach teams of interns and students. They had the balm of each other, but also the challenge of maintaining the relationship. Times when he was on call Monday-Thursday-Sunday and she was on the juxtaposed Saturday-Tuesday-Friday they saw each other only at meals and when one or the other of them was exhausted after a night on call. But when it ran, the roller coaster still went to the top.

"Rothstein," Edwards said, "She's such a petite thing. You really think she can smack a chest hard enough to start a heart?"

"One way to know, Teddy. Let her smack you; see if she can start yours."

Days they both had off (rare, but they traded their on-call around with sympathetic colleagues) they spent walking around the city or browsing the numerous bookstores in Harvard Square ("Where," Ben said, "If you need a Hungarian-to-Cambodian dictionary you would have five choices"). On a rare weekend when they had coinciding days off they drove into the fall foliage in New Hampshire. They stopped to hike in a state park, decided to climb the mountain trail to a famous rock formation. "Too muddy for outdoor sex," Ben joked as they trudged uphill in thick woods.

"We share a bed now. No need to brush sand out of our asses." They worked their way up the moderately steep slope. "But Ben, you know what? Sometimes I'm so exhausted, as much as I'd like to, I'm just not that up for it."

"It's a way to recharge, Dr. Mautner. Didn't I once tell you about R&R?"

"Sex isn't always the answer," she said.

"No," he said. "Sex is the question. Yes, is the answer."

She laughed, but said, "It was, in college. This is different."

Around her she heard praise of Ben. That he didn't so much lead his teams as collaborate with them. And the nurses liked and respected him. She found this reassuring.

He heard she was being given shit. *She wants to find her way Stay out of it*

The reason Ben eventually bought one of those fancy bagel slicers is, one Saturday morning when he surprised Lisa with bagels and lox he was holding a bagel in his left hand while slicing it with a bread knife with his right. She heard him shout "Shit," and ran into the kitchen to find him rinsing a three-centimeter laceration in his left palm in cold water. "Must have hit an air pocket," he said. "Going to apply pressure."

"Let's see that." She opened his hand, looked at the welling blood. "Might need suturing, Pooh Bear." She brought him some sterile 4X4s and some tape for a temporary bandage; he held it while she wrapped. Blood quickly soaked the 4X4s. "So much for pressure. Come on. ER."

"Stupid," he grumbled as they walked the few blocks. The ER was as usual quiet on a Saturday morning, but they didn't want to bother anyone with this. "Just need a sterile room for some advanced first aid," he said to a nurse.

They took an empty cubicle; together (he one-handed)

gathered lidocaine ampoules, syringe, betadine and a suture kit. She drew up the first amp of lidocaine and unwrapped the makeshift bandage. Blood still welled. She expertly dabbed it up. "Deep breath, Rothstein," she said, and dumped the betadine over it. "Crybaby," she said when he winced. He picked up the lidocaine syringe with his right hand and put in the first injection himself. "Was that really necessary?" she said. "Tough guy." He grinned. She shook her head. "How about I take it from here." She injected through the numbed spot and the successive numbed areas, creating an anesthetized zone surrounding the laceration. "Assist," she said, and he dabbed away blood with a clean 4X4 as she opened the suture kit. "Keep my field clear," she said. He nodded as she pulled the curved needle through the flesh of first one, then the other side of the laceration with the hemostat, looped the thread around the tip and pulled through with the forceps. "Sponge," she said.

By the third stitch they had an audience of colleagues. "Come see this," Mortenson called. "This is unique. How the hell did you manage that, Rothstein?"

"Duel," she said, cutting the fourth suture. "He fought off two of the Capulet bravos but sustained a flesh wound." She finished stitching the laceration closed.

"Jewish breakfast wound," Ben said. "Slicing a bagel." The bleeding had stopped. They collaborated on a clean bandage.

"You know," a surgical chief resident he recognized said, "One of us could have taken care of that for you."

"I wanted a doctor I could trust," Ben said. "I've seen her suture a bear."

"My step-niece's teddy bear," she said as she bandaged him. "We'll bring another suture kit home and I'll take them out in a few days." Walking home she said, "Nice one, Rothstein. Wanting a doc you could trust."

"You have good hands, Dr. Mautner. I know that. Now they all do."

As she approached with her lunch tray Edwards was holding forth on his Army experience. "The tropics are quite a shock to a New Englander," he was saying. "You had to say a daily prayer that the A/C wouldn't quit, because you were wearing a white coat on top of a uniform." She took a seat far down the long table, next to a pretty First-Year. Edwards sat forward. "Mostly what we were dealing with was exotic forms of gonorrhea, so add a daily prayer that the penicillin supply held up…"

"How do you deal with this?" the First-Year murmured to her.

"Same way you deal with construction workers whistling at you in the street."

"…because Manila, the whole PI, is nonstop pussy, 24/7/365."

Acres of pussy "Or you could try this," she murmured to the First-Year, and turned toward the rest of the table. "So, Dr. Edwards, it got a rest every Leap Year?" Into the laughter she said, "This being an Evac Hospital, I assume there were some complicated casualty cases from that misbegotten bit of foreign policy in Vietnam?"

Edwards sat back. "Yes. Terrible wounds, of course, and we had to detox them, and treat malaria because when they were high they got lax about their antimalarials. And we had to work with the Trickcyclists on the dreams. Combat Fatigue…"

"PTSD, they're calling it now, at the Philly VA," she said…

"This is a bullshit admission," she said.

"I know it," Mortenson said. "Pre-eclampsia, but GYN is scared to have her on the floor with that high a blood pressure. Want us to bring it down before delivery. Edwards okayed it. Keeps good relations."

"What'll bring it down is having this baby. Which, she's gravida 8, could be any second. It could just walk out." She turned to the woman on the gurney. "Tienes dolor?"

"No mas," the patient said *hopefully meaning the headache.*

"Take her to the floor," Mortenson said. "I'll see what else is in the ER and meet you there."

She pushed the gurney onto an elevator, almost running Ben down. "We have to stop meeting like this," he said.

"Too late," she said, pushing the button for the Medicine floor. The doors shut and the elevator headed up. And just short of their floor, stopped. "Shit," she said.

He examined the control panel. "Have to hope the phone works." She moved around the gurney to give him room. He called the operator, asked for Engineering to deal with a stuck elevator. "And it would be nice if they hurry. We have a very pregnant woman aboard." The patient smiled contentedly. "Como se llama?" he said. She continued to smile contentedly at the elevator's roof.

"Señora Estevez," Lisa said. "She's a gravida 8, Ben." She saw his eyebrows rise. She put her hand on the patient's shoulder. "Señora Estevez?"

The phone rang. "They say at least ten minutes," Ben said.

Señora Estevez chose that moment to say, "Baby coming."

Lisa dropped the chart and pulled back the thin blanket. "No," she said. "Baby here." Anyway, the head almost was. She reached in to free the baby's shoulder and was rewarded with a lusty cry and a gush of fluid as it emerged. Ben whipped the blanket off, wrapped the baby and placed him on his mother's chest. Señora Estevez smiled broadly.

"We're going to have to cut the cord and deliver the placenta," Lisa said.

He pulled out his Swiss Army knife. "We need clamps," he said.

"Got it," she said, already pulling clips and hairpins from her hair, which cascaded out of its French twist as she clamped the cord close to the baby's navel with the hardware. Ben severed the cord and they worked together to pull the placenta out.

When the phone rang to tell them five more minutes the baby was crying enthusiastically. "You have a pregnant woman aboard?" the Engineering guy asked.

"Not anymore. A little speed please, and call Pediatrics, will you?" He opened his black bag and passed Lisa the blood pressure cuff and gauge; Senora Estevez raised her arm so Lisa could slip it around her bicep. "BP's down to 130 over 85. I don't see any sign of hemorrhage. Felicitades, que bonito bebe, Señora Estevez."

The elevator began to move. "Better hold the baby, Leece. Don't want him rolling off when we push this rig out of here. This is going to be a story for our grandchildren."

"For *her* grandchildren, Rothstein."

When the doors opened there was quite an audience. Lisa, her hair down, was cradling the now-peaceful baby. Ben was standing beside her, maneuvering the gurney. A Pediatrics intern took the baby; an OB resident took over at Señora Estevez' side.

"You guys work fast," Mortenson said. "When you got on the elevator you weren't even pregnant."

Even Lisa had to laugh. "I'm going to have to run downstairs to the gift shop for some hairpins. The ones I started up with clamped the cord."

"What the hell did you cut it with?"

Ben held up the Swiss Army knife. "Standard issue in the Mautner-Rothstein Obstetrics Pavilion."

"Shit," Edwards said. "You realize, you just did a jungle delivery in the middle of Massachusetts General Hospital? You did everything but christen it."

Walking home that night she said, "That really was pretty cool, Ben." She laughed. "Mautner-Rothstein Obstetrics Pavilion."

"That elevator will be known by that name for a few years at least. While our cohort are here. I should ask the parents to send my Boy Scout woodburning set so I can make a plaque."

She laughed again. "We really did do everything but christen him."

"Yeah. We used to be better at finding baptismal fonts when we needed them. You looked great cradling the baby, Leece." He didn't see her frown.

Winter closed in again, the famous New England winter. Skies varied between the colors of aluminum, iron, platinum, silver; all the gray metallic elements. "Only consolation," Ben said, "Is Tricky Dick Nixon looks to be on the way to getting his." Their lives were mostly confined to the hospitals and the apartment. The roller coaster still went all the way to the top, just not every time. Sleep was occasionally interrupted by their dreams from the Occupation. "I guess any anxiety triggers those," she said. They began sleeping spooned, his arm around her, and the dreams receded.

They were in a tough spot. The pneumonia patient's breathing (complicated by intravenous heroin use) was more and more labored. They'd been over all the numbers; she'd even gotten a radial arterial blood gas, a moderately difficult procedure, but his peripheral veins were shot and they couldn't seem to keep up with his fluids. Edwards was senior resident, Matthews the junior; they conferred outside the room. Edwards was irritated, anxious; this patient was the son of someone important to the Attending who had arranged the admission. "A cut-down is what we need. We should call the surgeons."

"Peripheral circulation's collapsing. He won't survive the wait," she said. "We don't know what's going on at the core. Wouldn't hurt to know central venous pressure. We should drop a central line, hydrate him that way."

"Just like hearing Rothstein." Edwards said.

She smiled sweetly, looked around. "Don't see him anywhere nearby. Amazingly I managed to think of that all by myself, with my own little lady brain."

"All right, Mautner, settle down. I'm just...It was a dumb thing to say, alright?"

"We could wait for him to die while we argue, or he can die waiting for the surgeons," Matthews said.

Edwards sighed. "Do it," he said. "Be careful. Hepatitis risk."

After, Matthews said, "It was a good idea. But it might have saved time and hassle if you'd let me suggest it."

"Why? Because I'm a woman?"

"Because for Edwards it's a hierarchy. Interns don't *suggest* to a Chief Resident, thinks Teddy, a resident does. It's

friendly advice I'm giving you. Will you take it?"
""Under advisement," she said. "Thanks."

They ate lunches with their teams, or both teams ate
together when they could. She was at lunch with her team
and they were discussing the Chinese patient they'd admitted
the night before. "Could have Chinese Black Cock Disease,"
Edwards said. When the table looked up he said, "So this guy
notices one morning that his penis is turning black, and he runs
to the doctor. Doctor says, No help for it old son, you have
Chinese Black Cock Disease, we're going to have to amputate.
Guy says, Not without a second opinion you're not, and he goes
to another doctor. He goes to three more doctors in a week, and
they all say the same thing, Have to amputate. Then he realizes,
Wait a minute, this is Chinese Black Cock Disease..." She was
holding her coffee cup poised at her lips, aware they were all
watching her surreptitiously. "...so I should see a Chinese doctor.
So he goes to Chinatown and there's a doctor's office, he goes in
the old building, climbs three flights of creaky stairs, and in the
office is this little old man, face full of wisdom, he shows him his
cock and says Doctor they all say they have to amputate..."
     She moved the coffee cup away from her lips and said,
"And the little old Chinese doc says, Oh no, no need to amputate.
In two days, fall off by self."
     That night she told Ben, who roared with laughter at
her poise, not at the old joke. "How do you like me?" she said
grimly. "Dr. Lisa Mautner, one of the boys."
     "One of the team," he said.
     "I don't know, Ben. Every time I start to feel like I'm
really a full member of a team Edwards does something to
undermine it, make me feel like an interloper."
     When one of them was on call and the other wasn't
they'd meet for dinner at the hospital cafeteria. One night, when
it looked like the Vietnam War might just heat up again, the
conversation came around to the Columbia campus occupation.
     "You were Class of '68 Rothstein," Firman said, "Where
were you?"

He looked over at her; she shrugged slightly *What the hell, we resolved, no more lying or secrecy* He kept eating, casually said, "In Mercer Hall."

"Half the campus claims they were in it. You're full of shit, Rothstein."

"Okay, I'm full of shit."

"He isn't," she said.

"How would you know?"

"Because so was I. Ben was our medic."

"Sure. Not buying it. At Mercer everyone was tear gassed and busted."

"Not everyone," she said. "Quite a few of us were behind where the gas landed and scattered around the building in the clouds."

"Is that where you guys met?" someone asked.

"No," Firman said. "I was there when they met. Rothstein was the student lab assistant at my and her Organic lab. We were giving her shit and Rothstein came in and broke it up. Confronted the asshole leading the hazing."

He saw the alarm in her eyes. "That was just a momentary thing," she said. "We didn't really meet until Mercer Hall. And, Firman, you're leaving out the part where I had already confronted the asshole. We met up again when I came up to interview for the internship. I asked to shadow an intern, recognized his name on the list..." she shrugged. Never missed a forkful. "Close one, Rothstein," she said later, in bed.

"Could have passed on it."

"I don't know. I get in these moods, I get sick of the whole self-control thing. One unguarded conversation. Just one. But we have to keep lying about our undergrad thing."

"I think it's a hoot when we tell them the truth and they don't believe it," he said.

"You think that's amusing? You find people that amusing, Ben?"

"Not our patients. I'm talking about our colleagues and co-workers. They're fools. Where it concerns you. Me. Us. In college they thought we were geeks and power tools.

They thought we couldn't possibly even talk to each other, much less…"

"There we agree. I never liked how everyone thought of me," she said. "I don't like how they think about you. About us. I don't like living to their expectations. Hah. Do you know Herodotus, the story about the Phoenicians that sailed around Africa? They told everyone the sun was in the north at high noon when they sailed far enough south, so no one believed them. But centuries later, when the earth was known to be spherical and tilted on its axis, it was the reason we know they did do it."

"So if they just had all the facts, we wouldn't be seen as geeks and power tools anymore? I don't think facts, even if we told them, are going to change fools' minds."

"I guess we have to suffer them, if we're to have friends. And we need friends. I do, anyway. This was easier at Woman's, with friends. Here, I'm not really part of any team. I know it. None of the few women here are. We're tolerated, treated like some exotic species, by the Attendings and the older Residents. The only time I ever felt like I was, was when Maggie Roth covered for Matthews one night. Introduced herself by telling me what a fan she is of my father." She was silent for a time. "I'd like to get away from thinking about this for at least a little while. I worry, Rothstein. No real friends but each other, nothing but the job and sleep. We need a life."

"Stop. This isn't life, Mautner. This is medical training. We all get force fed ten years of experience in every year and go quietly crazy. If they wanted us to have friends they'd have given us some. Most of us have no one. We have each other. Marry me."

"There's a romantic proposal. You know what the divorce rate is among medical trainees? I damn well do. Plus, how would I ever get to be seen as an individual person in this profession, independent of you? A man doesn't ever have to think about that."

"Well, it isn't a proposal, it's an invitation. Always open. Always."

"It isn't the answer."

* * *

New Year's Eve, which was typically a quiet time (because of Attendings' vacations and patients not wanting elective procedures during the holidays) the House Staff staged a floating party in the cafeteria. "Tradition," Ben told her. "Revived by Teddy Edwards upon his return from the military. Catered by his family of ex-Deans and Department Chairs. No booze, of course. Everyone who's off call's invited, and if you're on call you can drop in and stay until your beeper goes off."

She was in fact off call, if tired after her previous night's On Call, and she went, hoping Ben (on call) could join for at least a little while. *We need friends Anyway I do* It was mildly boisterous, waiting for the midnight Ball Drop; some off-call people had snuck some liquor in. Unaccompanied women gradually gathered in a corner.

Maggie Roth was there. "Will Ben be here?" she asked.

Here's a friend I could make "I hope he can drop by. He's on call upstairs."

"How in the world did you two get together? I heard, you met in college?"

Her alarm went off. "Just casually, really. There might have been some sparks. When I came up here for interviews I asked to shadow an intern, recognized his name on the list, spent the day with him…the sparks ignited."

Edwards, off call and mildly buzzed, convivial, making the rounds, stopped long enough to say, "A Happy New Year to you two. I think, if we are ever to have an answer to The Woman Question, here in this corner is where we'll find it."

"Groton to Harvard," Maggie Roth said. "Too much time in monasteries, Teddy. Not enough opportunity to meet women as *people*. Or Blacks or Hispanics, if they weren't carrying mops. We weren't allowed in the treehouse."

"True, I suppose. You're two of the ones who broke in."

"Broke in?"

"I mean it as a compliment, Mags."

"Is Medicine a profession, Teddy, or a priesthood? Women are allowed to join, despite what you often seem to think."

"Look, of course I...it's all just...hazing. Everyone gets hazed..."

"It isn't a fraternity either," Lisa said, just as Ben found them. Teddy walked away. "What is it with him, anyway?" Lisa asked.

Maggie, shook her head. "One horrifying possibility is, he wants us, and he doesn't know how to do anything but stick our pigtails in the inkwell."

"Allow me to offer a second theory," Ben said. "With a name like Colson Bradford Edwards, the Bradford going back to the fucking Mayflower...It's a lot to live up to. And, live down. Colson Bradford Edwards, the Fourth no less, of Groton and Harvard. He's constantly trying to maintain credibility with his peers. Easiest way: the jock dash frat boy manner endemic in those institutions of learning."

"With male peers, you mean. Joining them in establishing and maintaining that jock and frat boy atmosphere we all so know and love, and writing off the women," Maggie said. "I feel so much better now."

"Iphigenias," Lisa said. "Sacrifices to further some man's career. So we get Teddy a fair wind for eventual Department Chairmanship?"

"He also writes off the male peers who get bullied the same way, for not being jocks or frat boys, or who prefer books to sports. I get where you're coming from because I never loved it either. I was the kid who loved science and literature, never good at sports, and I got bullied in the same way. The trick is to not be intimidated. Damn," he said as his beeper went off. He looked at the number. "Off to Admission land. Well. Happy New Year. Nice almost seeing you, Maggie. See you in the AM, Leece."

"So we should learn judo?" Maggie said to Lisa.

"He had the advantage of an older brother, big guy, something of a brawler, in his anti-Semitic little town. I try not to tolerate humiliation or intimidation either."

"Explains how he acted at our Chest Examination lab." She told Lisa the story.

"That's Ben. He always puts it as hating bullies." She hesitated, took a plunge. "I came to see something else. He was a chem major in college, and he thinks about things in chemical terms. He thinks what we all are, is complex organic chemistry, and more than 99% of our chemistry is identical. No other man I was ever with was like him, acting like there isn't a nickel's worth of difference between men, women, Black, brown, white. He sees in chemical terms variant ways of being human. Right and left isomers. Or complimentary strands of DNA. You're into my father's music. Ben seems to me to see male and female, white, Black, and brown as variations on a theme. Or, different arrangements of the same music. A violin and an oboe can both sound a perfect 440 cycle A and tune the orchestra, right? Ben always *acts* like he knows this, without being told. He just does it. Considerate without being *patronizing*. Well. Maybe except when he's *explaining* Teddy Edwards. Or maybe when he's being brotherly-protective."

"That's how he was about the Chest Examination exercise." Maggie said. "He took a fair bit of ribbing for helping me out. Gave it right back. And he takes no shit from Teddy Edwards, either." She told Lisa about Ben's response to Teddy's remark about her.

"Touching," Lisa said. "Look, it's outrageous that the women aren't given their own room. How would the men feel if they had to take their pants off to learn how to examine the genitourinary system? There are more of us every year, but we're still a tiny minority in this boys' club. If I ever have time for anything but work and sleep I'd love to start a woman's support group. Trainees from all levels. What do you think? With enough of us, and more women faculty every year, we could protest. Among other things, set up a room of our own, for that exercise. With female instructors, too. "

"I'm in. It would be nice to know when we're talking to our colleagues they aren't thinking *I've seen her tits*. We'd have male sympathizers. Well, one we can count on."

"Yes. But it might be important to do it ourselves."

Ben got home in time to see her wake New Year's Day,

to hear what Maggie had told her about the Chest Examination exercise and his responses to Teddy. "Said you were very gentlemanly, Ben. Knightly. Standing up for her personhood. And mine."

"I was angry for her. And for you. I'm glad at Woman's you were spared any such crap." Her sudden stricken look took him by surprise. "What?" he said.

She got up, forced herself to control her voice, her face. "I wasn't. Spared, I mean. We had a visiting lecturer from Penn. Nister. Big expert on burns. Told us to call with any questions, so I called him. He was very accommodating, the bastard, invited me down, to his office. And." She stopped. Caught herself. He went to her, but she motioned him away, grabbed a robe and paced. "He offered me exam answers and a job in his lab if… Then…he tried to grab me. The son of a bitch."

"Shit. I…You got out okay?"

She began to shake, and he put his arms around her. "The things that almost happen. I got up and slammed the door on him. Nister. Professor fucking Nister. I thought I got out okay, but obviously it's left a scar. I didn't know I was still so angry."

"On Adolescent I saw a surgical resident pull something nearly like that on a patient, a seventeen year old girl. I threatened to report it to the head of Peds. Dragged him in to apologize to her. Holy shit, Leece. I'm sorry. Did you…what did you do?"

"What could I do, Ben? I never told anyone, until now. I wanted to report it, but who to? And, no witnesses, so who would believe it? Believe *me*? He could always say it was me who tried to seduce *him*. A woman can't risk that. I didn't want to end up like my Barnard schoolmate, in the New York Times." He nodded, and hugged her to him.

Edwards was already there with her team at lunch; no choice but to join the table. The minute *the second*, she sat down and settled her tray he said, "It's World War Two, and this Boston women's club is having a speaker, a Free Dutch pilot, Blitz veteran, big handsome blonde guy, all the young ones are lubricating, and one of the old biddies gets up to introduce him, says (here he did his best Old Boston Brahmin Talking-Through-Her-Nose), Ladies this is Captain Hans Brinker of the Royal Air Force, here to tell us what it's like to shoot down Germans, and the guy gets up and says, Vell, I'm on his tail, und I shoot down one of ze fokkers, and here's anozzer, und I shoot down anozzer vun uv ze fokkers, and the old biddy gets up and says, 'Ladies, a Fokker is a type of German aeroplane, and the Dutchman says…"

"No, zese fokkers vas flying Mezzerschmitts," Lisa said tiredly.

Edwards glared at her. "Has Rothstein told you *every* dirty joke?"

"No, Teddy," she said, "I heard them all in elementary school."

"Oh, *sound*," someone said.

"He does it to intimidate," she told Ben over dinner. "I refuse to be intimidated."

"Way to go, Dr. Mautner. You're tough."

"Am I, Ben? I'm goddamned sick of being tough. I'm smart, and I'm skilled, and I'm capable. Why should I have to be *tough*? Why?"

She leaned her head against the cold ward window, eyes closing. She may have actually slept for a long moment, roused by a friendly hand on her shoulder. "Want to go down for a cup of coffee? We're going to need it." She knew he was right; the snow was letting up, the plows were out, and the ambulances full of new admissions would be right behind them. She followed Firman to the cafeteria. "You've been looking more and more unhappy, Lisa. What gives?"

She looked out at the freezing night. "I'm sick of winter. And of being so tired."

"This is my fifth Boston winter," Firman said, sipping his coffee, "And my last. I'm applying for Residencies in the sun. Florida. Arizona. Southern Cal."

"Why not, Mickey? With Harvard credentials you can

probably get in anywhere."

"You'll have them now too. Why not come along? And not see another winter in your life." She laughed. "I'm serious, Lisa. You look so unhappy, I've been wondering if your thing with Rothstein's starting to unravel."

She snapped fully awake. "Why would you think that?"

"I know him, Lisa, have for four years. None of his relationships last longer than a few weeks. You hold the record, but I know him. A word to the wise."

I'm tired And I'm tired of "You know nothing," she said. "We were secretly going together the whole time in Organic. And after. For over a year. Almost two."

He looked into her face, trying to see how deep the joke ran. "Christ, Mautner, you almost had me going there." *Maybe Ben had a point Fool I'm too tired to care*

"You know what we used to call you?" *Yeah Mouthner. Mount Her* "The Jewish Natalie Wood. Maria in West Side Story, the movie version."

Jesus "Are we flirting, Mickey?"

"Yes. We definitely are. Not for the first time. Senior year. Embryology study group. You wouldn't give me the time of day." He laughed. "I consider Ben to be a very lucky man, running into you here. I was right next to you at that lab table. If it wasn't for that idiot Boland putting you off all of us… Then you gave off this vibe, in Embryo, senior year, shot me down, shot all of us down before we could even get off the ground."

"I think I kept expecting Ben to turn up on his bike." *Huh I guess I did*

"Right. On his bike…wait. Wait a minute. He didn't have the bike until med school. How would you have known about the bike?"

"Because he had it all through college, but he couldn't afford to park it up on the campus so he kept it behind his parents' store on Orchard Street. Kept it registered in Jersey, too, for the lower insurance rates. We used to take runs up to Bear Mountain for picnics. To study together." She smiled. "Among other things."

He gaped at her. "You're full of…You didn't get together until you got here, you both said. Hopped into bed with him, like the others. I don't know what he's got…"

That does it "I didn't *just hop into bed* with him here. And we didn't just go to Bear Mountain. We spent days, whole weekends, at the Hotel Pennsylvania, across from the station, Friday night to Sunday morning, when he had to help out at the store. Our parents thought we were on the campus and our roommates thought we were home. We read, and talked, went to movies and museums, or just spent days in bed. Until we had this stupid fight about him coming up here instead of staying in the City for med school. I applied up here partly hoping to restart a relationship that should never have ended."

"Wait, I remember. There was a rumor about you two. But he denied it."

"Of course. We both did. I could have been expelled, remember?"

Firman continued to look skeptical. "Okay. Sure. What kind of bike?"

"Honda CB450. Also known as a Black Bomber." Firman looked at her. Hard. "And I bet he kept those Jersey plates in Boston. Cheaper insurance."

"Jesus Christ, Mautner." He shrugged. "Almost good enough. So he told you about the bike. And the Jersey plates. So. Describe the bike and the plates."

"New Jersey motorcycle plate. About the size of a small textbook. Orange numbers on black, E over H, 436T. Cranky. You had to kick it down twice to start it."

Firman rocked back in his chair. Looked at her. "Holy shit," he muttered. "You two were really…? Wow. Under that power tool façade, Lisa Mautner, Outlaw Biker Chick. No wonder you aced Organic."

"There's the other reason we kept it secret. That people would think that. I aced Calculus before I met him. And Embryo too, remember? I have a brain, Mickey." *Jerk* "So let's see, I have two choices to explain how I'm with Ben. Either I'm a slut who hopped into bed with a guy I barely knew, or I somehow

owe all my academic success to him. Which is it, Mickey? I
mean, before I run off with you because it's cold outside."
  "Jesus, Lisa, I only meant…I'm sorry. Well. I always
thought you had a lot of nerve." He looked away. "So, all that,
just from taking Boland on?"
  "Sure, Mickey. You slay the dragon, you get the
princess." She took a sip of coffee. "Schmuck. Do you really
think it was that simple? What Ben Rothstein *has* is that he's
as interested in what's between my ears as what's between my
legs." She stood to leave. "Tell anyone any of this and I'll deny
it." She checked her watch. "Mickey. Here's the time of day: It's
2:36 AM, and I have work to do."
  "Our secret's out," she told Ben bitterly. "I was stupid
sleepy. I got to choose between being thought of as a slut, or a
clever cheat at Organic Chem. Can't win, Ben. It was a relief
to confront it openly, how women are judged. I said I'd deny
it if he talked. He's leaving for sunnier climes, so it should be
no problem."

  It felt to them sometimes as if every morning they woke
and assumed the Doctor mask, the Doctor persona, like a role, a
theater they were trapped in, every day a matinee, some days also
an evening performance. Sometimes it felt to each like a cage.
With time it felt like a uniform, a suit of armor, they donned
every morning. After enough time, they knew, when they had
been doctors longer than they hadn't been, it would feel like
a self.
  They got a membership at the Museum of Fine Arts and
went when they could. They were on call for their birthdays,
but For Valentine's Day he gave her a battered ex-Boston Public
Library copy of Asimov's *World of Carbon* he'd found at a
used bookstore, with a suitably romantic card. She laughed and
hugged him tight. *Good enough for the moment But* It was a
thought she couldn't ever completely banish, and could ignore
for only so long. A thought love could not completely banish. A
thought everything always came back to. *Are we equals or not* It
made a distance…

The old man knew this recurrence of his leukemia was the last; he was, they all knew from his bone marrow biopsy, terminal. She thought he was asleep when she tried, as gently as she could, to change his IV without waking him, apologized when she thought she'd wakened him. Eyes still closed, he said, "It's okay. I'll have all the sleep I'll ever need soon."

"But you need rest now," she said, as sincerely as she could. *God knows I do*

"Don't worry," he said. "The Universe will go on. I don't run it."

It did just go on and on. Even aching with fatigue, they often could not sleep, kept awake by an unstoppable stream of thought, anxiety about what might come the next day. Or dreams of the last. One night he found her in bed fully dressed, staring at the ceiling. "This must be the afterlife," she said, "Because I'm dead. Not dead tired, dead."

"You need sleep."

"Been trying. Brain won't stop."

"Okay. This is easy. What got you to sleep when you were a kid?"

He thought she'd say something like counting sheep, or ask to be held, but she said "Bedtime story. Winnie the Pooh. But even he was once my patient."

"We'll have to get a copy. Want a chapter from *The World of Carbon*? No? Snow White? That's one I know. You're certain I'm not going to hear something about infantilizing you, at some future point? I may require consent in writing."

"Moments when I am totally regressed, you are allowed to infantilize me at my request, Rothstein." She patted the bed. "Sit."

"Okay. So. Snow White was a beautiful princess who lived in a beautiful castle with her beautiful mother the Queen and her beautiful father the King. Until one day her evil aunt, her mother's evil sister, gave her mother a poisoned apple, optioned the autopsy and married the King. Snow was pretty bummed.

Plus she had a problem. She was now about Tanner Stage VII: built like a brick shithouse."

"So this isn't the Disney version."

"No. The original. From the Bible. So her aunt slash stepmother is a prize narcissistic personality, who can't stand the competition for Fairest, her Magic Mirror tells her Snow is the Fairest Of Them All, so she gets out some flasks and condensers and such and injects another apple with..."

"Strychnine. Cyanide. No. Thallium. Mercury..." she said.

"...the stuff they used to put on the meat loaf at Jack's," he said, "And feeds it to Snow and turns her over to her faithful evil henchman, whose name actually *was* Henschmensch, to dispose of the body. Henschmensch hasn't had a raise in like forever, he notices the body is still breathing, notices the apple didn't go all the way down; big chunk is lodged in the upper airway." Her eyes were closed but she was starting to grin. "So he figures, the best place for a princess in a vegetative, or rather, fruitive, state is with a set of round-the-clock, three-shifts caregivers: The Seven Dwarfs. He brings her there, and they roll out a gurney, put her to bed, start an IV, and put in a consult for a handsome prince to do royal CPR, which is the nonsurgical approach to this condition. A handsome prince shows up and kisses her..."

"And her eyes open and she marries him," she said. "Nice try, Rothstein."

"Nope. Wrong procedure. One of the dwarfs, Doc, pushes the Prince out of the way, listens for breath sounds, grabs a laryngoscope, takes a look down her throat, calls the Prince an idiot, calls for a pair of sterile tongs, fishes out the piece of apple and pulls the laryngoscope. Snow wakes up, takes a look at the Prince, then sees Doc with the piece of apple. Bang. Love at first sight. Big wedding. Moral: Don't waste your time with handsome princes. Find a short doc who knows what he's doing."

"Or become one." She looked at him. "Did you ever reach the burnout point?"

"I did. Almost a year ago. I was saved by a fairy tale.

A beautiful princess I thought was gone forever suddenly turned up."

The next time she was on call on a Saturday he succeeded in finding a Best of Glenn Miller album in decent condition at a used record store off Harvard Square. Then they could, when really low, dance. Which worked. Briefly.

She knew something was wrong the minute she saw him out the window. He dragged himself out of the VW, kicked the door shut *Jeez Ben don't do that* His usual brisk pace was a trudge, as if through deep snow. Or deep grief. When he came in he silently emptied his pockets, slowly and carefully, as if taking inventory. His turn to stretch out and stare at the ceiling.

"Do you want to tell me about it, Rothstein?" she said. And when he didn't answer, "Ben?" When he still didn't answer she put a hand on his shoulder. Then on his cheek. Kissed him. "Talk to me, Ben."

As if from a great distance he said, "I killed someone today Leece."

"You did not."

"I did. I was putting in a central line and it must have kinked and I must have pulled back a touch, and I felt it go. Felt the tip snap. Embolized straight to her lung. Breathing was already compromised. Couldn't get her restarted."

"How old?"

"Does it make a difference? As old as she was going to get. I had to fill out the death certificate. I'm supposed to have good hands, Leece."

"You have good hands, Ben. When we were apart it was your hands I thought of."

"Nice try, Leece, really nice try, but…"

"Ben, you know those trochars have burrs. Everything we do, a certain number of times it's going to slit the tubing. And we know …"

"Yes we do. We know to not pull back. I mean, I know I've probably killed patients before, something I did or didn't do, and the next day the bed's empty and I'll never know what, but then…this one, I know what I did. "

"Ben, I think we, us, not just the drugs and the equipment, we have a certain failure rate. It's supposed to curve down, but it never goes to zero. Nothing biological does. We're just flesh, Ben. You always say: Just chemistry."

"I'm supposed to know what to do. Always supposed to know something to do."

"There was nothing to do. Not this time."

"Then I'm supposed to know that. And I don't seem to."

"It's a big universe, and it doesn't necessarily like us, and Benjamin Rothstein doesn't control it. Let yourself know it, Ben. Let yourself. It's okay. It's okay that sometimes there's nothing you can do." She knew he was thinking of Morty. "We're just chemistry, Ben. It's okay." He reached for her then. She lay next to him and held him. Finally he cried. Just a few dry sobs, really, but it was enough.

In early spring, trees beginning to be in leaf, she began the dreaded, exhausting ER rotation; 24 hours on, 24 off. With weather warming, people were out doing stupid things to themselves and each other; ambulances were able to make it through the streets so recently closed by record snowfalls. It was busy, without surcease.

Dinner with the entire team, plus Teddy Edwards, making himself felt as Chief ER Resident. *He could have sat anywhere, with other teams, with Attendings* she thought. Everyone except Teddy was eating as quickly and efficiently as possible, hoping to have eaten enough before a beeper went off, but Teddy insisted on telling a joke. "So this 80-year-old nun is admitted, end stage renal disease, she knows she's going, and all she keeps saying is, I wish I was Sarah Pipilini, I wish I was Sarah Pipilini. No one can figure it out. So she dies, and they're cleaning out the bedside table, and there's a week-old newspaper, and the headline is: Sahara Pipeline Laid by 100,000 Men."

There was laughter Lisa didn't join. "Don't you ever get tired of it? Don't you ever give it a rest?" She stood and walked off, leaving her tray.

"Goodness," Edwards said, grinning. "What'd I say? One you don't know?"

She was teamed with a female Third-Year that night when they brought in the fourteen-year-old boy with severe electrical burns. The ambulance radioed; all hands on deck. Teams from Pediatrics, Surgery, Medicine…they needed some of everything. "Because," she told the Third-Year as they readied a sterile room, "Electrical burns are especially nasty. A subject I got to know well. I saw them in Philadelphia. The big expert was a guy named Nister…" The Third-Year watched her shake her head as if to clear it. "The kids play on the tracks, climb on the tops of the boxcars, reach out to steady themselves and grab the eleven-thousand-volt overhead line that runs the trains. It's night; he might have been trying to break into freight cars looking for, like, bicycles."

"Oh shit," the Third-Year said.

"Yes, shit. Electricity travels down conductive tissue; nerve, muscle, blood vessels, exits whatever is touching a conducting surface. It heats and coagulates blood, choking off circulation to tissue all along the way. It's third-degree burns all along its path. We have to hope it entered and exited close together."

But it hadn't. It was as she said; the kid had grabbed the catenary line and had been touching metal parts on the roof of a boxcar at both ankles. The current had blasted through the arm, both legs, chest, back and abdomen. By the Rule of Nines, she told the Third-Year, the kid didn't have a chance. "You add it up. Each leg 18%, the arm 9%, the chest plus abdomen plus back, 36% of body surface…"

"It's hopeless," Edwards said. "It's 81% third degree burns. Not survivable." Something they all knew. "It doesn't matter what we do. You ladies take this."

The boy was conscious when they brought him in, conscious and talking. *God, I even wish Nister was here* Burnt flesh hung in sheets, pink dermis, even muscle, exposed in places. He smelled like burned popcorn. The surgeons went to work immediately to relieve the pressure on blood vessels closed by the swelling of surrounding tissue, trying to forestall gangrenous necrosis. The pediatricians tried to find a vein in the unaffected arm, even knowing a routine IV would never keep up with the massive fluid and electrolyte loss of 81% third-degree burns. The Peds resident tapped her on the shoulder. "Word is you're the go-to for central lines," he said.

She went for the equipment. "Ever seen a central line put in?" she asked the Third-Year, who was barely keeping back tears.

"No."

"You're about to."

"He's dying. Why do this?"

"Because he's fourteen, and maybe he isn't. Because maybe he got to us in time. Because maybe the World's Best Hospital will make a miracle. Because we don't get to make that call. And if he does die, you're going to learn something, a procedure or two that may save someone else's life next week. What should we hang?"

The Third-Year shaped up. "D5NS?"

"Right. Good." She pierced a bottle of 5% Dextrose in Normal Saline solution, hung it, opened the line to make sure it ran, closed it and looped it over the bottle. She gloved up and felt along the right clavicle for the notch. She leaned over the boy. "Nathan," she said. "I'm going to numb it up here to put a needle in a big vein (she touched him at the spot) so we can get fluid into you." She rubbed the area with Betadine, let the Third-Year raise a bleb of lidocaine at the clavicular notch, and opened the trochar pack. She felt once more for the notch and pushed the big needle through. Blood was there when she pulled out the obturator. "Now," she said, "We feed in the tube, pushing forward through the trochar. And we do NOT pull back, because there's a bug in these things, sometimes the trochar has a little burr at the tip, a manufacturing problem, and if you pull back you risk cutting the tube and it floats off into the bloodstream, through the right heart to become a pulmonary embolus." *Which for this kid would be a mercy*, she thought. She concentrated on pushing the plastic tubing, guiding it by feel and by wish into the superior vena cava. When she judged it was there she signaled the Third-Year to push a 4X4 gauze pad down as she slowly, gently, rotated the trochar and pulled it back out along the tubing. They hooked up the IV. She put her hand on the boy's shoulder. "You okay, Nathan?"

"I can't feel anything."

A surgeon looked up. "That was pretty slick, for a Medicine resident."

"I'm an intern," she said, and opened the sliding valve to start the fluid.

They worked on him all night, taking turns talking to him as he drifted in and out of consciousness. But at dawn he died anyway.

She came home around 8:30. Ben had been on call the night before too, for his Cardiology elective month; a tough consult had taken him over to Boston City but he'd gotten back just as the sky was lightening at around 5:15. He'd considered picking her up at the ER but knew it could be hours before everything was locked down and she could leave. He caught a nap and woke when he heard her come in, got up to make coffee. Whatever had happened she would have had a harder night at the ER than anything a specialty consultant, no matter how junior, could have had, and her face told him it was, whatever it was, even worse than that. She threw her keys and black bag on the table; the keys went skittering off onto the floor. He started to retrieve them but she just walked on and he followed her into the bedroom. "Rough one."

"Yes."

"Want to talk?"

"No."

"Want coffee?"

"No." She started to undress, and he went over to hug her. She shrugged away from him. "Get away from me, Ben. This isn't the time."

"For a hug?"

"A hug? And that would be all? Get out of here, Ben. Don't touch me."

"I just wanted…"

"You just wanted what? It's always sex with you, isn't it. All of you. That's what it comes down to. And always did. Oh, the poor Barnard girl is being bullied, rescue her and get laid. She wants help with Organic Chem, tutor her and get laid. She wants to go to medical school, keep tutoring her, score again. She wants to go to Harvard for post-grad, wow, jackpot, move her in and get laid whenever you want. Only not now, Ben."

He was open-mouthed with astonishment. "Is that what you really think? Is that what you think I'm about? Only for the sex? Do you really think that's me?"

"I don't know, Ben. No, I don't think…I think more than anything I need to sleep, and so do you; then maybe we can talk…"

"Yeah, you get some sleep." He slammed out of the room, the feeling of regret a sudden memory. *Calm down. Something really terrible must have happened.* To slow his heart he counted to ten chemically *methane, ethane, propane, butane, pentane, hexane, heptane, octane, nonane, decane*…How right was she? *You wanted her from the first time at Jack's.* Yes. *From the time she came to the supply room window about the missing piece of glassware?* Maybe. *You think you have to justify wanting to get laid little bro?* So what? No matter how pure, Love has to start somewhere. In the chemistry. Loving begins in desiring. Caring begins in loving. A wave of tenderness, of caring for her, washed over him *No, Mautner, this time you don't get rid of me so easily.* He had some orange juice, tried to read some abstracts from the latest New England Journal of Medicine, but his eyes kept closing. After half an hour of nearly falling into a doze he heard her stir and went to check on her. She was wide awake, staring at the ceiling. She had obviously been crying. She was in bra and panties, having gotten no farther toward a nightgown when whatever it was overtook her. "You're still here," she said.

"Still here."

She shook her head. "I probably wouldn't be, if you talked to me like that."

"I thought about it," he said. "Once was enough."

She nodded. "I'm so sorry. I hope you know that was despair and exhaustion talking."

"Been there myself."

"Help me, Ben. I can't sleep. I haven't really slept in a few nights."

He pulled a quilt over her. "How can I help?"

She smiled, patted the bed beside her. "You can start by forgetting that woman who was here a little while ago. I don't know who she was, but she has an awful temper. Hold me?" He took off his pants, got under the quilt beside her and put his arm around her shoulders. She snuggled down and leaned into his chest. He kissed the top of her head, stroked her hair. It smelled of alcohol, betadine and hospital cleaning fluid. "Tell me a bedtime story, Ben. I've tried everything else."

He was silent for a few minutes, stroking her hair, looking down the length of her. "I don't know, Leece. I'm at least half asleep myself. If I had a story it would be about a terribly lonely young alchemist, and one day a brilliant, beautiful young woman alchemist comes to his door… Are you still awake?"

"Mmmm."

"A short version is, she wants to learn alchemy with him, and she wasn't like any alchemist he'd ever met; she cures his terrible loneliness." He could feel her body making the small jerks and shudders he knew meant she was beginning to fall asleep. He continued gently stroking her hair. "Aside from alchemy, he's a complete idiot and she asks him to leave her alone." His eyes were closing again. "She begged him. And he did. He told himself he would find another. But not one was like her."

Her eyes were closed now; he thought she was asleep. But she murmured, "How does it end?"

Half asleep, he said, "I want it to end happily. But I don't know how it ends."

She slept. And, after a few minutes, so did he.

He woke to an ambulance's wail. *Will this be our lives' soundtrack?* They had rolled apart. She was propped on one elbow looking down at him, her hair cascading over her face and onto his chest. "Did you sleep?" he said.

"Yes. And I may have a story," she said. "It starts with Once upon a time, there was a King and a Queen and a Princess. She shifted slightly. "I think a short version is: The Queen is a sorceress who could bring calm and love with her lute, which was the way she had enchanted the King. But the King roamed. The sorceress queen began to doubt her powers, which the young Princess…"

"A very intelligent girl."

"…Yes indeed, a very intelligent girl, can see, but since she's so young, understand only imperfectly when the King roamed and didn't return. At least the screaming fights were over. The King sends the Princess gifts, many from quite far away, but he never gives the greatest gift she could wish: Himself. She didn't know he never could. Hoping to summon back his love and regard, she goes to study alchemy at a great school for sorceresses."

"Not to study the calming lute?"

"It's not *that* simple. So, nearby is a school for sorcer*ers*, whose spells she figures might be powerful enough to bring back the King. So she decides to study alchemy at the boys' school. The boys harass her mercilessly. She resists as best she can…"

"And triumphs over their childish…"

"Hey. Whose story is this?"

"I apologize. Go on."

"A boy steps forward to be her champion, in such a way that he enhances her standing."

"In spite of his constant interruptions…"

"Are you going to let me do this? It's important." He made the gesture for zipping his lips. "He helps her, always protesting that she doesn't need help. They fall in love, despite his constant explaining and interruption, because the boy seems to need no enchantment beyond the joy of learning with her; not the things learned, but the learning with her itself. But he's on a Quest, and she fears turning him from it, or turning from hers. She fears abandoning her goal, even *herself* entirely, to become only a man's appendage, always wondering what she could have been, and she fears his quest would always mean more to him than she ever could, so when he reveals his love for her, a love which burns down his school, she's frightened of her own need for him, and when it was clear you would do anything for me, Ben, I asked you to leave me, needed you to then, and I damn near did the same thing again today. All because of Teddy Edwards, and what happened. And what I need now…I haven't worked it all out yet. I need to walk and think, and not alone. What time is it?"

"Mid to late afternoon, I think. Lisa, I love you. I sat out there and I thought, you aren't getting rid of me so easily this time. Or ever. I know something really bad must have happened in the ER last night."

"Yes. And I need to tell you, and figure out what to do about it. What to feel, and to do, now. Figure out what I need now."

"Want to walk and tell me it over a very, very late brunch? I can bring the latest New England Urinal. We haven't had a chance to look at it yet."

They showered and dressed; no whites, no beepers, and wandered across downtown Boston, into the North End, just walking, holding hands in mid-afternoon warmth. He had the Journal in a backpack. It had turned into a fine day. Over big sandwiches, espresso and pastry at a little coffeehouse that reminded them both of the Reggio, she told him.

"You talked to him the whole time?"

"When he was conscious. I just felt him fade away." He was silent. "No words of wisdom?"

He just shook his head. "No. That's uniquely awful. I was hoping you had some."

"I told the Third-Year we knew he was dying, that this wasn't survivable and we all knew it, but that this was a teaching hospital, that we'd maybe pull off a miracle, and if we didn't, what we learned would maybe make a miracle tomorrow or next year. At the time, and in that place, it sounded wise."

"I think it was, Leece."

"By the time I got home it felt like a load of crap. Now, I don't know...I want for it to mean something. I wish I'd told the kid a bedtime story. That would have meant more..." That was when she cried. He came around the table, put his arm around her, waved the waitress away. "Ben, I got that central line in perfectly, just like I've done a dozen times, just like I taught that Third-Year. I know all about burns, Ben. From a so-called expert professor who even after what he tried to do to me, I had to wish was there." She paused, overwhelmed. "But the poor kid died anyway. They all die anyway. It isn't about how good, how powerful our spells are. And I can't stop to cry. I can't let them see me falter. Instead I get mad, and I came home and took it out on you. I understand, I'm sorry, I accused you of being your brother, of being just another ..."

"It's okay," he said. And added, "Sometimes we pull them through."

"Only sometimes."

"Yeah."

"I'm crying about all of them. Not just him."

"Maybe it's always for all of them," he said.

She slipped into the restroom to repair the damage while he paid the bill. "Bad day at the office," he reassured the waitress. "The office is an ER." They walked, crossing back past Faneuil Hall, on down to the Public Gardens, and. sat on a bench.

"I always wanted to be a doctor. I just never realized it would be every minute," she said.

"I had other plans. The Kerouac idea. Ride to Frisco on the bike. Further..."

"What happened to that dream?"

"I met this girl."

"Well, I met a guy. We could drive somewhere together."

"Tell me what Teddy Edwards had to do with it."

"That's the part...He told this joke at lunch..." she told it. "If you told me that joke I'd probably grin, but Teddy—it's non-stop with him. Not a shared joke. It's intimidation. Keep the little lady in her place. All the little ladies. And Black and brown people. Only the *right* people can be doctors."

"You're tougher than that, Mautner."

"Am I, Ben? Maybe I am. But you know what? I told you, I'm tired of being tough. Having to be. Sick and tired of it."

"You can be proud of it."

"I can? Tough like you, Ben? Because…all your experiences in East Orange, in college; all mine at Bronx Science and college... They're all abusive environments..."

"We learned to be tough enough to survive, succeed in abusive environments."

"Yes, but why is being able to succeed in abusive environments an advantage? Abusive environments produce the Bolands and the Edwardses that we have to survive. It does nothing to eliminate the abusive environments. Our first instinct is to revenge ourselves on the bullies, instead of attacking the system that creates them, the cultural bullying system itself."

He thought. "So what's the solution? Do you have one? I don't."

"I don't either. I'm not that good or wise a person."

"It didn't turn me into Boland, Leece. Or into Teddy Edwards."

"I'm pretty sure Ben, but how do I know for absolutely sure? How am I supposed to *know*? You came up in that environment too, stink-bombing the lockers, threatening Boland. I want out of it, Ben. What I need now… How do I know you do too?"

"Because I'm a man, a male human, it's in my DNA? In the chemistry?" He saw it suddenly, from inside her head. "I don't know," he said softly, carefully. "I know you've been on the receiving end of even more crap than me, without being able to fight back, so…I don't know. You'll have to trust. Trust me, knowing the worst about me."

"I want out of it, Ben. You were a chem major, to get out of the pre-med crap. What do you want to do after training? Clinical or research? Practice? Or academia?"

"I hadn't thought that far ahead. I like teaching, but I know…Here's what I know about Teddy Edwards. Or rather, Dr. Colson Bradford Edwards, The Fourth Of that Name. Which carries very powerful juju here in Bahston. At Hahvahd…"

"Every time I start to feel like maybe I'm a member of the team he does something to undermine me. Make me feel like an outsider again."

"You're a member. You're *here*. And I'm a very lucky man, they all say."

"Yes. Lucky. They might all just want to sleep with me. Firman even gave it the old college try. Why do they look at me, and Maggie Roth, and all the female students, and see *woman*, not *doctor*?"

"When I look at you I see both. Always did."

"Well. You're the only man I license to do that. The others get to see The Doctor, and that's it." They sat quietly for a time, until she said, "The Fourth? Seriously?"

"Very. A walking stereotype. Exactly the kind of jerk my father had for a commanding officer in France. And loathed. I told you, they moved to Jersey so we could be Americans, but found out they wouldn't let us. Some of Teddy's ancestors and cousins are probably in Hawthorne stories. At least two hacked off limbs at Gettysburg. Two more, in the direct line, were military docs in the world wars, all later on the Harvard Med faulty, one a Chairman of Medicine. So will he try to be, probably will be. He's a legacy. So much for academics."

"So he's untouchable? It wasn't just the joke, Ben. That wasn't it. It was…he said, the patient was hopeless, so the ladies, me and the woman student, should take him."

"Jesus, Leece. He really said that? In front of everybody?"

"He did. So when I'm in your place, on a consulting resident rotation…" She stopped, gazed off a minute, or gazed *in*. "I think what I'm struggling with is this, Ben. Will they listen to me? Do what I advise? When I'm in practice will they ever refer patients to me? Why should I have to earn their respect as a doctor? Respect they automatically get just from the title?" Ben was silent. "After he told the joke, I got pretty steamed, asked him if he ever let up."

"Payback, you think?"

"If I'm honest, the mental picture of your brother skinning Teddy and his frat brothers at a poker table gives me pleasure. Despite, or perhaps because of, the distinguished lineage and being a pretty good physician, let us say Teddy the Fourth lacks *noblesse oblige*," she said.

"Pretty fancy way of saying he's a perfect dick."

"Nonsense. Nobody's perfect." She arched an eyebrow. "And, Dr. Rothstein, if you employ such sexist terminology, how would a woman know *you* aren't one? Seriously, Ben. I know I have your love, your devotion. Do I know, really *know*, I have your *respect*? In this culture, how can a woman ever know? You can say it, but it's just words. I don't know, maybe it can't be put in words."

"So this isn't only about being a doc. A woman would just have to know and trust me, know I completely lack distinguished family lineage and didn't come to Harvard to become a Jewish Teddy Edwards. Beyond that, I don't know. Seriously, Leece, Teddy *is* a pretty good doc, and he's profoundly loyal to and caring of an institution, Harvard, and a guardian of its traditions. And America's. He never learned what we learned at Columbia. A lot of people think it was a lark. A big panty raid. We watched the cops drag kids down the stone steps of Low Library feet first, banging their heads on the stone, before they got to us at Mercer. Teddy *loves* Harvard. That culture. We know all about the benignity of beloved institutions and cultures. You can love them as much as you want, but they won't love you back. Only people can do that. They're organic. I, as you know, have no, and can have no, faith in cultures or institutions. My loyalty is to its students and its patients. To individuals. To persons. A view stemming from experiences we share." He looked around the park; suddenly remembered it overrun with cops and fleeing students. "Here endeth the sermon."

They were quiet for a considerable time, gazing around the greening park, the soft grass, the blossoming trees, the ducks, the swans, the happily-playing children. A butterfly landed briefly, fluttered away. "It's nice to take off the white coats for a little while," she said. "Just be Lisa and Ben for a little while."

It was too early for Swan Boats but the ducks were pairing off. "There'll be ducklings."

"Every year," he said. "You know, there will come a time when we will have been docs longer than we haven't. I calculated it. It'll be when we're fifty and forty-eight." It began to cloud over.

She took his hand, pulled him up to walk. "Mike the nice policeman will help Mrs. Mallard get her ducklings to the Charles."

"Right. Mike the nice policeman. I never asked, do you know if they ever found that dud tear gas canister in the library?"

"No. If they did it never got around. They did decide it was a police riot, like Chicago, and you know they never let city cops back on campus again. Do you know if they had to re-sanctify the font at Saint John's?"

"No idea." They walked on, the mass of Mass General looming ahead.

"I would have done anything to save that kid, Ben. At the end, when he was fading, he just kept whispering 'Sweet Jesus'."

"There was nothing more you could do. Other than work to make a world where a kid doesn't have to get killed trying to have a bike." She made no reply. "Disenchanted, Leece?" he said. "Look. The ones we pull through get a second chance. Something you and I are experts on, second chances."

"But maybe we're treating the wrong kind of sickness," she said. "We treat the casualties of the world's sickness. Just like at Mercer. And we're the walking wounded."

He nodded. "Eliot's wounded surgeons. 'The wounded surgeon plies the steel That questions the distempered part; Beneath the bleeding hands we feel / The sharp compassion of the healer's art'."

"Resolving the enigma of the fever chart," Lisa completed the line.

"Remember my idea about The Freak? It's work toward that better world. Something a person could do something about. Something two people could do something about. Think about it. No worries about anyone referring you patients. *You'd* be referring patients to *them*." They walked on toward the hospital.

"Interesting," she said. "Also a good place for a Women's Group to meet. I'll take it under advisement. Now, I'm just an intern."

"Only for a few more weeks, Dr. Mautner. Gonna be a rezzie."

"Damn straight, Dr. Rothstein."

"Decided on a specialty rotation?"

"I was thinking Cardio. I really do have a good ear."

"That'll be fun. And think of the savings. We'll both be using the same books."

"You always were a cheap bastard, Dr. Rothstein."

"Frugal, Dr. Mautner. So are you. We had a lot of practice."

"I'll be at all the conferences with you. I'll have my eye on you, Rothstein."

"Leece. I know you're teasing, but I also know how deep this goes for you."

"What if someone better shows up? Someone less neurotic? More...trusting?"

"Could happen, I suppose. But she'd have to live with disappointment. *You* showed up. I'm taken. Leece. Even if such an impossible creature existed, chemistry be damned, she would lack one thing I only have with you: History."

"Even if...when...I get crazy?"

"If we get crazy, it shouldn't be about sex. Can we talk about this, Leece? I don't mean physical sex..."

"That's the part we get right," she said.

"I'm glad you think so. Leece. I wanted you so much. I was that much Morty..."

"Must have been pheromones."

"We decided that's just the chemistry, a code. Pheromones don't *make* desire. Didn't we figure out, they *evoke* desire? This morning, I figured out that desiring *evokes* loving. And loving *evokes* caring."

"Not in everybody. We're lucky. Ben. I've never made it easy for you. I have a lot of defenses but you snuck through all of them. Inside the perimeter before I knew it."

"You made it interesting. Want to know why I wanted you so much?"

"Risky question, Rothstein. I'll have to pretend I never heard what my mother and my camp counselors and the culture said about there being only one thing men want."

"Seriously. This was something that came before anything else. I was on the train going back to school from the Reggio, and I thought, this girl has guts and brains, and that's what I want. I didn't know that until I met you. A woman with that combination. Which was sometimes a pain in the ass, for my nineteen-year-old self."

"I think you wanted someone you could fight bullies and make stink bombs with."

There was silence for a time, except for the distant wail of an ambulance. He finally said, "Maybe. I can't know if that's how it started. Unconsciously. How long have you been sitting on that insight?"

"Pretty long time. Since about when I figured out I wanted, more than I would admit, someone. A man. Who could care about me without patronizing me. An equal."

He stopped. Said softly, "You risked everything just to be with me."

"I didn't shout it to the New York Times. And we were always so careful."

He looked away. "The truth? That first night, I wasn't sure I was up to the job. I was a nerd, Leece. Still am...I..."

"Well, so was I."

"I used to hear Morty's voice in my head. Telling me how to grow up. In ways I didn't want to follow. Leece, you always made me feel...competent. Also, occasionally, courageous. I stopped needing him. Needing his...Mortyism."

"You did that for me, too." she said. "You know, I got my driver's license because I heard your voice in my head urging me. So, even when we weren't together..."

"Really? My voice in your head?"

"Really. The thought came to me to do it, in your voice. The sex was wonderful, but it wasn't the most important thing. How much time have we spent in bed, versus how much working? Talking? Ben, my childhood…I think, at first, I maybe just loved knowing I was loved. You gave me that feeling. It took longer…no, it took losing you, to know it was *you* I wanted, not just that feeling. You've made me feel loved, Ben. You liked me as I was. As I am. And I liked you. Our conversations. The things we do together. Smart, funny, resourceful, caring Ben. Adoring me. And. Helping me be me."

"Same as you do for me, Leece. Just returning the favor," he said.

She stopped. "And I wanted you. I didn't know why, and I didn't care. Your eyes are the blue I like. The sex…wanting you…was a bonus."

He looked away. "At the hotel, the first time we made love…I didn't know I could ever generate such passion in anyone."

"Neither did I, Ben."

"Well, you do. Leece, I never told you this…"

"What?"

"It was our first night. At the Pennsylvania. Remember?"

"Yes, Ben. Every detail. Every time brings it back."

"For me too. Here's a detail you don't know. When I woke, and woke you…"

"I always thought you waited for me to fall asleep and then…"

"No. I fell asleep too. Feeling like a nerd who'd only earned a C+. I dreamt about you, Leece. I dreamt we were in some place with, it was like, no gravity. We just floated. Like we were chemicals, huge molecules, in a warm ocean. And I was kissing you, we were wrapped around each other, kissing each other, caressing, all over. And we fit together perfectly. And I woke up, and you were right there beside me…"

"I dreamt too. I dreamt, or maybe I was, I must have been, half awake, I don't know, that I was being kissed, touched, all over, and it set me on fire. And I woke up, and it wasn't a dream."

"Kekule's snakes," he said. "Leece, I figured something out this morning. Tell me if I have it right. When I feel like crap

I want to make love with you to feel better, but you have to feel better first so you can make love. I promise to remember that."

She stopped to hug him. "Yes," she said. "That's it exactly. Thank you, Ben."

"Why, 'thank you'? You were running on empty this morning. I know what that feels like. I should have known." They continued walking.

"I could have just said that, not fly into a rage. But it touched a nerve." She paused to collect her thoughts. "Teddy. Nister. Even…My longish relationship, in Philly. He wasn't *considerate*. I don't mean he hurt me, or anything, I just mean… he didn't always pay attention or listen to me. Everything happened on his schedule. According to his needs. I think maybe I started believing…this is the way men are. I guess I mean, men when they're beyond passionate puppy love."

"So, trust: How can you know it isn't in the male chemistry?"

"I guess. I'm sorry Ben. But you figured some of it out… here I am. Still here."

"Me too," he said. They were at their door. He didn't know what to do or say. "We forgot the Urinal." He started to hand her the Journal, but she pushed it away, put her arms around him and kissed him "Now look what you've done," he said.

She went into the bedroom; when he didn't follow immediately she popped out the door, blouse unbuttoned. "You coming, Rothstein?"

"You sure?"

She nodded, smiled. They undressed quickly, hungrily; embraced, kissed, fell across the bed, kissed everywhere. "Ben," she said.

He rose from her. "What?" he half said, half gasped.

"I want to ask…I want to be on top."

He grinned. "Sounds like fun." They'd never tried this before (*Why not?* both thought); it took a minute to figure out exactly how, but she was astride him, leaning back slightly, supported behind by his raised knees. He opened his eyes wide, took in the sight of her there, her hair cascading over her breasts. He reached out to gently hold them, and she leaned forward, caressing the most sensitive parts of him with the most sensitive parts of herself. She heard him moan, took him in, gingerly, finding that he could move so she didn't lose him even if she leaned over all the way…and she thought, remembered suddenly, *this isn't something he takes from me, this is something we share.* She leaned back again; he moved with her, supported her, and she raised herself from her knees, sliding up and back down him. Did it again. Watched him close his eyes, and open them.

"You like?" she said.

He closed his eyes, smiled, nodded, said, "You're leading." She did it again, watching him respond, and again. *This isn't something either of us gives or takes,* she thought, *this is something we do together, like dancing,* and then the roller coaster took her, took them both high, higher than it had in a while. She collapsed forward onto his chest and he hugged her to him, crying her name. And they both thought *Why did we never think to do this before* and in the silence he said, "Marry me Leece," and she said, "I don't *know.* When I was a kid I wanted someone to love and want me more than anything else, and that's just childish, a child's wish. Now I don't know if what I want is possible. That plus I don't know if what I want is possible to put into *words.* But I'm thinking about it," and he said, "Whenever you're ready just say yes, it's an open invitation."

WBCN popped on. Light was creeping in. They lingered as long as they could, disentangling limbs. "Morning," she whispered to him. "I want to do that again."

"Me too," he said. "Not, unfortunately, now. Work, alas, calls."

"Ohhh, noooo…" They got up, regretfully showered, ate, put on their whites, and activated their beepers; Ben his, plus the cardiology service's long-distance pager.

"You see how you outrank me, Rothstein," she teased him.

"In what possible way?" he said.

"You have a second beeper. You're a two beeper man."

They kissed at the ER doors and went their separate ways.

* * *

Many weeks later, after leaving a Boston municipal office (there would be, weeks later, a gathering of parents and cousins in Kurt's capacious home, to which they submitted somewhat reluctantly) they followed fiery turning leaves through New Hampshire and Vermont and what was less a road map than a catalogue of minor Catholic saints to Quebec City. High in a tower room of the Chateau Frontenac they got back to selves they remembered from a much shabbier hotel, and he asked her, in afterglow, "Why, just when you did, did you decide to *marry* me?"

"Because right then I knew I could trust and depend on you to know my worth. No matter what my rank or title. Just trust you, period. Because you trusted me."

"Right then? That moment?"

"Because you did what nobody else in that ER, in that hospital, would have done. Can you imagine Teddy doing what you did? He even tried to stop you."

"Billy Mortenson probably would have."

"He might have, but he would have asked me why first. And probably let Teddy stop him. You didn't. You just did what I asked. What I said."

"I knew you were on to something."

"You trusted me."

"Of course I did. Always have."

"And you didn't care how anyone else in that room would see that."

"Oh. I see. No. It wasn't important. It was the patient that was important."

"I saw that it's what you'd have done for anybody. Even for a girl intern. I saw that I would always be able to trust you to be who I thought you were. In any situation."

The patient rolled in about mid-afternoon, usually the low point before the PM rush. Found on Storrow Drive, by the Charles, by a bench, unconscious, face down in the grass. Almost pulseless; when she auscultated she heard a faint beat, at under 30 per minute, a very serious bradycardia. Practically no blood pressure; diastolic was close to 40. No other notable findings. Mortenson was ER First Year Resident; he pulled the curtain and stuck his face in. "What have we?"

"Maybe 50-year-old black female, unresponsive, serious bradycardia, almost no BP. Already pushed glucose and naltrexone. I'm just hooking up EKG." He came over and they read it together. "Shit," she said, "Runs of trigeminy, she's going to…" And as they watched she went into ventricular tachycardia.

Mortenson shouted "Get the cart." Nurses, other residents, interns, and students arrived with the crash cart, along with Edwards, the day's ER chief, who took the EKG strip out of her hands and looked it over, handed it to the med students.

"V tach. We're going to need to shock her," he said. Nurses were already pushing IV bicarb; Mortenson was part way through getting an endotracheal tube in. She listened for breath sounds, gave a thumbs-up and stepped back. "Clear." Edwards shocked her back into sinus bradycardia. They clustered around the EKG. There were still runs of trigeminy, other escape rhythms. Edwards showed the Third-Years: "You see? Her pacemaker, the sinoatrial node, is running so slowly lower centers are starting to beat on their own, creating the risk of, or actual…" he pointed to the female Third-Year.

"Escape rhythms. Ventricular tachyarrythmias, fibrillation," she said.

"Good. V fib. The wing beats of the Angel of Death. So the question is, why the bradycardia?" He whipped around. "She hypothyroid?"

"No nodules or goiter," Lisa said. "Skin's not dry, no obvious hair loss. Labs are cooking. Also, left fourth digit callus, but no wedding ring, so I wonder if…"

"Sick Sinus Syndrome?" a Fourth-Year said.

"Could be," Edwards said. "We're not going to find out in the ER."

"Whatever it is, she's going to need an external pacemaker," Lisa said, "We should call Cardio." Which she knew, and knew Edwards knew, meant *Call Ben*. She thought Edwards gave her a look, so she turned away, pretending to check the IV.

Firman stuck his head in, said "What's going on?" They never heard him.

"Somebody page Cardio." Edwards said.

When the phone rang Mortenson answered and passed it to him. "It's Rothstein."

"Benjamin. We have a mysterioma. Fifty-some-year-old black female, unresponsive, no response to glucose/B$_{12}$/ Naltrexone push, severe sinus bradycardia with escape rhythms, one episode of V tach already. Not obviously hypothyroid. Yeah." He hung up. "He's on the way."

She knew that as far as Edwards was concerned Ben was just the portal to the Cardiac Care Unit, that he hated having to have Ben make this call. *Probably hates Ben, period.* She watched the EKG tape unspooling, saw the premature ventricular contractions. "We have PVCs," she said, and as she watched, "Bigeminy. Runs of three...we have trigeminy."

"Shit," Edwards said, "Good thing we left the airway in. Push Bicarb."

Ben walked in just as the patient went into V fib again. The nurse began squeezing the Ambu bag; Lisa began pumping the patient's chest as Edwards charged the defibrillator. "We can't keep her beating fast enough to prevent escape rhythms," he said to Ben.

"Gonna need a pacer," Ben said. "Any chance this is toxic?"

"We emptied her handbag," Mortenson said. "Nothing there but lipsticks, compact, wallet, some letters; no answer at the number on her ID."

Lipsticks? she thought, pumping the still chest. "Ben," she said suddenly. "Take over for me." He moved over to pump; she ran to the table where the patient's purse had been emptied out and picked up the two lipsticks.

"Mautner. Rothstein," Edwards shouted. "What the hell are you doing?"

"Thought so," she said, pouring a few tablets out of one. "This one's a pill keeper. Somebody get a PDR. I bet it's Inderal."

"I bet you're right," Ben said, pumping. "No blood pressure, sustained bradycardia." He gestured to Mortenson. "Billy, pump, will you? I'll call CCU, get her set up for an external pacer."

"Accidental overdose or suicide attempt?" Mortenson said, taking over pumping.

She had the PDR open to the pill pictures. "Inderal," she said. "Positive ID." She rummaged in the pocketbook, found what she was looking for. "Suicide. She'll need a psych consult when she wakes up."

Ben flashed a quick thumbs-up as he made the call to CCU.

"Clear," Edwards called, and shocked the patient back to sinus bradycardia. "Suicide? What is that, woman's intuition?"

"No, Teddy," she said, tearing open the blank one of the four envelopes she'd found in the pocketbook's hidden compartment. "Three are overdue bills. Utility, phone, credit card. This one's the note." She put the suicide note on the gurney. "For the chart," she said to Ben.

"Let's roll, people," Ben said, and he and a nurse rolled the patient out to the elevator bank.

He didn't even think He just did what I asked.

She pushed past Edwards and opened the door to the corridor. The elevator door was just opening. "Ben," they all heard her shout.

"What?" they all heard him call back.

"Yes. I'm saying yes, Ben. Let's do it." She saw him give another thumbs-up and grin as the elevator doors closed. When she turned back they were all gaping at her. "What?" she said. "He asked me to marry him."

From the Introduction to *Fundamentals of Medical Biochemistry*, by Benjamin Rothstein, M.D. and Lisa Mautner-Rothstein, M.D., Boston, Harvard University Press:

All biochemistry relevant to Medicine is about stereochemistry: molecular shape and fit, the active molecules acting in chains of reactions. Inorganic reactions and bonds are largely the result of electric charge and chance. Carbon atoms, on the other hand, cannot be alone. They must affiliate by sharing electrons, forming covalent or resonant bonds. The resulting organic molecules can be extraordinarily complex, such that their shapes, at the nano level, can catalyze chemical reactions. Each reaction is like a tiny jigsaw puzzle, in which a coenzyme (usually a vitamin or mineral) might fit into an enzyme molecule, deforming it in such a way as to allow two reactants to attach. The reactants, thus brought together, then bond with each other to form a new molecule, which moves on to the next reaction in the chain. Many such coordinated chains are a mechanism capable of running the processes, tissues and organs that make life possible. They are the processes of self-assembly, reproduction, and maintenance we call Life. At higher levels of organizational complexity, these processes underlie the interactions with the world that evoke the phenomena of consciousness and behavior best understood by psychology and sociology.

Disease and dysfunction occur when there is interference with the chains of chemical reaction. It is the physical fit of molecules together, at the nano level, and at the cellular level, that cause the chemical reactions that make life possible. Allow Life to *happen*. Imagine a ball in a Jane Austen novel. The young people, the reactants, circle the floor, where the dance will occur. Parents, aunts, uncles, hosts and hostesses, play the role of enzymes, creating the occasion, organizing, and the dancing begins. The young people are brought together in couples, and when the fit is right, a bond might be created. The most complex manifestation of organic chemistry is a chemical dance, which in its complexity evoke the phenomena we call Life and Consciousness.

The physician must never forget that while disease is occurring at the level of the patient's chemical mechanisms, it is *experienced* by the patient at the level of consciousness and suffering, Medicine is the art of addressing all the levels of existence simultaneously.

Author's Notes

This is a work of fiction. Events at Harvard Medical School in the 1960s and 70s, and in 2018 are entirely fictional, and the picture of it presented is entirely the feelings of two fictional young people, and the adults they became, at a time when Harvard Med was a cynosure for pre-meds everywhere. Educational procedures (e.g. the chest auscultation exercise) and training atmosphere were common to many medical schools, not necessarily Harvard. The state of American Medicine in 2018 as presented here is accurate in general, but not, in fact, at Harvard and in Boston. The Boston Health Care for the Homeless Program, founded shortly after my fictional Freak, serves the poor of Boston through Massachusetts General Hospital and a network of clinics and active outreach. It has the benefit of foundational and charitable support, something such programs in most other places lack. The story can be found in: *Rough Sleepers: Jim O'Connell, M.D's Urgent Mission to Bring Healing to Homeless People* (Random House, 2023), excerpted at: https://www.nytimes.com/2023/01/05/magazine/boston-homeless-dr-jim-oconnell.html. Free clinics staffed by volunteer physicians and students were common in the 1960s, and many evolved, as did the fictional Freak, into community health facilities.

Similarly, there is no Mercer Hall at Columbia University. If it did exist, it would occupy the space in the campus bounded by the very real Hamilton and John Jay Halls to the north and south and Wallach and Hartley Halls on the east, just northeast of Butler Library. There was no tear gas used in clearing the protesting students from the occupied buildings at the 1968 campus occupation; contemporaneous and historical accounts (from which some details of my story are drawn) and official reports agree that the New York City Police Department relied on, quite literally, brute force. As noted, there are some reports of use of tear gas at the Gym Crow demonstrations that preceded the occupation.

In March 1968 the *New York Times* ran the story of an anonymous Barnard sophomore who lived with her boyfriend (a Columbia student) despite Barnard's "housing policy," and of how Barnard administrators quickly identified her and initiated disciplinary action. Columbia had no such rules, setting off a debate on the Columbia and Barnard campuses and in the national press, and hearings by the student-faculty disciplinary body. Very light punishment, and a review of college *in loco parentis* policies, was recommended but overruled by Barnard's president; the girl was expelled at her orders. Her boyfriend suffered no penalty whatever. The story (followed in the *New York Times* and other newspapers) was soon eclipsed by the April campus occupation, but not forgotten. In a survey of students, 73% admitted to breaking at least one "housing" rule. By the 1970s such *in loco parentis* and "housing" rules remained as quaint relics at some church-affiliated colleges. Contraceptives were freely available as well, regardless of marital status. True coeducation became almost universal.

Events in Boston and Cambridge, and at the Harvard Campus Occupation are also taken from real events. WBCN, Boston's "Voice of the American Revolution" operated as a free-form "alternative" station from 1968 to 1975, evolving from its previous classical music format. A film history can be found through: https://www.pbs.org/show/wbcn-and-american-revolution/

Stuyvesant high school in New York admitted its first female student in 1969.

Once the largest hotel in the world, the Hotel Pennsylvania, designed by McKim, Mead and White, opened in 1919 across 7th Avenue from Pennsylvania Station. The Glenn Miller orchestra immortalized it in song, but as of this writing, after years of planning, its demolition is underway.

The Honda CB450 was not actually available in the year Morton Rothstein would have started riding it; it came to the U.S. market about a year later than my story required. It was one of the few road bikes at that time that could be ridden comfortably by two drivers of such disparate size as the Rothstein brothers, and by a petite passenger.

The Medical Committee for Human Rights, was formed in the late 1950s to provide medical support for the marches, Freedom Rides and Freedom Summers of the Civil Rights era, and left many free medical clinics in its wake. It, and its student wing, the Student Health Organization, similarly provided medical support at the Columbia campus occupation, the demonstrations at the 1968 Democratic Convention in Chicago, and at many peace demonstrations, including the numerous Marches on Washington (Spring and Fall Mobilizations) throughout the Vietnam War.

The Physicians for a National Health Plan, PNHP (http://www.pnhp.org), has its headquarters in Chicago. It is as of this writing active in promoting a single-payer American national health service, or a national health insurance plan, Medicare For All.

Medical procedures and slang are accurate for the times portrayed. Whites have been replaced by scrubs. The Roberts and Caserio textbook was, in the 1960s and beyond, a standard text for the undergraduate Organic Chemistry course required of all pre-medical students. Clear, comprehensive and well-written, it has gone through numerous editions. Likewise Baldwin's *Dynamic Aspects of Biochemistry*. The T.S. Eliot quote on page 250 is from his *Four Quartets*. The quote on pages 4 and 13 is Pound's *In a Station of the Paris Metro*. The lyrics on page 119 are from John Lennon's *Imagine*.

I must thank all my friends and classmates for, over many years, supplying (sometimes inadvertently) many inspirations and anecdotes of pre-medical and medical education in the 1960s and early 70s, to supplement my own. And note that women comprise 63% of my alma mater's class of 2026.

My thanks to Dave Worrell, who gave me the following advice: "The state of medicine is not the story. The love story is the story."

ABOUT THE AUTHOR

Andrew Levitas, M.D, is retired Professor of Psychiatry at Rowan University-SOM in Stratford, New Jersey. He is a 1972 graduate of the Albert Einstein College of Medicine, Bronx, New York, did his Medical internship at Montefiore Hospital, Bronx, New York, his residency in Psychiatry at Downstate/Kings County Hospital Center, Brooklyn, New York, and his Fellowship in Child Psychiatry at the University of Colorado Health Sciences Center, Denver, Colorado. He maintained a private practice in Denver and was a member of the Volunteer Faculty of the University of Colorado Health Sciences Center for eleven years, during which he travelled extensively in the Rocky Mountains and the Southwest. In 2017 he retired as Professor of Psychiatry and Medical Director of the Center of Excellence for the Mental Health Treatment of Persons with Intellectual Disabilities and Autism Spectrum Disorders at Rowan University-SOM, Stratford, New Jersey.

Dr. Levitas is Board Certified in both Psychiatry and Child Psychiatry. He is the 1999 recipient of the Robert D. Sovner Award for psychiatric services to persons with intellectual disabilities. He is an emeritus member of the Scientific and Clinical Advisory Committee of the National Fragile-X Foundation, past Associate Editor of *Mental Health Aspects of Developmental Disabilities*, a member of the Advisory Board and scholastic contributor to the Diagnostic Manual on Intellectual Disabilities: A Clinical Guide for the Diagnosis of Mental Disorders in Persons with Intellectual Disability (DMID), and co-author of three chapters of the DMID and two chapters of the DMID-2, as well as author and co-author of numerous scientific papers and book chapters on psychiatric aspects of intellectual disability and autism spectrum disorders, and two previous novels, *Alumni Notes* (Star Cloud Press), and *The Third Book of Samuel* (Amazon). He is a former member of the Student Health Organization and a member of Physicians for a National Health Plan.

He maintains a research interest in Autism Spectrum Disorder especially as it relates to Fragile-X and other intellectual disabilities syndromes, as well as other behavioral phenotype issues. He is a member of the Volunteer Faculty of Rowan University-SOM.

Printed in Great Britain
by Amazon